THE EMMERDALE GIRLS

Also published in the Emmerdale *series*

Christmas at Emmerdale
Spring Comes to Emmerdale
Emmerdale at War
Hope Comes to Emmerdale

THE EMMERDALE GIRLS

KERRY BELL

TRAPEZE

First published in Great Britain in 2020 by Trapeze
an imprint of The Orion Publishing Group Ltd
Carmelite House, 50 Victoria Embankment
London EC4Y 0DZ

An Hachette UK Company

1 3 5 7 9 10 8 6 4 2

A CIP catalogue record for this book is
available from the British Library.

ISBN (Hardback) 978 1 4091 9588 7
ISBN (eBook) 978 1 4091 9590 0

Typeset by Born Group
Printed and bound in Great Britain by Clays Ltd, Elcograf S.p.A.

MIX
Paper from
responsible sources
FSC® C104740
FSC
www.fsc.org

www.orionbooks.co.uk

To the best features team ever – Claire, Carena and Laura.

Part One

Chapter One

5TH JUNE 1944

Portsmouth

'I've never seen so many boats,' Annie Pearson said, looking out over Portsmouth Harbour from where she stood on the hill. 'It's like an armada.'

'Do you think it would be possible to walk all the way to the Isle of Wight?' her friend Patricia said, squinting into the horizon, where more ships bobbed gently on the waves.

'Hopping from deck to deck like a seagull looking for food?' Annie said with a smile. 'Maybe.'

'Imagine how they're all feeling now. Squashed inside, waiting for the order.' Patricia shuddered and Annie couldn't blame her. It had been an odd few days in Portsmouth, seeing the harbour fill up with ships and landing craft, and the streets full of tanks, guns and troops. And then the soldiers all disappeared, crammed into the boats ready for what was going to happen next.

'It must be tonight,' Annie said thoughtfully and Patricia nodded.

'Has to be.'

The two women exchanged a glance full of trepidation and fear and just the smallest bit of excitement. They'd known something was planned – an invasion of occupied France – for ages and, thanks to tide tables, they'd managed to work out, the day before, that it would be happening. Both women had been disappointed when they realised their shift pattern as Wrens meant they wouldn't be involved. But a storm last night meant the boats were still here and that meant the invasion was bound to take place that very night – with Annie and Patricia right in the thick of it.

'Shall we go?' Patricia said.

Annie nodded, taking one more look at the harbour. It felt like something monumental was happening and she wanted to remember everything about this.

Inside Fort Southwick, where Annie and Patricia were based, it was as busy as usual, but there was something else, something new. A feeling of nervous energy that fizzed around the communications HQ and made Annie's stomach flutter.

She gave Patricia a small smile and squeezed her friend's hand.

'See you on the other side,' she said.

The Wrens worked a shift pattern that was twenty-four hours off, then forty-eight hours on, though Annie always found it hard to keep track of the time when she was working. Fort Southwick was tunnelled out of the rocks overlooking Portsmouth and there was no natural light inside. Today, though, time was speeding past because she was so busy, she barely had time to breathe. Like all the Wrens based at Southwick, she and Patricia worked in communications, and today they were under more pressure than they had ever been before.

But, oddly enough, through all the running around and the snatched ten-minute breaks, and the occasional nod and smile to Patricia as they passed each other in the corridors, the person Annie kept thinking about was Jacob Sugden.

Jacob would be interested in this, she thought as Patricia – who worked with the meteorologists – passed her a weather report to send to the commanders in the boats. As a farmer, Jacob always paid attention to the climate and could predict when a storm was coming better than any chart. Annie smiled at the thought of him staring at the horizon over Emmerdale Farm and saying, 'We need to bring the cows down early tomorrow,' or, 'Best mend that barn roof before the rain comes.'

Of course, everything was different at Emmerdale Farm now. They were working harder than ever, Jacob and his mother Maggie, alongside their Land Girl, Audrey. Jacob's letters told of them turning previously barren land into fields for flax, endless rows of potatoes and other vegetables, and regular inspections to make sure they were doing everything they could. Annie was proud of her friends back in Yorkshire putting so much work into keeping the nation fed. She was proud of Jacob, who'd put the death of his brother Edward – Annie's fiancé – behind him and stepped up to keep the farm running when it was needed most. And almost more importantly than that, she knew Jacob was proud of himself.

'Pearson, we need you on the VHF,' the coxswain said.

Annie jumped to attention, startled out of her daydreams about home, and followed the officer to where she was needed. She enjoyed working the VHF – a high-frequency machine that meant she could relay messages to troops – and she tried hard to stay calm and unflappable, knowing how important the information she was passing on could be.

And never more than today. They had no windows in Fort Southwick, but somehow a murmur had flown round the Wrens earlier on in the shift and they'd all known that meant the boats had set off; leaving the safety of Portsmouth Harbour and sailing for Normandy to face goodness knows what. Lots of the women Annie worked with had sweethearts or husbands or brothers on board the vessels and she'd felt a pang of agony for them, seeing their pale, drawn, worried faces. She knew the heartache of losing someone she loved. She knew how she'd felt when Edward had been killed at sea, early in the war, and how she thought for a long time that she would never again feel the same joy or contentment she'd felt when she was with her love.

But now she knew that while a part of her would always love Edward and always feel sad for her loss, life could be good again. She'd even found herself thinking about what she might do after the war, because now there did seem to be an end in sight. She felt a sort of lurch in her stomach when she thought about it, like when she was little and missed a step when she was running down the stairs and thought she might fall. She loved being a Wren, she had friends both here in Portsmouth and back home in Beckindale, and she knew that being part of the war effort as she had been had changed her forever. She thought she probably would return to Beckindale. She loved Yorkshire and farming. But she thought if she did, she would be going back as a different Annie Pearson. Mind you, the war had changed everyone, she thought. She saw the changes in the regular letters she received from her mother Grace, her friend Lily, and, of course, from Jacob. She smiled again, thinking of how she'd describe today to him.

'All set?' said the officer.

Annie checked her equipment and nodded. 'All set.'

And she was off, suddenly thrust into a whirlwind of flipping switches and passing on messages that she didn't always understand. It wasn't always easy to hear, or to be heard, and she had to concentrate so hard that the hubbub around her receded into the distance.

At one point, the message she was receiving was drowned out by a persistent and deafening rat-a-tat-tat.

'Hold on,' the commander shouted, and she heard him panting as he ran and took shelter. The sound was still there, in the background, but she could hear him better now. And it was only later, much, much later, when she realised that the sound had been there the whole time like an insistent drumming, that she understood it was gunfire.

When the first wave was over, Annie, Patricia and some of the others collapsed into the narrow bunks in one of the hollowed-out rooms at Fort Southwick and slept for an hour or so. Then they were woken and the whole thing started again. Annie thought she had never been so tired, or so hungry, or so nervous. She was running on adrenaline and cups of tea. But being a part of this – Operation Neptune, as she now knew it was called – was really something. She looked at herself in the mirror in their tiny bunk room, smoothed down her hair and straightened her hat, imagining telling her children, or grandchildren, about it one day. 'It was a team effort,' she saw herself saying to the imaginary child on her knee. 'There were troops from all over the world, working together to beat the Nazis.'

7

With a start, she realised that in her imagination she was sitting at the table in the kitchen at Emmerdale Farm, where she'd sat so often and chatted to Maggie over a cup of tea. Why on earth would she imagine herself living there? Edward was gone and he wasn't coming back.

'Pull yourself together, Annie,' she said sternly to her reflection. 'There's work to do.' And so there was.

Annie carried on with her work on the VHF machine. She couldn't quite believe that the men's voices she was hearing were coming all the way from the beaches in France. Couldn't imagine what they were seeing or doing as they went from village to village, checking for German troops. It sounded terrifying from where she was sitting, safe in the depths of Fort Southwick, so she could only guess how scared those men were; running towards the gunfire of the enemy when surely all their instincts would be telling them to run the other way.

Annie had no idea from the messages whether the operation was proving successful. Everyone around her just looked harried and concerned. No one was smiling.

As she sat at her desk, hunched over her VHF machine, Patricia hurried over from the meteorological office and handed her a weather report to relay to the commanders in France. While Annie scanned the information, her friend bent down so she could speak into Annie's ear. 'I half expected someone to say it was all over,' she said. 'That they'd neutralised all the Germans and the boys were coming home.'

Annie looked round at Patricia and gave her a quick smile. 'I think we've a while to go yet.'

'Wishful thinking.'

And then there was another message coming in, and Annie had to turn her attention back to the troops in France.

Eventually, Patricia and Annie's work was over. Two whole days – forty-eight hours – after they'd started, they handed over to the Wrens who were just beginning their shifts, picked up their belongings and emerged, blinking in the morning sunlight, out on to Portsdown Hill.

'Bloody hell,' said Patricia, looking out over the harbour. 'I knew they'd gone, but it's strange to see it, even so.'

Where once the harbour had been that solid mass of ships, now it was empty. Every one of the boats and landing craft had gone across the Channel to France. Annie shivered despite the warmth of the early-summer sun.

'Wonder how many will come back,' she said, thinking of the sounds she'd heard over the past few hours. The gunshots and the shouts and the cries of alarm.

Patricia looped her arm through Annie's and squeezed. Annie returned the squeeze gratefully.

'Look,' Patricia said. 'There's one ship left.'

Annie turned to her left, looking to where Patricia pointed, down towards the end of the harbour. And there, as majestic as ever in the sunlight, was HMS Victory, Lord Nelson's ship. She was looking a bit more battered than usual, because she'd been damaged by a bomb earlier in the war, but Annie thought she'd never seemed so beautiful.

'Victory,' she said, almost to herself, though Patricia was standing right there. 'I hope it's a sign.'

Chapter Two

LATE JUNE 1944

Beckindale

Betty Prendagast checked her watch for the tenth time, and sighed. It was clear her fiancé Seth wasn't coming to meet her in The Woolpack like they'd arranged. He was supposed to have been here an hour ago and there was still no sign of him. Meanwhile, Betty had been sitting here like a lemon, all alone. Again.

Mind you, she should be used to it by now. Seth had been so busy at work for the last few months that he often forgot their arrangements. Betty wasn't sure why he was working so hard. He was only a gamekeeper, for heaven's sake. It was hardly life or death. But whatever it was, it was keeping him busy for all hours.

She looked down at the dregs of her gin and orange, swirled it round in the glass and drained it. It wasn't all bad, she thought. The pub was buzzing this evening, with Jacob Sugden entertaining the drinkers with stories about Annie Pearson's involvement with the Normandy landings.

Betty slid out from behind the table where she'd been sitting and went to the bar to order another drink.

Larry Dingle, who ran the pub with his cousin Jed, grinned at her.

'Same again?' he said.

'Thanks,' said Betty. She gave him one of her best smiles and was pleased when she saw a flush rise up on his cheeks.

The Woolpack wasn't a big pub, just one room with a bar in the middle. So it always felt busy, even when there were only a few drinkers inside. This evening, though, it was standing-room only and there was a celebratory feel as everyone toasted Annie's efforts earlier in the month. And even though it was getting late, there were some older children around – Stan Dobbs, and his sister Ruby were there, hanging off Jacob's every word.

'So the whole harbour was empty except for HMS Victory?' Ruby was saying, her eyes wide with awe. 'All the boats had gone to Normandy?'

'That's what Annie says,' Jacob Sugden said proudly.

Betty paid Larry and took her gin back to the table where she'd been sitting. She could see how proud Jacob was of Annie. His chest was swelling and he was standing up so straight, it was like he'd been commanding the troops himself. It was quite sweet, really, she thought. And he was right to be proud. Betty couldn't believe Annie had been right in the thick of it, when the soldiers landed on the beaches. Mind you, she'd always been a bold one, Annie. She'd not given up when Edward Sugden died, nor when there had been all that nasty business with Oliver Skilbeck. Betty wondered if she'd be as bold as Annie, if she had to be. She had a horrible feeling she wouldn't.

'Annie's so brave,' said Ruby now, in wonder.

Jacob nodded. 'She really is.'

'Carry on then, Jacob,' said Mick Dingle, who was sitting by the bar. 'What else does she say?'

'So she says that she and her friend Patricia thought the sight of HMS Victory would be a lucky sign,' Jacob said.

'You read that already,' said Stan, Ruby's younger brother, impatiently. His adopted mother, Meg Warcup, put a hand on his shoulder to calm him, making Betty smile. Stan was always a little ball of energy. 'Read the next bit.'

'"That first week is a blur,"' Jacob read. '"We were so busy, and whenever we had a break, we would just flop into bed and sleep like the dead. But then things started to settle down and we could see that our troops were gaining an advantage. And it all began to seem worthwhile."'

Jacob looked up from the notepaper. 'And then she just asks after everyone here, and sends her love.'

Betty watched Jacob with interest. He'd always been on the miserable side, had Jacob Sugden. Surly, some might say. His brother Edward had been the nice one. Edward was the charmer with the sense of humour, the good looks and the pretty girl – Annie – on his arm. But Jacob was softening. Look at how he'd taken the Land Girl, Audrey Atkins, under his wing. And he'd really worked hard on the farm, and looked after his mother Maggie when she was ill. Betty had been impressed by that. She tilted her head to one side, looking at the young man appraisingly. He was even becoming more handsome nowadays. And he was clearly smitten with Annie Pearson, whether he knew it or not. Betty wondered if Annie felt the same. Probably. She shifted on her chair slightly, feeling a tiny prickle of irritation.

She looked round as her boss, Nancy Tate, sat down next to her. 'What's up with you?'

Betty forced a smile. 'Nothing. Just thinking about Annie.'

'I hope I get a chance to get to know her better when the war is over,' said Nancy. 'She sounds like a real character.'

'She certainly is.'

'Mind you, we're not short of them round here. Speaking of which, where's your Seth?'

Betty tried to smile again, but this time it was harder. 'Don't know,' she admitted. 'He said he'd be here, but he must have got held up at work.' She checked her watch again. 'Don't think he'll make it now.'

Seth worked up at the estate, training to be a gamekeeper. He loved his job. In fact, he loved it so much that Betty often thought he loved it more than he loved her.

Nancy looked at Betty, her sharp eyes taking in every inch of Betty's face and making her feel uncomfortable. 'Are you all right?'

Betty shrugged. 'Not seen much of Seth lately, that's all.'

'These are difficult times for everyone,' Nancy said. 'I've heard they're very busy up at Miffield Hall.'

Betty thought Nancy was just being kind. She may have been Beckindale's vet, but she didn't have much to do with Mr Verney and his team up at the hall, so she wouldn't know how busy they were, not really. Nancy spent most of her time at the farms that surrounded the village.

'I know,' she said half-heartedly. 'He's working hard.'

She was being unfair, she thought. Seth was busy. And it wasn't that long ago that Betty herself had been the one who was out all hours, dancing with ENSA and entertaining the troops. She smiled to herself, remembering her time on the stage and how much she'd loved it. She'd almost joined them permanently, but then Seth had proposed and she'd decided to stay in Beckindale instead.

'Goodnight!' called Meg Warcup, gathering up Stan and a complaining Ruby. 'Bedtime for us.'

Betty gave her a quick wave and looked up optimistically as the door opened again as soon as Meg had left. Was this Seth? But no, it was just Audrey – the Sugdens' Land Girl – and her sweetheart Ned Barlow. Betty let out a small snort of irritation. Those two were so in love, it made Betty want to vomit.

'Did we miss Annie's letter?' Audrey asked. 'You should have waited, Jacob.'

Jacob looked at Audrey fondly. 'You can read it yourself. Where have you been, anyway? You left Emmerdale Farm before I did.'

Audrey looked round at Ned and giggled. 'We got distracted,' she said. 'Ned wanted to show me something.'

Betty raised an eyebrow. She and Seth were fond of getting 'distracted' behind a convenient hedgerow – at least they had been once upon a time – but she'd never been one to declare it to the whole Woolpack.

Audrey was glowing with happiness and sort of jiggling from one foot to the other. 'Can I tell them?' she said to Ned.

Ned beamed, his broad smile lighting up the room. He was a very good-looking chap, Betty thought. He had wide shoulders and a narrow waist and strong arms. And he was the sweetest, most devoted man she'd ever met. She snorted again. He'd never leave Audrey sitting waiting in the pub.

'Earlier today,' Ned began, putting an arm around Audrey's shoulders, 'I asked Audrey if she'd do me the honour of becoming my wife, and I'm pleased to say that she accepted.'

The pub erupted in cheers of congratulations. Betty joined in, even though she felt a bit flat. It wasn't so very long ago that everyone had been toasting her engagement, and here she was, still not married, sitting in the pub all alone. She pasted on her smile again, not wanting to seem petulant.

'Betty, isn't it wonderful?' Audrey stood in front of Betty, her eyes shining with happiness. She held up her right hand to show Betty the ring that was on her finger. The Land Girl was missing her left hand – she'd been born that way – though she never liked people to make a big thing about it.

Betty, who was a performer at heart, got to her feet, threw her head back and gave Audrey her best film-star smile. 'It's the most gorgeous news,' she said. 'Let's have a look at that ring.'

Audrey flashed her hand at Betty. 'It was Ned's grand-mother's. Isn't it perfect?'

Betty oohed and aahed over the pretty jewellery, pushing away the resentment she felt because she didn't have an engage-ment ring at all. Not many people did, she knew that. And Seth had said that as soon as the war was over, he'd get her all the sparkly trinkets she wanted. Betty tried to believe him.

'We're going to get married at Christmas,' Audrey was saying. 'That way, I've got time to save my clothing coupons for a dress. I'm hoping it might snow.'

'I can do your hair and make-up for you, if you like?' Betty said and Audrey looked delighted.

'Would you? That would be so kind. You always look so beautiful, Betty.'

Betty brushed off the praise modestly, but she was touched by Audrey's compliment.

'And I'll teach you a dance for the party,' she said.

Audrey looked pleased. 'I'd love that,' she said. Then she frowned. 'Ned might not be so keen though.'

'I'm sure you can persuade him,' Betty said. She gave Audrey a kiss on the cheek. 'Congratulations,' she said. 'Will you excuse me, I just need to pop to the lav.'

She nodded to Nancy, whose turn it was to admire Audrey's engagement ring, and headed towards the toilet. But instead of going in the door, she changed direction and went outside. She needed some time away from all the celebrations and frivolity.

It was a gorgeous summer's evening. The sun was still warm and the breeze was soft on Betty's bare arms. Everything should have been perfect, but it wasn't. She sat down on the steps by the pub and rested her chin on her knees.

Once upon a time, she'd have been in the centre of all the fun in The Woolpack. She'd be the one pushing back the tables to clear a space for dancing, getting Mikey Webb from Hotten to play some jaunty tunes on the pub piano and pulling people up to join in. But now she just felt tired and sad. She wished Seth was here, though deep down she knew if he was, he'd just spend the whole evening laughing with the other men at the bar.

Through the pub's open windows, she could hear Audrey telling Lily Dingle from the garage about her plans for a Christmas wedding.

'Won't that be wonderful?' Lily was saying. 'I hope it snows.'

Like a child, Betty put her hands over her ears so she didn't have to hear about Audrey's ideas for her big day. She and Seth had been engaged for more than a year now, but they'd not so much as talked about when they might tie the knot. All around them, people were marrying in a hurry, desperate to pledge their love to one another before they were forced apart by the war. But with Betty and Seth both in Beckindale for the foreseeable future, there seemed to be no rush.

Except . . .

Betty sighed. Except she'd given up her chance of dancing with the ENSA to stay in the village and wed Seth. She'd turned down the offer of going on stage every night, whirling and twirling, and bringing joy to troops all over the country, so she could settle down in Beckindale with the man she loved. She'd chosen making appointments for poorly kittens and injured calves and pregnant pigs over stage make-up, costumes and dance shoes. And that was fine. She was fine with it. She really was. Or she had been, when she had thought she and Seth would walk down the aisle and live happily ever after. But now it seemed they might never actually do it. Neither of them seemed to be in a hurry to make things official. Neither of them was keen to talk about why. They barely saw each other. It was all just one big mess.

Dramatically, Betty, buried her face in her hands. What on earth was she going to do?

A gentle hand on her shoulder made her look up. It was Wally Eagleton. He'd been a few years ahead of her at school, but she didn't know him well.

'How do, Betty?' His face was furrowed with concern. 'Are you ill?'

With what felt like an enormous effort, Betty gave Wally her best, most dazzling smile.

'Wally, how lovely to see you,' she said brightly. She held out her hand and he grasped her fingers and helped her get up. 'I'm not ill at all, just worn out with all the fun.' She nodded her head towards the pub, where the sounds of the celebrations still rang out. 'Jacob's been reading Annie's latest letter, all about her part in the Normandy landings, and Ned Barlow's asked Audrey to marry him.'

'Sounds like it's all happening,' said Wally, drily.

Betty looked at him, remembering how at school he'd always been one for a sharp, funny aside. Often at the teacher's expense.

'I've not seen you for ages,' she said.

'Been away,' Wally said. His eyes flashed with mischief. 'Been spending some time in North Africa.'

'And how was North Africa?'

'It was quite nice,' said Wally. 'Not sure I'd visit again though. Full of bloody Germans.'

Betty giggled. Her laughter felt strange in her mouth, as though she'd forgotten how to do it.

'And,' Wally went on, 'one of them shot me. Which was unpleasant.'

'I can imagine,' Betty said. 'Are you healed?'

Wally shrugged. 'Good as I'll ever be. Not well enough to go back, though.' A shadow crossed his face. 'So I'm home to Beckindale.'

'I'm glad,' said Betty truthfully.

'Me too,' Wally said. He grinned. 'Coming in for a drink?'

Betty thought about the jollity in the pub and, though she was enjoying talking to Wally, she shook her head. 'Bedtime for me,' she said. 'Got an early start tomorrow.' She paused. 'At the vet's. I'm the receptionist there.'

She had no idea why she was telling Wally where she worked, but he gave her that mischievous smile again. 'Righto,' he said. 'Nice to see you, Betty.'

'Nice to see you too, Wally,' she said.

As she walked down the steps by the pub, she felt his eyes on her back. And she liked it.

Chapter Three

Seth's heart was pounding. He could feel it thumping against his ribs as he lay face down in the long grass, hidden from view by a clump of gorse bushes.

It was late in the evening, but it was still light, though the shadows were growing longer. Seth was taking advantage of the fading sunshine, hoping he couldn't be seen where he lay.

The sound of quiet footsteps made him freeze, breathing slowly out and in, biding his time. The other man wasn't walking fast, rather pacing in a deliberate rhythm, looking from left to right, scanning his surroundings. He was looking for Seth.

Seth flattened himself down even more, waiting for the right moment, and then, as the man's boots came into view, Seth leapt to his feet and, in one fast move, he'd taken the man's legs from under him and pinned him to the ground.

There was a pause. All Seth could hear was his own breathing and then the man spoke.

'Geroff, you bugger.'

Seth chuckled and stood up, dusting off his trousers. The other man – Sid – did the same. He rubbed his neck.

'I thought I had you this time.'

'Never,' said Seth in triumph.

Sid aimed a playful punch at him and Seth darted out of the way.

'Well done, lads.' Paul Oldroyd, an older man with a stiff-backed stance, appeared from the undergrowth where Seth had been hiding. Seth always thought Paul looked like a bank manager, even when he was dressed in camouflage. 'Let's head back to base for a debrief.'

The two younger men followed Paul as he picked his way through the wood. Seth was grinning broadly; he loved this. He loved being outside, being with the other men, doing something useful – he loved it all.

He'd not believed Paul when he'd first approached him about joining the Hotten Operational Patrol of the Auxiliary Unit. Paul was something of a joke to Seth back then – too old to join up, and too fond of his Home Guard uniform for Seth's liking.

So when he'd come to Seth one day and explained that he was recruiting for a team of men to form a sort of British resistance in the event of a German invasion, Seth had laughed.

'Nah, you're all right,' he'd said, thinking Paul had enjoyed one too many pints in The Woolie and wasn't thinking straight.

But then Ernie – Seth's best friend – had joined up and Seth started thinking perhaps it was time he did his bit. So he took Paul aside one day and asked him if the offer was still there. Even then he'd been a bit bewildered about why Paul had come to him. Seth was many things, but he knew better than anyone that he wasn't the sort of man who'd do well as a soldier.

Paul, though, had brushed aside his concerns.

'We need men who know the countryside inside out,' he'd told him. 'Men like you, who know every tree in the forest, every clearing, every stream. Who can track a deer, or a man. Who can listen to birdsong and tell us what we're hearing.'

Seth had nodded slowly. 'That's me,' he'd said eventually. And before long he was on a training camp with men from all walks of life, learning about things that Seth was pretty sure didn't come under the normal rules of warfare.

Until Ernie had been killed, Seth still treated the patrol like a game. He larked about and showed up late. Paul often scolded him for not taking it seriously enough. But when Ernie died, Seth had found that being part of the operational patrol had helped him through – given him something to focus on. Now he spent just about all of his spare time with the other members of the patrol, keeping everything they'd learned in their training fresh, and making sure they were ready to leap into action if the Germans invaded. It felt good to be part of something bigger than him. He was proud to be doing his bit, even if he wasn't allowed to tell anyone about it.

Of course, the threat of an invasion happening had receded so much now that every time the men met, there was a sense that it was all coming to an end. Seth was concerned the powers that be might disband the Auxiliary Unit altogether – he wasn't sure how he'd go back to just being a gamekeeper and living his normal life again. He worried that everything would seem dull in comparison to being part of this. Every day he worried that today would be the day Paul told them to stop training. But it hadn't happened yet.

'Right, caution,' said Paul as he always did when they approached the entrance to their base. They all paused and checked no one was around and then crawled inside.

The base had been created by soldiers from the Royal Engineers. That had been the first clue for Seth that this wasn't just boys playing war games – it was real. Paul had shown him the base, deep in the woods near Beckindale, and his jaw had dropped. It was big, well-stocked with ammunition and weapons, and completely invisible from outside. There was even an escape tunnel, in case they needed it.

Sometimes Seth thought they really were just pretending, especially now that the Allies were pushing into occupied Europe. But he pushed those thoughts to one side because he knew his life would be a little bit emptier if he stopped being part of the operational patrol.

'Eh up,' said George, the final member of their team, who was inside the base already.

Seth, Paul and Sid settled down for a debrief on the training exercise. Seth was listening, but his mind was elsewhere. He knew exactly what to do now and he knew that chances were he'd never have to use the things he'd been trained for. Fortunately, he supposed. If he was ever called on to put those skills into practice, it would mean things were very bad indeed.

'So, all in all, another successful evening,' Paul was saying, in his usual self-important way.

Seth hid his smile. He knew people in Beckindale thought Paul was a bit pompous, but Seth knew he had a good heart.

'Things are changing, aren't they?' George said. Seth looked at him. He was fairly young, was George, and he hadn't grown up round here like the rest of them had. He had cropped blond hair, he was sharp as a tack, and because his mother was Austrian, he could speak fluent German. He had been recruited because he would be a real asset to the patrol should the Nazis invade. 'Why are we still spending time here? The Germans aren't going to win the war. They're certainly not going to invade. Why are we here?'

Seth felt a tug of disappointment. He knew George was right, but he didn't want to think about life after the unit disbanded. Not yet.

Paul, though, nodded. 'You're right,' he said. 'And I have been told that if any of you want to join up elsewhere, I am to let you go.'

George looked pleased and Seth thought this evening might be the last they saw of the clever youngster. Suddenly, he wanted to mark the occasion. It felt like a farewell, and he thought they should make something of it.

'We should have a drink,' he said. 'There are some bottles of beer down the back. Let's crack them open and drink to the four of us.'

Paul looked like he was going to say no, but then he nodded. 'Good plan, Seth.'

Sid found the beers and handed them round and they opened them and shared stories about their training and the exercises they'd been on. It was only when he was halfway down his second bottle that Seth remembered he'd said he would see Betty in The Woolpack tonight.

'What's wrong, Seth?' Sid was watching him. Sometimes Sid reminded Seth of Ernie – the way he could read Seth's moods and know when he was mithering over something. Seth quite liked that. He thought Ernie would too. 'What's up?' Sid said.

Seth shrugged. 'Forgot I was meant to be meeting my Betty.'

'She won't mind if you're late.'

Seth checked his watch. He wasn't just late, he was very late. Poor Betty might even have got fed up with waiting and left the pub already. Mind you, she was never one to be alone for long. He smiled, thinking of his sweetheart. She was the life and soul, was Betty. Always first up to dance, and with her film-star good looks, he felt like the cock of the walk with her on his arm.

He'd been so proud when she'd agreed to marry him. Like he was set up for life. Mind you, they'd not got round to setting a date yet. But he'd been so busy with the operational patrol, and his job at the Miffield estate, that it just hadn't been a priority. He'd talk to Betty, he thought. Make some plans. Especially if all this was coming to an end. A wedding might take his mind off having no training to do or patrols to mount. Stop him feeling useless and like he had no purpose, like he was afraid he would feel when the unit was disbanded.

Yes, that's what he'd do. He'd go and find her now, and say it was time for them to set a date. They could go to church on Sunday and have a word with Reverend Thirlby. The thought of Betty walking down the aisle towards him, looking like Judy Garland in one of those fancy white frocks, made him beam with pride. She'd make the most beautiful bride, he thought. She'd be delighted when he told her they should make plans. Over the moon.

'I should head off,' he said, throwing his empty bottle on to the pile. He stood up. 'I reckon this is the last we'll see of you, George.'

George stood up too and the men shook hands rather stiffly and then embraced, slapping each other on the back. 'Stay for another drink,' said George. 'We can tell Paul about that lad on the training camp who said he was a pacifist.'

Seth chuckled. 'That officer's face when he said he would prefer to talk to any invading soldiers and not fight.'

Sid held out another beer to Seth and he took it, almost without thinking, and opened it with his knife. 'And he wouldn't do any of the demolition training because he said it was too destructive.'

He and George were both laughing now. Together, they sat back down on the bench.

'Honestly, he was the worst patrol member I came across,' George said. 'Apart from that chap we met who was at least eighty years old. Remember him?'

And they were off, trading more stories about their training, laughing as Sid – who was an excellent mimic – did impressions of the various people they'd met, and gently ribbing Paul, who was always reluctant to join in with their silly stories. At first.

Betty would understand, Seth thought a couple of hours and many beers later. She'd have caught up with her friends and had a drink or two herself. She wouldn't have missed him. He'd see her tomorrow and they could have a chat about the wedding. She'd be over the moon, he thought again. Over the blooming moon.

Chapter Four

AUGUST 1944

Annie had done nothing but sleep since she'd got back to Beckindale. She'd tumbled off the bus from Leeds and dragged herself up the hill to the shepherd's cottage her parents lived in, close to Emmerdale Farm. She'd gone straight to her old bed in her tiny bedroom and only woken for the occasional cup of tea or slice of toast.

But now, almost two whole days after she arrived home, as she yawned and stretched and tried to work out the time from the patterns the sun was making on her bedroom wall, she felt more like her old self.

It was morning, she decided, watching the rays dance on the pink patterned wallpaper. Suddenly ravenously hungry, she got out of bed, hoping she hadn't slept through breakfast, and pulled on an old dress she'd left behind in one of her drawers. It was soft from being washed so many times and smelled of the bars of soap her mother always tucked into clothes. Not that there was soap to spare now, of course, but the scent lingered.

In bare feet, Annie skipped downstairs and found her mother sitting at the kitchen table, reading the *Hotten Courier*.

'Oh, thank goodness, I was starting to worry you'd never wake up,' Grace said.

Annie grinned at her, feeling so much better for catching up on her sleep that she didn't even mind her mother's disapproving glance at her bare legs.

'Is there tea in the pot?'

'I'll freshen it,' Grace said. 'You sit down.'

Annie was quite capable of making her own tea, but she let her mother fuss round her, bringing a clean mug and some toast for her. The bread was delicious – a big improvement on the solid grey stuff they were served in the Wrens' billet in Portsmouth. There were definitely some advantages to living in farming country. Her eyes widened as Grace put a boiled egg in front of her. Definitely advantages.

'Everyone will be so excited to see you,' Grace said, sitting down again. 'Jacob's been reading your letters out in The Woolpack. You're like a returning hero.'

Annie's cheeks reddened. 'That's sweet of him.'

'He's proud of you,' Grace said. She looked down at the tablecloth. 'We all are,' she muttered.

Annie reached out and patted her mother's hand. The Pearsons weren't ones to show a lot of emotion, but she was pleased to be home, even if it was just for a couple of days, and she knew her mother was glad to have her.

'Where's Dad?'

Her mother shrugged. 'Working.'

'WarAg business?'

Sam had always been a farmer, running his own farm until some bad luck had seen him working for the Sugdens instead of being his own boss. But when the war broke out, he'd been snapped up by the WarAg – the War Agricultural Executive Committee – sharing his knowledge with farmers all over Yorkshire.

'He's got a busy week actually, but he said he would try to move things around if he could. He wants to spend time with you.'

Annie nodded. Things weren't always easy between her parents, and her mother had made choices that Annie wasn't happy about, but the war had made her realise that life wasn't always straightforward.

'I might go for a walk when I've had this,' Annie said. 'Go and see Lily. And Meg, maybe. Are they well?'

Her mother's face softened. 'That little Hope is a real character,' she said. Hope was Lily Dingle's two-year-old daughter. 'She's such a chatterbox already.'

'Like her mam,' said Annie. 'How about Meg?'

'Getting on with things quietly, you know Meg. Same as always,' Grace said.

'And Stan? And Ruby?' Annie was fond of her friend's adopted children.

'Ruby's never off her bicycle,' Grace said with a frown. 'She says she wants to ride in races. Imagine that. That's no sort of ambition for a girl.'

Annie thought it was an admirable ambition for a girl, but she kept her mouth closed.

'And is Stan still playing his music?'

'Beautifully,' said her mother. 'It's the only time he's still.'

Her mother took a breath. 'Oliver Skilbeck is still stepping out with Elizabeth Barlow.'

Annie stared very hard into her mug of tea. 'I don't care what he does.'

'I know,' Grace said. 'I just wanted to let you know he's around, that's all. You might bump into him while you're here.'

Oliver Skilbeck had tormented Annie when she was with Edward. Teased her and taunted her, and then one awful evening when she was walking across the fields on the way home from her friend Sarah's wedding, he'd jumped out at her. Annie had tried to fight him off, but he'd been too strong. He'd pushed her to the muddy ground and raped her. It had been the worst experience of Annie's life – until Edward had been killed a short while later. One of the best things about being in Portsmouth was that she never had to worry that Oliver Skilbeck would show up.

She shook her head to get rid of the memories and shovelled another piece of toast into her mouth. 'I'll go up to Emmerdale Farm and see Maggie.' She paused. 'And Jacob.'

As she said his name, she felt a little flutter of something – nerves? Surely not. She'd known Jacob almost as long as she'd known herself.

Her mother was looking at her with sharp eyes. 'Been writing to him a lot, have you?'

Annie picked up the crumbs she'd left on her plate with her forefinger. 'Him, you, Lily,' she said casually. 'I had a lot to say about the Normandy landings.'

'It sounded right frightening.'

'It wasn't really,' Annie said. 'Can I have some more tea? Not at the time. It was sort of exhilarating. It was only afterwards when I realised how dangerous it was for our troops.'

'And for you,' her mother said, pouring the remains of the tea in the pot into Annie's mug.

Annie chuckled, thinking of Fort Southwick, with its thick stone walls and centuries-old rooms. 'I was never in danger, Mam. Not for one minute.'

Grace looked unconvinced and Annie thought it was time for her to go. She drained her mug and stood up.

'I can't tell you how much better I feel for having a lot of sleep and some proper food,' she said. She dropped a kiss on to the top of her mother's head. 'Thank you.'

With a spring in her step, she picked up her handbag, shoved her feet into an old pair of pumps that were still in the rack by the front door, waved goodbye to her mum, and went outside.

It was the most glorious day, Annie thought as she walked down the lane. Warm and sunny, with bees buzzing round the flowers in the hedgerows and rabbits darting across the fields. She paused at the road, deciding which way to go. Would she head to the village and find Lily and Meg? Or should she go to Emmerdale Farm and see Maggie?

And Jacob, a small voice in her head said. She ignored it.

She'd go and see Maggie, she thought. The woman had been like a second mother to Annie over the years and she deserved to be top of Annie's list.

Mind made up, she bounced her way along the lane to the farm, enjoying the feel of the sun on her bare legs.

In the farmyard, she was greeted by a cacophony of barks. Annie recognised Jacob's dog, Bella, and Maggie's old boy, Ben, lumbering behind, the fur on his snout grey with age. And leading the way was a small, excitable black dog with a white patch over his eye and a misshapen foot.

'Get away,' a voice called. 'Get away, Winston. Come here, boy.'

The small dog bounded away from Annie, leaving her free to rub Bella's ears. Ben waddled over too and pressed himself against her legs. Wasn't it extraordinary how animals remembered people? she thought. She smiled wryly as she thought of how the donkey she'd rescued, Neddy, had remembered Oliver Skilbeck, and then she pushed away the horrible memories his name stirred up.

'Annie, how lovely.'

Annie looked up from the dogs to see Jacob smiling broadly at her, Maggie standing behind looking just as delighted, and by the barn, crouching down and clutching the little black dog, was Audrey, the Sugdens' Land Girl, waving enthusiastically and trying to stop the dog chewing her sleeve. Like she was being wrapped in a blanket on a cold night, Annie suddenly felt completely at home. As though she was back where she belonged.

Disconcerted at such a rush of emotion, she straightened up and smiled at everyone. 'Hello,' she said, feeling uncharacteristically shy. 'I've got some leave.'

Obviously she had leave. Why on earth did she feel the need to say that?

'Mam's washing my uniform.' Or that.

There was a tiny pause and then Maggie rushed forward and gathered Annie into her arms. 'Oh my girl, it's good to see you.'

Maggie's embrace felt strong and familiar and full of love. Annie relaxed into it, squeezing the older woman tightly.

'Let me look at you,' Maggie said, holding Annie at arm's length and appraising her with her sharp eyes. 'Bit thin,' she said. 'But you look well.'

Annie beamed at her. 'Food's rubbish in the billet,' she said. She tilted her head to one side and looked at Maggie, who didn't seem to age. She had a scarf tied round her head, but Annie could see there were a few grey hairs round her temples, and there were a couple more creases on her forehead, but she looked the same. Her eyes still shone with determination, despite the hardships she'd suffered over the years.

Jacob hovered nearby and awkwardly patted Annie's shoulder. 'It's right good to see you,' he said.

Annie untangled herself from Maggie and grinned at Jacob. It was lovely to see him too. His hair was a bit longer, and his face was ruddy from the sun. He looked good, she thought. He looked – and this was unusual for Jacob Sugden – happy. Their eyes met and Annie felt that flutter again. She took a step backwards, feeling oddly like it was important to put more space in between herself and Jacob.

'How's Joseph?' she asked and was relieved when Maggie began talking.

'He's doing well,' she said, of her husband. He'd never been the same since he'd been injured in the Great War and it hadn't been easy for Maggie, or Jacob and Edward, to live with him. But he'd mellowed and Annie was fond of the curmudgeonly old fellow.

Maggie chattered away, about the farm and Joseph, and the dogs, and Annie listened. At least, she half listened. Most of her mind was fixed on Jacob, who was standing next to her. He smelled of hay and horses and the sun, and she found it was hard to pay attention to Maggie's chit-chat while he was there, so present and so physical, after months of just being words on a letter.

'How about you show me round the farm, Maggie,' she said, suddenly desperate to move. 'I'd love to see all the changes you've made.'

Jacob gave her a small smile. 'I'll show you,' he said. 'Mam can make some tea.'

That hadn't been what Annie intended, but she supposed it would be nice to spend some time with Jacob. She nodded. 'That would be good.'

'Come on then, I don't have a lot of time to spare.' Jacob strode off and Annie followed him with a smile. He may have changed a lot, but he was still the same old grumpy Jacob when he wanted to be.

The farm was so different, Annie couldn't quite believe her eyes. Emmerdale was a large farm and before the war they'd grown crops and farmed sheep and cows. But now most of the animals were gone. There were no sheep any more; just dairy cows. The fields were full of flax, sugar beet and a huge amount of wheat, as far as Annie could see.

'I didn't think anything would grow down there?' she said, pointing to a patch that had always been waste ground before the war, as they walked up the hill. 'The soil is so thin.'

'WarAg says we have to make use of every patch of land we can,' Jacob said. Annie couldn't tell if he thought that was a good thing or bad. 'There's always something that'll grow if you plan it right.'

Annie was impressed. 'I can't believe you're growing so many rows of vegetables,' she said. She was out of breath trying to keep up with Jacob's long strides. She definitely wasn't as fit as she once had been – sitting at a desk underground all day certainly wasn't as energetic as farming. 'It's astonishing,' she gasped. 'But harvest won't be easy.'

Jacob nodded. 'Last year's harvest was the biggest ever,' he said. He sounded like he was reading from a book. 'Farmers in Great Britain grew the biggest acreage of crops in history.'

'No wonder you need that tractor,' Annie said.

Jacob grimaced. 'I still think horses are easier.'

'How will you manage the harvest?'

'Audrey's here. And her Ned's going to work with us for a couple of weeks. Plus I've got schoolchildren coming to help. I weren't keen on having them at first, but they worked really hard last year.'

Annie was impressed. 'You've made it work, Jacob,' she said. 'I know it's not been easy for you.' She paused. 'Edward would be proud.'

Jacob looked away from her, but she thought she could see a gleam of emotion in his eyes. 'I owed it to him to make it work,' he muttered.

Annie slipped her arm through his and gave him a squeeze. 'I know,' she said.

Jacob and Edward, Annie's fiancé, had been brothers, but they'd not always been friends. They'd drawn straws to decide which of them would stay at the farm and which would join up, but Jacob had fixed it so Edward had joined the navy. When his ship went down, Jacob had been crippled with guilt. And Annie had been furious. But Jacob had changed. And Annie had too. The war had made things that once seemed hugely important less so. And vice versa.

'He'd have gone anyway,' she said to Jacob now. Edward had never wanted to stay in Beckindale. He'd always had itchy feet and an eye on the horizon.

Jacob turned to Annie. 'I know,' he echoed.

Their bodies were close together, Annie's arm still looped through Jacob's. They looked at each other and Annie felt that flutter again, stronger this time. Her heart thumped and she looked at Jacob, and he looked back at her.

Was he going to kiss her? she thought wildly. Surely not. What would she do if he did? She didn't know. They gazed at each other for a second and then Jacob bent his head, his face was close to hers, and she could feel the warmth of his breath on her skin . . .

With a start, Annie pulled her arm from his and stepped away. Her head was spinning. She wanted him to kiss her, and yet, it was suddenly too real. Memories of Oliver Skilbeck pushing her to the ground as he unbuckled his trousers sprang into her mind, making her feel queasy. She shoved her trembling hands in the pockets of her dress so Jacob couldn't see her reaction. She'd always thought it would be the memory of Edward that stopped her getting close to another man, but it turned out it was Oliver Skilbeck's brutality that was causing her trouble.

Jacob cleared his throat awkwardly, obviously thinking the problem was with himself, not Annie.

'You know Audrey's marrying Ned?' he mumbled.

Annie couldn't speak. She wanted to tell him that he'd done nothing wrong, but instead she just blinked at him.

'Audrey?' she said vaguely.

'And Ned. Christmas wedding.' Jacob headed off at a cracking pace down the hill towards the farmhouse. 'I'll show you Mam's bees. Come on.'

Her head spinning and her heart still pounding, Annie touched her lips gently with her fingertips, and then she took a deep breath and raced after Jacob.

Chapter Five

Betty didn't want to go to The Woolpack to see Annie Pearson, even though everyone else was going. She liked Annie well enough. In fact, more than once she'd smiled to herself, thinking how funny it was that they got along, because they were about as different as two women could be. But, though she would like to say hello, she wasn't keen on a night out. Truth was, Betty seemed to be getting more miserable by the day. It was as though the further the troops advanced into France, and the more hopeful everyone became, the bleaker Betty felt. It was very unlike her and she wasn't enjoying it one bit.

Susan Roberts, who helped out in the vet's when she wasn't at school, looked across Betty's reception desk, suspicious at Betty's lack of enthusiasm.

'What's up with you?'

Betty forced a smile. She was doing that a lot these days – forcing smiles. 'Just got a headache, that's all,' she lied. 'Of course I'll be at The Woolpack. Is Nancy going?'

Betty was fond of Nancy and Susan, and the vet's part-time nurse, Cathy. In fact, there was lots Betty liked about being the receptionist in the surgery. She enjoyed meeting people, and chatting to the animals' owners. She was organised and quick with numbers and, all in all, it was a good job. Better than working in the factory where she'd been at the start of the war. But that didn't stop her dreaming of her time on stage with the ENSA dancers and wishing things had turned out differently.

'Nancy's coming,' Susan said. 'She's just finishing up with Miss Whittaker's cat. Though she's exhausted as usual, so I bet she's asleep in a corner before the night's out.'

Betty smiled more genuinely this time. Nancy was such a hard worker, she deserved some time off.

'What about your Seth?' Susan asked, making Betty frown.

'Might be working,' she muttered. 'Dunno.'

She felt the younger woman's curious eyes on her, but she didn't want to talk about Seth now, so with a big effort she tossed her hair back and raised her chin.

'Should you be going to the pub?' she said to Susan in a teasing tone. 'Shouldn't you be studying?'

Susan wanted to be a vet, like Nancy, and was usually poring over her schoolbooks somewhere. She'd got top marks in her school certificate the year before and it seemed she was on track to do the same in her higher certificate. Betty had never been one for books really, but she was fiercely proud of what Susan had achieved. Especially after the heartache she'd been through. The young woman really had blossomed since she'd come to Beckindale.

'It's the summer holidays,' Susan said now, rolling her eyes. 'I'm free as a bird. Though Ruby keeps nagging me to go on bike rides with her.'

'You should go.' Betty's appraising gaze took in Susan's pale face and scrawny, long-legged frame. 'Would do you good to get out in the fresh air. My Seth always says fresh air is the best tonic.'

'Maybe,' said Susan. 'It could be fun. I could get my gran to make us a picnic.'

'There you go,' Betty said, a touch wistfully. She wished she could be seventeen again like Susan and be content with a picnic and a bike ride.

'So are you coming?' Susan said. 'Nancy said she'd see us there.'

Betty straightened her desk, picked up her handbag and followed Susan out of the surgery and across the village to the pub. Seth had said he would be there this evening and even though he'd let her down such a lot recently, she still hoped he might be true to his word.

So her heart lifted a bit when Susan pushed open the door and the first person Betty saw, sitting in his usual spot at the end of the bar, was Seth. And it lifted even more when his face lit up at the sight of her.

'Betty!' he said in delight. He jumped off the stool and came over to wrap her in his strong arms. Betty melted. All the doubts she'd been having disappeared and she enjoyed the feeling of Seth's embrace.

'I wasn't sure you'd be here,' she said into his chest.

Seth didn't hear – or he didn't seem to, any road. Instead he just kissed the top of her head and asked what she wanted to drink.

'Gin and orange, please,' she said.

'Coming up,' Seth said. 'What about Susan?'

'Just a lemonade for me,' said Susan. 'Oh, there's Annie, look.'

Betty looked over to where Annie Pearson sat, with Jacob and Maggie Sugden, Audrey Atkins and Ned Barlow, all hanging on her every word. Ned and Audrey's fingers were entwined under the table and they were sitting so close to each other that Audrey may as well have been on Ned's lap. Jacob was gazing at Annie as she talked in a way that made Betty feel like she was intruding, even though she was right at the other side of the pub. She took her gin and, together with Susan, went over to say hello to Annie.

They all chatted for a while. Annie's stories about the Normandy landings were pretty exciting, Betty had to admit.

'Were you scared?' she asked.

'Not one bit,' Annie said. 'Not for myself. I was scared for the lads over in France. I could hear the gunfire and the shells exploding.'

Betty shivered. She looked at Annie, with her neat hair and make-up-free face, and her smart Wrens uniform. She was so different from Betty, who painted her lips with beetroot juice and her legs with gravy browning, and slept in curlers. For the first time ever when it came to Annie Pearson, Betty felt a tiny glimmer of envy and a flash of guilt thinking about how much Annie had done for the war effort and how little she'd done. 'I think you're ever so brave,' she said.

Annie held Betty's gaze and then she smiled. 'Thank you,' she said. 'That means a lot, Betty.'

Betty returned her smile. 'So, tell us more about the landings,' she said.

To her surprise, Seth sat down next to her, asking Annie questions about the troops on the beaches, what equipment they had, and if it was true that they had tanks that floated on the water. Betty had never known Seth to be interested in military strategy before. It was the countryside that was his great passion, as far as she knew. She felt another uncharitable

39

flicker of envy. Annie was holding Seth's attention, she thought. Why couldn't she?

Eventually, after an hour or so of chat, Seth turned to her. 'I need to go,' he said.

Betty stood up and pulled him to one side. 'What?' Her tone was icy. She felt like she'd barely seen him even though he'd been sitting next to her.

'I need to go.'

'Where?'

He paused. 'Work.'

'Seth Armstrong, you're a gamekeeper, not a nightwatchman. Why on earth do you need to go to work at this hour?'

Seth shifted from one foot to the other, looking uncomfortable. Susan and Nancy, who were nearby, had heard Betty's sharp tone and they were now very obviously pretending not to have noticed that she was annoyed with her sweetheart. Betty found she didn't care what anyone thought, so cross was she with Seth.

'Where,' she said again, very slowly and clearly, as though Seth was hard of hearing, 'are you going?'

Seth opened his mouth and then closed it again, like a goldfish.

Betty pulled herself up so she was standing very straight. Her stomach felt like the bottom of it had dropped out, and her hands were trembling, but she was determined to say what was on her mind.

'Have you got another girl, Seth? Is that what all this is about?'

Seth looked horrified. His eyes darted about him, as he cast about for what to say. Then, to Betty's surprise, he took her hand and pulled her out of the pub. Once they were outside in the soft summer evening, Betty made to sit down in front of The Woolpack, but Seth shook his head and instead pulled her down the steps and round to the side a bit, hidden from the view of any passers-by.

'What's going on?' Betty said, her voice shaking. 'What's this all about?'

Seth sighed. He took Betty by the shoulders and stared deep into her eyes. Betty stared back, wondering what he was going to say.

'Betty Prendagast, you're the only girl for me,' he said. 'I meant it when I asked you to marry me and I was just thinking the other day we should set a date for the wedding.' He kissed her softly on the lips.

Placated slightly, Betty smiled at him. 'Really?'

'Really,' he said vehemently.

'So what's with all this rushing off then, if it's not another girl? I don't believe it's work.'

Seth swallowed. 'It's work of a sort.'

'Is it black-market stuff?' Betty was shocked. Seth had his faults, but he was an honest man. 'Is it illegal?'

'No, course not.' Seth frowned. 'I can't tell you, Betty. I wish I could, but I can't.'

'Is it dangerous?'

Seth's frown deepened. 'I can't say anything. I've told you too much already.'

'Seth . . .' Betty began, but he silenced her with another kiss.

'Just remember you're my girl,' he said.

He turned and walked away, leaving Betty leaning against the wall of The Woolpack feeling completely confused. What was going on?

'I need another drink,' she said to herself.

Back inside the pub, Nancy had arrived and was chatting to her friend Lily Proudfoot and the village schoolteacher Meg Warcup. Susan was laughing with her pal Ruby Dobbs – Meg's adopted daughter – and Annie Sugden still had a crowd around her.

Feeling a bit like a spare part, Betty almost turned and went home, but instead she took a deep breath and went to the bar, where Larry Dingle was serving.

'What are you having, pet?' he said. 'Gin and orange?'

Betty nodded.

'I'll get this,' a voice behind her said. 'And a pint please, Larry.' Betty turned to see Wally Eagleton standing behind her.

'Hello, Wally.' She smiled at him – a genuine, old-Betty smile – and he grinned back. 'That's really kind.'

'On your own?'

'I came with Susan and Nancy from work,' Betty said, gesturing with her head to where her colleagues sat.

'Would they mind if I stole you away for a while?' Wally put his hand on her arm. It felt nice.

'I don't think they'd even notice,' said Betty.

'I doubt that, but their loss is my gain.' Gallantly, Wally picked up their drinks and led the way to a table at the side of the pub, tucked away behind the door.

Betty sat down and took a swig of her gin, feeling it warm her throat. 'That's better,' she said.

'Rough day?'

She shrugged. 'Same old.'

'Want to talk about it?'

Betty shook her head, but suddenly she realised she did want to talk about it. With her sister Margaret off nursing in Birmingham, and Nancy always so busy, she had no one to confide in really.

'Just some trouble with my . . . fiancé,' she said.

'Seth Armstrong.'

Betty was surprised he knew. Had he been asking around about her? The thought warmed her more than the gin had.

'That's him.'

Wally leaned over the table towards her. 'Tell me everything,' he said.

So Betty did.

Chapter Six

Lily Proudfoot watched Betty chatting to the handsome man at the bar with a frown. Where was Seth? Why was Betty fluttering her eyelashes at that man?

Lily knew that where respectability was concerned, she didn't have a leg to stand on. Hadn't she had an affair with a married man – not that she'd known he was married of course – and got pregnant out of wedlock? But the fact was, she just wanted everyone to be happy. Lily loved love stories and romantic films where the hero whisked the heroine off her feet. She didn't want to think about broken hearts, or her friend Betty giggling in a corner with a man who wasn't her fiancé.

'Where's Betty gone?' Nancy asked, having noticed her absence too.

'She's over there.' Lily nodded to where Betty was deep in conversation with the handsome man. He looked vaguely familiar, but Lily couldn't remember his name.

Meg raised an eyebrow. 'That's not Seth.'

'Seth's here, though, isn't he?' Lily looked over to his usual spot by the bar, but Seth's stool was empty. She shrugged. 'He must have gone.'

'Who's gone?'

Annie appeared in front of them and Lily squealed with happiness. She jumped to her feet and threw her arms round her. 'I'm so pleased you're home,' she said. 'And that Jacob's let you sneak off for five minutes.'

Annie flushed. Lily watched her, wondering what she'd said that had caused such a reaction. Surely it wasn't the mention of Jacob? Was it?

'Sit down and tell us all your news,' Meg said. 'You remember Nancy?'

'Of course I do,' said Annie, sitting down next to Meg. 'Hello, Nancy.'

'Come on then,' Lily said. 'What's new?'

Annie threw her head back in mock despair. 'Please don't make me talk about the Normandy landings again,' she said. 'I've told the story that many times, my head's spinning.'

Lily was only slightly disappointed. 'Tell us all the other stuff, then. Any romance with those handsome sailors?'

'Give over, I don't have time for that,' Annie said. She reached across the table and took Lily's hand, gripping her fingers tightly. 'It's you lot I want to know about. How's Jack? And little Hope? And how are you, Meg?'

Lily grinned at the mention of her husband and daughter. 'Jack's great,' she said, truthfully. Her husband was the village policeman, a loyal and supportive man. He'd proposed to her when she was pregnant with another man's baby and he loved Hope as much – more even – as he would have if she'd been his own daughter. Lily thanked her lucky stars every day that she'd met him, because Derek – Hope's biological father and the man she'd had an affair with – had been a real cad. A married man and a liar. But now she had Jack, and Hope, and . . . She leaned forward. 'We want to have another baby,' she told her friends. 'I wanted to wait a while after Hope, but she's almost three now and she'd love a little brother or sister.'

Annie clapped her hands together in joy and Meg and Nancy both grinned. 'That's wonderful,' said Meg. 'I'm often glad that Ruby and Stan have each other. Goodness knows they needed to rely on each other when their mam was killed.'

'And now they have you,' Annie said fondly, looking at Meg. 'They're lucky you stepped up and took them in.'

Meg waved away Annie's praise, though Lily could see she was pleased. 'I'm the lucky one.'

'What about you, Nancy?' Annie turned to the vet, who'd been sitting quietly.

'What about me?' Nancy's eyes widened in surprise.

'Do you have a sweetheart?'

'Goodness, no,' said Nancy quickly. 'I'm much too busy for any of that nonsense.'

Lily nudged her friend. 'You won't always think it's nonsense.'

Nancy took a sip of her drink. 'Won't I?' she said, in a tone that made Lily think she really meant it. Lily made up her mind to find someone who might suit Nancy. There had to be someone in the village who could catch her eye. It was hard, mind you, with so many of the men away fighting, or back but recovering from injuries . . . Oh, now she knew who it was.

'It's Wally Eagleton,' she said.

'Who?' Meg frowned.

'Over there, talking to Betty. It's Wally Eagleton. I knew his face, but I couldn't remember his name. He was injured,

I think. That's why he's here. Ooh, look at the way he's looking at her. He's hanging on her every word.'

Meg looked round and Lily thumped her arm. 'Don't look.'

'You just told me to look,' Meg said. 'How was I supposed to know you actually meant don't look?'

The women all giggled and, subtly, Annie peered over her shoulder. 'You're right, Lily. He's smitten.'

'Betty's engaged to Seth,' Lily said firmly. 'They've been planning their wedding.'

But, as she said it, she wasn't sure it was true. Had they been making plans? She'd not seen Seth and Betty together much recently.

She looked at Betty again. 'She looks downright miserable,' she admitted.

'Let's hope Wally can cheer her up,' Meg said.

Lily grimaced. 'Might just make everything worse.'

Annie nodded. 'That's true.' She stifled a yawn. 'Oh, goodness, I'm sorry. I'm still so tired.'

'You've been busy,' said Lily, full of concern for her friend. 'Why don't you head off home?'

Nancy suddenly yawned too. 'I think I need to go home as well, I'm sorry.'

'I'll walk with you, Nancy,' Annie said. The two women both stood up. Lily grabbed Annie and squeezed her in a hug.

'Come and say goodbye before you go back to Portsmouth,' she said.

'Of course.'

The women all waved, and Nancy and Annie headed for home.

'Do you have to go, or will you stay for another?' Lily asked Meg. 'Jack's at home with Hope, so I don't have to get back.'

47

'Stan's with Mrs Roberts,' Meg said. 'So why not.'

Lily signalled to her cousin Larry, who was behind the bar, and he nodded to show he'd bring their drinks over. Lily grinned at him. There were some perks to being part of the family that ran the pub, that was for sure.

'You've been quiet,' Lily said to her friend. 'Is everything all right?'

'Everything's fine,' said Meg. But then she frowned. 'Actually, no. It's not fine.'

To Lily's alarm, Meg's eyes filled with tears and she buried her face in her hands, just as Larry put their drinks down on their table.

'I'll pay you later,' Lily said, shooing him away. He glanced at Meg and scarpered – he wasn't fond of emotional women. Not that Meg was emotional, not usually. Concerned, Lily put a gentle hand on her friend's shoulder. 'What's the matter?'

Meg looked up.

'I'm in trouble, Lily.'

Lily was shocked. 'You don't mean . . .' She glanced at Meg's midriff, which was neat and slim as ever, and Meg shook her head.

'Not like that,' she said. 'I've done something stupid.'

'That would be stupid,' said Lily wryly. 'Believe me.'

Meg gave her a weak smile. 'Remember Rolf?'

'The prisoner of war?' Early in the war, there had been a prisoner of war camp close to Beckindale. Some of the local farms – Emmerdale Farm for one – had used the prisoners for labour and Meg had got to know Rolf. He'd even taught Stan to play violin. But he'd left the village when the camp had been moved.

'That's him,' Meg said. She bit her lip. 'I've been writing to him.'

Lily shrugged, not understanding why Meg was making a big deal about this. She'd known that they'd kept in touch. The German had been fond of Stan and Ruby, and Meg had promised to keep him updated with their progress.

But Meg was shaking her head. 'I don't mean every now and then,' she whispered. 'We've been writing a lot. Every week.'

Lily's jaw dropped. 'Every week? What on earth do you say?'

'I've told him all sorts,' Meg said. 'About Stan and Ruby, about me and what I think about things. About my family. I've told him things I've never told anyone else.' She paused. 'Even you.'

Lily was put out. 'Why?' she said, feeling prickly. 'Why would you confide in him like that?'

Meg looked into her glass, avoiding Lily's stare. 'Because I like him,' she said. 'I really like him.'

'Oh Meg,' Lily said. 'Oh no.'

Meg stared straight at Lily, her expression defiant. 'He likes me too,' she said. 'I think . . .' She breathed in deeply. 'I think we might love each other.'

Lily felt completely at a loss. She wanted to support her friend, who'd been there for her through all the awful business with Derek, but not with this. She almost felt angry with Meg for telling her. What did she expect Lily to say? Lily loved happily ever afters, but how could this ever end well? Meg was deluded. She opened her mouth to speak and then closed it again without saying anything.

'I know,' said Meg, her defiance deserting her. 'It's hopeless.'

'He's German,' Lily whispered. 'How could you ever . . .'

'He's just a man.'

'A German man.'

'They're not evil,' Meg said.

'Aren't they?'

'No,' Meg almost shouted.

At the bar, Larry looked over, raising an eyebrow at Lily and checking she was all right. Lily nodded to him, letting him know things were fine.

'Meg . . .' she began. But then she trailed off. Because she knew Meg was right, really. There must be good German soldiers, just as there were horrible British ones. And Lily knew Rolf. She'd met him many times when he was at the camp locally. She'd seen how lovely he was with little Stan. How quiet and thoughtful and caring he was. But even so. He was German. A Luftwaffe pilot. 'Edward Sugden died,' she said. 'And Ernie Hudson.'

'I know . . .' Meg began.

'People won't ever accept it, Meg.'

'Lily . . .'

Lily paused. 'I know Rolf is a good man,' she said, choosing her words carefully because she didn't want to break her friend's heart. 'But this war isn't over yet, and even when it is, the scars will be deep. I just can't see how an English woman and a German man could be happy together.'

Meg looked wretched. 'I know,' she said. 'I know you're right. But I keep dreaming that one day we'll be a family – me, Rolf, Ruby and Stan. Maybe a baby of my own.'

Lily felt awful. 'The Germans killed Ruby and Stan's mother,' she said.

'And the Allies killed Rolf's mother,' Meg snapped.

'See?' Lily said. 'The scars are too deep.'

Meg's eyes filled with tears. 'I hate this war.'

'Me too.' Gently, Lily reached over and wiped away Meg's tears. 'But it's nearly over. The Nazis can't win now. Jack says it could be over and done with by Christmas.'

Meg snorted. 'I've heard that before.'

'Well, maybe this time it's true. And once it's all over, and Rolf's back in Germany, you'll feel better. Ready for a new start.'

'Maybe,' Meg said. 'Christmas feels like a long way off, yet. And so does the end of the war.'

'We must have hope,' Lily said. 'Because without that, we have nothing.'

Chapter Seven

Meg couldn't sleep. She lay in bed, thinking about what Lily had said. She knew her friend was speaking sense. How could she ever have dreamed of having a life with Rolf? The war may have been on its last legs, but there could be no future for them.

She rolled over and punched her pillow hard. It was so unfair, she thought. Of all the men in England, why did she have to go and fall in love with the one she couldn't have? The one she could never have.

Lily had been right, though, she thought. She had to get over this. She wouldn't write to Rolf any more. Half of her letters didn't get through anyway, even though he was only across the Pennines in Lancashire.

She sat up in bed and hugged her knees, feeling tears weren't far away. She would stop writing to him and move on with her life.

Meg had always tried to be a good person. Her twin sister Rose had died when they were fifteen and since then she'd tried to be twice as good, as though she had to make amends for being the sister who survived. She'd even become a teacher – the job Rose had wanted to do – because she felt she owed it to their parents. Now, of course, she loved her job and she thought, proudly, that she was rather good at it.

Early in the war, she'd been thrown in at the deep end when, as the village schoolmistress, she'd been given the job of finding billets for evacuees who'd come from Hull – where the bombs were falling heavily – to rural Yorkshire. It hadn't been easy. Meg had stared at the ragtag bunch of children in the school hall and wanted to cry – for them and for her. She knew a lot of the farmers nearby had volunteered to take on an evacuee or two, thinking they'd get good strong lads who could help with all the extra work the WarAg had landed on their shoulders. She'd even heard a couple of them boasting to Sam Pearson in The Woolie, telling them how impressed he'd be at their next inspection because they'd have extra hands to help out.

But Meg had looked at the scrawny, hollow-eyed children in front of her and thought she'd never find homes for them.

She had, of course, in the end. Not all of them were happy. Not all of their billets were right. Some of them were downright dangerous. And a few kids had gone back to Hull, preferring to take their chances with the bombs. But lots of them had been transformed into healthy, ruddy-cheeked country children, indistinguishable from the kids who'd grown up in Beckindale.

And then there was Ruby and Stan.

They'd been left behind that first day. The pair of them standing hand in hand in the hall, skinny, scruffy and defiant. Ruby had been horribly aggressive, Stan so sad he could barely talk. And because there was no one left to take them, it had fallen to Meg to put them up.

Those first few months had been really hard. The children hadn't wanted to be with Meg. Ruby in particular had been awfully prickly. She'd run away, and made life very difficult for everyone – Meg especially. She had even dragged her brother home to Hull, before their mother brought them back to Beckindale. Meg hugged her knees tighter, thinking of Brenda, the only parent the children had known. She was neglectful and dismissive, and not remotely worried about her offspring. But even so, when she'd been killed in a raid on Hull, Ruby and Stan had been devastated. Ruby had been furious with the world, and Rolf – not surprisingly – had borne the brunt of her anger.

Meg smiled to herself, thinking of how Rolf had reacted. Meeting Ruby's fury with love, and compassion. He was such a caring man. So calm and sweet-natured. A million miles away from the angry Germans in everyone's minds.

But no. She shouldn't be thinking of that now. Rolf was in her past.

Ruby had grown to adore him, of course, she thought, ignoring her own warnings to stop her reminiscing. And it was thanks to Rolf that Ruby had been given her first bicycle to ride. And now she spent all her spare time on two wheels, whizzing through the country lanes, and telling anyone who'd listen how one day she'd race in the Olympic Games and win medals for Britain. And Stan. Well! He was Rolf's biggest fan.

She thought about Stan as he'd been. Tiny, shy, barely speaking. And how he'd reacted when he'd heard Rolf play the violin for the first time. Rolf was a beautiful musician. He'd almost joined an orchestra in America before the war. He'd picked up a fiddle at a village party, back when he was labouring at Emmerdale Farm, and changed Stan's life in that minute.

Music had been the making of Stanley. Rolf had taught him how to play violin and he was now so accomplished himself that he dreamed he'd one day be a professional. He had a different teacher now, but he still talked about Rolf. His talent at music had helped him come out of his shell and now he had an enormous group of friends, played cricket whenever he could, or football, or climbed trees, and he really was the apple of Meg's eye.

Because, of course, the children were hers now. When Brenda had died, Meg had taken them on officially – become their adopted mother. Before the war, she'd never dreamed she'd one day have two kids of her own, but now she wouldn't be without them. She was prouder of those children than of anything else she'd ever done. She loved them so fiercely she couldn't remember how it felt to be without them, and she thanked her lucky stars every day that they'd come into her life.

People always said that she'd done a good job with Stan and Ruby. That she'd given them a life they couldn't have had in Hull. But Meg knew that, really, they were the ones who'd done a good job with her.

Before they'd fallen into her life and turned it upside down, she'd been sort of half living. Still grieving for her sister Rose, blaming herself for her death, doing a job she'd never intended to do. She had been less living and more simply existing.

But the arrival of the children had changed all that. Suddenly she had a reason to be a better person. To live her life to the full. To make the most of every minute. They'd made her whole world a nicer place to be and she would always be grateful for that.

Rolf loved them too, she thought. He'd been such a steady influence for them in those chaotic early days. And his letters were always full of questions about them.

She leaned over the side of her bed and pulled out the shoebox that she kept all of his letters in. Then she tipped it out on to her counterpane and leafed through all the envelopes.

She'd read every letter so many times she could almost recite them by heart. There was one where Rolf had described his attempts to join the POW camp football team that had made her laugh so hard. There was another where he'd written of his sadness that he'd never see his mother again – she'd been killed in an Allied bombing raid on Berlin. Another where he'd sent pages of information to Stan about records he should listen to that would help his violin playing. Another where he'd drawn a picture of Ruby with a gold medal around her neck. Ruby had that sketch on her wall now.

And then there were the letters where he'd told Meg how he felt about her. How she was the last person he thought of at night and the first person he thought about when he woke up in the morning. How when things were tough at the camp – and they were tough, even though Meg liked to pretend they weren't – he thought about Meg's smile and that helped him through . . .

She buried her face in her hands. He was just such a nice man, she thought sadly. The kind of man she could have been really happy with. But no. Lily was right. She had to put it all behind her and move on. Stop writing to him altogether and forget about him. Rolf Schreiber was in her past.

Although . . .

He was so interested in the children, that surely it would be cruel not to keep him updated on their achievements? After all, it was down to him that they'd discovered their talents and now had goals to reach for.

Surely it would be all right to keep sending letters, if she focused on Ruby and Stan? There was no harm in that, was there? And, actually, didn't she have to tell him that Stan had learned a new piece of music just last week, and that Ruby had been doing really well helping Lily at the garage?

Those snippets of news were definitely worth a letter. She nodded to herself. She'd write to him now, she thought, leaning over and getting a pen and some writing paper from her bedside table. She'd keep it breezy and friendly, all about the children. No declarations of love. No outpouring of emotion. None of that. Just two friends, sharing news.

She picked up her pen.

'Darling Rolf,' she wrote.

Chapter Eight

DECEMBER 1944

Lily came out of the bathroom and shook her head at Jack sadly. 'Not this month.'

She tried to smile, but it wasn't easy, and Jack gathered her into his arms and kissed the top of her head.

'We'll keep trying,' he said. 'I'm rather enjoying it.'

This time, Lily's smile was easier. Jack always knew what to say to cheer her up. 'I know,' she said. 'I just hoped it would happen sooner than this.'

She'd thought she would fall pregnant easily this time. After all, last time had been an accident, and that little mistake was now playing happily with her dolly on the rug, her curly hair caught up in two adorable bunches.

Jack saw her looking at little Hope and grinned. 'We've got our hands full with that one,' he said. 'Her brother or sister will arrive when he or she is good and ready.'

Lily nodded. 'You're right.'

But she still felt a bit sad as she got ready for work. Jack loved Hope, there was absolutely no doubt about that. And she loved him too. In fact, she had picked up so many of his mannerisms that people who didn't know the truth about her father often commented that she was just like Jack. Lily liked it when that happened.

'Come on, Hope,' she said now. 'We need to go and see Grandma Nina.'

Nina was Lily's stepmother. She'd married her father Mick just before Hope was born, and the couple were very happy. Lily hadn't been keen on Nina at first, worrying her dad was trying to replace Lily's mother. But Nina had been so supportive and kind when Lily discovered she was pregnant – and that her lover Derek was married – that the pair had struck up a firm friendship. Nina looked after Hope when Jack was working and Lily was busy at the garage.

'Grandma Nina,' Hope cooed. She loved Nina and liked to dress up in her bohemian clothes. Lily thought it was nice for Hope to have a grandma who was as glamorous as Nina was. Especially when her mother wore overalls most of the time and spent her days tinkering with bicycles.

Once they were bundled up in their coats, hats, scarves and gloves – it was a cold day – Lily kissed Jack goodbye, took Hope by the hand, and together they wandered through the village to Mick and Nina's cottage. It was frosty outside, and the puddles left by recent rain had frozen. Hope was three now and very chatty, so it took them a while to get there because she liked to stop and say hello to everyone they passed.

'Hello!' she called to Nancy, who was hurrying into the vet's.

Nancy called a greeting back. 'I've got some kittens, Hope,' she said. 'Would you like to come and see them later when they've woken up?'

Hope clapped her hands excitedly. 'We go and see the kittens,' she said. "Lo, Betty.'

Betty was following a few steps behind Nancy. She was walking quickly through the cold morning air, hunched down into her scarf. She was so deep in thought that she didn't even hear the little girl's greeting.

Hope's happy face fell, and Lily quickly distracted her. 'I think I can see Grandpa Mick,' she said. 'Is he at the garage?'

Hope looked over to where Mick was just opening up.

'Grandpa!' she bellowed.

Mick pretended to be surprised, putting his hands up in mock fright and staggering backwards. Hope giggled.

'Can I run?' she said to Lily, and when Lily nodded, she took off, dashing across to where her besotted grandfather stood waiting with open arms.

Smiling, Lily followed at a more sedate pace.

'I'll take her to Nina,' she said to her father.

'Don't worry, love. I'll keep her here for a minute. Nina wants to talk to you.'

Lily frowned. 'Is everything all right?'

'Nina's fine, nothing to worry about there,' Mick said. 'She's just got some news.'

Feeling unsettled, Lily went round to the cottage and opened the door – it was never locked – calling for Nina as she entered.

Her stepmother came out of the kitchen, looking worried. 'Oh Lily, come in, love. Let me make you some tea.'

'I don't want tea. What's happened?' Lily could tell by Nina's face that something was wrong.

'I've just got a bit of news for you,' Nina said vaguely. 'Sit down.'

Obediently, Lily plonked herself down on one of the kitchen chairs that had been in her father's house for donkey's years but which Nina had re-covered in a bright gingham fabric that Lily thought might have been potato sacking once upon a time.

'What?' she said, really worried now. 'What's wrong?'

'Lily love, I had a letter from my friend Sylvia. She was the woman who arranged the billets for the training camp, remember?'

Of course Lily remembered. It was Sylvia who'd billeted Derek Mortimer – Hope's biological father – with Nina.

'I remember,' she said cautiously. 'And?'

Nina took a breath. 'I'm very sorry, Lily. She said that Derek's been killed in action. In France, I believe.'

Lily was glad she was sitting down because her legs suddenly felt like jelly.

'He's dead?' she said. 'Derek's dead?'

'I'm afraid so.'

'I'll have that tea now, please,' Lily said.

Nina put a comforting hand on her shoulder and set about filling the kettle. Lily watched her, but her mind was elsewhere. Derek had proved himself to be an awful person. Cheating on his wife, lying to Lily, and even offering to pay for Lily to . . . she swallowed . . . 'deal with' her unexpected pregnancy. He was, she thought, the opposite to lovely Jack in every single way. But that didn't mean she'd wished him dead. Far from it.

'Hope will never meet her real father,' she said, to herself really.

Nina put a cup of tea in front of her and sat down at the table. 'She will never meet her biological father,' she said. 'But Jack's her real father in every way that matters.'

Lily nodded. 'You're right. It just feels a bit odd, you know?'

'I know, love,' Nina said. 'It's all right to be sad. You're not being disloyal to Jack.'

Nina had summed up how Lily was feeling so precisely that Lily could only blink in surprise.

Her stepmother smiled at her. 'Your dad has his moments when he's missing your mum,' she said. 'At first I felt prickly when it happened. Like he was cheating on me, which is ridiculous. But then I learned that he loves us both in different ways. And that him loving your mother made him the person I'd fallen for.'

'But my mother was a good person,' Lily said, annoyed that Nina was comparing her beloved mam to horrible Derek.

'I know,' Nina said quickly. 'I don't mean that she and Derek are at all alike. Just that the things you went through with Derek have made you the Lily that Jack loves. And Jack understands that. He's a very clever man, I think.'

'He is,' Lily said, proud as punch at the compliment.

'So he won't take it as a snub if you mourn Derek.'

'It's not Derek I'd be mourning,' Lily said, thoughtfully. 'More the idea of Derek.'

'Exactly.'

There was a little silence as they both drank their tea. And then Lily spoke again.

'I've always worried, you know, that one day Derek might turn up. That he might suddenly decide he wanted to be part of Hope's life. Or try to take her from me.'

'I can understand that worry,' Nina said. 'He was a horrible man, right pleased with himself. With his chest puffed out all the time, like a peacock. It had crossed my mind that he might show up, too.'

'Really?'

'But now we don't have to worry about that at all, do we?'

'No,' Lily said. She sipped her tea. 'We don't.'

Suddenly, she felt as though a weight had been lifted from her; a weight she hadn't even known she was carrying. Jack was free now to love Hope and care for her without any fear that she could be taken from him. Lily was free to build her life and her family without looking over her shoulder, or feeling guilty. It was sad that Derek had been killed, there was no doubt about that. Lily felt sorry for his widow – she'd seen her once and felt bad enough then, but this was worse. But she felt no sorrow for herself or for Hope, because they had Jack and he was the best husband and father they could ever have.

Nina was looking at Lily carefully. 'Feeling better?'

'I am,' Lily said. 'I'll speak to Jack later, but for now, yes, I'm all right.'

'Good.'

'I'll go and get Hope.'

'Oh, no rush,' Nina said. 'She's fine with your dad. I'll top up your brew and let's keep chatting.'

Lily relaxed in her seat, smiling at her stepmother. 'I'm not going to say no to that.'

They sat happily for a while. Lily told Nina about Betty and how odd she'd been recently. 'I'm worried about her, Nina,' she said. 'She's not been herself for ages. And I've barely seen Seth Armstrong. She said they were going to set a date for their wedding, but she's not mentioned it again.'

'Perhaps she's got cold feet,' Nina suggested.

'Perhaps.'

'Speaking of weddings, are you going to Audrey and Ned's?'

'Of course I am,' Lily said. 'I wouldn't miss it. I've made the sweetest dress for Hope. Imagine getting wed on Christmas Eve.'

'It's a lovely idea,' Nina said. 'I'm hoping it'll snow.'

Lily rolled her eyes. 'That's what Audrey wants. She keeps looking at the sky and asking Jacob whether he thinks there's going to be a freeze.'

'It's definitely cold enough,' Nina said. 'Ah, it'll be nice to have some fun, won't it.'

'It will,' said Lily, nodding her head vigorously. 'I really thought the war would be over by now. I can't believe it's another Christmas and it's still going on.'

'I know,' Nina groaned. 'It's not going to be easy, doing another Christmas on rations, that's for sure.'

'We'll get through it, we always do,' Lily said. 'And we can all have a good old knees-up at The Woolpack on Christmas Eve to celebrate Ned and Audrey's wedding.'

Nina groaned. 'Larry's got some home brew going, apparently. Make sure you steer clear of that.'

Lily giggled. 'Jed will keep an eye on him, don't worry.' Lily was devoted to her older cousin, who'd been like a brother to her growing up. 'Are you doing the decorations?'

'In the church and the pub,' Nina said. She had a real knack for making simple things look beautiful. 'I thought holly and ivy as it's Christmas. I'm going to rope all the kids in the village into collecting it for me.'

'Wonderful.' Lily was pleased that everyone was pitching in to make Audrey's big day a success. She was such a lovely girl, she deserved it. 'Maggie's making Audrey's dress, and

Betty is doing her hair. Though she was supposed to be teaching Audrey to dance, but last I heard, she was being rather unenthusiastic about it.'

Nina frowned. 'That's not like our Betty.'

Lily shrugged. 'What about the food?'

'We've got a spread planned,' Nina said proudly. 'Everyone's helping out.'

'And music?'

'Stan's playing his fiddle, and Mikey Webb's promised to play the piano.'

'It's going to be perfect,' Lily said. She finished her tea, stood up and put the mug in the sink. Then she kissed Nina on the cheek. 'I must go and get some work done,' she said. 'Ruby Dobbs has been nagging me to fix her handlebars, though quite how she thinks she's going to do any cycling in this icy weather, I don't know.'

'I'll come with you and collect Hope,' Nina said. She stood up too, but as Lily pulled on her coat, Nina took her hand. 'You're really all right?' she asked. 'About Derek.'

Lily bit her lip as she tested her feelings, but she found, to her surprise and her relief, that she really was. She smiled at Nina. 'I'm fine,' she said. 'Derek Mortimer is history.'

Chapter Nine

CHRISTMAS EVE 1944

Betty didn't want to go to the wedding ceremony. She couldn't face it. Couldn't face all that joy and happiness when she was feeling so miserable. Though, actually, even though she knew she could avoid other people, she found herself wishing she could avoid her own company, because frankly she was getting boring.

'Our Betty's got a right sad on,' her dad kept saying. And he was right, but she couldn't shake it off. She just had a horrible, clawing, desperate feeling that she'd given up her chance to be a dancer for Seth, and now he didn't even love her.

She'd gone over and over his explanation about what he'd been doing. Not that it really was an explanation. Not illegal, he said. So not poaching, or black marketeering. Was he doing something for Mr Verney? Seth thought the world of his boss, and Betty knew he went above and beyond to please him. Plus Seth was old-fashioned in some ways and was a stickler for knowing his place in a pecking order. The way he saw it,

Mr Verney lived in the big house, so Seth did his bidding. Betty had no doubt that if he was asked to do something on the wrong side of the law for Mr Verney, he'd do it.

But Mr Verney was a lovely man. He'd been so good to Beckindale and its villagers over the years. It seemed very unlikely that he'd suddenly turn to crime. Even less likely that he'd drag Seth into it, too.

Betty sighed, as she put the few bits of make-up she still had, and the substitutes she'd gathered throughout the war, into her bag. She was about to go up to Emmerdale Farm to do Audrey's face and hair, despite her glum mood.

It was, she thought, looking more and more likely that Seth was cheating on her. What was that Sherlock Holmes quote? 'Once you'd eliminated the truth . . .' No, that wasn't it. What was it? She shook her head. She'd never read a Sherlock Holmes novel in her life, but Margaret was fond of a detective story. Anyway, she was pretty sure it just meant that the truth was often staring you in the face.

'If it walks like a duck, and quacks like a duck, it's a duck,' her dad always said in his brusque Yorkshire way. And he was right, she thought. Seth was quacking like a duck all right. A cheating duck.

She zipped her bag closed with a flourish. Tonight was his last chance, she'd decided. She was going to give him one last chance to prove that he wanted to be with her. That her choosing Seth over a life on the stage hadn't been a big mistake. He'd sworn blind he'd be at the wedding party and Betty was really hoping he didn't let her down this time. She'd told herself that if he didn't turn up then she'd do something. Though she wasn't sure what. Sometimes she pictured a big confrontation, like in the films. Betty sobbing

– but Hollywood sobbing so her face didn't go blotchy – pulling off her engagement ring and throwing it at Seth, telling him it was over. And then Seth grabbing her and kissing her passionately . . .

Except she didn't have an engagement ring to throw, and Seth had never been one for passionate kisses.

Betty plodded down the stairs.

Her mother poked her head round the kitchen door. 'Off to Emmerdale Farm?'

'That's right.'

'She's a nice girl, that Audrey.'

Betty smiled. 'She is.'

'Give her our best,' her mum said. 'And take a coat, it's bitter out there.'

Betty nodded. She took her coat and scarf from the hook and started putting them on, while her mother chattered.

'Ned Barlow is a good lad,' she said. 'Shame his sister's not so fussy about who she spends time with.'

'Sarah or Elizabeth?' Betty asked, pulling a hat on. She knew her mother was too fond of gossip, but she couldn't help being interested.

'Elizabeth,' Nora said firmly. 'Seems she and Oliver Skilbeck are planning to get wed themselves.'

'Urgh.' Betty shivered. Oliver Skilbeck was a horrible man. 'Stupid woman. She'll regret that. Mark my words.'

'I know,' Nora said. 'Oh, I forgot to say, we had a letter from our Margaret this morning.'

Betty smiled. She missed her sister and wished she got to come home more often. 'What did she say? Is she all right?'

'Busy as ever,' Nora said. 'But she said to remind you about what she said.'

'She said that?' Betty was amused at Margaret's perfect timing.

'She did. What did she mean?'

'I have to go,' Betty said, even though she was early. 'I'll tell you later.'

She picked up her bag, blew her mother a kiss and headed outside, gasping with the cold.

Tucking her chin into her scarf, she started walking towards Emmerdale Farm. Her sister Margaret didn't like Seth. She'd always thought he wasn't good enough for Betty. Had always tried to persuade Betty to do more with her life than settle down with Seth in Beckindale. Now she was on at Betty to come and stay in Birmingham with her for a while. She lived in a house with two other girls, but one had joined up, so they had a spare room. Betty had said no at first. She had a job in Beckindale. She had friends. She had Seth. Why would she leave all that and go to Birmingham?

But now . . . Well, it was an option, wasn't it?

She plodded up the hill, still thinking about what she'd do if Seth didn't show up to the wedding. She'd see him tomorrow anyway. Betty wasn't a big churchgoer, but she always went on Christmas Day and Seth would be there with his family, she assumed. And if she didn't see him there, she'd go and see him at home. They could have a chat and maybe she'd say she was going to Birmingham. Not forever, not at all. Just for a week or two. She could do with a break anyway and perhaps she and Seth just needed a bit of space.

Feeling more in control, she walked faster as she approached the farm. A bit of space, that was it. They'd be good.

The farmyard was a bustle of activity. Maggie was in her overalls with her hair in curlers, feeding the chickens, and Jacob was stomping about, looking grumpy as usual.

'Morning, Jacob,' Betty called, pretending to admire his flannel shirt and dirty britches. 'That what you're wearing to the wedding?'

He grunted at her. 'Cows don't know it's a wedding day, do they?'

Betty chuckled. 'Reckon they do, Audrey's told everyone.'

That got the ghost of a smile from Jacob, as he headed off to see to the herd. Betty felt slightly triumphant, having made him grin. She was good at making people happy, she thought. A memory of standing on stage, taking a curtain call as the troops whooped and cheered popped into her head and she pushed it away. Today was Audrey's day.

'She's inside, Betty love,' Maggie called. 'There's tea in the pot.'

Betty let herself into the farmhouse, where a fire burned in the grate, and warmed her freezing fingers by the flames. My goodness it was cold today. Perhaps Audrey would get her snow after all.

With her fingers thawing out, she poured herself a mug of tea and took it and her bag upstairs.

'Audrey?' she called.

'In here.'

Audrey was in her little bedroom, lying on her bed, still in her nightgown. She looked extremely relaxed, and very happy.

'Oh Betty, it's exciting, isn't it?' she gushed. 'I'm so looking forward to today. I can't wait to walk down the aisle, and Jed and Larry have got the pub all ready for afterwards.

Maggie's been really lovely, and my parents came up from Sussex yesterday. They're staying in Hotten.'

Betty couldn't help smiling at Audrey's enthusiasm. It was sweet, how much she and Ned were in love. They were going to run their own farm, Audrey had said. Once the war was over and she could leave the Land Army. She was so obviously looking forward to her life with Ned that it was adorable, and only a tiny bit annoying.

Audrey paused to breathe and, seeing her chance, Betty jumped in.

'Did you get the ivy?' she asked.

Audrey nodded. 'It's in a box in the cold store.'

'Great,' Betty said. Audrey wore her hair short because her missing hand made complicated styles too hard to manage. So Betty had decided to make a sort of crown out of green leaves and weave them into Audrey's hair somehow. 'Can you get them?'

Audrey skipped off downstairs and Betty drank her tea and gazed out of the window across Emmerdale Farm. It was big, she thought. Much bigger than it used to be. She'd heard people talk about how Jacob had been clever about using every inch of land for food, and it was impressive. It seemed everyone was doing their bit for the war effort. Jacob, Maggie and Audrey, Annie Pearson, Margaret . . . Everyone except her.

She shook her head, getting rid of her miserable thoughts, and turned to Audrey as she came into the bedroom holding a box of ivy leaves.

'Right then,' Betty said, giving her a beaming smile that almost managed to reach her eyes. 'Let's make you the most beautiful bride Beckindale has ever seen, shall we?'

Chapter Ten

Lily thought she'd never seen a bride look as happy as Audrey Atkins did. She was every inch the blushing bride as she paused at the door of the church and waved joyfully at Ned, who was waiting, fidgeting with the sleeves of his unfamiliar shirt.

Audrey was on the arm of her father. He looked proud as anything of his beautiful daughter – and so did Jacob Sugden, who had a grin on his face as wide as the River Emm. Lily wasn't sure she'd ever seen Jacob looking so happy before. He was so fond of Audrey, she'd heard him say it was like having a little sister. Lily liked that. It was a bit like how she felt about her cousin Jed. Family didn't always mean blood, in Lily's opinion. After all, Jack was Hope's real father, even if it had been Derek who was biologically her dad.

Mrs Briars, the church organist, struck a loud chord. The congregation got to their feet – Hope stood on the pew so she could see – and, much to Lily's amusement, Audrey almost ran down the aisle to where Ned stood, virtually dragging her poor father behind her.

'Were you that keen to get wed when it was our turn?' Jack said to Lily out of the corner of his mouth. 'I don't remember you running like that?'

She poked him in the ribs. 'I was as big as a house and about to give birth,' she whispered, stifling her giggles. Hope had been born on their wedding day, which just underlined how dramatic her pregnancy and her and Jack's courtship had been. Lily snaked her arm round her husband's and gave him a little squeeze. 'I'd have run there if I could have,' she said. 'I was desperate to marry you and I'm very pleased I did.'

Jack gave her a quick kiss, as the strains of the organ died away. 'Me too,' he said.

The congregation sat and Hope clambered into Jack's lap.

'We are gathered here today,' began Reverend Thirlby.

Lily watched happily as Ned and Audrey made their vows. Now and then she glanced at Jack, remembering the promises they'd made to one another, and smiling when he looked at her. He really was a good husband. He'd been so kind when she'd told him about Derek being killed, understanding her mixed feelings, just as Nina had predicted. Now all Lily wanted was to fall pregnant again and bring a new baby into their perfect family.

Audrey looked beautiful. Betty had done a good job of pinning some tiny ivy leaves around her head like a natural crown for a farming princess. Her dress was simple: an ankle-length, gathered skirt and a plain bodice with long sleeves. Maggie Sugden, who was clever with a needle and had a real eye for make do and mend, had gathered clothing coupons from anyone who'd donate them for the fabric and had even added some extra bits from some dresses the women of Beckindale had given. Betty had painted her lips, too. Lily peered at Audrey, wondering if Betty had used actual lipstick or the boiled beetroot lots of women were resorting to nowadays. Either way, the end result was really lovely and Audrey was every inch the blushing bride. Especially considering she was only ever seen in her Land Army regulation green sweater and brown britches.

Lily looked round for Betty. She'd obviously been up at Emmerdale Farm earlier, getting Audrey ready, but she couldn't see her now. Where had she got to? There was no sign of Seth either. Perhaps they were together? Lily hoped so. She'd been concerned that Betty seemed to be spending lots of time with Wally Eagleton, which didn't fit with Lily's love of happy ever after at all. Subtly, she looked round the church and, with a slight relief, she spotted Wally sitting at the back with an older man who looked so much like him it had to be his father, and a younger lad in uniform. His brother perhaps. Lily eyed Wally appraisingly. He was very handsome, she thought. And she'd asked around and found out he'd been shot at El Alamein, which gave him the status of a hero. She hoped Betty's head wouldn't be turned by his attention while Seth was busy elsewhere. Though quite what Seth was busy doing, Lily couldn't imagine. The estate at Miffield Hall seemed to take up an extraordinary amount of his time.

She turned back towards the front of the church as Reverend Thirlby declared the happy couple to be man and wife, and the church broke into applause. Audrey and Ned shared a lingering kiss, then they skipped down the aisle, waving to their friends.

'Wasn't that simply perfect?' Lily said to Jack as they strolled across the village to the pub, where the party was going to be. 'A perfect wedding.'

Jack swung Hope up on to his shoulders. 'It really was,' he said.

Lily shivered, pulling her woolly hat on to her head as the December wind whipped her hair around her face. She looked up at the steely grey sky. 'I think Audrey might get her snow, you know?' As if by magic, a fat flake drifted past her nose. 'Oh,' Lily said, delighted. 'Look, Hope, it's snowing!'

And then suddenly the snowflakes were falling fast. Hope whacked Jack on the head with her podgy little hands. 'Down, Daddy,' she demanded. Jack let her down on to the ground, which was rapidly being covered by pristine white snow, and she ran around madly, trying to catch the flakes.

Lily and Jack linked arms and watched, laughing, while Hope played for a few minutes.

'Goodness me, it's really coming down now,' Lily said eventually. 'Let's get into the pub and out of the cold.'

Up ahead, The Woolpack's lights were glowing in the gloom of the December afternoon – Jed hadn't yet shut the blackout blinds, so it looked warm and cosy from the outside. And the Christmas tree Larry had put up outside was sparkling as the snow landed gently on its branches.

'It's so beautiful,' Lily said in wonder. But then the wind blew again, Hope let out a little gasp, and she clapped her hands together. 'Into the warm, let's go.'

But inside the pub was just as cold as outside. Everyone was standing around, still wearing their coats, and poor Audrey – just clad in her thin gown – was shivering.

Lily found Jed, who was looking worried. 'What's happened?' she asked him.

'Everything's frozen,' he said with a grimace. 'The pipes have burst out the back.' He glared at Larry. 'Because Larry didn't lag them.'

Larry ignored him, pretending to be staring out of the window at something terribly interesting, which made Lily smile as it was very typically Larry to avoid a problem. But it didn't solve the problem of what to do with a pub full of shivering customers and a bride and groom with no wedding reception.

Jacob and Maggie Sugden were deep in conversation, Maggie gesturing wildly with her hands, and Jacob nodding eagerly. Maggie cleared her throat and spoke to Audrey – who was now wearing her father's coat – and Ned.

'We've just been thinking, pet. If you want, we've got the space up at Emmerdale Farm. We could take the food and . . .' she looked at Jed. 'The beer?' Jed nodded and Maggie grinned. 'And go home for the party. What do you say?'

Audrey and Ned didn't even have to check with each other, they both smiled broadly and Audrey threw her arms around Maggie.

'We'd love that,' she said.

'Thanks very much,' Ned added. 'It's really kind.'

Maggie shrugged. 'Audrey's one of ours now,' she said. 'We'd be lost without her, isn't that right, Jacob?'

"S'right,' said Jacob, giving Audrey a good-natured punch on the arm. 'Shall we all head up the hill then?'

Jack, who'd been looking out of the window, spoke up. 'Might be tricky,' he said.

Ned frowned. 'What do you mean?'

'Have a look.'

Jack pushed open the door to the pub and everyone gasped. The village was completely covered in a soft blanket of snow, even The Woolpack sign, which swung in the wind, had an inch or so of white on top.

'Oh my goodness,' said Audrey, delighted. 'I got my snow.'

'You did,' Ned said fondly. 'But it might mean no party.'

'Rubbish.' Mick, Lily's father, stood up. 'We've got carts and horses, right? Lily love, you can help. Let's get some runners on a couple of carts. We'll make our own horse-drawn sleigh.'

Within an hour, Lily, Mick, Jacob, Ruby Dobbs and a few others had transformed two carts into sleighs. Nancy helped hitch the horses to the sledges.

'It's not an easy journey, so keep an eye on them,' she said sternly, always the vet, even when she was dolled up for a wedding. 'We can swap them over if the horses get tired.'

Jacob saluted as he climbed into the driving seat and picked up the reins. 'Will do, Nancy.'

Audrey and Ned clambered up, looking like a fairy-tale prince and princess from one of Hope's storybooks. The snow was dusting Audrey's ivy crown and her cheeks were flushed pink with the cold and happiness. Ned put his arm around her, Jacob tugged on the reins and they were off.

Some of the villagers had found other sleighs in their garages, or vehicles that could make it up to the farm without too much trouble. It seemed a wedding was worth using the petrol ration for. Jed and Jack loaded barrels of beer into one cart, while Nina helped supervise loading the food into another.

And soon, the whole wedding reception had been moved, lock, stock and barrel, to Emmerdale Farm.

Lily and Jack stood next to the window of the large lounge in the farm, watching the lights on the Christmas tree reflecting on Hope's awed face. She'd never seen a tree that big before and she was fascinated by the presents underneath too.

'She's going to remember this Christmas,' Lily said. 'When she's an old lady, she'll tell her grandchildren about the last Christmas of the war, when everyone celebrated a wedding and we all felt like we finally had something to look forward to.'

'Hello, Lily.' Meg appeared next to her, holding a mug of mulled cider that made Lily's nose tingle.

'Meg,' she said, sweeping her friend into a hug. 'Happy birthday!'

'Thank you,' Meg said. 'Lots to celebrate today.'

'That's what I was just saying to Jack.'

'Ruby and Stan are celebrating too,' Meg reminded Lily. They'd never known when their real birthdays were, so when Meg adopted them, she'd told them she'd share her birthday with them.

'Of course,' Lily said. 'Happy birthday!' she called, waving across to where the children were gathered in the corner of the room. Ruby and Stan both waved back, happily.

On the other side of the room, Jacob Sugden banged a glass with a spoon to get everyone's attention.

'Ladies and gentlemen,' he said. 'Please clear a space in the centre of the room, as the new Mr and Mrs Barlow share their first dance.'

All the wedding guests clapped and cheered as little Stan Dobbs picked up his fiddle and Ned swung Audrey on to the tiny space in the middle of the floor.

'I want to see,' said Hope, tugging on Lily's leg.

Lily bent down and picked her up and, in delight, the little girl jiggled along to the music.

'Happy, happy Christmas,' she said in Lily's ear. Lily squeezed her precious daughter tightly and leaned over to give Jack a kiss.

'Merry Christmas, my darling,' she said.

Chapter Eleven

Betty hadn't gone to the wedding ceremony. She'd found herself so weary after spending all morning plastering on a smile and being enthusiastic about weddings and romance that she just couldn't bring herself to watch as Audrey and Ned said their vows.

Instead, when Audrey was ready – looking beautiful – and Jacob had taken Maggie and Betty down to the village first of all, before going back for the bride, Betty had let the mask drop.

'You go in,' she said to Maggie. 'I've just got to pop home and grab some lippy.'

'Shall I save you a seat?'

'No, best not. I'll sneak in at the back.'

She knew Seth wouldn't be there until later and she couldn't bear to be alone again. She could sit with Nancy, of course, or squeeze in with Ruby and Susan, but she would be a spare part, like always.

Full of self-pity, she'd stayed at home, hiding in her bedroom. She lay on her bed, watching the snow falling. Seth loved the snow. Betty preferred summer. She'd always thought that was why they were so good together – they complemented each other. She sat up, suddenly. They were good together. They were. Perhaps they'd just lost each other for a while, but they were meant to be.

Maybe, she thought now, she just needed to remind him how they belonged together. Seth had been neglecting her, there was no doubt about that, but Betty knew she wasn't entirely blameless. She'd been busy with ENSA and then distracted and cautious, wondering if she'd done the right thing when she turned down the chance to entertain the troops. They were in a pickle, her and Seth, but it was nothing that couldn't be fixed.

She jumped to her feet and flung open her wardrobe doors. She was going to dress up to the nines and remind Seth why he'd fallen for her in the first place.

She threw aside the pretty frock she'd been intending to wear and instead found a deep, grass-green dress that she'd made but never worn.

The fabric had taken weeks of saving her clothing coupons and she'd sent off for the pattern from a magazine that her friend Pamela from ENSA had given her. It was cut low at the front, with short, puffy sleeves and nipped in at the waist. Then it hugged her bottom and thighs, before kicking out into a soft flare at her knees. The advert in the magazine had called it a wiggle dress, and there was no wondering why it had been given that name. When she wore it, it was so tight that she had to walk in a certain way.

Now she pulled it out of her wardrobe and held it up in front of her. She'd intended to wear it when she went to London to visit Pamela, but Pam had been so busy that the trip hadn't happened. Betty bit her lip. Could she wear it in Beckindale?

'It's a party, Betty,' she said out loud. 'Course you can.'

She had a quick wash and then wriggled her way into the dress. It fitted like a glove and the colour flattered her. She carefully drew kohl round her eyes and painted her lips with the same actual lipstick she'd used to add colour to Audrey's. She'd had this one tube since the start of the war and tried to save it for special occasions. She thought today fitted the bill.

She brushed her hair until it gleamed and teased it into glossy victory rolls, then she slid her feet into her best dancing shoes and headed downstairs – with some difficulty, it had to be said, because the dress did not allow for steps – to go to the party.

'Mam,' she called. 'It's snowing. Can I take your stole?'

Her mother came out of the lounge, frowning. 'My stole, Betty? It's precious, is that.' Then she stopped, looking her daughter up and down. 'By 'eck, you look like a film star.'

Betty threw her arms out and bobbed a curtsey.

'Thank you, madam,' she joked.

Her mother rolled her eyes at the theatrics. 'Go on then. Take the stole.'

'Can you get it please,' Betty begged. 'I can't walk in this bleeding dress.'

Smiling, her mother ran upstairs and came back down with her precious fur stole.

'Do not leave it in a puddle of beer in The Woolie,' she warned.

Betty blew her a kiss. 'As if I would.'

She arranged the fur around her shoulders, picked up her handbag, and feeling like the cat's pyjamas, she headed out into the snow.

It was freezing, even with the fur draped across her arms, and Betty was soon shivering. And she was horrified when she realised the wedding guests were all crowding out of the pub and jumping into sledges, carts and cars.

'Where's everyone going?' she asked Ned's sister Elizabeth, pointedly ignoring her beau Oliver Skilbeck who stood nearby.

But it was Oliver who answered. 'Pipes are frozen at the pub,' he said. 'We're all going up to Emmerdale Farm instead.'

'Have you seen my Seth?' Betty asked, addressing Elizabeth again. Oliver made a face and Betty ignored him. She didn't have much time for the Skilbeck family and Oliver was the worst of the lot.

'Jed's leaving a note on the door, so he'll know where to find us,' Elizabeth said. 'Come with us if you like.'

Betty didn't really want to share a lift with them, but she was really cold, so she accepted gracefully and piled into the Barlows' fruit and veg truck. She had to ease herself into the back seat, bottom first, because her dress was so unforgiving, and she did not like the way Oliver watched her as she did it.

Still, she was here now, she thought, as she accepted some mulled cider from Jed Dingle, who'd set up a makeshift bar at one end of the Sugdens' kitchen. She just had to wait for Seth to arrive.

She said hello to Lily and Meg, and watched Ned and Audrey dancing. She remembered with a start that she was supposed to have taught them something. She'd have to apologise for that later.

'Betty, you look wonderful,' Nancy said, kissing her on the cheek. 'How you do it, when the rest of us are dressed in sacks and old curtains, I'll never know.'

Betty smiled at her boss, who was wearing a rather nice suit with a little frilled blouse underneath and looked very smart. 'If that's made from curtains, I'll eat my hat,' she said to Nancy. 'Are you wearing mascara?'

Nancy fluttered her eyelashes. 'I thought I'd make the effort,' she said. 'Everything feels more hopeful, don't you think?'

'I do,' Betty said, with a vehement nod. 'I really do.'

'Is your Seth here?' Nancy asked.

'On his way.'

'Lovely.'

Betty looked at Nancy. 'Any romance for you? Are you all dolled up for someone special?'

Nancy flushed. 'No,' she said, so firmly that Betty felt she couldn't tease her any more.

They chatted for a while longer, and still Seth didn't arrive. They joined Lily and Meg, laughing about Hope's latest escapades and enjoying more mulled cider, and still there was no Seth. Betty found Audrey, shared her congratulations, and apologised for forgetting the dance lessons, but Seth wasn't there. Time ticked on, and Betty was still looking up every time someone came in the room. But it was never Seth. Feeling foolish and sad, and sort of untethered, Betty was beginning to accept he wasn't coming. But still she hoped.

'I'm going to fetch another drink,' Betty said eventually. 'Fancy one?'

Nancy hiccupped softly. 'Think I've had enough,' she said. 'I'm going to find somewhere to sit.'

Chuckling, Betty wandered through the farmhouse, swinging her hips in her dress. She pretended she wasn't looking for Seth, but she was really. And then, as she entered the kitchen and walked over to Jed, she felt eyes on her.

Finally! Confident it was her Seth watching, she took her time turning round. And there, his gaze on her where he stood leaning against the wall in the corner of the room, running his eyes over her curves, was Wally Eagleton.

Betty was so surprised to see him that she let out a little gasp of air. She looked round for Seth, but he wasn't there. Had never been there. It had been Wally all the time.

Slowly, Wally gave her his customary lazy smile. He really was very handsome, Betty thought. She drained her cider and held out the mug for Jed to fill it up again, as Wally made his way across the room.

'Betty,' he said. 'You look beautiful tonight.'

Betty ducked her head and looked up at him from under her eyelashes. She wondered how long it had been since Seth said she was beautiful. Right now, she couldn't remember him ever saying it.

She glanced at the clock over the fireplace in the Sugdens' kitchen. It was eleven o'clock already. Seth wasn't coming, that much was obvious. She felt that same feeling again. Like she'd been released from something that had been keeping her steady.

She smiled up at Wally. He was a big man. Tall and broad, with wide shoulders. Betty wondered for a second what it would be like to rest her head on his chest. Goodness, how much cider had she drunk? What was she thinking?

'Having fun?' he asked.

Betty gave him a small smile. 'I am now,' she said. 'I was waiting for . . . someone. But he's not coming. So there we are.'

'There we are,' said Wally. He looked her up and down again and his gaze fizzed on her skin. She liked the way it made her feel.

Betty swallowed. 'It's snowing,' she said.

Wally nodded. 'It is.'

Was it her imagination or had he moved a fraction closer to her? His hand brushed her hip and she felt dizzy for a second.

'I thought I might go outside and see how deep it's got,' Wally said.

Betty looked straight at him, thrilled and appalled in equal measure at how bold she was being. 'Good idea,' she said.

Without another word, Wally turned, ducked past Jed Dingle and went outside into the snow.

Her heart hammering in her chest, Betty waited a few minutes, finishing her drink. Then, casually, she put her now empty cup down and headed for the kitchen door. She slipped outside without anyone seeing her and paused for a moment in the frosty evening air. Her breath made clouds as she looked around for a clue about where Wally had gone. Then she saw footprints in the snow, so, following the trail, she tiptoed across to a barn on the other side of the farmyard.

There was no one there. Disappointed, she stood just inside the barn, looking into the gloomy interior. Maybe he had just wanted to see the snow after all.

But then suddenly he was there, in front of her, looking – Betty was pleased to see – just as nervous as she was feeling.

Gently, Wally took her hand. She let him, liking how strong his fingers were. He led her up to the back of the barn where no one could see them. She liked that too.

And then, finally, he kissed her. All of Betty's senses exploded. Her heart was thumping, her skin aching for him to touch her. She melted into him, falling backwards on to a hay bale and enjoying the feel of his body on hers.

'You're the most beautiful girl I've ever seen,' he murmured.

Betty kissed him deeply, all worries about Seth, and the war, and ENSA forgotten. For now.

Chapter Twelve

'Told you it was going to snow,' Seth said as he and Sid tramped through the woods. He lifted his face up, looking at the sky and feeling the biting wind on his cheeks, then gave Sid a triumphant wink. 'Didn't we have a bet?'

Sid sighed. 'We did.'

The men had been bickering about the weather earlier, with Seth adamant it would snow and Sid equally convinced it wouldn't. But now the sky was steel grey and the flakes were drifting through the trees, which meant Seth was the winner.

'Pay up,' Seth said.

Sid looked at his watch. 'We're nearly done for this evening.'

Seth grinned, knowing what was coming. 'Are you coming down to the wedding party in The Woolie when we're finished here?'

'I am.'

'So the ales are on you.'

'Sounds fair.'

The men shook hands and carried on. Seth was chuckling to himself as they walked. Sid always made bets with him about the weather and, so far, he'd never won. Seth didn't mind the snow. He liked being outside whatever the weather. Though his fingers and toes were freezing right enough. He was looking forward to sitting in the pub, pint in front of him, and Betty on his arm.

'What have you got your Betty for Christmas, then?' Sid asked. 'My Elaine wanted a hat, right, so I got one of my dad's old ones . . .'

But Seth wasn't listening to Sid; his eye had been caught by something on the ground. He stopped walking and threw his arm out to warn his friend to stay quiet. Sid was on the alert straight away.

'What?' he breathed at Seth, pulling out his pistol. 'What is it?'

'Someone's been through here,' Seth said. He pointed at the snapped twigs and bent foliage that showed that someone had passed by recently.

'Deer?' said Sid hopefully, but Seth shook his head. That wasn't a deer. He pulled out his own gun and, holding it carefully – he'd grown up around guns, but he was more used to shotguns than these small pistols – crouched down for a better look.

'Definitely a person,' he said. 'Another half-hour and the snow would have covered this trail.'

'Could just be someone having a walk.' Sid sounded casual, but they both knew there was no reason for anyone to be this deep into the woods in this weather.

Very slowly and quietly, they began creeping through the woods, following the trail of broken branches until they came to a small clearing. The snow was falling heavily now they were out of the cover of the trees.

Sid froze, throwing an arm out to stop Seth moving, his face twisting with fear. 'Shhh,' he said. 'Listen.'

Seth strained to hear what Sid was hearing. He had ears like a bat, that one.

'It sounds like talking?' Sid said under his breath.

'Where?'

Sid pointed and, inch by inch, the men crept towards the sound. Seth could hear it now too. It was voices all right, and to his ear, it didn't sound like English they were speaking. His heart was pounding. The Germans were in retreat across Europe, so he wasn't imagining an invasion, but perhaps it was an escaped POW.

They left the clearing behind and headed back into the woods, the voices getting louder. But as they walked, Sid shook his head. 'It's just one,' he said. 'One voice.'

Seth wasn't sure. But his hearing wasn't as sharp as Sid's and before he could argue, the voice – or voices – stopped.

'Damn,' he whispered. He stood for a moment, his eyes scanning left and right, and suddenly he saw something heaped under a tree.

'What's that?' he said to Sid.

Sid looked. 'An old coat?'

Very carefully, Seth approached. With his foot, he prodded the pile of rags and jumped back, his gun raised, as it moaned.

'It's a man,' he hissed at Sid. 'In a bad way, by the look of it.'

Sid frowned. 'Could be a trap. Be careful.'

Seth laid his gun down on the ground, wondering if there was someone else in the trees, waiting to pounce, and gently turned the man over. He was hunched down in a huge but threadbare coat and his face was skeletal, beneath his shaved head. He was jabbering softly to himself, but Seth couldn't make head nor tail of what he was saying. His lips were blue and his breathing shallow.

'He's freezing,' Seth said. 'We need to get him indoors.'

'What if he's a German?'

'Don't matter. We can't leave him here to die.'

'We can take him back to the base,' Sid suggested. 'Can we carry him, the two of us?'

Seth looked at the man, who was skin and bone, and nodded. 'Reckon I could do it myself. I'm Seth and this is Sid. Can you stand?' he said to the man.

His eyes flickered open for a second, but then they closed again. Seth felt a lurch of fear. Unless they got him out of the cold, the poor lad didn't have long.

'Come on,' he said to Sid.

Together they hoisted the man up, and between them, they carried him through the woods and back to their base.

'Paul,' Seth called quietly as they approached. 'We need help here.'

Paul's head appeared out of the door, his eyes wide with shock as he saw the man.

'What's this? What's going on?'

'Found him in the woods. He's freezing. We need to get him warm.'

Paul opened the door wide to let the men through. 'Is he English?' he said. 'I need to radio this in.'

'Let's just get him set first, shall we. We need blankets.'

Paul darted across to where there was a pile of regulation blankets. He spread one out on the bench and, gently, Seth and Sid laid the man down. Paul put another blanket on top of him, and another.

'What about the oil heater? Is that handy?' Sid looked round. The base was very nearly packed up now. All the operational patrols were being stood down and the Hotten Auxiliary Unit wouldn't exist a week from now. Already someone had come to collect most of the ammunition and weapons from the store, and a lot of their other equipment.

'It's in the escape tunnel,' Seth said. 'I put it there yesterday.' He quickly went and fetched it and they put it on, enjoying the warmth it spread through the freezing base.

Paul was looking down at the man, checking his pulse and watching his chest rise and fall. Seth was glad he was there. Paul had had more medical training than he or Sid had.

'He's warming up,' Paul said, sounding relieved. 'Look, his lips aren't so blue now and his breathing is becoming deeper.'

Seth sat down on the bench opposite their patient. 'I thought he were a goner.'

'Me too,' said Sid in a quiet voice.

The men all sat for a long while, looking over at the heap of blankets that was rising and falling with the man's breathing. They chatted quietly about what they would do when the operational patrol was finally disbanded, but they were just trying to distract themselves. All of their focus was on the man as he slept.

'What should we do?' Seth said, eventually, after a good couple of hours had gone by. 'We can't just sit here and look at him. What if he's German?'

'Should we wake him up?' Sid asked. 'We need to speak to him, and we can't leave him here all night.'

The younger men both looked at Paul for guidance. He thought for a moment and then he nodded.

'Let's make some tea,' he said. 'A hot drink will do him good. And then we can wake him up and see what he was doing out here in the snow. I'm going to have to report it in the morning.'

Sid busied himself making the drinks.

'Shame George is gone,' Seth said, almost to himself. 'He'd have been useful, seeing as the rest of us don't speak German.'

Sid almost dropped the mug he was holding. 'Do you really think he's a Jerry?'

'Don't know, do I?' said Seth. 'But what if he is.' He was more curious than scared like Sid. He didn't think the chap was German – after all, what would a German be doing in the woods outside Beckindale? But he had obviously been through some sort of dreadful experience and Seth wanted to know what had happened to him. 'Maybe he's gone AWOL,' he said. 'Maybe he's run off from the army or somewhere.'

'Wouldn't he be in uniform if that's the case?' said Sid doubtfully. 'Is he in uniform?'

Seth shrugged.

'Right, men,' Paul said. 'Weapons out, let's be prepared for him to run, or to be aggressive. All ready?'

Seth and Sid drew their pistols and stood guard as Paul very carefully shook the man's shoulder.

'Hey there,' he said. 'What's your name, mister?'

The man's eyes opened and he jerked awake, making all three of the patrol members jump. Scrabbling to sit up, the man looked around himself, clearly bewildered about where he was or who they were.

'Easy now,' Seth said, putting out a hand to calm him. 'Calm yourself.'

'Don't be frit,' Sid said in his broad Yorkshire way. 'Is thou English?'

Seth glared at him. Even if the poor lad was English, chances were he wouldn't understand Sid's broad dialect.

Paul took charge. 'We're the Hotten Auxiliary Unit,' he said in his best BBC voice. 'Paul Oldroyd.'

The man relaxed the tiniest bit, his shoulders dropping slightly. Assuming that meant he wasn't a German, Seth stepped forward. 'Seth Armstrong.'

'Sid Mosby,' said Sid.

The man opened his mouth and tried to speak, but just a croak came out.

'Sid, the tea.'

Sid passed the man the enamel mug and, gratefully, the fellow wrapped his bony fingers round its warmth and sipped. After he'd drunk about half the mug, he looked up at Seth, Sid and Paul's curious faces.

'I'm Nick,' he said. 'Got any biscuits?'

Seth's laughter was tinged with relief. He grinned. 'No biscuits, but there's some chocolate?'

'Chocolate,' Nick said, his eyes wide. 'Yes please.'

Sid found it and handed it over, and Nick munched away happily.

Paul cleared his throat. 'I'm sorry to ask,' he said. 'But who are you and why are you here?'

Nick looked at him. 'What's an auxiliary unit?' he asked.

Paul shifted from one foot to the other. Seth didn't blame him. They had all signed important documents saying they would never talk about the work they'd done on the operational patrol. No one was supposed to know they existed. And now Paul had blurted it out to the first person who came their way.

'Wildlife,' Paul said quickly, much to Seth's amusement. Paul didn't know much about the countryside. 'I'm a game-keeper and these lads are helping me with a scheme I've cooked up to catch poachers.'

'And the guns?' Nick raised an eyebrow. Seth was torn between annoyance and amusement. This man was sharp and observant.

'Who are you?' Paul said, clearly losing patience.

Nick looked at Paul for a minute and then he shrugged. 'I'm Nicholas Roberts,' he said. 'I was a POW in Rouen and I escaped.'

'Rouen in France?' said Sid in wonder. 'How did you escape? How did you get across the Channel? Why are you in Beckindale?'

Nick rested his head against the wall of the base. Seth thought that though he was quite a young man, his eyes looked tired and old.

'They moved us when the Allies got close,' Nick said. 'Put us on a train. But we stopped because a bridge had been blown up . . .'

Paul nodded approvingly. 'That's our chaps slowing down any German response, you see. Taking out railways, bridges, radar . . .'

'Go on,' Seth said.

'I just opened the train door and got out,' Nick said. 'Still can't believe it really. I kept walking, thinking someone would stop me, but they didn't.'

Seth was astonished by Nick's bravery. 'And the Channel?'

'I walked to Dieppe,' Nick said. 'It took me four days because I was weak. And when I got there, there were boats going back and forth all the time. I just sneaked on board one

95

and hoped no one would find me. Once I was in England, I got on a train and then another and then another. It took a while because I had to keep getting off them when a ticket inspector came.'

'Why didn't you just tell someone?' asked Sid.

Nick looked blank. 'No idea,' he admitted. 'I felt like I wasn't sure who to trust.' He took a breath. 'So I eventually got off a train at Bradford a couple of days ago. I walked from there.'

'No wonder you were frozen,' Paul said.

'Why here, though?' Seth said. Nick's accent told him he was a Londoner, not a native Yorkshireman like the rest of them. 'Why have you come to Beckindale?'

'I've come to see my daughter,' Nick said.

Suddenly all the pieces of the jigsaw fell into place for Seth. He pointed at Nick in delight. 'I know who you are,' he said. 'You're Mrs Roberts's son. Susan's da.'

'You know her?' Nick said, his voice raspy with tears. 'You know my girl?'

'That I do,' Seth said. 'She's a right bright spark. Works at the vet's with my Betty.'

Nick buried his face in his hands and his shoulders shook.

'Ee,' Seth said awkwardly, patting the man on his back. 'How about we get you sorted out with some warm clothes and we can take you into the village to find her and your ma?'

Nick looked up. 'That would be great, thank you.'

'I'll go home,' Paul said. 'Fetch the Home Guard car. We can't expect you to walk any further. And we should wait until morning, I suppose, to take you down to Beckindale. We can't get everyone out of bed at this hour.'

Sid looked at the clock.

'It's after midnight,' he said. 'It's Christmas Day.'

With a start, Seth realised he'd missed Audrey and Ned's wedding celebrations. Somehow, though, that didn't matter. He slapped Nick on the back once more.

'Reckon you'll be the best Christmas present that girl of yours has ever had.'

Chapter Thirteen

Paul went home to fetch his car, while Seth, Sid and Nick stayed in the base. They had planned to sleep, but as Nick warmed up and relaxed, they ended up chatting.

'I'm sorry about your family,' Seth said to Nick. He hadn't been sure how to bring it up. He was horribly aware that Nick's wife and three of his four children had been killed in a bomb in London. That was why his daughter Susan had come to Yorkshire to live with her grandmother. Seth felt the tragedy hanging heavily between them and decided it was better to mention it. 'Your Susan's a top lass,' he added.

Nick's face contorted in pain and then, with what was clearly a lot of effort, he managed to smile. 'I can't wait to see her.'

'Did you know?' Seth said, feeling a bit awkward. 'Did you know what had happened when you were in France?'

'We got letters, every now and then. Via the Red Cross. I got one from my mum, telling me what had happened. But it was a year or so afterwards. I wrote back to her, but another lad said our letters never got out. We were only allowed one or two postcards a year and he reckoned the guards binned them.'

'I'm sorry,' Seth said again. 'That's rotten.'

There was a pause and Nick looked round at the base once more, taking in the well-engineered shape of the bunker, the last bits of equipment and the food stores.

'Gamekeeper, eh?' he said to Seth.

'Aye.'

Nick nodded. 'But this is different. What is it? The other bloke mentioned the Home Guard.'

Seth and Sid exchanged a glance. 'Sort of,' Seth said. 'Reckon Paul will have let them know we've found you now. He'll explain.'

Nick gave him a long look. 'Fair enough.'

They chatted some more about Nick's time in the prison camp, and, Sid found some more chocolate, which they shared, and, eventually, the grey icy dawn crept through the entrance to the base.

'When Paul comes, he'll park on the road,' Seth said. 'He can't park right close because of all the trees, so we'll take you out, if you can manage it. Reckon you'll be all right to walk?'

'Should be,' Nick said. He swung his legs out from under his blanket and Seth saw his feet were bruised and bleeding. He was wearing boots, but the soles were worn through and they obviously didn't fit right as they had rubbed and blistered his feet. Nick saw his horrified look and winced. 'Not much choice of footwear in the camp,' he said.

'Here,' Seth said. He bent down and unlaced his own boots, while Sid – realising what he was doing – dug into his backpack.

'I've got some socks,' he said. 'And I'll find the first-aid kit. Let's see if we can bandage you up a bit, eh?'

With his feet out of his boots, Seth checked a billycan to see if there was water and was relieved to find it full. He poured some into a tin and ripped off a piece of blanket to use as a cloth.

Then, together, he and Sid gently bathed Nick's poor feet and bandaged the heels and the toes and the balls of his feet where the blisters were worst. Nick tried to protest, saying he could do it himself, but Seth insisted.

Once his feet were less painful, Nick shrugged the blankets from his thin shoulders and took off the enormous coat he'd been wearing the whole time. Underneath, he had a thin shirt and threadbare trousers.

'I stole that coat,' he said, torn between shame and pride. 'Off a bloke at the dock in France. He took it off while he went to the toilet and I nicked it.'

Seth chuckled. 'Should have chosen one more your size.'

'I was glad of it, when I had to sleep outdoors,' Nick said.

'Here.' Seth held out his boots. 'Might help with the walking.'

Gratefully, Nick took them, and Seth helped him loosen the laces so he could fit them over his bandages.

'And have this,' Sid said. He had taken off his sweater and now he offered it to Nick.

'Sure?' Nick said. 'I don't want to think about how long I've been wearing this shirt.'

Sid nodded, so Nick peeled off his shirt and put on the jumper. Seth tried not to look at his protruding ribs or the backbone that stuck out like a mountain range. The poor bugger was covered in bruises and bites from lice, but Seth couldn't help thinking he'd be right as rain once his mam got him home with her.

'Car,' said Sid.

Seth rolled his eyes. 'Sid's got ears like a blooming bat,' he said.

And, sure enough, a few seconds later, he heard an engine.

'Ready?' he asked Nick. He looked terrified for a moment, but then he nodded his head. Seth patted his arm. 'Reckon it must seem strange, meeting your daughter and your mam for the first time in years. But soon as you see them, it'll feel just like normal. Mark my words.'

Nick nodded again. Seth took his left arm and Sid his right and, together, they helped him to the car. He was still very weak, and for the umpteenth time that night, Seth thanked god they'd come across him when they had. Imagine if he'd died in the snowy woods, so near, yet so far from his family.

The roads were covered in snow and Paul had driven up not in the Home Guard car, but a jeep that Seth had never seen before.

'Where did you get this?' he asked as they approached.

'Don't ask,' Paul said out of the corner of his mouth. Seth was amused. Paul was a stickler for the rules generally.

They helped Nick into the passenger seat and headed off down to the village. Nick was silent the whole way and Seth didn't blame him.

Beckindale was quiet. It was still very early and Christmas Day was just beginning. Paul parked by the pub and the men got out.

Reverend Thirlby was hurrying past wearing his cassock and Paul tipped his hat to him.

'Merry Christmas, Reverend,' he said.

Reverend Thirlby waved gaily. 'And to you, Mr Oldroyd.'

Mrs Roberts and Susan lived in a small cottage at the end of the village. The curtains were still closed, but smoke was snaking out of the chimney.

'Probably in the kitchen out back,' Paul said.

Sid was shivering without his sweater and Seth was trying not to wince with each step as the snow soaked through his socks and froze his toes. Despite his borrowed boots, Nick was taking smaller and smaller steps.

Paul turned to him.

'Nervous, lad?' He nodded and Paul patted his back kindly. 'We're all right here with you, son.'

They reached the cottage and Nick took a deep breath.

'I'll knock, shall I?' Paul said. Seth and Sid stayed standing at the front gate, with Nick between them, while Paul walked down the path and rapped firmly on the door.

Mrs Roberts answered, her hair still in last night's curlers.

'Oh, hello, Mr Oldroyd,' she said. 'Merry Christmas. What can I do for you?'

Seth had never seen Paul short of words before, but suddenly the man, who was always so sure of himself, looked lost as to what to say.

'Mrs Roberts,' he began. 'We found . . .'

Mrs Roberts looked at him blankly. 'What did you find?' she said.

But Paul didn't get to answer because Nick left Seth's side and walked down the path towards his mother.

'He found me,' he said.

Paul stepped aside and Mrs Roberts came face to face with the son she'd thought was dead. She breathed in sharply, standing stock-still.

'Hello, Mum,' Nick said. 'It's really good to see you.'

With a trembling hand, Mrs Roberts reached out and touched Nick's face, his sunken cheeks and his closely cropped hair.

Nick caught her hand in his and held it and then he held out his arms and his mother rushed to him and hugged him so tightly Seth wondered if he should step in and tell her to be gentle.

'My boy,' she was saying over and over. 'My boy.'

Seth put his hand up to his face and found it was wet with tears. He looked at Sid, who was the same, and they both grinned.

'Soppy sods,' said Sid happily.

'Mum,' Nick said. 'Where's Susan? Where's my little girl?'

Mrs Roberts put a hand to her chest, and then she turned and called into the house. 'Susan,' she said. Her voice was croaky with emotion. 'Sweetheart, can you come here?'

Susan appeared in the doorway, still in her nightdress with her hair round her shoulders.

'Nan, it's freezing,' she said. 'Why are you standing here with the door open? You're letting all the heat out. What's going on?' And then she stopped suddenly as she saw Nick and steadied herself on the door frame. 'What's this?' she said. 'Is this . . .? Are you . . .?'

Seth thought his heart might break with the hope in the girl's voice.

Nick and Susan stared at each other for a moment, both speechless. Then Nick smiled at his daughter.

'You're so tall,' he said. 'Taller than your nan.'

Susan jumped at the sound of his voice. She covered her mouth with her hand and looked at her grandmother.

'Nan?' she said, shakily. 'Nan?'

Mrs Roberts reached out her hand and Susan took it. 'It's your dad, sweetheart.'

Susan's eyes filled with tears and she suddenly looked much younger than her seventeen years. Seth thought how sad it was that Nick had left behind a little girl and come home to a young woman and he'd never get to see those years he'd missed.

'It's my dad,' Susan whispered. 'It's my dad.'

She took a deep, juddering breath and then she barrelled into her dad, throwing her arms round him, crying and laughing and talking all at once.

'Daddy,' she kept saying. 'I knew you weren't dead. I knew it.' Nick let out a small involuntary groan as she squeezed him and Susan loosened her grip. 'I'm sorry, is that too tight? Does it hurt? You're so thin. Are you cold? Where have you been?'

Nick laughed at the endless questions and tried to answer as Mrs Roberts looked over to where Paul, Seth and Sid all hovered by the garden gate. 'You found him, did you?'

'Seth and Sid did,' Paul said. Seth held his breath. What would he say? 'Seth was working.'

Seth breathed out slowly. That was good. It was a plausible excuse.

'They asked me for help,' Paul went on.

'I was in a bad way, Mum,' Nick said, still holding on to Susan tightly. 'I don't even remember them picking me up and taking me to . . .' He looked at Paul and stopped talking. 'They brought me here.'

Mrs Roberts cast a sharp eye over the men. 'You gave him your boots, Seth Armstrong?' Seth nodded. 'And I suppose that's your sweater, Sidney Mosby?' Sid dipped his head in agreement, and Mrs Roberts beamed at them. She came up the snowy garden path and pulled all three men into an enormous hug, covering their faces with kisses. 'You brought my boy home,' she said. 'I will never forget that.'

Seth and Sid ducked away from her embrace, embarrassed at the show of emotion. Paul tolerated her kisses for a second longer, before he untangled himself too.

'You need to get Nick inside,' he said, back to his efficient self. 'He's warmer now, but he's been very cold. He needs a hot bath, and a good meal.'

'You're heroes,' Mrs Roberts said. 'You deserve the George Cross.'

Seth chuckled. 'I'll settle for my boots back.'

'Thank you,' Nick said simply to the men.

Paul gave him a tiny salute. 'No problem.'

As the men turned to go, the church bells rang out, making them all jump.

'It's Christmas Day,' Susan said in wonder. 'Dad, it's Christmas Day.' She gasped. 'I've not got you a present.'

Nick kissed her on the top of her head as they walked inside the cottage. 'I've got everything I need, right here,' he said.

Mrs Roberts blew the men a kiss and shut the door, leaving Seth and the others outside.

'I could do with some sleep,' Paul said. 'I'm too old for this excitement.'

Seth nodded. He was exhausted too. And, now he came to think of it, really bloody cold.

'You did well, lads,' said Paul. 'You saved that man's life tonight. You did yourselves proud.' He paused. 'Talk about going out on a high note.' His voice cracked a tiny bit and he slapped both younger men on the back. 'Well done,' he said again. 'I'm proud of you both.'

Chapter Fourteen

The sound of church bells woke Betty with a start. It took a moment for her to realise where she was and then she remembered, last night's party coming back to her in fits and starts. Seth not turning up. The mulled cider . . . Wally.

She opened her eyes. She was lying on a surprisingly comfortable and cosy hay bale, snug under a blanket and tucked into Wally's broad chest. Wally, bless him, was fast asleep still, snoring softly. Seth didn't snore, Betty thought, and then felt appalled with herself for the comparison. Urgh, her mouth was furry and her head ached. Why on earth were the church bells ringing so loudly and so gaily?

She sat up suddenly, making Wally moan and turn over, taking the blanket with him.

'It's Christmas Day,' she said out loud. 'Flaming heck.'

Oh this was bad. This was really bad. It must still be early if the bells were ringing, but her parents were bound to be awake already. Hopefully they'd go out to church and she could sneak in the back door and pretend that she'd been home all night – not curled up in a barn with a man who was definitely not her fiancé. She felt a rush of guilt so huge it made her dizzy. Yes, she'd planned to do something drastic if Seth hadn't turned up. But she'd been thinking two weeks staying with Margaret in Birmingham. She hadn't meant . . . She looked at Wally. Oh goodness, she thought. What had she done?

She watched Wally sleeping, his chest rising and falling rhythmically. He was a nice man, she thought, this wasn't his fault. It was all her.

Very slowly and carefully, she slid out from under the blanket, shivering as the cold air hit her bare skin. She picked up her clothes and wiggled into her figure-hugging green dress. It was very much an outfit for a party. There was no way she could pretend she was just heading for church dressed like this. She hoped she could make it back to the village without bumping into anyone. She didn't want word of her . . . indiscretion . . . getting back to Seth.

She picked up her mother's fur stole from where she'd draped it over a beam and slung it round her shoulders, then she put on her shoes and tiptoed out of the barn.

It was freezing. Absolutely freezing. The snow was at least three or even four inches deep. Betty could feel it soaking through her shoes as she stood there. What on earth was she going to do? She could barely walk in this stupid dress and her shoes had thin soles that would see her sliding down the hill to Beckindale. Shame hit her like a tonne of bricks. What a terrible, terrible person she was. Spending the night with a man, cheating on the man she loved, drinking so much cider, dolled up like some cheap tart. She snorted. A cheap tart was exactly what she was, wasn't she? What else did you call a girl who slept with men she hardly knew?

Head bowed against the wind, she started to walk across the farmyard, slipping and sliding as she went. Her eyes were stinging from the cold, and from the tears that were gathering. She felt absolutely wretched.

'Betty Prendagast, did you get lost?'

Betty jumped to see Jacob Sugden standing in front of her, a smug grin playing on his lips. She paused for a second, gathering herself, then she lifted her heavy head and gave him her best, most dazzling, Judy Garland smile.

'Darling Jacob, I'm so pleased to see you,' she gushed. 'I'm so embarrassed. I had too much cider at the party and fell asleep.' No need to say where she had slept. Let Jacob assume she'd found a corner in the farmhouse.

Jacob nodded. He reached out a hand and plucked a piece of hay from Betty's hair and handed it to her without a word.

She took it, feeling her cheeks flush.

'Need a ride down to the village?' Jacob asked.

Betty would have kissed him, if she hadn't done quite enough of that already. Instead she beamed at him. 'That would be wonderful.'

She stood, shivering, in the icy wind as he brought his cart round. It had been adapted for the snow, with runners nailed over the wheels.

'Climb in,' Jacob said. Betty did as he said, slightly awkwardly because of how tight her dress was, then settled down on the wooden seat. Jacob looked at her shivering and frowned in concern. 'Do you need a blanket?' he asked. 'There's one in the barn. I'll fetch it.'

'No!' Betty almost shouted, then she caught herself. 'No need. I'm snug as anything, thank you.'

Jacob gave her an odd look, but he didn't argue.

Betty rested her head against the back panel of the cart as Jacob set off. Her head was thumping and the smell of the horse was making her feel decidedly queasy.

Jacob glanced round at her. 'All right there, Betty?' he said. 'You've gone a bit green.'

Betty closed her eyes. 'I'll be fine,' she lied. She wasn't actually sure she'd ever be fine again. What on earth was she going to do? Tell Seth what she'd done? The thought of confessing made her feel even sicker. What about Wally? What if he told someone? She'd made some mistakes in her time, but this was the worst.

As they reached the edge of the village, Jacob turned to her. 'I need to get some hay from the barn,' he said. 'Thought I might give it an hour or so before I go in there. What do you think?'

Betty swallowed. He knew exactly what she'd been up to and who he'd find in the barn if he went in there. 'I'd definitely give it a little while,' she said.

Jacob nodded. 'You'll be all right, Betty,' he said. 'Don't worry.'

Grateful at his kind words, Betty could only pat him on his arm. She was worried that if she tried to speak, she'd start crying. Or throw up. One or the other.

'Can I drop you here?' Jacob asked, pulling up the horse.

Betty nodded. 'Thank you,' she whispered as she climbed awkwardly out of the cart. She could see people heading out of church, and desperate to avoid everyone, she thought she'd go round the back way.

Jacob waved goodbye to her and drove off, and Betty paused for a second. Then she pulled her skirt up to above her knees so she could walk and quickly darted round the back of Grange Cottage, along past the pub and the garage, and finally, with her heart beating loudly, she reached her own back door.

Very slowly, she turned the handle, listening for any sound that would mean her parents were home and not at church. But all was quiet. Quickly, she slid into the kitchen and dashed upstairs, unzipping her dress as she went and pushing away the memory of Wally doing the same thing last night.

Upstairs, she kicked off her soggy shoes, threw her dress into the corner, changed her underwear and washed in icy water that made her gasp. Then she pulled on a demure skirt, thick stockings and a warm sweater, slathered cold cream over her face to take away the kohl that was smudged under her eyes, and brushed out her drooping victory rolls.

Just as she finished tidying her hair, there was a knock on her bedroom door and her mum stuck her head round.

'Oh good, you're up,' she said. 'Merry Christmas.'

Betty ran over and gave her mother a hug, wondering if she could tell that something was different about her daughter. If she could sense the shame that Betty felt was pouring out of herself in great waves. 'Merry Christmas.'

'Come downstairs when you're ready, we've got some presents to open and I could do with some help with lunch.'

'Will do,' Betty said. She waited for her mum to go back downstairs and then opened her bedside drawer and took out the presents she'd made for her parents. A scarf she'd knitted for her father, carefully unravelling the wool from an old jumper her sister Margaret had left behind. And there were two jars of delicious-looking strawberry jam that had been given to her by a grateful dog owner at the vet's for her mother. She shut the drawer quickly as her eye was caught by the gloves she'd made for Seth. They were an old pair of her father's, but Betty had darned the holes neatly and cut them down so they stopped at Seth's knuckles, trimming the edges with a different colour of wool. Seth's hands got cold when he worked, but he needed to be able to load his gun, or fiddle with machinery, and Betty thought the gloves she'd made would be just the thing. She'd started making them back in the summer, because she was slow at sewing and knitting and wanted them to be just right. She stifled a sob as she thought about all the time and love she'd devoted to making them in the spare time she had when Seth was off working all hours. Guilt about spending the night with Wally stabbed her again, making her breathe in sharply.

'Come on, Betty,' she told herself sternly. She practised her smile in the mirror, and satisfied she looked normal, even if she felt anything but, she ran downstairs to see her parents.

Her father was standing by the fireplace, looking very pleased with himself.

'Merry Christmas,' Betty sang.

He hugged her. 'Merry Christmas, sweetheart. Bet you're the proudest girl in Beckindale today.'

For a terrible second, Betty thought he knew where she'd been last night and was making a barbed comment about it. But he was smiling so broadly that couldn't be the case. So, ignoring the lurching in her stomach, she gave her dad a quizzical look. 'What do you mean?'

'Your Seth.'

None the wiser, Betty stared at him. 'What about my Seth?'

'You've not heard?' her father exclaimed. 'Nora, she's not heard.'

Her mother appeared at the living-room door. 'She's not heard?'

Betty thought she might scream with frustration. 'What?' she snapped. 'What has Seth done?'

'He's a hero,' said her dad.

Betty stared at him. A hero? What on earth did he mean? Seth was lots of things – funny and kind and knowledgeable about the countryside – but she'd never thought of him as a hero. A sudden memory of Wally's gunshot scars flooded her, and she steadied herself on the arm of the sofa as guilt made her reel once more.

She took a breath. 'A hero?' she repeated.

'He were out in the woods last night. Christmas Eve. The snow was falling and it was freezing cold,' her dad began, adding to Betty's inner turmoil. Her father loved to tell a story, embellishing and adding to it. Usually she enjoyed his tales, but today she just wanted to know the facts. She threw her head back in despair and her dad rolled his eyes at the drama. 'He and his friend Sid were in the woods, working . . .'

'Sid who?' said Betty. 'Sid Mosby? Seth's not friends with Sid. Sid works over in Hotten.'

Her father frowned. 'It was Sid, wasn't it, Nora?'

'Definitely,' her mum agreed. 'Because Sid's mam Janet is a friend of Mrs Roberts, and I heard her telling Nelly from the shop.'

Betty blinked, not following the story. 'Go back to the woods,' she told her father. 'Seth was in the woods, possibly with Sid Mosby, who, as far as I know, he's never spoken to . . .'

'And they came across a man, skin and bone, he were. Frozen half to death. So they picked him up, and took him . . . Where did they take him, Nora?'

'Ee, I'm not sure,' her mother said. 'Up to the estate, perhaps?'

'I don't think it could have been the estate, because they were on the far side of the woods, weren't they?'

'They took him somewhere,' Betty said, hurrying him up. 'And . . .'

'Well, they warmed him up and bandaged his wounds.'

'Seth gave him his boots,' her mother added proudly. 'Walked into Beckindale in his socks, he did. In all that snow.'

'And who was it?' Betty said, just wanting the story to be over. 'Who was the man?'

'That's the best bit,' her dad said. 'It was Nick Roberts.'

'Who?'

'Young Susan's father – Vera Roberts's son. They thought he was dead, but he's been in a POW camp. He walked all the way from France and he'd have died in the woods outside Beckindale if your Seth hadn't saved him.'

'Him and Sid,' her mother put in. 'And Paul Oldroyd.'

'Paul Oldroyd?' Betty said. For the life of her she couldn't imagine why Seth would be spending any time with stuffy old Home Guard Paul Oldroyd, because he always said he was pompous. And, what's more, he was right. Paul Oldroyd *was* pompous. And way too pleased with himself. Betty's head was spinning. None of this made any sense to her.

'Are you all right, Betty love?' her mother said. 'It's a shock to all of us. Apparently Vera thought he was a ghost. The Spirit of Christmas Past or summat. Susan's thrilled, of course. Dr Black's with them now.'

'Seth saved the man's life?' Betty muttered. 'Last night?' While she was out at Ned and Audrey's party, flirting – and goodness knows what else – with Wally Eagleton, Seth was bandaging wounds and giving a stranger his boots? She felt hot and cold all at once and so dizzy. She put her hand to her forehead and then felt the floor come up to meet her as everything went black.

Chapter Fifteen

Betty opened her eyes to see her concerned parents standing over her.

'What happened there, love?' her mother said, helping her to her feet and settling her on to the sofa.

Betty rubbed her head, which was still pounding from the cider and now ached from hitting the floor, too.

'I'm just hungry, I think,' she muttered. She wasn't hungry really, it was just the guilt and the shock of Seth's heroism that had made her faint.

Her mother rushed off to make her some toast and a cup of tea, while her dad sat next to her and frowned.

'Maybe we should get Dr Black?' he said. 'You look right peaky.'

'I'm fine,' Betty said. 'Honestly.'

Her mother came back with the food and, obediently, Betty ate her toast while Nora stood next to her, checking every mouthful.

'Arthur, can you put the kettle on for another brew,' Nora said. Betty's father looked pointedly at the full mugs on the coffee table, but he got up and went into the kitchen. Nora looked at Betty through narrowed eyes and Betty flinched. Had her mother realised what she'd been doing last night? 'Betty Prendagast, you're not in trouble, are you?' Nora said bluntly. 'That Seth Armstrong will have me to answer to if he's got you in the family way without a ring on your finger.'

Betty's eyes widened. She gave her mum a small smile. 'No,' she said. 'I'm not in trouble.'

Nora's shoulders slumped in relief and she grinned at Betty. 'Good girl.'

Ha! Betty thought. *She was anything but.* She finished her toast – actually it had made her feel a bit better – and stood up.

'Where are you going?' her mum said, her brow creasing with worry.

'I need to see Seth,' Betty told her. 'I need to find out what happened last night.'

Ignoring her mother's protests, Betty grabbed her coat from the peg, pulled on some boots and headed out into the snow.

There were quite a few people around – children pulling each other on sledges, their rosy cheeks shining, or families hurrying to exchange gifts.

'Merry Christmas,' they called as she passed. Betty gave them each a cursory wave, ignoring the beautiful Christmas tree outside the pub and the carol singers huddled in the middle of the village. She didn't feel any joy, just the weight of guilt and confusion, so she rushed by them and marched on to the edge of the village, to the row of tiny ramshackle cottages where Seth lived with his mother and his sister.

Betty knocked on the door and then suddenly felt foolish. What was she doing here? This wasn't going to make her feel better. How was hearing that Seth had stood her up because he was saving a man's life going to stop her feeling guilty? It was just going to make her feel worse. But she had to know. She took a deep breath and waited. She was a terrible person and she had to face the music.

Seth's mother opened the door. 'Hello, Betty love,' she said. 'Happy Christmas.'

'And to you,' Betty said politely. 'Is Seth here?'

'He's asleep,' his mother – Lorna – said. She looked very proud. 'He's been out all night.'

'He's awake, Ma,' Seth's sister Briony said, coming down the stairs. 'Shall I shout him?'

'Please,' said Betty.

Lorna gestured for her to come inside and shut the door and she and Betty stood, close together, in the narrow hallway as Briony pounded upstairs and bellowed for her brother.

'You heard what he did?' Lorna said.

Betty nodded. 'He saved a man's life.'

'He's a hero.' Lorna grinned broadly. 'You're lucky to have him.'

Betty leaned against the wall, worried she might faint again. 'I am,' she muttered.

Eventually, Seth appeared. His face lit up when he saw Betty, making her heart twist with guilt – again. 'Betty, Merry Christmas!'

'I forgot your present,' Betty said.

'That doesn't matter one jot,' Seth said. He bounded down the stairs and grinned at her. 'You're my present.'

Briony made sick noises at Seth's mushiness, which would have usually made Betty laugh, but today she couldn't find the humour in anything.

Seth punched his sister on the arm and turned back to Betty. 'Shall we go for a walk in the snow?'

Betty could only nod. She had a very unsettling feeling that everything was about to change. That everything she'd thought was solid and unchangeable was suddenly different.

She waited for Seth to wrap up warmly – noticing he had his boots to put on, so either that had been a rumour or Nick Roberts had returned them – and then they went outside again.

Betty normally liked to link arms with Seth when they walked, but today she kept her hands in her pockets.

For a while they didn't speak. Betty was trying to work out what to say. 'Everyone's saying you're a hero,' she began eventually. 'It all sounds terribly exciting. Can you tell me what happened?'

Seth paused. 'Shall we sit?' he said.

The pub was closed, but he led the way over to where there was a bench, sheltered under the jutting roof of The Woolpack, and they sat down. Betty couldn't help but notice there was a gap between their legs, when normally they'd be touching.

'I was in the woods,' Seth began. 'Just working.'

'On your own?' Betty said.

'No,' Seth was clearly choosing his words carefully. 'Sid Mosby was there. He's been helping out.'

'I didn't know that.'

'Well he has.'

Betty folded her hands into her lap, noticing one of her gloves needed darning. 'Go on.'

'We came across this fella, in a right bad way, he were. Frozen stiff and barely breathing. So we bundled him up and took him to get warm.'

'Where did you take him?'

Seth stared at her. 'What?'

'Where did you take him?'

'To the estate.'

'That's not true. Mam said you found him on the other side of the woods, so the village would be nearer. Where did you take him?' Betty's voice sounded shrill to her own ears. Nothing was adding up. Nothing about this story made any sense. She took a deep breath, trying to calm herself, and looked straight at Seth. 'I know this isn't the truth and I think you've been fibbing to me for ages. Months and months. I need you to tell me everything again, but this time tell me what really happened.'

There was a long pause. Betty's heart was pounding. She no longer thought Seth was cheating on her – there was only one cheat in their relationship, and it wasn't Seth. But she was absolutely sure that he'd been lying about something. And she needed to know what it was.

Seth nodded slowly. 'I will tell you, Betty. But you have to understand that if I do, you can't tell no one.'

Betty started to talk, but Seth held his hand up to quieten her.

'If you tell anyone, I reckon I'll be in a lot of trouble. They might even shoot me.'

'What?' Betty said. She felt close to tears. 'What's this all about, Seth?'

Seth looked straight at her. 'A while back, Paul Oldroyd came to me,' he began.

'Paul Oldroyd from the Home Guard?' Betty said, wanting to check that's really who he meant.

Seth nodded. 'He was recruiting for the Hotten Auxiliary Unit. We were to form an operational patrol.' He swallowed. 'We were trained to defend England in the event of a German invasion.' He parroted the words in a way that made Betty realise he really was telling the truth this time, even if that truth sounded totally unbelievable. 'I went on training week-ends,' Seth said. 'That's why I wasn't around much.'

'Training for what?' Betty couldn't believe what she was hearing.

'Guerrilla warfare,' Seth said. 'Unarmed combat, demolition, sabotage . . .' He looked straight ahead. 'Assassination.'

'Assassination,' Betty squeaked. Her hands were shaking. Of all the things she'd expected Seth to say he'd been doing, forming some sort of British Resistance with pompous old Paul Oldroyd hadn't been among them. 'Seth . . .'

But he was still talking. Betty had the slightly odd sensation that he was talking to himself.

'We were told never to surrender,' he said. 'To fight on. Sometimes it felt like being in a comic-book story. But other times I felt like we were doing something really important, you know?'

Betty did know. She'd felt exactly like that when she was dancing with ENSA. That mix of doing something useful but also frivolous and unimportant.

'Now the Germans are in retreat, there's no chance of an invasion, so we're all but finished,' Seth went on. 'We've packed up the base, and George has gone. It's just Paul, me and Sid now. Come January, the Hotten Auxiliary Unit won't exist any more.'

'Where's the base?' Betty stuttered. 'Who's George?'

'George was one of the patrol. Clever bloke. Fluent in German. Each patrol had someone who could speak it, just in case. Sid and I have picked up a fair bit too. George used to teach us when we were out on patrol of an evening.'

Betty thought she might be dreaming. This was all

completely bewildering. Seth was there next to her, looking just the same as he always had but talking about speaking German, and guerrilla warfare.

'And the base?'

'Royal Engineers built it. It's in the woods. You'd never know it was there, though, if you weren't looking for it.'

'So that's where you took Nick Roberts?'

Seth looked at her, as though he'd forgotten she was there. 'Aye,' he said. 'We warmed him up. Sid found some chocolate. And we bandaged his feet – he'd come all the way from France. Walked miles, he had, and he's skin and bone, poor lad. Then Paul brought a jeep from somewhere, and we took him home to his mam.'

Betty was speechless. Completely and utterly speechless. She and Seth had been sweethearts for so long and yet she hadn't known him at all. She looked at him in awe.

'I'm sorry I've not been around much,' Seth said. 'I know your Margaret thought I was neglecting you. And I was. But now you know why.'

Betty let out the breath she hadn't even realised she was holding.

'You've done a brilliant thing,' she said, meaning it. 'Not just rescuing Nick Roberts. All of it. All that training. Learning all that stuff. Folk in The Woolie would fall off their bar stools if they knew.'

Seth gave a small smile. 'They can't ever know. We're not allowed to talk about it.'

'I won't breathe a word,' said Betty. She looked at Seth's lovely, familiar face. 'I'm really proud of you. And I'm glad you told me the truth.' She swallowed, trying to get rid of the lump in her throat. 'But I'm afraid it's too late.'

Seth turned to face her. 'What do you mean, Betty?'

Betty felt a tear dribble down her cheek. She pulled her glove off her left hand and brushed the tear away with her finger.

'I turned it down,' she said. 'I turned down my chance to be a dancer so I could stay here with you.'

Seth stared at her. 'What are you talking about, love?'

Betty had never even told Seth that she'd applied to be a permanent part of ENSA, let alone that she'd been accepted and turned it down.

'They said they'd have me,' she said. 'Dancing in the shows for the troops every night. It could have been the start of something, you know? Pamela said I could be a Tiller Girl one day. In a theatre in London. But I said no to them and yes to you.' She stared down at her bare ring finger. 'I said I would marry you instead.' She was crying properly now. 'I thought you were just working at the estate. I thought that was our life – me at the vet's, you up at the hall. And it was fine. But all the time you were doing this amazing, incredible, brave thing . . .' She paused. 'And I was making appointments for cats to be castrated.'

'I thought you liked it at the vet's,' Seth said, confusion etched on his face.

'I do,' wailed Betty. 'But I want to be a dancer, not a receptionist.' She couldn't find the words to express how she was feeling. That she'd stayed in Beckindale because she thought that was what Seth wanted – the two of them plodding along together. But now she'd found out that wasn't what he'd been doing at all. She felt the sharp sting of betrayal, swiftly followed by the realisation that if Seth had betrayed her, she most certainly had betrayed him too. This was an enormous mess.

She looked up at the stark white sky, wondering if she should tell him about Wally, but deciding against it. She had a horrible feeling that she was about to break Seth's heart – why make it more painful than she had to?

'I'm proud of you,' she said. 'And you should be proud of yourself, Seth.' She tried to smile, but it was too hard. 'You may not have fought off a German invasion, but you were ready for it. And you saved Nick Roberts's life and brought him home for Susan. You've done so much. You've proved what you can achieve.' She took a deep breath. 'And now I have to go and do the same.'

Seth frowned. 'What do you mean, Betty?'

She wiped away another tear. 'I think I need to leave Beckindale for a while. Maybe even for good.'

'What about us?'

She shook her head. 'I think we're done, don't you?'

Seth's expression darkened. 'How can we be done?' he said.

'We just are.'

Seth looked furious. 'I've been doing my bit for the war effort,' he spat. 'Working all hours, learning all sorts. And this is how you repay me?'

Betty glared back at him. 'This isn't about you, Seth Armstrong. It's about me wanting more than a life in Beckindale.'

'Aye, well that's always been the trouble with you, Betty Prendagast. You're never happy with your lot.'

'I am happy,' Betty said. 'I was happy. Until you started ignoring me and leaving me sat in The Woolpack on my own.'

'I was on patrol,' Seth growled.

'I know,' Betty said. 'And that whole time you were on patrol, I could have been on stage. I could have been doing my bit for the war effort like Gracie Fields.'

'You should have gone,' Seth said bitterly.

'I should have gone.'

Seth sniffed loudly and turned away from her. Betty thought he might be crying. 'Will you join ENSA now?'

Betty shook her head. 'I think that ship has sailed,' she said. 'War's almost over and I doubt they'd have me now. I think I'll go and stay with our Margaret in Birmingham for a while. See if I can get a job in a theatre down there.'

Seth gave her a look that was half regret, half disgust. 'I was never enough for you, was I? Me, Beckindale, this life? Never enough.'

Betty thought about it. Should she lie? There had been enough falsehoods between them to last a lifetime.

'No,' she said. 'It was never enough. But you made it feel like it was for a while.'

Seth shook his head. 'You were never the right girl for me.'

Betty felt a wave of sadness crash over her. She felt so tired, she thought she could lie down right where they sat, outside the pub, and sleep for a week. 'Probably not,' she said.

Seth gave a snort. 'Good luck, Birmingham.' He sounded bitter and his angry tone made Betty wince.

They sat in silence for a moment, then, with nothing left to say, Betty stood up and straightened her skirt. 'I'll be seeing you, Seth Armstrong.'

Seth didn't reply.

Betty walked down the steps from the pub and paused for a minute at the bottom, but she didn't look at Seth. Then she headed for home.

'In the bleak midwinter,' the carol singers were singing, as she passed by. But, much to Betty's surprise, she didn't feel bleak. Instead she felt lighter, as though a weight she'd been carrying around with her had been taken away.

'Ta-ra, Beckindale,' she whispered. 'Merry Christmas.' And the snow began to fall.

Part Two

Chapter Sixteen

7TH MAY 1945

'Thank you so much, Dr Black,' Lily said as he showed her out of his office.

He smiled at her. 'My pleasure.'

As the door shut, Lily clasped her hands together and bounced on her tiptoes in excitement.

'Everything all right, is it?' asked Phyllis, Dr Black's extremely nosy receptionist.

Lily beamed at her and then, realising she didn't want any rumours spread around the village before she'd had a chance to speak to Jack, arranged her face into a frown.

'Fingers crossed,' she said to Phyllis in her best sombre tone.

She bowed her head and left the doctor's house slowly, but as soon as the door was closed, she raced across the village to the police station and burst through the entrance.

'Jack?' she called, as she ran in. 'Jack?'

Jack appeared from the back office, his face etched with worry. 'What is it? Are you all right? Is it Hope?'

Lily shook her head, panting with the exertion of her hundred-yard dash from the surgery. 'No,' she gasped. 'Everything's fine. Oh blimey, I need a second to catch my breath. I've run all the way from Dr Black's.'

Jack came round the side of the wooden counter and took his wife's hands. 'Dr Black?' he said. 'Are you . . .?'

Lily couldn't contain her glee for a second longer. 'I'm pregnant,' she said. 'We're having another baby.'

Jack threw his arms around her and hugged her so tightly Lily couldn't breathe and had to wriggle free.

'Why didn't you tell me?', Jack said.

'I had a feeling, but I didn't want to get your hopes up again only to be disappointed.' Lily looked at her feet. 'And last time was so awful, I was so worried about what everyone would think, that I just wanted to make it right. Have a nice experience of hearing the news.'

Jack, lovely, kind, clever Jack, looked into her eyes and nodded. 'I can understand that.' He hugged her again, more gently this time. 'When is the baby due?'

'A couple of weeks before Christmas,' Lily said with delight. 'A wonderful Christmas present for us.'

'How do you feel?' Jack said. 'Sick? I remember you being sick before.'

'A bit,' Lily said. 'But not as bad as last time.'

'Should we tell Hope?'

Lily made a face. 'I think she's too small to understand for now. And Christmas seems like such a long way away at the moment. Closer to the time, I think.'

'What about your dad? And Nina?'

'I thought we'd go and see them now, if you can spare the time? I have to collect Hope anyway,' Lily said, loving how excited he was. 'And maybe we could write to your parents later, too?' 'They'll be over the moon.' Jack pulled down the grille over the counter and picked up his hat. 'I'm finishing early,' he announced. 'If anything happens, they'll have to come and find me at home.' He took Lily's hand and kissed her fingers. 'Let's go.'

'Do you know what would be the icing on the cake?' Lily said, as Jack locked up the police station and they began sauntering, hand in hand, towards her dad's garage. 'The end of the war.'

'Wouldn't that be wonderful?' he agreed. 'A peacetime baby.'

They knew the end was coming, but Lily found she couldn't think about it really. Couldn't even imagine what it would be like. She hardly dared to hope that this was the final few days of the war, and though she knew other people were making bunting and streamers and other decorations ready for what they were calling Victory in Europe day, Lily couldn't do it. She was over Derek now, of course she was. But her mother's death, and Derek's betrayal, had taught her at an early age that happiness could be pulled away from her without warning. Now, even though she was content with Jack and Hope, and the new baby, and she loved her job working alongside her father, she never wanted to assume that good things would happen. Just in case.

They found Mick working on the engine of a tractor.

'Hello, love,' he said. 'Hello, Jack. You just missed Ruby. She's left a bike for you. Wants you to have a look at the gears or something.'

Lily rolled her eyes. 'She can do that herself,' she said. 'She knows what she's doing.'

'She was racing off to Emmerdale Farm, I think,' Mick said. Ruby had been working with the Sugdens since she'd left school. Mick dropped the bonnet lid and wiped his oily hands on a rag. 'What are you two doing here? Hope's with Nina.'

Lily couldn't stop smiling. 'I know,' she said, bouncing on her toes. 'We just had something to tell you before we pick her up.'

Mick looked at her through narrowed eyes. 'What is it? What are you up to?'

'We're having another baby,' Lily declared.

'You never are.' Mick's face broke into a broad grin. 'You clever thing.'

He pulled Lily into his arms and she relaxed into his embrace. She was so lucky to have such strong, kind men in her life.

Mick reached over Lily's shoulders and shook Jack's hand. 'Well done, son,' he said.

Jack flushed with pride. Lily thought that was the first time her dad had called Jack 'son'. She quite liked it.

'We've not told anyone else yet,' she said to her father. 'We're going to let Nina know now. But we're probably going to wait a while before we tell Hope.'

'Sensible,' her dad said, nodding his head. 'A week's a long time for that one. She'll be desperate for a little brother or sister straight away.'

Lily gave Mick a big smacker on his cheek. 'We'll go and find Nina now.'

Nina was delighted for them. She fussed over Lily like a mother hen. While Lily had grown to love her stepmother, she'd always thought of Nina as more of a friend than a mother. Her kindly concern now, though, together with how lovely she'd been when she shared the news of Derek's death, made Lily realise she was a mum of sorts. Of course, she'd never forget her mother, Rose. She'd loved her so much and missed her every day. But Nina made Mick happy – and Lily was very glad to have her, too.

Jack went off to find Hope, who was playing in the garden, and Lily sat down with a groan, suddenly exhausted by all the excitement.

'You look after yourself,' Nina said sternly.

Lily grinned at her. 'I will. And I've got a lot of people looking after me, too.'

Nina stroked the top of Lily's head. 'You deserve it,' she said. 'I'm so thrilled for you, darling. You're the strongest person I know and you have come through all that Derek business with your head held high. After all the darkness comes light.'

And it seemed Nina was right, in more ways than one.

Jack and Lily took Hope home, gave her tea, and a bath, and tucked her up snugly. As Lily kissed her goodnight, she thought about how wonderful it would be to have another baby to love and tuck into bed and read a story to. She stroked her stomach gently. She hoped it would be a little boy, who looked just like Jack. Or a little sister for Hope would be wonderful too.

With Hope fast asleep, Lily went downstairs and found Jack dozing in a chair, listening to the wireless. Lily made them both a cup of tea, put Jack's by his arm and settled down in her own chair to do some mending. She was just concentrating on unpicking the hem of one of Hope's little dresses – she'd grown so much in just a couple of weeks

– when the music that was playing on the wireless suddenly stopped.

Lily sat up straight and Jack's eyes sprang open. They looked at each other, without speaking, hardly daring to hope.

The announcer apologised for interrupting the programme and then he went on: 'This evening, the Ministry of Information has confirmed that an official statement declaring the end of the war will be made simultaneously in London, Washington and Moscow tomorrow.'

Lily put her hand over her mouth. She wanted to cry and laugh and scream and shout and jump for joy and lie on the floor and sleep for a hundred years, all at once. Her eyes were brimming with tears and Jack's looked much the same.

'The day has been declared a national holiday to mark Victory in Europe Day – VE Day,' the announcer continued.

Lily dropped her mending on the floor.

'It's over,' she said to Jack in wonder. 'It's over.'

She started to cry, and Jack did too. Both of them standing in the middle of the living room, sobbing and holding on to each other.

'The war's over,' Jack said. And then he shouted, 'The war's over!' and suddenly their tears turned to laughter and they jumped around the room like little children.

'Mama?' a voice called from upstairs – their celebrations had woken little Hope.

'Oops,' said Lily, giggling wildly.

'Go and fetch her,' said Jack, who was usually quite strict about bedtime. 'She needs to be part of this. She might remember it when she's older.'

Lily bounded upstairs to find Hope sitting up in bed, clutching her rag doll.

'Is it a party?' the little girl said hopefully. She was a real social butterfly and loved being among friends.

'It is,' sang Lily. 'It's a party, because the war is over.' She scooped Hope out of bed and covered her face with kisses, making her laugh. 'Come on.'

'Downstairs?' said Hope, hardly daring to believe her luck. 'In my nightie?'

Lily laughed. 'In your nightie.'

They went down, hand in hand, and found Jack had opened their front door and gone outside into the warm early-summer evening.

'We need to tell everyone in the pub,' he said as Lily and Hope followed him outside. 'They won't have had the wireless on.'

'Let me,' Lily said. Jack took Hope, and Lily darted across the village and into The Woolpack, slamming through the doors so loudly that everyone looked up.

'Lily?' Jed said, looking worried. 'What's up? What's the matter?'

Lily looked round at the concerned faces of the drinkers in the pub. Seth Armstrong and Sid Mosby were on one side of the bar, Jacob Sugden was standing by the window, Betty's parents were sitting at a table, chatting with Ned Barlow's dad. Everyone was gazing at Lily expectantly.

'Is it . . .' said Jacob in a strangled voice.

For a second, Lily couldn't speak, because the emotion of what she was about to say was too much. Everyone gazed at her, and she looked back, gathering herself.

'The war's over!' she announced. 'It's over!'

The roar from everyone in the pub was like a football crowd.

'Drinks are on the house!' Jed shouted and everyone roared again. Then everyone was laughing and shouting and talking all at once. The noise made Lily's head spin.

She pushed her way through the people and went back outside into the village to find Jack. Everyone was drifting out of their houses, blinking in the twilight as though they'd just been woken from a six-year-long sleep.

'It's over,' people called. 'It's all over.'

Lily saw her dad and Nina and she and Hope ran over and they all shared a cuddle.

'What a day,' her dad kept saying. 'What a day.'

Jed emerged from the pub and gave them a wave.

'Watch this!' he shouted. 'Watch!'

Inside, Larry was pulling down the blackout blinds. Lily watched in delight as Jed counted down and Larry flicked a switch. The pub's lights shone out, lighting up the dim centre of the village.

'And the other one!' Jed called. There was a pause and then, with a hum, the light above The Woolpack sign switched on, making the gold-painted name glow in the twilight.

'No more blackout,' Lily breathed. 'No more war.'

'Come and have a drink, Uncle Mick!' Jed shouted as they all gazed at the pub, beaming its light out like a beacon. 'On the house!'

Lily exchanged a look with her dad, raising an eyebrow.

'Best go,' said Mick. 'Chances are that won't happen again.' He hoisted a delighted Hope on to his shoulders, and he and Nina wandered off towards The Woolpack.

Lily waited for Jack, who'd been chatting to Ned Barlow, and took his hand.

'We'll remember this day for the rest of our lives,' she said. 'First the baby and now the end of the war.'

Jack gave her a kiss. 'It's one of the happiest days I've ever had.'

Lily smiled. 'And this is just the beginning,' she said. 'It's only going to get better from now on.'

Chapter Seventeen

VE DAY

Lily was up with the lark the next day. She was regretting her reluctance to make bunting ahead of the end of the war now that she wanted to deck the house in red, white and blue for the village celebration, so now she was quickly cutting out triangles from some old clothes, sacking and other bits she'd found, and stitching it all together.

She couldn't quite believe the war was over. She knew it would take a while – years probably – for the country to get back to normal, but, oh, wasn't it just wonderful to know that it was finished? Annie would be back. The troops would be coming home. Some of them at least. She thought about how the celebrations would be bittersweet for Maggie Sugden, whose beloved son Edward wouldn't be returning. And for the family of Ernie Hudson – Seth Armstrong's best friend – who'd been killed in Syria. Or for the other families in Beckindale who'd lost loved ones. There would be more names to put on the village war memorial and that was sad.

'Making your bunting?' Jack said behind her.

'Thought I'd get it done before Hope wakes up.'

'It looks lovely.'

Lily admired her handiwork. 'It's almost there. Can you get the ladder out so I can hang it up?'

'Erm, no,' said Jack. 'I'll hang it. You shouldn't be climbing ladders in your condition.'

'Well you'd better hurry up,' said Lily. 'Because I'm finished.'

With a flourish, she held up a string of bunting and showed it to Jack. She'd sewed scraps of red, white and blue fabric together. It wasn't perfect, but it would look lovely.

And it really did. The whole village looked wonderful. Some people had strung bunting right across the centre of the village, looped between houses and the pub and strung between trees. The sunshine made the decorations shimmer and glow and Lily thought she'd never seen Beckindale looking so beautiful.

'Lily, give us a hand?'

She turned to see Meg struggling with a long table and darted over to help her. Everyone was bringing out tables, kitchen chairs, stools and even old doors propped on trestles so the whole village could sit down together and have a good old celebratory feast – well, as much of a feast as could be managed on rations and at short notice. For the thousandth time since the war began, Lily thanked her lucky stars that she was living in the countryside and that some things that were in short supply in towns and cities were still available for them.

Lily and Meg set the table down.

'Are you all right, Lil?' Meg asked. She was looking at Lily in that way she had – as though she could see right into Lily's mind and tell what she was thinking.

'I'm fine,' Lily said. 'I'm better than fine, in fact.' A little bubble of happiness rose up and she let out a tiny squeal of excitement. 'I'm pregnant!'

'Oh Lily, that's wonderful news,' said Meg. The women hugged and Meg smiled broadly at Lily. Lily couldn't help noticing, though, that her friend didn't seem as jubilant as the rest of the revellers.

'What's up?' she said.

Meg shrugged. 'Nothing.' She glanced round. 'Oh, there's Nancy. I must catch her.'

She hurried off as Ruby wandered over, leaving Lily looking at the young woman in bewilderment.

'What was that all about?'

'Search me,' Ruby said. 'She's been right funny since the announcement last night. I thought she'd be over the moon.'

'It's a strange thing, the end of the war,' said Lily thoughtfully. 'Because it's been awful, but it's brought good things too. My Hope, for one. And Jack coming to Beckindale. And you and Stan.'

Ruby's face clouded over for a second. 'But we lost our mam.'

'You did.'

'And Susan lost her whole family.'

'She did.' Lily shuddered at the idea of poor Susan's family all being killed. 'But then there was the joy when she found her father.'

Ruby looked over to where Susan sat in the sunshine, kicking her legs like a little girl and chatting animatedly to her dad.

'She's so much happier,' she said. Her fondness for the older girl was clear. 'She's not got that sadness inside her any more, know what I mean?'

Lily actually did know what Ruby meant. Susan had been silent and skittish when she first arrived in Beckindale but had gradually grown in confidence, thanks mostly to Nancy. The vet had really taken her under her wing and helped with her studying and later with her applications to university. But even so, Susan had had a sorrowful air about her that had remained – until Nick had turned up on Christmas Day. It had been lovely to see.

'She's working so hard for her exams, I'm glad she's having a break for today,' Ruby said. She made a face at Lily. 'Rather her than me. I wasn't sad to leave school.'

'Help me put out these tablecloths,' Lily said. Obediently, Ruby took two corners and together they wafted the cloth into place. 'I know how you feel about school, Ruby. I was the same. How are you getting on at Emmerdale Farm?'

'It's good,' Ruby said thoughtfully, smoothing out a wrinkle in the cloth. 'I like being outdoors. But farming's not my thing.'

Lily grinned at her. 'Your thing is cycling.'

'It is.' Ruby loved bicycles, which had made things difficult when she first moved in with Meg. Meg's beloved twin sister had died in a cycling accident when they were young and she'd blamed herself for a long time. But she'd grown to accept Ruby's passion and had even encouraged her to join the local club. 'Now I'm part of Hotten Wheelers, I just want to spend all my time with bicycles,' Ruby said. 'I'm grateful that the Sugdens gave me a job, but I want to race.'

Even though women didn't ride in cycling races, Lily had absolutely no doubt that Ruby would do it anyway. She grinned at the enthusiastic young woman in front of her.

'You will,' she said. Then she gasped as a thought occurred to her. 'I've had the most brilliant idea.'

'What?' said Ruby, who had finished arranging the table-cloth and was clearly desperate to be off.

'I'm having a baby,' said Lily.

Ruby grinned. 'I heard you tell Meg earlier. That's great news.'

'You could fill in at the garage, when I'm too big to bend down over bikes and when I've got my hands full with the little one. I imagine it won't be so busy up at Emmerdale Farm by then, so the Sugdens won't mind.'

Ruby stared at Lily, as though she couldn't believe her ears. 'Seriously?'

'Of course.' Lily had started using the garage to run her own branch of her father's business when Hope was a baby. She mended the bicycles that were vital for people getting around thanks to petrol rationing – and it had been Ruby's idea. 'I owe you. And you're the only person I'd trust anyway. You know more about bicycles than I do.'

Ruby threw her arms round Lily and hugged her. 'Thanks, Lil,' she said. 'Can I tell Susan?'

'Go on then,' Lily said, laughing. 'We're done with these cloths anyway.'

Ruby darted off, and Lily gave the cloth a final smoothing and stood back to admire it.

'Looks great.' Lily turned to see Maggie and Jacob Sugden arriving, laden with food. They had bowls of salad, and – was that ham? How exciting! There was cooked chicken and Maggie's home-made bread. This was going to be a real feast.

'Thanks, Maggie,' Lily said. She felt awkward suddenly. This was supposed to be a celebration, but how could the Sugdens celebrate when Edward wouldn't be returning with the rest of the troops. 'Bet you're looking forward to having Annie back?' she babbled.

'It will be lovely to see her,' Maggie said carefully. 'Shall I put these down somewhere? Maybe in the middle of the table?' She went off with her plates.

Lily turned to Jacob. 'How is Maggie doing? It can't be easy seeing everyone celebrating when you're missing Edward.'

Jacob glanced over to his mother and shrugged. 'She's not brilliant.'

'And you?'

'Same.'

At a loss as to how to comfort him, she reached out a hand and patted his upper arm gently. 'I know,' she said. 'There's a lot to be sad about.'

He shook his head. 'Ma's in a state,' he said. 'She's been crying.'

Lily looked over to where Maggie was talking to Nina. That was good, Nina was always comforting in hard times. 'I saw Jimmy Jenkinson's mum in tears too,' she said. 'Jimmy's in the Pacific with the navy. Still fighting. She says she won't celebrate until he's home.'

Jacob winced. 'Can't blame her.'

'Me neither,' said Lily. She looked round at the hustle and bustle of people setting out the party food, hanging the bunting or just standing round chatting. 'There's a bit of grief for everyone today, I reckon.'

'You're right there, Lil,' Jacob said. 'But there's happiness too. We should let ourselves celebrate, because lord knows we need it after all these years.'

Lily relaxed slightly. She'd felt so guilty being joyful when others were sad, but Jacob was right, they did need some fun. She smiled at the usually surly farmer. 'Not like you to be so upbeat,' she teased.

He winked at her – Jacob Sugden, winking – and smiled. 'War's brought a lot of changes to Beckindale.'

Without another word, he wandered off, calling a greeting to Jed, who was staggering out of the pub laden with bottles of beer. Lily eyed them suspiciously. They looked very much like her cousin Larry's own brew, rather than anything official. Not that she'd be having a drink herself. She stroked her abdomen gently. Not now she had this little one to think about.

Across the village, her eye was caught by a woman. She was standing very still at the edge of the makeshift barrier some of the men had built to make sure no cars came through the party area. She was very thin, and her dress was billowing around her legs in the summer breeze. It looked like she might be lifted off her feet by the wind. She was on her own, no one around her, which was unusual because everyone else was standing in groups or carrying furniture in pairs, or helping each other to pin up decorations.

Trying not to look like she was staring, Lily pulled down the brim of her sunhat a little so it shielded her eyes and, to her surprise, realised the woman was staring right at her. She wasn't sure who she was; she definitely wasn't one of the villagers, but she looked vaguely familiar. Lily lifted her hand to wave, but the woman didn't respond. She just stood there, in her too-big dress, her eyes boring a hole into Lily.

'Lil, is Larry bringing a table out for drinks?' Jack asked, appearing at her elbow.

She turned and gave him a kiss before replying. 'Already done,' she said, gesturing to where Jed and Jacob were arranging the bottles of questionable beer on a long table at the front of the pub. 'Do you know that woman, over by the vet's?'

Jack looked. 'What woman?'

Lily glanced up and down the street, but the woman had vanished.

'Oh, she's gone,' she said. 'That's odd. I thought I recognised her, is all.'

The sun disappeared behind a cloud and Lily shivered in the sudden coolness, feeling unsettled.

'Where's Hope?' she asked Jack, her voice slightly shrill.

'She's with your dad.'

Lily looked and there was Hope, 'helping' Mick put out some chairs. She shook her head. Today was supposed to be a joyful day. There was no point worrying about strange women. She hooked her arm through Jack's. 'Let's see if we can make a space for people to dance, shall we?'

He grinned at her. 'Lead the way, twinkle toes.'

Chapter Eighteen

Meg was feeling flat. She was trying so hard to join in with the excited preparations for the VE Day party, but she couldn't quite muster the enthusiasm.

Thank heavens for Ruby and Stan. They'd been so excited when they'd heard that the war was over, and that there was to be a huge party to celebrate, that their happiness had made her smile, for a while at least. There had been some tears, too. The children's real mother hadn't been the most attentive parent. Goodness knows she'd been quick enough to send them to Beckindale as evacuees, and Meg had always suspected it had been less about the kids' safety and more about having them off her hands. But despite her failings, they'd loved her, and when she'd been killed, they were devastated. Now the war was over and their mother was dead and Meg thought it must feel like they were losing her all over again.

That was how she felt about Rolf. Which was ridiculous, because she had never 'had' him in the first place. He was just a friend. And a German one at that. But still she felt like she was losing him.

She sighed as she shook out a tablecloth. She wondered what it was like in the POW camp. Would they just open the doors and let them all go free? She shook her head at her silly imagination. Hardly, she thought. No doubt there would be reams of paperwork and forms to fill in before they could all be returned to their grateful families in Germany and Italy.

Arms circled her waist and she turned to see her adoptive son Stan. He was growing up fast and sometimes she could see the young man he'd be one day, but today he was like an excited little lad again. And as affectionate as ever.

He squeezed her tightly and grinned at her. 'It's great this, in't it?'

Despite her mood, Meg couldn't help but smile back. 'It really is.'

'Do you know what I was wondering?' Stan said.

'Something about food?' Meg teased. She was constantly amazed by how much Stan could eat, despite his skinny frame.

Stan nudged her good-naturedly. 'No,' he said. 'I was wondering if Rolf can come back to Beckindale now the war's over? And maybe teach me violin again?'

Meg's heart leapt at the mention of Rolf's name, and then twisted with sadness as she looked into her son's hopeful face.

'Oh, Stan. I'm not sure, sweetheart.'

'But, Meg, the war's over now. So he can come home. He's the best teacher I've ever had. Mr Barron is good, but Rolf was better.'

'Stan . . .' Meg began, but the boy hadn't finished.

He looked at Meg with his best puppy dog eyes. 'Please, Meg,' he said. 'I really want to go to the music school in Bradford and if Rolf teaches me, I'll have more chance of getting in.'

Meg pulled the boy close and gave him a hug. 'Now, that's not true, Stan. You're very talented.' She wasn't just saying that. The young lad played violin like a dream – thanks to Rolf's lessons earlier in the war – and he'd taken up piano too. Now he was twelve, he was desperate to go to school in Bradford and study music more seriously. Meg marvelled at how far Stan and Ruby had come since they'd arrived in Beckindale and she knew that for a boy from Stan's background to be considering going to music school was astonishing. Sometimes she thought she would burst with pride.

The only way Stan could achieve his dream was to pass an audition. Meg had every confidence in her son, but she knew he was right about Rolf's help. The German was also a talented musician and he'd been such a good role model for Stan. She felt her gloomy mood descend again. If only he could come back to Beckindale and teach Stan. She touched the necklace she always wore – a simple pendant that Rolf had made and which she treasured. He could come back to Beckindale for Stan – and for her.

'Meg, are you all right?' Stan said, gazing at her with a mixture of bemusement and concern.

She forced herself to smile at him. 'I'm fine, son,' she said. 'Just thinking about your audition.'

'Will you ask him?' Stan begged. 'Will you ask Rolf if he'll teach me?'

Meg ruffled his hair. 'I'll do my best,' she promised. 'Now go and help your sister with those tables before she falls over.'

Satisfied with what Meg thought was a very unsatisfactory answer, Stan raced off to help Ruby, and Meg sank down on to the grass beneath a tree and leaned against its thick trunk. She was being silly, behaving like a lovesick young schoolgirl. She was a grown-up. A mother, for goodness' sake. She had no business mooning around over a man who, chances were, she'd never get to see again.

'Taking a break?' Nick Roberts – Susan's father – stood in front of her, smiling down. 'Mind if I sit? I could do with a rest.'

'Of course,' said Meg, shuffling over so he could lean against the trunk too. He sat down with a grunt. 'Are you all right?' Meg said, concerned. Nick was a different man from the one Seth Armstrong had come across in the snow, all those months before, but he was still feeling the effects of his imprisonment and escape.

'Just a bit tired,' he said with a weary smile. 'It's a wonderful day, but it's not easy.'

'My children Ruby and Stan lost their mother in a raid on Hull. We had some tears this morning.' Meg put out a tentative hand and patted Nick's knee. 'I understand.'

Nick bit his lip and looked away, and not wanting to push him, Meg stayed silent for a few minutes, watching the villagers scurrying back and forth. Beckindale was looking marvellous, she had to admit. Bedecked in bunting and red, white and blue streamers, with the tables all laid out and the sun shining. It was . . . What was the word?

'It's idyllic, isn't it,' said Nick, following her gaze.

'That's it,' said Meg in triumph. 'I was trying to think of the word and you said it. Idyllic. Everyone in good spirits. All together.'

'It's a shame the troops aren't here to see this,' Nick said. 'This party's for them, really.'

'We'll do another one. When they're all back. After six years of war, goodness knows we deserve some fun.'

Nick looked at her carefully. 'You don't look like you're having fun, if you don't mind me saying.'

Meg leaned her head against the rough bark of the tree. 'I'll get there,' she said. 'Like you say, it's not an easy day.'

'Have you lost someone?'

'In the war? Not family, thank the lord. But friends, yes. Edward Sugden, and Ernie Hudson, and others . . .' she trailed off. 'So how are you getting on in Beckindale?'

Nick, thankfully taking the hint that she didn't want to talk about the war, grinned. 'Bit different from London.'

'I bet it is. Do you think you'll stay?'

Nick rested his arms on his knees and looked round. His gaze fell on Susan and Ruby, laughing together, and he nodded thoughtfully. 'I reckon I will. Sue's happy as Larry up here and she's doing great in her studies.'

'She's such a lovely girl,' Meg said. She'd grown very fond of Ruby's friend. 'My Ruby will miss her terribly when she goes off to university.'

'She'll be back for holidays,' said Nick. 'And Nancy says she'll have a job in the vet's whenever she wants one.'

'Nancy's really looked out for her, hasn't she?'

Nick beamed. 'She's a really nice girl.' He pronounced it 'gal', which made Meg smile. She liked Nick's London accent. 'I've been helping out in the surgery. That Betty left them in the lurch a bit, by all accounts.'

Meg made a face. Betty's break-up with Seth and her swift departure from Beckindale had come out of the blue, but she couldn't say she'd been surprised. 'Betty always had her sights set on something more than Yorkshire could offer,' she said tactfully. She knew Nick and Seth had struck up a strong friendship and she didn't want to tread on any toes. 'I'm glad you're able to help Nancy, though.'

'I'm a bookkeeper,' Nick said. 'Least I was, before the war. Thought I might ask around, see if I can get started up here. I've been sorting out Nancy's accounts for her, and she said she'd recommend me to some of the farmers.'

'That's a wonderful idea,' said Meg. She looked at Nick sideways. 'Getting close to Nancy, are you?'

'Like I said, she's a nice girl.'

Meg hid her smile. Nancy worked so hard and she hadn't expressed so much as a hint of interest in anyone since she'd arrived in the village. It was about time she had some romance.

'What's your story, Meg,' Nick said, snapping her out of her dreams of matchmaking. 'Two kids, no bloke?'

Meg blinked at him. 'You don't beat around the bush, do you?'

He chuckled. 'No point.'

She rolled her eyes. 'Well, you know that Ruby and Stan are adopted?' He nodded. 'They came to the village as evacuees and because I'm a teacher, I was the billet officer. No one else wanted them, bless them.' She looked fondly over at her kids, now healthy and happy and a million miles away from the lice-ridden scrawny urchins who'd landed on her doorstep. 'Then their mother was killed and it made sense for them to stay with me. I'm very glad they did.'

'They're great kids,' Nick said.

'Ruby wants to race bicycles, wouldn't you believe?' Meg said proudly. 'She wants to be a champion and win medals. And Stan's a musician. He's got an audition coming up for a music school in Bradford.'

'Sounds like they're going to do you proud.'

Meg nodded. 'Ruby was hard work at first, I must admit. But we muddled through together.'

'Can't have been easy.'

'It wasn't,' Meg admitted. 'But I had help.' Rolf, she thought. Rolf had helped her in those early days. Not flinching when Ruby's mother was killed and the grieving girl lashed out at him. Teaching Stan about music. Staying strong even when his own mother and two of his four sisters were killed in a bombing raid on Berlin.

'You're a million miles away again,' Nick said. He looked amused. 'What are you thinking about?'

'What was it like?' Meg said suddenly. 'In the camp?'

If Nick was surprised by the sudden change of subject, he didn't show it. Instead he took a breath. 'Highs and lows,' he said. He picked up a stick and dug it into the ground next to where they sat. 'The other POWs were a great bunch of blokes. Everyone looked out for each other, even though some of them were injured or poorly.' He smiled, lighting up his still gaunt face. 'We'd play football most days, if we were up to it. We had a league going and everything. And we had cards, so we'd play a lot of rummy.'

Meg was almost afraid to ask. 'And the lows?'

'At first it was hard, just being there,' Nick said. He was talking quietly and Meg had to listen carefully to hear him over the sound of revelry in the village. 'I felt ashamed, you know. Most of the lads on my ship drowned. I was dragged from the water by the enemy. I felt like they'd died a noble death and I'd surrendered.' He dug his stick into the dry earth harder. 'And then once we were in the camp, it wasn't easy.'

'What did you have to do?'

'Hard labour,' Nick said. 'Really physical stuff. Building walls. Shovelling gravel, clearing rocks.' He smiled at her again. 'Not what this soft bloke from Sydenham was used to. And not much grub. I used to go to bed at night dreaming of a bacon sarnie and wake up licking my lips.'

Meg understood that feeling. She would dream about her favourite meals sometimes. Occasionally she'd even dream she was washing her face in soap, lathering up the bubbles. Wasn't it silly, the things you missed?

'The guards weren't all bad,' Nick said. 'You got to know which ones you could have a laugh with, and which you couldn't.' He looked straight at her. 'I'd look at some of them, and think "he's just like me". Missing his wife and his kids, doing his job. The only difference was, he was born in Germany and I was born in England.' His expression darkened. 'But there were others that I thought were proper bad'uns. Devoted to the Nazi cause, they were. They were harder to cope with.'

He looked off into the distance. Meg thought he wasn't seeing the children gathering to play games, or the bunting fluttering in the summer breeze, but his friends in the camp, or the guards, or the men on his ship drowning as the vessel slipped beneath the waves.

Meg nudged him very gently. 'If you're finding it hard today, you come and find me,' she said. 'We'll get through it together.'

Nick nodded. 'Thanks, Meg,' he said. 'Everyone's been so great to me, here in Beckindale.'

A shadow fell over them and Meg looked up to see Nancy standing there. She was wearing a floral summer dress and looked pretty as a picture. Nick's face lit up. He had it bad, she thought with amusement. But it was Meg who Nancy wanted.

'Phone call for you,' she said.

Meg frowned. 'For me?'

'At the surgery,' Nancy said. 'Lucky they caught me really, because I only popped in to check on Mr Tulliver's dog. I'm not working today, not properly.'

Meg struggled to her feet, wondering who on earth was phoning her, at the vet's, on VE Day. 'Are you sure they asked for me?'

Nancy gave the customary frustrated sigh that meant someone was annoying her. '"Meg Warcup", he said. Though the line's not great, and I had to get him to repeat it, because he had an accent.'

Meg's legs turned to jelly. 'An accent?'

Nancy rolled her eyes. 'Door's open,' she said, pointing to the surgery. 'Lock it when you leave, will you?'

But Meg wasn't listening, because she was already halfway across the grass towards the vet's. She burst through the door and saw the telephone receiver lying on the desk. With shaking hands, she picked it up and put it to her ear.

'Hello?' she said.

'Meg?' said a voice at the other end. A beautiful, familiar voice. 'It's Rolf.'

Chapter Nineteen

THREE DAYS LATER

Meg was trying to pin her hair up, but she was shaking so violently, she couldn't manage. Ruby, who was lying on Meg's bed, telling her something complicated about the Hotten Wheelers cycling club, eyed her in the mirror. 'What's the matter?'

Meg tried to jab a hairpin into a roll and gave up. 'Nothing,' she said, faking a smile. 'So tell me about the race. You thought they wouldn't let you race because you're a girl? And then what happened?'

Ruby sighed. 'I raced. And then I won,' she said. 'And I just told you that.'

Meg put down her hairbrush and turned to face her daughter. 'Well done, sweetheart. I'm so proud of the way you're fighting to be allowed to enter all these races.'

Ruby beamed at her. 'Yeah, well, the lads don't all like it, but I'm going to keep going.'

'Of course you are.' Meg blew her a kiss.

'So what's up with you then?'

'What?'

'You've been jumpy for days and days,' Ruby said. 'And now you're getting all dolled up to go where? Hotten? What are you doing?' She rolled over on to her stomach and looked at her mother with a gasp. 'Are you seeing Rolf?'

Meg thought about fibbing, about saying she was going to the bank, or to meet an old friend, but she looked into Ruby's lovely, excited face and found she couldn't do it. 'Yes,' she admitted. 'I'm seeing Rolf.'

'Can I come?' Ruby asked. 'And Stan? Is he all right? Is he free? Can he come back to Beckindale?'

Meg put her hand up to stop the relentless questions. 'He's been released,' she said to her daughter. 'And he is coming back to Beckindale, but he's just passing through, Ruby. He won't have time to see anyone else. He has to go home, to Berlin.' She took a breath. 'For now, at least.'

Ruby looked outraged. 'Doesn't he want to see us?'

'He does, of course he does. But he needs to see his sisters, Liesbeth and Ingrid. He's not seen them since their mother and their other sisters were killed.'

'Killed by a British bomb,' said Ruby.

Meg shifted on her dressing-table stool, feeling uncomfortable. 'Perhaps,' she said.

There was a little pause. 'Will he come back from Berlin?' Ruby asked.

Suddenly close to tears, Meg got up and sat next to her daughter on the bed. 'I don't know,' she admitted. 'But I hope so.'

Since Rolf had phoned on VE Day, her mind had been a whirl of possibilities. She'd burst into tears as soon as she'd heard his voice on the phone.

'Don't cry, Meg,' he'd said to her in his usual calm way. 'Today is a good day.'

'I know,' she'd sobbed. 'I'm happy.'

Rolf had chuckled. 'Then I'd hate to make you sad.'

He'd sounded different, she'd thought. His English was better, but he sounded tired and weak. She'd thought about Nick, forced to do hard labour on meagre rations, and had shuddered. 'Are you all right, Rolf?'

The pause was so long she'd thought the telephone call had been cut off. Then eventually he'd spoken. 'I'm not all right, no,' he'd said slowly. 'I have a lot of feelings in my head. Like when strings are . . .' he'd trailed off, not knowing the word.

'Tangled,' said Meg immediately. She felt the same. 'Your feelings are tangled.'

'Tangled,' Rolf repeated. 'Yes.'

He went quiet again.

'Rolf?' Meg said. 'Are you still there?'

'I'm in Lancashire,' Rolf said. 'But I can return to Germany when I want. I can get a boat from Hull. I can come through Beckindale.' He paused. 'For one day.'

Meg breathed in.

'Will you come to meet me?' Rolf said. 'Please.'

Meg hadn't had to think about it. She'd wanted to see Rolf for so long and now he was coming to the village. Of course she would meet him.

'Just you,' Rolf had said. 'No one else. Emotions are . . . running high. I don't want to see anyone.'

Meg understood. Even her best friend Lily had been unimpressed about her feelings for Rolf. If this was goodbye, she didn't want anyone else to be involved.

'Meg,' Ruby said impatiently now, jolting Meg from her thoughts. 'When will he come back from Berlin?'

'I don't know, sweetheart. I don't know if he'll be allowed. He might have to go and live in Germany.'

'Will you ask him?'

Meg put her arm round Ruby's shoulders and squeezed her tight. 'Of course I will.'

'Do you love him?'

The question took Meg by surprise. She turned and faced Ruby. Her daughter had grown up so much, Meg sometimes forgot how close she was to being an adult.

Ruby stared at her, unflinching. 'Do you love him?' she asked again.

Meg nodded, very slowly. 'I do.'

'You should tell him that,' Ruby said. She slid off the bed and stood up. 'Make sure you tell him.'

Meg smiled. 'I'll see.'

'Want me to help you do your hair?'

'Yes please.' Meg held her hands out to show Ruby how much they were still shaking. 'I'm too nervous to make it neat.'

Ruby was no hairdresser, but she'd done a fair enough job, Meg thought as she looked at her reflection in the window of the vet's later. She looked nice. Not glamorous like Betty Prendagast, but nice. Her dress was clean and nicely pressed, and though it was old, she didn't wear it often, so it wasn't frayed. She'd put some make-up on, and she'd found some smart shoes and polished them until they shone. And she'd put on the pendant Rolf had made her. She touched it gently now, as she often did when she was nervous. She felt sick and excited and full of dread and everything in between. She couldn't wait to see Rolf, and she wanted time to slow down so she didn't get there at all. She was a mess of emotions.

Meg and Rolf had arranged to meet just outside Beckindale. Rolf was getting the bus and he'd planned to get off a stop before the village, so they could walk down by the river and not bump into anyone. Meg wasn't sure what time Rolf would arrive – he hadn't known – so she'd brought a book to read in case she had to wait. Not that she could concentrate on the words. All she could think about was him and the way his lips had felt on hers, when they'd shared their one and only kiss, all those years ago.

She found a comfy spot under a tree a little way from the bus stop and settled down to wait, concentrating on her breathing, forcing herself to look at her book, even though she wasn't reading it. She didn't want to look up every time she heard a car pass by.

Even when she heard an engine that she knew was the bus pulling up, and the hiss of the doors opening, she kept her eyes firmly on the page. It might not be him, she told herself. It might not be Rolf. But then, as the bus drove off, there was a shout. 'Meg!'

Before she knew it, she was on her feet and running, and there he was. Rolf, thinner and older, of course, but his smile was the same. He held out his arms and Meg fell into them and they held on to each other tightly.

'Rolf,' Meg said, tears streaming down her face. 'It's so wonderful to see you.'

Rolf was crying too. He wiped away a tear with the heel of his hand, reminding Meg of Stan, and squeezed her even tighter. 'And you,' he said. 'It's wonderful to see you, Meg.'

They stood there for a while, clutching each other.

'Should we walk?' Rolf said. 'Let's not spend our time together standing by the side of the road.'

'Let's go this way.' Meg steered him up the verge to where there was a fence with a stile. 'We can go to the river this way.'

Rolf went first, and when she followed, he held out his hand to help her jump down and then didn't let go.

They walked through the fields, hand in hand. Meg thought it was astonishing how his fingers fitted perfectly with hers, even after all this time.

'So you're going back to Berlin?' she said as they walked.

Rolf looked down at her and nodded. 'To see Liesbeth and Ingrid,' he said.

'It must be hard, knowing Hanna and Klara and your mother won't be there.'

'It is,' Rolf said. 'I was sad when I found out they had been killed, but I fear I will feel it all over again when I return and they're not waiting for me.'

They'd reached the river and he looked around for somewhere to sit. Meg realised he must be exhausted. Worn out by years of imprisonment.

'There,' she said, seeing a patch of grass in the shade of a willow tree. They both sat, their legs touching and their hands still intertwined. It was so peaceful there, watching the dragonflies darting around the water and hearing the birds in the trees. The branches of the willow waved gently in the breeze as they drooped into the river. In the distance, she could hear cows lowing and, next to her, Rolf's breathing.

Meg inhaled him; the closeness of him, his very presence, making her feel more alive than she'd felt for months. Years, perhaps. She longed to kiss him, but she was nervous.

'Meg,' Rolf said, sounding rather like he was reading what he was saying from a script. Meg wondered if he'd practised it. 'I asked you to meet me because there is something I need to ask you. Something I need to tell you.'

'Go on,' she said.

Rolf took a deep breath. 'I love you,' he said.

Meg's head span. How long had she waited to hear him say that? She thought about Ruby, telling her to say the same to Rolf and she smiled. 'I love you too.'

Rolf bent his head and his lips met hers in a deep, dizzying kiss. Meg didn't want it to end, but eventually they broke apart, both smiling and laughing uncontrollably.

'Come with me,' Rolf said.

'What?'

'Come to Berlin with me. I can get a job, and you can teach. Everyone needs teachers. Ingrid has a large house. She said we can stay with her for a while until I get back on my feet.' A shadow crossed his face. 'She says the city is changed, broken, but it will recover.'

'Rolf . . .'

'It's so beautiful, Meg,' he said excitedly, not letting her speak. 'You'll love Unter den Linden. The trees are glorious in the summer, and you can stand under the shade and look back at the Brandenburg Gate.'

Meg shuddered, picturing the building adorned with Nazi swastikas, and Rolf smiled.

'It was there long before the Nazis, and it's still standing, you know. Despite the damage. You'll see it for yourself.'

But Meg shook her head. 'I can't come to Berlin,' she said. 'Darling Rolf. You know I can't come to Germany. What about Ruby and Stan?'

Rolf sighed. 'Could they come too?'

'No,' Meg said firmly. 'No.' She played with Rolf's long skinny fingers, where they lay on her leg. 'Rolf, it's going to take us all a long time to recover from the war. All of us. But I think Germany's going to suffer the most.'

There was a pause. 'I know,' Rolf admitted. 'It will be difficult for everyone.'

'I can't uproot the children and take them to Berlin. It's just not happening. I love you, but Ruby and Stan come first.' She paused. 'Come back. Go to Berlin, see your family and then come back. Could you do that? Would you be allowed?'

The sound of footsteps made them both stop talking and look up. A little way along the path was Wally Eagleton and another man who Meg only knew as Sparky. She'd not seen Sparky for years. He'd obviously been away fighting, too. Both men waved in greeting.

'How do, Meg?' Wally called.

Meg felt her stomach lurch with nerves. Wally didn't know Rolf – he'd joined up before Rolf had come to Beckindale, but Meg knew that Wally had been shot at El Alamein. She wasn't sure of the details, but she knew he'd been injured badly enough to be invalided out of the army, and she'd heard people say that Wally had been changed by what happened to him. He was always good-natured, but his jokes about what he'd suffered had an edge. Meg wasn't sure he'd take kindly to a German being in Beckindale, and she wasn't sure if Wally had been close enough to hear Rolf talking.

'Hello, Wally,' she said. 'Hi, Sparky.'

Wally looked at Rolf. 'How do?' he said.

Meg felt Rolf shift next to her. He didn't speak, but he raised his hand to wave at Wally and Sparky.

'Lovely day for a walk,' Meg said politely. 'Are you off to the cricket pitch?' Oh, was that the wrong thing to say? Could Wally still play cricket? She wasn't sure where he'd been shot. 'Stan's down there,' she added quickly. 'You might see him.'

'We'll look out for him,' Wally said. 'See you later.'

He and Sparky walked on by. Meg and Rolf watched them go, breathing out in relief. They didn't speak until the men were further down the path, and when Rolf talked again, it was in a quieter voice.

'At the camp, I made friends with a chap called Bernd,' Rolf began. He sat back against the tree trunk and looked out over the river. 'Bert, the guards called him. He was a footballer. Loved the game. He'd organise the men into teams, play matches. They even played against local sides.'

Meg raised an eyebrow. 'Did you join in?'

Rolf chuckled quietly. 'I was on the entertainment team,' he said, miming playing a violin. 'Not the sports team.'

'What about Bernd?' said Meg, wondering where he was going with the story.

'He loves England,' Rolf said. 'He said he feels at home here, and he loves playing football with the men here. He wants to stay.'

'In England? Is he able to?'

'He told me we were offered repatriation to Germany.'

'And?'

'And it was just that – an offer. We don't have to take it.'

Meg felt her heart lift. Was it possible, then, that Rolf could live here? That they could make a life together? Would he want to?

'Does that mean . . .' she began.

Rolf kissed her. 'I could stay,' he said. 'We could be together in England.'

Meg was speechless with delight. 'Would you?'

'It wouldn't be easy,' Rolf said.

'I know.' Meg remembered the hostility of the villagers in Beckindale towards Rolf. Heavens, even her own hostility at first. She wondered how Wally would have reacted if he'd heard Rolf's accent.

'And I do need to return to Berlin first of all. I must see my family.'

'Of course.'

'But I shall find out how to go about making a life in Britain. I will write to Bernd. Ask his advice.'

Meg threw herself into Rolf's arms. 'I can't tell you how happy this makes me,' she said.

He looked at her fondly. 'And me also,' he said. 'But now, I'm afraid, I must go. I need to get to Leeds so I can catch my train to Hull.'

They strolled, holding hands, away from the river and back towards the bus stop. But as they approached the road, Meg froze. Up ahead, a group of men – Wally, Sparky, and some others – were sitting on the fence beside the stile.

'It's fine,' Rolf muttered. 'They won't bother us.'

As they got nearer, though, Meg realised the men were bickering between themselves. 'They're bored and resentful,' she murmured to Rolf. 'It's hard for the men who have been away. They're changed, and the world's changed.'

Rolf nodded, understanding.

'Let's just get past them and we can walk down to the other bus stop,' Meg said.

They carried on towards the stile, just as Wally and Sparky both slid off the fence and stood toe to toe, like a pair of boxers ready for a fight.

'Come on then,' Wally said. The sinews in his neck were tensed.

Meg stopped walking, pulling Rolf to a standstill too.

'We'll go the other way,' she said.

Wally shoved Sparky hard, and Sparky shoved back. Both men fell on to the grass, wrestling. For a second, Meg felt relief, thinking they were just playing, but then Sparky raised his head, and she saw that his nose was bleeding.

'Come on,' she urged Rolf, tugging his hand again. But Rolf was watching the men. Wally and Sparky were still rolling around on the ground. The other men looked on, amused. Occasionally one of them aimed a kick at their friends on the ground.

One of the kicks landed on Wally's ribs, and he looked up to see who'd lashed out and yanked his leg so he fell to the ground too, hitting his head hard on the fence as he tumbled. Wally struggled to his feet and started pummelling the man where he lay.

'Oh goodness,' Meg gasped. 'Goodness.'

She looked round desperately for some help, hoping there would be a car coming along the road, or someone walking by, and as she did, Rolf dashed over and pulled Wally away, holding his arms.

'Stop that,' Rolf shouted. 'Leave him be.'

The other man crawled along the grass to get away from Wally's fists and turned to stare at Rolf, while Sparky pulled himself up to standing on the fence post.

Suddenly it seemed to Meg that the men were united once more and it was Rolf who was their enemy.

'What's it got to do with you?' Wally spat, puffing his chest out as he looked at Rolf. 'Kraut?'

Meg winced, as the man on the ground, the one Rolf had stopped being beaten by Wally, looked disgusted. 'You German?'

'Evil bastard,' Wally said.

And then here was Sparky joining in too.

'Stinking Nazi,' he said. He stumbled and half fell, half launched himself into Rolf, flailing with his fists and catching Rolf on the side of his face. It wasn't a hard punch, but Rolf wasn't expecting it and he turned his face at the wrong time, meaning it landed right on his nose. Blood spurted and Meg cried out in shock. Sparky whirled away, triumphant, and the man on the ground aimed a kick at Rolf's leg.

'Stop it,' Meg shouted. 'Help! Someone! Help!' She pushed in between the men and Rolf, facing the attackers and trying not to show how completely and utterly terrified she was. 'Stop this at once,' she said in her best schoolteacher voice. 'Leave him alone.'

There was a pause, long enough for her to think they'd listened to her pleas. And then, quick as a flash, Sparky reached out and grabbed the hair on the back of her head, twisting his hand so it pulled hard and made her gasp in pain. Then he yanked his hand back, pulling Meg's head on to his shoulder.

'What are you doing with a Kraut?' he said. His breath smelled of stale beer. 'You disgusting Nazi slag.'

Meg was crying now, trying to get away from his grip.

'You make me sick,' Sparky hissed.

Rolf tried to step forward and stop Sparky, but Wally put his bulk in between them. Sobbing, Meg tried to catch his eye and tell him to run and, to her relief, she saw a van pull up next to the bus stop and heard doors slamming. Someone was coming to help.

'What the flaming heck are you lot doing?' a voice shouted.

As suddenly as he'd grabbed her, Sparky let go of Meg's hair and she fell forward into Rolf's arms.

'Sparky Brooks? Wally Eagleton? What do you think you're doing?' Meg looked round and saw Jed and Larry Dingle coming towards them. Her legs felt weak. Jed would sort this out; he was no stranger to trouble.

Like a sulky child, Wally faced up to the Dingle men. 'Just an argument got out of hand, is all,' he said.

Jed took a step towards him. 'An argument with Meg?'

'No,' Wally admitted.

Still looking at Wally, Jed reached out and grabbed Sparky's collar. 'If I ever see you touching a woman like that again, Sparky Brooks, you'll wish you'd never been born.'

Larry helped the other man to his feet and then gave him a shove that made him stumble. 'And you, Griff Evans,' he said. 'Get out of here, before we give you a taste of your own medicine.'

The men didn't hang around. They all set off towards Beckindale at a cracking pace.

'Thank you,' Meg jabbered to Larry and Jed. 'Oh thank you. I was so scared. You can see what a state we're in.'

Rolf was holding a bloodied handkerchief to his nose, and Meg was horribly aware that her victory rolls, so carefully pinned up by Ruby, were tumbling down her face.

Jed looked at Meg and then at Rolf, then back to Meg.

'Rolf,' he said. There was no friendliness in his voice.

Meg's sense of relief vanished. She didn't know what to say.

'Jed,' said Rolf, matching the other man's tone. 'Larry.'

'What are you doing here?'

'I'm not staying,' Rolf said. 'I just came to say goodbye.'

Jed nodded. He looked at Meg, who was standing still, frozen with dismay. 'He can't be here, Meg.'

Meg bit her lip.

'Folk have lost sons and husbands,' Jed said. 'Sparky lost his brother. Wally's lost a chunk of his arm. Griff Evans worked at Ephraim Monk brewery before the war. But he can't go back, because the sound of the bottles clinking together makes him into a nervous wreck.'

Meg looked at her feet. She could hear Rolf breathing next to her and desperately wanted to reach out and take his hand, but she didn't.

'He can't be here,' Jed said again.

Meekly, Meg nodded. She and Rolf stood as Jed and Larry got back into the van and drove off.

'I'm sorry,' Rolf said. 'I'm sorry.'

Together, they walked to the bus stop and sat down. Meg felt numb.

'I have to go,' Rolf said, looking along the road where the bus would come.

'But you'll be back.' Meg's voice sounded shrill and frantic to her own ears.

Rolf shook his head slowly. 'I don't think so.'

'Rolf . . .' Meg was panicking now. 'Rolf, please.'

'How can we be together?' Rolf said. 'How can we make a life here if that's what happens? That man attacked you, Meg. And Jed Dingle spoke the truth about what people have lost.'

Meg rubbed her aching head where Sparky had pulled her hair. She looked at Rolf's swollen bloody nose and she thought about Sparky's dead brother and Wally's useless arm and Griff's nerves. She thought about a life where something like this happened every time she left home. And then she slowly nodded her head, tears streaming down her cheeks.

'I don't want you to go,' she sobbed, gripping the lapels of Rolf's jacket. 'I don't want this to happen.'

Rolf kissed away her tears and held her tight. 'I know, *liebchen*. I know,' he soothed. And then, eventually, he unravelled himself. In the distance, Meg could see the bus trundling along the road. Rolf followed her gaze and breathed in sharply as he saw the bus too. 'I have to go, Meg.'

They kissed again as the bus pulled up. 'Good luck,' Meg said. 'Have a good life.'

Rolf swallowed. He didn't speak, simply pinched his lips together and nodded at Meg. Then he hoisted his backpack higher up on his shoulder and got on board.

Meg watched him through the window as he found a seat at the back. The bus pulled away and Meg stayed at the stop until it had completely disappeared from sight. Then she walked back towards Beckindale, crying the whole way home.

Chapter Twenty

JUNE 1945

Annie felt odd being on the bus to Hotten without her uniform on. She kept thinking her hat had slipped off her head, only to put her hand up and realise she wasn't wearing it. Being back on Civvy Street, as the girls in Portsmouth had been calling it, was going to take some getting used to.

She couldn't wait to get home, though. She wanted to see her parents, and Lily and Meg, and Maggie, and all the animals, and . . . She took a breath, staring out of the bus window. And Jacob.

She'd been thinking about him a lot this past year. Their letters had become more frequent as the Allies pushed back across Europe and the end of the war started to seem like it would happen sooner rather than later. Jacob wrote about the farm, and his plans for the future, and Annie found herself imagining being a part of it all.

She wriggled on the hot seat of the bus impatiently. The war was over, and she wanted to start the rest of her life and put the sadness behind her.

There had been some tears, she wasn't ashamed to admit it, when the news came that Germany had surrendered. She wasn't the only one. So many of her fellow Wrens had lost someone in the conflict and they'd all suffered and mourned. She and Patricia had clung on to each other and cried and laughed all at the same time. It was an odd feeling.

But now it was really all over. For Annie and Patricia, and the rest of her friends in Portsmouth. How strange to think she might not see some of them again. That the women she'd been living with and spending every hour of every day with for years would go back to their own lives and carry on and she would return to Beckindale.

The bus pulled to a rather juddering halt, startling her out of her thoughts. She grabbed her bag and clambered down, looking round at Hotten. It was so familiar to her, yet everything was different. The people especially. How could they not be, after six long years of war. And she herself was different too.

She crossed the road and sat down to wait for the bus to Beckindale. Hotten was busy and she wasn't surprised. So many people were being demobbed all at once. She wondered if they were all feeling as odd as she was. Probably. The thought of them all sharing the same emotions comforted her.

Luckily she didn't have long to wait for the next bus. She hopped off just before the village, took a shortcut over the fields, and she was soon walking up the path to her parents' cottage. Her mother Grace – who wasn't given to big shows of affection – flung the front door open before Annie could even knock and gathered her into her arms.

'It's good to have you back, love,' she said.

Annie breathed in the smells of home. Her mother's talcum powder, something cooking in the kitchen, her father Sam's tobacco. She felt tears welling in her eyes and buried her head in her mother's neck.

'It's good to be back.'

And, actually, the oddest thing about it all was how quickly it stopped feeling odd. How fast she felt like she'd never been away. Once she'd had some food, and unpacked, and helped her mother with the washing up, and drank gallons of tea, and answered all her father's questions, she was feeling like her old self again.

'I might go and see Lily,' she said.

'She were in the garage, when I walked past,' said Sam. 'I saw the light on.'

'Then I'll go and find her there.'

'I'll come with you, lass,' Sam said. 'See what's happening in The Woolpack.'

Grace sighed, but she didn't argue. Annie had a sense that despite their troubles over the years, the Pearsons had found a way to rub along together, for now.

She put her arm through Sam's.

'Come on then, Pa,' she said. 'Let's go.'

Sam was right, Lily was indeed in the garage. She was sitting on a chair, watching Meg's daughter Ruby tinkering with a bicycle.

'There must be something in the way of the gear cable,' Lily was saying. 'So we need to work out what the problem is.'

'Hello, Lily,' Annie said.

Lily looked up and, with a gasp of delight, slid off her chair and bounded over to Annie.

'Oh my goodness, I didn't know you would be home so soon,' she exclaimed, pulling Annie into a hug. 'Let me look at you.' Lily held Annie at arm's length and gave her an appraising glance. 'You look so well.'

'I look well?' Annie said, laughing. 'What about you?'

Lily's blonde hair was shining, her pretty face glowing with happiness and there was a very slight thickening around her usually trim middle.

Annie prodded her. 'Got something to tell me?'

'I'm expecting another baby,' Lily declared, her smile broad. 'Round about Christmastime.'

Annie hugged her friend again, thrilled to bits with the news. 'Congratulations. Is Jack excited?'

'Oh he's treating me like I'm made of glass,' Lily said. 'It's very sweet, but it's wearing me out a bit, isn't it, Ruby?'

Ruby gave her spanner a firm twist. 'That's it,' she said in triumph. She stood up and grinned at Lily and Annie. "Lo, Annie,' she said. 'Nice to have you back.'

'Hello, Ruby,' said Annie. She felt a tiny bit awkward, talking to the young woman. She knew she'd been working up at Emmerdale Farm since Audrey and Ned Barlow had taken on their own farm. Annie knew it was silly, but she felt as though Ruby had taken her job. 'How are you getting on with the Sugdens?' she asked, trying to make it sound as though she didn't care.

Ruby blew a strand of hair away from her face and rolled her eyes. 'It's fine,' she said. 'Won't be there much longer, anyway.'

'Why not?'

'Ruby's going to help me with the garage, when I'm too big to work on the bikes,' said Lily. 'She wants to be a professional cyclist, so it makes sense for her.'

'So they'll be needing another pair of hands up at the farm?' Annie said casually.

Ruby shrugged. 'Audrey's still helping when she can.'

Annie felt a flicker of nerves. What if she couldn't walk straight back into her job? Of course, there were a lot of farms around, but her heart belonged to Emmerdale.

'A professional cyclist,' she said, trying to distract herself. 'Do women do that?'

Ruby shrugged again, looking more like the sulky school-girl she'd been when she first arrived in Beckindale than the young woman she was becoming. 'I reckon they'd have a hard job telling me I couldn't,' she said. 'Women have been doing all sorts during the war. Flying planes, driving ambulances . . .' She looked at Annie, with what seemed to Annie to be a sort of wonder. 'You were right in the middle of the Normandy landings,' she said. Annie nodded. 'They'd have been stuffed without you Wrens.'

'That's true enough,' said Annie with a chuckle.

'So if someone tells me I can't ride in a race because I'm a woman, I'll tell them about you, and all the others like you, that won the war for us.'

Annie and Lily exchanged a glance. Ruby Dobbs certainly knew her own mind. It would take someone bolder than Annie to try to stop her cycling, that was for sure.

'Glad you're back though,' Ruby said, picking up a different size of wrench and studying the bicycle carefully. 'Might cheer Meg up.'

'What's up with Meg?' Annie said with alarm. 'Is she all right?'

'Fancy a brew?' Lily said, giving a tiny shake of her head, showing Annie they shouldn't discuss it in front of Ruby.

Annie made a face. 'Drowning in it,' she said. 'Shall we go to The Woolpack instead?'

Lily grinned. 'Good idea. Ruby, can you lock up? Post the keys through my letter box when you're done?'

'Will do, ma'am,' said Ruby, giving the older women a mock salute.

They were both smiling as they left the garage and walked towards the pub.

'Ruby is such a character,' said Annie.

'She's wonderful,' Lily agreed. 'Meg's such a wonderful mother.'

'So what's wrong with Meg? What didn't you want to tell me in front of Ruby?'

Lily took Annie's arm and led her to the bench in front of the pub. They both sat down and Annie looked at her friend quizzically.

'Remember Rolf?' Lily said.

'The German POW?'

'That's the one.'

'What about him?'

Lily took a deep breath. 'He and Meg were good friends, weren't they, when he was here?'

Annie nodded. 'He was a nice chap, I remember. Maggie Sugden got quite fond of him when he was working up at Emmerdale Farm.'

'Well, turns out he and Meg were more than fond of each other.'

Annie's jaw dropped. 'What are you saying?'

'They've been writing to each other since he was moved over to Lancashire. And Meg says they fell in love.'

'But . . .'

Lily grimaced. 'I know,' she said. 'I know. But Rolf decided he was going to stay here and be with Meg.'

Annie's eyes widened. Was that even possible? 'I'm not sure about that,' she admitted.

'Me neither,' Lily said. 'He's a nice enough lad, but he's German, Annie. It's weird.'

Annie had a sudden memory of hearing the gunshots from the beaches in Normandy. She shivered, even though it was a warm day. 'I don't think it would work,' she said. 'How could it?'

'That's what I said.' Lily looked worried. 'And Jed said the same.'

'Jed knows?'

Lily sighed. 'It's such a mess, Annie. Rolf came back to Beckindale, a couple of days after VE Day.'

'He came here?' Annie made a face, but Lily shook her head.

'Not into the village. He and Meg met up along the river a little way. That was when they talked and decided Rolf was going to stay.'

'Where does Jed fit in?' Annie was confused.

'They came across Wally Eagleton and some of his mates and there was a bit of a scuffle,' Lily groaned. 'Jed broke it up, but he told Rolf he had to go.'

Annie's heart twisted with sadness for her friend. 'That's not fair, but he's right, I think.'

'I know,' Lily said. 'People are sad and angry about the war – you can't blame them, not really. And Meg and Rolf realised this was just too difficult and decided they couldn't be together.'

'So where's Rolf now?'

'Back in Germany, according to Meg. His mother and two of his sisters were killed by a bomb.'

'One of our bombs,' Annie said thoughtfully. How vicious this war had been. Rolf was grieving his mother and sisters, just as Maggie and Jacob grieved for Edward.

'I imagine the Germans think of us the same way we think of them,' said Lily. 'There's no way Meg and Rolf can be a couple. Not here, nor there. Not now, and maybe not ever.'

'It's so sad,' Annie said.

'It is. Meg's taken it really hard. She's barely eating. Ruby said she's not sleeping much either, just sits at the window, looking out over Beckindale. The children are sad, too. Stan's devastated. He had an audition for a music school in Bradford last week and he wanted Rolf to teach him. Meg blames herself for them being sad, too.'

'Poor Meg,' said Annie. 'I'll go and see her tomorrow.'

'She'd like that.' Lily looked at Annie, her blue eyes piercing. 'What about you?'

'What about me?'

'With Ruby working at the garage, I reckon the Sugdens would be pleased to have you back.'

'I really hope so,' Annie confessed. 'I can't imagine working anywhere else. I'll have to pop in on Maggie.'

'And Jacob?'

Annie's heart jumped a beat at the mention of his name. 'Him too,' she said casually.

Lily was still looking at her, but Annie pretended not to notice.

'Are we having that drink, then?' she said.

Annie couldn't go and see Meg until the following evening, because she was the village schoolteacher and the children were in lessons. So, instead, she took a stroll up the hill to

Emmerdale Farm. She desperately wanted to see if Maggie would let her have her job back, and she was keen to catch up with the Sugdens' news, though Jacob's letters had kept her up to date with everything that had been happening at the farm.

She felt a bit strange just letting herself into the farm kitchen, as she always used to, but even stranger about knocking on the heavy front door. So, with some trepidation, she gave a tiny rap on the back door and then went inside. Joe Sugden – Jacob's father – was sitting in his usual chair by the window. He had been badly injured in the last war and his wounds had changed his life and made him a nicer person, by all accounts. His damaged face lit up when he saw Annie.

'Hello, Joe,' she said, bending down to give him a kiss. He patted her hand with his gnarled fingers.

'Annie . . .' he said in his stilted speech. 'Nice to . . . see you.'

'It's nice to be here. How are you getting on?'

'Can't complain,' said Joe with a half-smile on his frozen face.

'Annie,' said a familiar voice. Annie stood up to see Maggie at the door of the kitchen, smiling broadly. 'I hoped you'd be home soon.'

'Maggie,' said Annie, rushing over and giving her a hug. 'It's so nice to see you.'

Just as she had at her parents' house, Annie took a moment, appreciating the things about the kitchen at Emmerdale Farm that she'd always taken for granted. The little grunts made by the two dogs, slumbering by the fireplace. The clean smell of the washing on the line outside, wafting through the open windows. The distant sound of the cattle, mooing to each other in the field nearby.

'Sit,' said Maggie. 'I'll put the kettle on and we can have a brew and a good natter. When did you get back?'

Annie sank into her usual chair, noticing how comfortable and familiar it felt, and let Maggie bustle round, filling the kettle and putting it to boil on the range, getting the large brown teapot down from the shelf, and finding Annie's favourite mug.

'So, Annie, what are your plans now you're back?' Maggie asked, putting the teapot on the table and covering it with a cosy. 'Do you want tea, Joe?'

'Please,' said Joe.

Annie looked at Maggie as she got another mug down from the cupboard. She didn't want to assume she could have her job back, but her mother always said if you didn't ask, you didn't get.

'Well,' she began. 'I'm going to need a job.'

'Come back,' said Maggie immediately. 'Come back to Emmerdale Farm. We could do with you now Audrey's demobbed from the Land Army and gone off to her own farm with Ned Barlow, and Ruby's going to be spending more time at the garage with Lily Proudfoot.' She poured some tea for Joe and smiled at Annie. 'You belong here.'

Annie felt a rush of warmth, like being wrapped in someone's arms. She was wanted. She was needed. She grinned at Maggie. 'I'm out of practice.'

'Like riding a bike, in't it?'

'I hope so,' said Annie. 'I've been sitting on my backside for so long it'll be a shock to be outdoors doing something physical again.'

'You'll be grand,' said Maggie. 'Here you are, love.' She put a mug down by Joe's hand and came to sit beside Annie at the table. 'So you'll come back, then?'

'Of course I will,' said Annie. 'There's nowhere else I'd rather be.'

Maggie looked relieved. 'Oh thank god for that. Jacob will be chuffed, too.'

'Where is Jacob?' Annie couldn't decide if she wanted to see him or not. She'd not seen him properly – spent time with him alone – since she'd come home after the Normandy landings and thought he was going to kiss her. How many times had she replayed that scene in her head? Them talking about Edward, and Jacob turning his face to look at her, and then her running off down the hill. How many times had she wondered what she would have done if he'd leaned forward and touched his lips to hers? Or if she'd made a move first. Put her hand up on the back of Jacob's head, wound her fingers through his thick dark hair and pulled his face down. Maybe if she felt more in control, she'd not be floored by the memories of Oliver Skilbeck, rolling on top of her, the weight of his body pushing her into the ground, or the smell of his breath as he tried to kiss her . . .

'Annie?' Startled, Annie jumped and looked at Maggie, who was frowning at her. 'Are you all right? You were miles away.'

'I'm sorry,' Annie said, embarrassed to have been caught in her daydreams. 'I'm just tired, I think.'

'That's understandable,' Maggie said fondly. 'Listen, Ruby's still with us for a while longer, so you can ease yourself back in gradually. It's going to take some getting used to.'

'I shared a room in my billet,' said Annie. 'There were three of us. Me, my friend Patricia and another girl called Mavis who snored so loudly she sounded like a tractor. When I first met her, I used to dream I was back here on the farm, bumping along on the tractor every night. But then I got used to her snoring, and it was quite comforting in a way. Now I can't sleep because my bedroom's too quiet. I never thought I'd miss Mavis and her snoring.'

Maggie chuckled. 'I bet it was a laugh, sharing with so many other women,' she said. 'Reckon you'll be friends for life?'

Annie wrapped her fingers round her mug, and nodded. 'Definitely,' she said. 'Can't imagine what it'll be like for the troops coming home. They've shared something, haven't they? No one else will really understand what it was like for them.'

'I remember when Joe came home,' Maggie said in a low voice, because Joe had fallen asleep in his chair. 'There was a look in his eye that I'd never seen before. War changes a man.'

There was a moment of silence and Annie thought they were both thinking the same thing – that they would never know how war would have changed Edward.

'Oh heavens, look at the time,' said Maggie. 'I need to feed the chickens.'

'I'll help.' Annie went to get up, but Maggie stopped her with a hand on her shoulder.

'You sit down,' she said firmly. 'I'll only be five minutes. You finish your tea.'

Annie obeyed. She knew better than to try to argue with Maggie Sugden.

Maggie went out of the kitchen door and Annie sat happily sipping her tea and thinking about how nice it would be to get back out on the farm.

A noise from out in the yard made her look up. She got to her feet and walked to the window to look out, and saw Jacob outside. He was carrying a ladder on his broad shoulders and she watched him for a moment as he set it down, admiring the ripple of muscles under his shirt and the way the sweat glistened on his brow. And then, as if sensing her gaze, he turned and looked directly at her, through the kitchen window.

Their eyes met, and they stared at one another. Annie's heart began to pound, thumping wildly in her chest, as Jacob raised his hand to wave and gave her a slow smile.

She raised her hand in response, and Jacob nodded and then turned to go. He whistled loudly, and one of the dogs who had been snoozing by Annie's feet jumped to her feet and plodded outside. With his hound by his side, Jacob walked off up to the fields, with Annie watching him go, her heart still beating fast.

'Oh heavens,' she whispered to herself. 'Oh heck.'

She sat back down at the kitchen table and put her head in her hands. There was absolutely no denying it; she was horribly, undeniably, head over heels in love with Jacob Sugden.

Chapter Twenty-One

Meg did not want to go to the pub. Of course she was happy that Annie was home. Yes, she wanted to see her friend and catch up with her stories and find out what she was going to do now she was back in Beckindale. But just the thought of getting herself ready to go out, and then to be around people, laughing and being happy, made her feel exhausted. Since that awful day when Rolf had come to Beckindale and then gone away again, more than a month ago now, Meg had gone to work, then come home, put on her pyjamas and spent her evenings reading her favourite books from when she was a little girl. She'd heard from Rolf just once. A seaside postcard with a photograph of Blackpool on it – he'd obviously taken it with him when he left Lancashire – but a Berlin postmark. On it, he'd simply written: 'I'm sorry.' He hadn't signed it, and he hadn't given her an address to write back to. Meg had tucked it under her pillow and at night when she couldn't sleep, she would slip her hand underneath and touch it.

So she didn't want to go to The Woolpack and put on a brave face. She wanted to go to bed early and read *Five Children and It* again.

Ruby, though, had other ideas. As Meg was half-heartedly preparing their tea, she marched into the little kitchen and stood, hands on hips, glaring at her mother.

'Lily says she asked you to go to the pub and you said no.'

Meg concentrated on slicing some bread. She didn't reply.

'Why did you say no?' Ruby said. 'It'll do you good to get out.'

Meg looked at the indignant young woman standing next to her and forced a smile. 'I can't go out, Ruby. I need to stay here with you and Stan.'

Ruby rolled her eyes. 'I'm going out on my bike and Stan's not even here. He's playing cricket.'

Meg blinked. She hadn't noticed Stan was out. She put down the bread knife and leaned against the counter. Ruby, sweetheart that she was, rushed over and put her arms round her mother. They were pretty much the same height now, though Ruby was all legs, and Meg thought she might still be growing.

'I hate seeing you so sad,' Ruby said. 'Rolf could still come back, you know. When things have settled down a bit.'

Meg had told Lily what happened with Rolf. She'd assumed Jed and Larry would have spilled the beans anyway, even if she'd not mentioned it. Meg had been disappointed, but not surprised, when Lily had said it was for the best. She knew expecting everyone in the village to welcome Rolf with open arms was a big ask. But Lily was so sweet-natured, so desperate to see everyone happy, that she had hoped . . . But no. It seemed a romance between a German man and an English woman was a step too far, even for Lily.

Ruby would be more accepting, Meg knew, but she hadn't told her daughter all the details about what had happened because she didn't want to upset her. She'd simply said that

Rolf had sent her and Stan his love, and that he'd gone back to Berlin for good. But Ruby was sharp as a tack and there was no disguising how miserable Meg was.

'He's not coming back,' Meg said now, as she stroked Ruby's hair. 'I just need time to get used to that.'

Ruby nodded. 'But as well as time, you need your friends.'

Meg started to protest, but Ruby jumped in.

'Lily's worried about you. She says you're moping. You should go and see her. Spend some time with Annie, and Nancy. It helps to be with people who love you when you're feeling sad.'

Astonished at Ruby's wisdom, Meg smiled for real this time. 'When did you start understanding people so well?'

'It's all the time on my bike,' Ruby said with a mischievous grin. 'I do a lot of thinking.'

'Apparently so.' Meg sighed. 'Fine, I'll go and see Lily and the others. You're right, it might cheer me up a bit.'

And, she thought later, it had done. A bit, at least. She'd knocked for Lily on her way to the pub and Lily had looked at her, obviously wondering what to say.

'I can't talk about it,' Meg muttered. 'Because I'll cry.'

Lily had squeezed her hand gently and very tactfully started talking about how she had found some of Hope's old baby clothes that she'd packed away and couldn't believe how small they were.

Meg had listened to her chatter gratefully, thankful that she didn't have to respond. And once they were in the pub with the others, she could simply let Annie talk. Because it seemed their friend had her own troubles.

'So you're going back to Emmerdale Farm, are you?' Lily said, putting down a drink in front of Annie. 'Annie worked at the farm before the war,' she explained to Nancy, who had arrived in the village after Annie had left to join the Wrens.

'Maggie's wonderful,' Nancy said. 'And Jacob's . . . very dedicated.'

'She means grumpy,' Lily teased.

Meg sat back against the seat, enjoying her friends' chit-chat. But she couldn't help noticing that Annie flushed when anyone mentioned Jacob. Lily clearly spotted it too, because she poked Annie in the ribs.

'What's going on?' she said. Meg watched as Annie avoided Lily's piercing stare. She exchanged a look with Nancy and they shared a small smile. Rather Annie on the end of Lily's questions than either of them.

'Nothing,' said Annie airily.

'Rubbish. You're looking all doe-eyed every time someone mentions Emmerdale Farm. What's it all about, Annie?'

'Nothing,' Annie said, sounding less sure this time.

'Annie . . .'

With a groan, Annie buried her face in her hands. 'Mmk mnnuff mmm,' she wailed through her fingers.

Meg stifled a giggle. Ruby had been right – she was cheering up. 'What?' she said.

'Mmk mnnuff mmm,' Annie said again.

Lily gasped. 'Oh my god.'

'What?' Nancy and Meg said in unison. Meg had no idea what Annie had said.

'You're in love with Jacob Sugden?' Lily said.

'Shhhh,' said Annie, looking round to see if anyone had heard.

Meg leaned forward. 'Are you?' she said. 'Are you in love with Jacob Sugden?'

'I think so.'

Lily clapped her hands, and Nancy grinned. Meg suddenly felt less alone in her heartbreak. Annie was in love with someone too – her dead fiancé's brother, no less. Maybe love was never easy. After all, look at Lily. First she'd gone head over heels for married Derek Mortimer, who'd turned out to be a total rat, and then she'd fallen for Jack while she was expecting Derek's baby.

And now Annie was in love with Jacob Sugden, who anyone with two eyes in their head knew had carried a torch for her for years. But could they really make a go of it, with Annie having been engaged to Edward Sugden?

Meg sighed. It seemed the saying was true – the course of true love never did run smooth. She smiled at Annie. 'I reckon Jacob's been in love with you for years. You just need to tell him how you feel.'

But Annie shook her head. 'It's not as easy as that.'

'You don't think he feels the same?' Lily asked.

'I think he might,' Annie said, her cheeks flaming. 'I think he probably does.'

Lily clapped her hands in delight, but Meg was watching Annie, who looked wretched and not in the least how a woman in love should look.

'What's the matter?'

'Last time I was home, there was a moment between us. We almost kissed,' Annie said. 'But I ran away.'

Nancy chuckled. 'You ran away?'

But Annie wasn't laughing. Instead she buried her face in her hands. 'It brought back some memories,' she said.

Meg understood straight away. She reached out and took Annie's hand. 'Oliver Skilbeck?'

Annie nodded. Out of the corner of her eye, Meg saw Lily turn to Nancy and explain what had happened in a low voice.

'You just need to take it slowly,' Meg assured Annie. 'It's bound to be strange at first, being close to another man, but Jacob will understand.'

'He knows?' Nancy looked surprised.

Annie nodded. 'He knows.' She snorted. 'Everyone knows.'

Meg felt a rush of sympathy for her friend. 'Nothing's ever straightforward, is it?'

Lily looked at her, sharply. 'Have you heard from Rolf?'

Meg shook her head.

'Who's Rolf?' asked Nancy.

Annie, obviously keen to share the spotlight, jumped in. 'He was a prisoner of war,' she told Nancy. 'German. He worked at Emmerdale Farm for a while before they moved the camp.'

Nancy looked at Meg curiously. 'And you and him?'

'No,' said Meg. 'Yes. Sort of.' She shifted on her chair, suddenly uncomfortable. 'But he's gone back to Berlin. We can't be together.'

'Meg,' Lily began, sounding weary. Meg didn't blame her really. They'd had the same conversation so many times recently. 'You know it wouldn't work. There's too much pain on both sides. No one would welcome a German into the village.'

'I know,' Meg snapped. 'You've made that very clear.'

'I'm just telling the truth, Meg,' Lily said, sounding annoyed. 'You can't expect Ernie Hudson's mother to queue up at the post office next to a Luftwaffe pilot who may or may not have fired the bullet that killed her son.'

'Ernie was killed after Rolf was imprisoned,' Meg said. She folded her arms across her chest like a shield. 'Rolf didn't kill Ernie.'

Lily pinched her lips together. 'You know it can't work.'

'Believe me, I know.' Meg rubbed her head. She could feel a headache forming behind her eyes. 'I think it's best if I go home.'

She went to get up, but Nancy stopped her with an outstretched hand. 'Don't go,' Nancy said. 'Please.'

Meg paused and Nancy went on.

'I think that life is complicated. It's not black and white, is it? The war's taught us that. No one's all bad, or all good.'

'That's true,' Lily admitted.

'And more important than that,' Nancy continued, 'is that life can vanish in a flash. Think of Susan. One minute, she's having tea with her mam and her brothers and sisters. Next minute, she's waking up in hospital and they're all gone.'

There was a brief pause as they all thought about what poor Susan had been through.

'So I reckon, even though it might be complicated, you should try and grab your chance of happiness,' Nancy said. 'Grab it with both hands. Tell Jacob how you feel, Annie, and tell him everything. Tell him about these memories you're having and how scared you feel. He's a grumpy bugger, but he's got a good heart.'

Annie stared at Nancy, and Meg blinked in surprise. She was speaking the truth, that was for sure. But she made it all sound so easy. Annie could tell Jacob how she felt, but Meg had already told Rolf that she loved him and she knew he felt the same.

'And, Meg,' Nancy said, turning to her. Meg felt her cheeks redden. 'If there's no way to be with Rolf, then you have to move on. Be glad that you met him, remember the good bits, and start living your life. Because it's short.'

Nancy stopped talking suddenly, squeezing her lips together, as the other women all looked at her in surprise.

'Where did that all come from?' said Lily.

Nancy looked into her drink. 'Just the war,' she said. 'And Betty. And a few other things.'

'Nick?' asked Meg, remembering how he'd spoken about Nancy on VE Day.

Nancy looked startled. 'Nick?'

'You've been spending a lot of time with him.'

'He's a friend,' said Nancy. 'He's doing the books for the surgery.'

'Nothing more?' teased Lily.

'He seemed very keen when I spoke to him,' added Meg.

But Nancy seemed oblivious. 'He's a nice bloke,' she said. 'But we're just friends.'

There was a slightly awkward pause. Meg felt a wave of misery again. She'd lost Rolf and now things were odd with her friends too.

But then Annie, bless her, leaned forward and said, 'Did I tell you about when my friend Mavis met Mr Churchill?' And the tension between the women eased as she told the funny story.

Later, when things were easier still between them, they talked about the party the village was throwing to welcome the troops home. Annie had been one of the first to return, but more servicemen and women were coming back to Beckindale every day and it had been agreed that the village was going to throw them all a big celebration.

'It will be lovely to see everyone,' said Annie. 'Some folk we've not seen since the start of the war. I heard Wally Eagleton was injured at El Alamein.'

'He was,' Meg said, with a shudder, not wanting to think about horrible Wally Eagleton and that awful day with Rolf.

Lily raised an eyebrow. 'He and Betty were friendly, but he's not been around much since she went to Birmingham.' She pinched her lips together as Nancy nudged her good-naturedly.

Meg laughed again, feeling more like herself. Nothing was easy, Nancy was right.

'June,' Annie shouted right in Meg's ear, making her jump.

'Blinking heck, Annie,' she said. 'Shout louder, can you? I think some people in Hotten didn't hear you.'

Annie stuck her tongue out and waved at a woman who'd come into The Woolpack. She had curly red hair and a sprinkling of freckles across her upturned nose and looked exactly as she had looked when she'd been at school with Meg and the others.

'Annie Pearson, as I live and breathe,' she said, smiling broadly. 'Hello, Lily, hello, Meg.'

'Good to see you, June,' Annie said. 'Fancy joining us?'

June looked over to a group of older men in the corner. 'I was meant to be fetching my da home, but why not?'

The women all shuffled round to let her sit down.

'I'm June Butterfield,' she said, sticking her hand out to Nancy.

'Nancy Tate.'

'Nancy's the vet,' Lily said.

'Ee,' said June, impressed. 'I heard there was a female vet in Beckindale. Didn't realise she was as young as you, mind.'

Nancy looked pleased. 'I'm older than I look,' she said.

'We were just talking about the party for the troops returning,' Annie told June. 'You'll be there, of course?'

'Wouldn't miss it,' said June. She turned to Nancy. 'I've been in the WAAF.'

'Bet you've got some stories to tell,' Nancy said, sounding to Meg as though she wanted to hear them all.

'You and Annie could probably write a book about what the women have been doing these last few years,' said Lily.

'And you,' Meg pointed out. 'You did your bit in the ATS.'

'And got a baby for my troubles,' grumbled Lily.

'Oi,' said Meg. 'You're happy as anything and don't pretend otherwise.'

Lily grinned. 'True.'

June gave a loud infectious laugh. 'Oh it's good to be home, isn't it, Annie?'

'So good.'

'I'd best go and see what Da's up to, but I'll catch you all at the party,' June said. 'Lovely to meet you, Nancy.'

Nancy beamed at her. 'Likewise.'

June wandered off and Meg sat back in her seat happily. She'd had a lovely evening, and Nancy was right. She needed to be happy she'd met Rolf, sad that it was not to be, but then move on.

She picked up her empty glass. 'Can I get anyone another drink?' she said, sounding upbeat and light-hearted, which pleased her.

As everyone shouted out their orders, Meg smiled. She was moving on, she thought. Living her life. Now all she had to do was to start feeling a little bit happier about it.

Chapter Twenty-Two

Seth was enjoying having the men back in the village. It sounded silly and of course there had been men in Beckindale all through the war, because farming was a reserved occupation so lots of local lads had stayed behind. But suddenly there were men everywhere. The soldiers had been coming home in dribs and drabs, all wearing the same suit – they were all given clothes to wear when they were demobbed – and looking different behind the eyes.

At the start of the war, Seth had felt faintly ashamed whenever he saw a man in uniform. As though he had to explain himself and drop into conversation why he wasn't fighting. But his time with the Auxiliary Unit had changed all that. Now he was proud to have done his bit – even if he couldn't ever talk about it. It had changed the way he saw other people, too. There must have been all sorts of secret organisations propping up the war effort. Who knew what people had done?

He straightened his cap as he walked into Beckindale. He was looking forward to today. He and Mr Verney had been involved in organising the celebration for the returning troops. If you could call it a celebration, because it was going to be poignant, too.

There was going to be a parade with the returning soldiers, and then the villagers were to gather round the war memorial and Reverend Thirlby was to say some prayers of remembrance. The Salvation Army were going to play and Seth had a feeling it would be a sombre affair. But he was strangely looking forward to it. It felt like a nice way to honour his friend Ernie. A proper goodbye to the lad he'd grown up with and who would never return to the village.

Once the memorial was over, though, the celebrations would start. There were going to be stalls and games and more music and lots of dancing. Betty would like it, Seth thought, and then glowered at the memory of her twirling her way across a dance floor.

Mr Verney was sitting at the side of the war memorial, looking thoughtful and, Seth thought, a little sad. It was still very early and the village was quiet, so he looked up as Seth approached, hearing his footsteps.

'How do, Mr V?' Seth said. He touched his hat, as was his habit when he spoke to his boss, and Mr Verney laughed.

'Don't doff your cap to me, Seth,' he said. 'Not now.'

Seth frowned. 'What do you mean?'

Mr Verney leaned forward and rested his arms on his knees. 'It's all changing, isn't it? The way we see the world.'

'Everything's changed,' Seth agreed. He looked at his boss. 'What's brought this on? You're not normally so thoughtful so early in the morning.'

Mr Verney laughed. 'That's true enough.' He sighed. 'I'm just thinking about all those lads, coming home. Who knows what horrors they've seen, Seth, or what awful things they've done?'

Seth nodded. 'War changes a man.'

'And they're the lucky ones,' Mr Verney pointed out. 'The ones who came home.'

Mr Verney was a lucky one, too, Seth thought. He'd been at university during the last war, so he'd not been conscripted. And this time he'd been given a job in one of the government departments. He didn't enjoy it much, and he hated having to travel backwards and forwards to London so often, but he'd often said how fortunate he was that he didn't have to go and fight. He could stay with Mrs Verney in Miffield Hall and see his children when they came home from school for the holidays.

Mr Verney turned and looked at the war memorial. 'There'll be more names on there soon,' he said.

Seth nodded again. He still wasn't sure what Mr Verney was on about. But he knew he'd get there eventually. He always did.

'What have I done, Seth? I sat behind a desk and moved bits of paper about.'

'Well, I think it was more than that . . .' Seth began, but Mr Verney hadn't finished.

'My father loved all the bowing and cap-doffing and the upstairs/downstairs business,' Mr Verney said. 'He loved being the lord of the manor. He really believed he was a notch above the people in the village.'

Seth rearranged himself on the stone step where they sat. He felt a bit uncomfortable at the tone the conversation had taken. Because he too had always liked the rules of a pecking order. He'd always been taught to respect the men in the big house, to be polite to their wives, and their children, and he'd always done it without question. But now . . .

'Men have died and been injured and seen things that I can't imagine,' Mr Verney said. 'They have proved themselves to be better men than me. I'm not a notch above them, now. Far from it.'

'There will be lots who feel the same as you,' Seth agreed. 'Working men won't settle for low wages or bad conditions now.'

'Nor should they,' Mr Verney said. 'I'm not better than them. Why shouldn't they have the opportunities I had?' He glared at Seth. 'So no more cap-doffing, Seth.'

Seth smiled at him. 'I didn't fight.'

Mr Verney held his gaze for a fraction too long. 'Maybe not abroad,' he said. 'But you played your part.'

'I wouldn't know about that, sir,' Seth said vaguely. Mr Verney was sharp and clever, and he was well-connected. Seth had absolutely no doubt that if anyone knew about the Hotten Auxiliary Unit, it would be Mr V. But he wasn't going to start talking about it. Not now, not ever.

'You're doing all right, are you, Seth? Now the war's over?'

Seth had a feeling Mr Verney really meant now the Auxiliary Unit was finished. He nodded slowly. 'It's taking a bit of getting used to,' he said. 'But we're getting there.'

'Good.'

Seth slapped his hands on his thighs. 'Should we mark out this parade route, then?'

'Let's go.'

The time passed quickly as Mr Verney and Seth marked out the way for the troops to walk. They were to start from the church, walk round past The Woolpack down Main Street, and then on to the Hotten Road and back to the war memorial, where the Salvation Army would be playing. It was a big loop of the village and, that way, people could line up and watch them as they passed by, or follow them to the memorial.

As Seth and Mr Verney reached the end of the route, marking it with rope to create a makeshift barrier, the Salvation Army band were setting up. Stan Dobbs was watching, asking questions about the instruments and following the band leader round, talking nineteen to the dozen.

'That lad's really something,' Mr Verney said.

'I heard he's hoping to go to that posh music school in Bradford,' Seth said.

Mr Verney nodded. 'He did the audition a while back.'

'Meg's done wonders with those kids.' Seth paused in tying the rope and looked over at Stan. 'Remember what they were like when they came to the village? All sulky and skinny. That boy barely spoke and Ruby, well, she was a holy terror.'

'The war's certainly given them opportunities they wouldn't have had otherwise,' Mr Verney said. 'Stanley won't doff his cap to anyone.'

'Nor Ruby,' said Seth fondly. He liked both of the Dobbs children. He thought they had real spark.

Mr Verney chuckled. 'That's the way it should be. It's a new world for those children.'

'New world for all of us,' Seth said. He tied the final bit of rope and stood back. 'That's all looking good.'

'Well done,' said Mr Verney. 'Shall we have a brew before the madness starts?'

'Sounds good.'

They strolled past the band setting up and Mr Verney stopped to talk to Mr Harrison, the leader of the Salvation Army locally. As they chatted, Seth noticed a small woman

– about his age – struggling towards him carrying a bundle of papers and two music stands.

'Here,' he said, dashing to help her. 'Let me take one of those.'

'Oh thank you,' she said gratefully. 'I was being lazy and trying to carry too much so I didn't have to keep going backwards and forwards.'

She brushed a strand of hair out of her eyes and smiled at him. Her face was glowing, as though she'd just scrubbed it. She looked fresh and happy and sweet. He smiled back.

'I'm Seth,' he said. 'Seth Armstrong.'

The woman laughed. The sound made Seth's heart fizz with happiness. 'I know who you are, silly,' she said. 'I sat next to you in arithmetic for a year.'

Seth stared at her. 'Meggy Harrison?' he said in amazement. The Meggy he remembered was quiet and shy – wouldn't say boo to a goose. This woman had a calm sort of confidence about her.

'That's me,' Meggy said. 'Nice to see you, Seth.' She made to walk away and Seth had a sudden urge to grab her hand and stop her leaving.

'Are you playing with the band?' he said hurriedly.

Meggy screwed up her nose. 'No,' she said. 'I just help out. It's my dad's thing really.'

Of course, her father was Mr Harrison, who Mr Verney was talking to.

'So perhaps I'll see you after the parade?' Seth said. He had a sudden image of how Betty would react to a pointed question like that. She'd give him that look she did, from under her eyelashes, and she'd say something like, 'perhaps you will,' and then she'd sashay off and make sure he was watching her go.

But Meggy didn't do any of that. Instead she grinned again. 'Oh I'd like that, Seth,' she said. 'It would be so nice to have a chat and hear all your news.' She tucked the music stand under her arm and rather ungracefully staggered over to put it with the others.

Seth stared at her, feeling warm inside. He would definitely find her later, he thought. Because, all of a sudden, he wanted to hear her news, too.

Chapter Twenty-Three

It was going to be a perfect day, Lily thought as she took Hope's dress out of her drawer. Nina had made it for her – it was a sweet little pinafore in red, white and blue stripes. Nina had collected scraps of fabric in the right colours and stitched them all together. It had been a real labour of love, and Lily was so grateful. She had already decided she would keep the dress forever, pack it away and give it to Hope when she was older as a memento of this extraordinary time.

'Are we going to a party?' Hope asked, her little face peeking out of her dress as Lily pulled it over her head.

'It's a sort of party,' said Lily, giving her a kiss on her nose. 'First we are going to see all the soldiers who have come home from the war and give them a big clap. But some people might feel a bit sad and that's all right, too.'

Hope nodded seriously. Lily wondered if she'd remember this day when she was an old lady. She thought she probably would.

'And then there will be music,' she went on. 'We're going to have so much fun.'

'Dancing?' said Hope.

'There might be dancing,' said Lily, thinking it was a shame that Betty wasn't here for the celebration. She'd have been the life and soul, no doubt. She'd have been up on the stage getting everyone on their feet. Lily hoped she was dancing every night in Birmingham.

'Chocolate?' Hope asked, her eyes wide. With sweet rationing in full effect even though the war was over, there was little chance of that, but Lily didn't want to disappoint her eager daughter.

'Perhaps,' she said. 'Grandad and Nina will be there.'

Hope clapped her hands in glee and Lily thought how lovely it was that she saw Mick and Nina every day and still greeted them like long-lost friends.

She put a hand to her swelling belly and smiled. This baby was coming into a family that was full of love, she thought.

'Ready?' said Jack, poking his head round the door. 'Well I never, Hope. Don't you look pretty as a picture?'

Hope beamed at her father. 'Chocolate,' she said.

Jack looked at Lily over Hope's head, and she rolled her eyes. 'I said perhaps, Hope.'

'Chocolate,' Hope said firmly and her parents laughed. She knew her own mind, that was clear.

With Hope's dress fastened and her hair pulled into two bunches and tied with blue ribbons, they were ready to go.

It was the most gorgeous day. The sun was shining brightly, and there was enough of a breeze to make sure it wasn't unpleasantly warm.

The villagers had put up the bunting from VE Day, and much, much more. The brightly coloured flags fluttered in the light summer wind, looking like the wings of a thousand butterflies. Lily, Jack and Hope found a spot near the war memorial and waited for the parade to start.

'Are you sure you don't want to join in?' Jack said. Lily had been asked to take part because she'd been in the ATS early in the war. But she shook her head, playing with Hope's ribbons.

'I don't regret my time in the ATS, but I'd rather not celebrate it either,' Lily said. 'And I was only in for a few months. I don't deserve a parade.'

'I think you deserve a parade just for being you,' Jack said with a grin. 'But I understand.'

It seemed that everyone in the village had come out to honour the returning troops. The crowds lined the short route from the church and people waved flags and cheered as they walked by.

'They all look so proud,' Lily murmured, watching the men and women march by. She saw Annie, marching with June Butterfield, and raised her hand to wave at her friend. Annie flashed her a quick smile, then turned her eyes to the front again. Most of the troops had put their uniforms on again for the parade. Some were wearing medals. All of them looked different from how they'd been before the war.

'There are so many of them,' Jack said. Lily nodded. Beckindale wasn't a large village, and the farmworkers hadn't joined up, but there were still more men and women in the parade than she'd expected.

When the procession reached the war memorial, Reverend Thirlby spoke. He talked about the pride everyone in Beckindale felt, and the sacrifices everyone had made. He listed all the people the village had lost during the war, and even gave a mention to Susan's family, and Ruby, and Stan's mother, which Lily thought was lovely. She saw Meg on the other side of the crowd, standing with Ruby, and found herself wiping away tears at the poignant words about her friends. Her hand searched for Jack's and she clutched his fingers tightly, thinking about how lucky she was that he was here with her and Hope.

As Reverend Thirlby finished his prayers for the fallen, the Salvation Army band struck up the 'Last Post', and Lily started to cry again.

Jack put his arm round her and Hope. 'I know,' he said. 'It's a strange mixture of happy and sad.'

'It really is,' Lily sniffed.

They watched the musicians for a while, Lily chuckling as she saw Stan Dobbs wearing his cricket whites, ready to play a game, but hovering close by the band, paying close attention to everything they did. And she smiled too as she saw Seth Armstrong chatting to Meggy Harrison. She was a sweet girl, Lily thought. Very different from Betty. Perhaps she was just what Seth needed.

After the sombre part of the day was finished, everyone began drifting away from the parade route. There were stalls set up all over the village, with games for the children or local treats to buy and taste.

At the pub, Jed and Larry had set up their outside bar again. They were both hurrying in and out of the building. Jed saw Lily and Jack and raised a hand in a quick hello, before he dashed off inside to fetch something. He looked a bit harassed, and Lily thought she'd better step in.

'I'll just go and make sure Jed's all right,' she said to Jack. 'He's going to be rushed off his feet today and he might need some help.'

Jack frowned at her. 'Don't lug any crates or lift anything heavy.'

Lily bounced on her toes so she could kiss her husband. 'I won't. Why don't you take Hope over to Dad and Nina? He's doing tractor rides up the hill – I bet she'd love that.'

'Fancy a tractor ride, Hope?' Jack said and the little girl's face lit up.

Lily wandered over to the pub, enjoying the sun's warmth on her face. 'Need a hand?' she asked Jed.

'Oh now she offers,' her cousin teased, putting down a final crate of bottles and sliding it under the table. 'Now we're finished.'

Lily chuckled. 'I can help serve or something.'

'Do not let this woman behind the bar,' said Larry sternly. 'Remember what happened last time?'

Lily gave him a good-natured punch on the arm. 'The floor was slippery,' she said. 'I didn't mean to tip that pint of beer into Mr Merrick's lap.'

'Pints,' said Larry with a dramatic grimace. 'Pints of beer.'

Lily winced, remembering poor Mr Merrick's shocked face when she tipped the drinks over him.

'That was years ago,' she protested. 'But you're probably right. Might be best if I steer clear.'

Jed slung an arm round Lily's shoulders and ruffled her hair. 'We're fine here, aren't we, Larry?' Larry nodded. 'You go and enjoy yourself. Spend some time with Annie and the others. You deserve a bit of fun.'

Lily kissed him on the cheek. 'If you're sure?'

'Course I'm sure.' He put his hands on her shoulders and turned her so she was looking straight at him. 'You're always so full of sunshine, Lil,' he said, his face serious for once.

'Always spreading happiness wherever you go. But this war's been tough on you and there's no harm in admitting that. All that stuff with Derek . . .'

'That's all in the past,' Lily said quickly.

'I know,' Jed said. 'But I know him being killed in action must have stirred up some awkward feelings, and then the end of the war must have done the same. I'm just saying . . .' He sighed. 'I'm just saying, go and enjoy today.'

Lily looked at her cousin – he was more like a brother really, as they'd been so close as they'd grown up – and nodded. 'You hide it well, but there's a good heart in there, isn't there, Jed Dingle?'

Jed stuck his tongue out. 'Don't tell anyone, will you?'

'Your secret's safe with me,' said Lily. She kissed him again, gave Larry another affectionate thump, and wandered off happily, looking for Meg or Annie or Nancy.

She found Meg first, surrounded by a group of over-excited children.

'Miss Warcup, Miss Warcup, when are we singing?' they were shouting. 'Miss Warcup, have I got time to have a wee?'

Lily watched, impressed, as Meg arranged the children into rows according to height, dispatched the ones who needed the toilet off to the school building, and then sent them off to wait by the stage with her assistant teacher, Franny.

'Flaming heck,' said Lily. 'I can't deal with Hope that efficiently. How do you do it with twenty of them?'

'Years of practice,' said Meg wearily. 'You'll probably just get the hang of it with Hope when it's time for her to leave home and get married.'

Lily gave her friend a hug. 'How are you?' she said. 'Bearing up?'

'I feel a bit better, actually,' Meg said. 'Happier. Moving on.'

'Really?' said Lily. Because in her eyes Meg still appeared tired and sad.

'Trying.'

'That's all you can do,' Lily said. 'I think . . .' she stopped talking as someone bellowed Meg's name.

Stan, pale-faced with his hair standing on end and with just one cricket pad on one leg as if he'd been interrupted as he put them on, came racing towards them, waving something in his hand.

'Meg!' he shouted. 'It's here! The letter's here!'

Lily had no idea what he was talking about, but Meg gasped. 'From the music school? What does it say?'

Stan skidded to a halt beside them and flapped the letter in Meg's face. 'I've not opened it,' he said. 'I can't do it. You do it, Meg.'

He thrust the letter at his mother and she took it. Lily saw it said 'Yorkshire School of Music' in large print on the front. So this was the result of Stan's audition. The one he'd wanted Rolf to help him with.

'Sure?' said Meg.

Stan looked sick, but he nodded. Lily put an arm round him, and they both watched as Meg slid a finger under the envelope and opened it. Painfully slowly, she pulled out a letter and unfolded it.

'Dear Miss Warcup,' she read. 'Thank you for bringing your son, Stanley, to audition for us . . . blah blah blah. We are delighted to inform you that we have a space for Stanley in our school, starting September 1945.'

Stan sat down on the ground with a thump. 'And the scholarship?' he said faintly, looking up at his mother.

'Full scholarship,' said Meg. 'You did it, Stan.'

She bent down and pulled him into a tight hug. Lily could see they were both crying and she wasn't surprised. He was a different child from the miserable, neglected boy who had come to Beckindale at the start of the war. Now, though he was still sad that he'd lost his mum, he had Meg, and his music talent had been discovered. Good things had come about because of the war, Lily thought. Even though there had been a lot of pain, too.

Meg and Stan stood up, and Meg brushed bits of grass and dust from Stan's cricket whites.

'Well done, Stan,' said Lily. 'Everyone in the village is so proud of you.'

Stan grinned. 'I want to tell Rolf,' he said to Meg. 'Can I write to him?'

Meg's face contorted with pain, making Lily's heart ache for her friend, and then she forced a smile. 'I'm not sure where he is, sweetheart. But why not write the letter anyway, and I'll find a way to get it to him.'

Stan looked pleased with that idea. 'Can I go and tell the cricket boys?'

'Find Ruby and tell her first, because she'll be thrilled,' Meg said. 'Then the cricket boys. I need to get my children on stage for their song now.'

She gave Stan a kiss, which he immediately wiped away, much to Lily's amusement, and he darted off towards the cricket pitch. Lily was fairly certain he wouldn't find his sister down there, but she didn't say anything. He was so excited, bless him.

'I must go and help Franny,' said Meg.

'Good luck.' Lily thought she'd need it. 'The children will do a great job.'

Meg rolled her eyes and went off to find her class. Lily stayed where she was, because she had a good view of the stage and she wanted to support Meg. She felt a little hand sneak into hers, and turned to see Jack and Hope next to her.

'Hello,' she said, delighted to see them. 'Have you had a lovely time on the tractor with Grandad?'

'We did go so fast,' said Hope. 'So fast.'

'Too fast for Daddy,' said Jack with a grin. 'I was holding on for dear life. This little daredevil loved every minute, though.'

Lily scooped up her daughter and covered her face with kisses. 'So there is some of me in there after all.'

Hope squealed with laughter, as Meg's schoolchildren all filed on to the stage.

'Look, Hope, this is Auntie Meg's class. One day she'll be your teacher.'

Hope wriggled to get down.

'Why don't you go to the front and sit with the other children,' said Lily.

There was a bit of a crowd of proud mothers and fathers gathering, and it was hard for Hope to see. But at the front was a group of small children, sitting on the grass. She helped Hope make her way through the audience and sat her down.

'Daddy and I are just behind you,' she said. Hope, already transfixed by the big children on stage, nodded.

Lily and Jack stood where they could see Hope's bunches bobbing around in time to the music, and watched Meg's children singing. It was actually rather good. Lily let the music wash over her, soaking up the atmosphere. She wanted to remember everything about today. It was a real milestone; something she could tell Hope and the new baby about, and maybe their children one day.

She caught Meg's eye as she stood at the side of the stage, and Meg smiled. She looked genuinely happy, Lily thought. Stan's news had obviously given her a much-needed boost, even if it had stirred up some unhappy memories.

Across the crowd of people, Lily saw Nancy Tate, sitting on a bench with June Butterfield. That was nice. She thought they'd get on well actually. They were both quietly strong, albeit in very different ways. Nancy was part of Beckindale now and it was good to see her making new friends.

On stage, Meg's class began singing 'We'll Meet Again'. They weren't as slick as Vera Lynn, obviously, but standing there in the sunshine, knowing the war was over, Lily felt a rush of emotions. Jed was right, it was a mixture of happiness and sadness, but they'd got through the hard times. She had Hope, and Jack, and the new baby on the way. Her father had Nina – and so did she. Everything was going to be all right, she thought, wiping away a tear.

'Lily?' Jack whispered, looking at her in concern.

'I'm fine,' she reassured him. 'I'm just happy.'

He put his arm around her and pulled her close. 'I love you,' he said into her ear, as the children sang.

'I love you too.' Lily rested her head on his chest and they swayed gently to the music.

At the end of the song, there was thunderous applause and the children gave an awkward bow.

The crowd began dispersing as people drifted off for a drink, or to have a go on the tin can alley, and Lily wandered over to get Hope from where she'd been sitting in front of them.

But Hope was gone.

Chapter Twenty-Four

'Hope?' Lily called, looking around. She wasn't worried. Hope knew just about everyone in Beckindale and everyone knew her. She'd probably gone to speak to Meg. 'Hope!' she shouted again.

Jack appeared next to her. 'Where's she got to?' he said, also unconcerned.

Lily made a face. 'I can't see her. Maybe she's with Meg?'

'You go and see, and I'll head to your dad. Maybe she fancied another tractor ride.'

'All right,' said Lily.

Quickly, because even if she wasn't worried, she did want Hope to be back with her, she walked over to the side of the stage, where a proud Meg was congratulating the singers.

'Meg?' Lily said. 'Have you seen Hope?'

Meg looked up. 'She was at the front of the audience, bless her.'

'She was, but she's not there now.' Lily felt the first stirrings of concern. Where was her little girl? 'She's not there, Meg.'

Meg patted the final child on the head and came over

to Lily. 'She can't have gone far, she's only got little legs. Maybe she's with your dad?'

'Jack's gone to see,' said Lily. Her voice sounded small and scared.

But Jack was running over to them now, his brow furrowed. 'She's not there,' he said. 'They've not seen her.'

Lily threw herself at Jack. 'Where is she, Jack? Where's she gone?'

Jack snapped into police constable mode. He gently unpeeled Lily from his arms. 'We'll spread out and look for her,' he said.

The stage had been put up next to the village hall, at the far end of Beckindale. Jack stood for a second, looking left and right, scanning the area and working out a plan. Lily's rising panic eased slightly; Jack was clever and capable and he was the only person in the world who loved Hope as much as she did. He would find their daughter, she was sure of it.

'Meg, you and Lily check inside the village hall,' Jack said. 'There are some games going on in there that Hope wanted to look at.'

Meg nodded and took Lily's hand. 'Stay with me,' she said.

Nancy appeared next to them. 'What's happening?' she said. 'What's wrong?'

'We can't find Hope,' Jack told her.

'I'll help you look,' Nancy said immediately.

June, who was hovering close by, came over too. 'I'll come with you,' she said. She was still wearing her WAAF uniform and Lily thought it gave her an air of authority.

She grabbed June's hand. 'Can you get everyone else?' she said. 'Everyone from the parade? All the soldiers? They'll help.'

'Of course,' June said. She nodded at Nancy and ran off.

'And could you go round and check in the surgery?' Jack said briskly to Nancy. 'You know Hope loves the animals.'

'Consider it done,' said Nancy. She dashed off too, calling Hope's name as she went.

Jack came over to where Lily stood and took her hands. 'We'll find her, Lil,' he said. 'I promise we'll find her.'

Lily nodded, numbly. She couldn't open her mouth to speak, because she was scared she would just wail.

'I'm going to go over to the cricket pavilion and see if she's wandered round there,' Jack said. 'I'll spread the word as I go. The more people we have looking for her, the better.'

'We'll check in the hall and then tell Jed,' Meg said. 'And if you're going to the cricket pitch, get Stan to look too. He loves Hope.'

Jack nodded. He kissed Lily on the cheek and ran off towards the pavilion.

Meg pulled Lily's sleeve. 'Come on, Lil, let's go and find your little girl.'

Lily shook her head. She wanted to stay outside, scanning the crowds for the ribbons on Hope's bunches to appear. Meg didn't argue. She just squeezed Lily's hand, then she went inside the hall and Lily could hear her shouting Hope's name. Lily just stood still, suddenly feeling cold despite the bright sunshine. She was frozen with fear; what if they didn't find her? What if Hope was gone?

It felt like forever, but Meg eventually came out of the village hall, followed by Ruby and Susan. Lily looked at her hopefully, but she shook her head. 'She's not there. Let's go to the pub.'

Lily let herself be swept along by the others. She was still looking from left to right, wildly, and she felt she couldn't control her breathing. Her chest was tight and she was dizzy.

'She's not here,' she said. 'I can't see her.'

'We'll find her, Lily,' said Ruby, slipping her arm through Lily's reassuringly. 'Remember when I got lost when I first came to the village? You found me.'

Susan took Lily's other arm. 'And when I got scared that time and ran off, you came to fetch me.'

Meg smiled at Lily and the girls over her shoulder. 'They're right, Lil. She must just be hiding somewhere. She can't have gone far.'

As they approached the pub, Jed took one look at Lily's face and vaulted over the table to get to her quicker. 'What's the matter? Is it the baby? Are you ill?'

Meg took over. 'We can't find Hope,' she said. 'She's wandered off somewhere.'

Lily clutched Jed's arm. 'We've been calling and calling, but she's not here.'

'She must be here,' said Jed calmly. 'Where else could she be?'

Nancy and June appeared, followed by several men in uniform.

'The surgery's locked up and she's not there,' said Nancy breathlessly. 'We checked all round the back way too. No sign of her.'

Lily's heart rate quickened again. She'd been so sure Hope would have been there, looking at the animals.

'Not at the cricket pavilion,' shouted Jack. He was approaching from the other direction, with Nina and Mick in tow.

'I just heard what's happened.' Maggie Sugden came over, with Annie and Jacob. 'Don't worry, Lily. We'll find her.'

Lily closed her eyes. In a second, she'd open them and

find out this was all a bad dream, she thought. Hope would be here, and everything would be all right.

'Lily?' said Meg, sounding concerned. 'Lily?'

With some effort, Lily forced her eyes open. Everyone was looking at her, identical worried expressions on their faces.

'We have to find her,' Lily said shrilly. 'She's only little. We have to find her. She can't be left alone for long.'

Once more, Jack took charge. Swiftly, he organised the group into search parties, one for each of the main ways out of the village, plus a group to sweep Beckindale.

'I'll fetch the car,' said Mick. 'And Paul Oldroyd will help. He's still got the Home Guard car.'

'See if you can find Seth Armstrong, too,' said Jack. 'He can track anything.'

Mick hurried off.

'Lily, you stay here with Maggie and me,' said Nina, looking concerned. 'You can't be rushing all over the countryside in your condition.'

'No,' Lily said. She was finding it hard to catch her breath, but she had enough to say that. 'No.'

'Lily, I think you should sit down,' Maggie said.

'She is my little girl,' Lily said through clenched teeth. 'I need to go and find her.'

Jack put his hand on Lily's arm. 'Are you sure?'

She nodded and he stepped back.

'She'll be fine,' he said to Nina.

Lily looked round at the people who'd gathered to help. 'Find Hope,' she begged. 'Please find her.'

The Sugdens and Annie headed off up towards Emmerdale Farm. Lily was pleased; they knew every inch of the country between here and there, and Jacob had keen eyes. If Hope had gone that way, they'd find her in no time.

Jed and Larry joined Jack, Stan and all the village cricketers, still in their whites.

'We'll go down past the church,' Jack said. 'Into the woods and down to the ford.'

Lily's breath caught in her throat as he mentioned the river. Surely Hope wouldn't go there by herself? It was quite a walk to the water, and she'd get tired before she reached it. Wouldn't she?

'Go quickly,' she urged her husband. 'Go.'

'Spread out,' Jack told the men. 'Look all around. And keep calling.'

Lily was left with Meg, Nancy and June, as well as Susan and Ruby.

'I'll fetch my dad,' Susan said. 'He'll want to help. And Midnight. She's such a clever dog, she'll be able to sniff Hope out.'

'Thank you,' Meg said. She turned to Ruby. 'Can you stay here in the village? Just in case Hope turns up? She knows you. If she's scared, you can look after her.'

'Course,' said Ruby. 'Susan and I can walk round a few times, make sure she's not hiding under the stage or somewhere. She might have fallen asleep in a little corner.'

Lily squeezed the girl's hand gratefully. 'Come on,' she said to the others.

The women fanned out and started heading out of the village, calling Hope's name.

Nancy and June were on one side of the road, marching through the fields, while Meg and Lily were on the other.

Lily tried to concentrate on her breathing, matching her inhalation and exhalation to the sound of her feet on the dry grass. In and out. In and out. Panic was sitting heavily on her chest. She needed to focus or she'd scream.

'Hope,' she called. 'Hope, it's Mummy. Come out, sweetheart. Don't hide any more.'

But there was no reply.

In the distance, they could hear other voices calling to her.

'Where is she?' Lily said. 'Where is she?'

'We'll find her,' Meg said again.

Lily fought the urge to grab her friend by the shoulders and shake her. How could she be so sure? Hope could be anywhere. She could have been hit by a car, or the bus to Hotten. Or fallen into a ditch. Or tripped over and hit her head. She let out a sob. This was too far, now. They'd been walking for ages; Hope could never have come this far out of the village by herself.

Lily was crying properly now, sobbing as they walked along. 'Hope,' she shouted again, her voice frantic. 'Hope!'

Up ahead, the road widened, and there was a little viewpoint, over the undulating countryside. It was a nice spot for picnics in normal times, close to where the fields ran down to a bend in the river. Now there was a car parked on the side of the road.

'I'll find the driver, ask if he's seen anything,' Meg said.

'I'll go,' said Lily. She pointed back along the road, where they'd come from. 'Nancy and June are coming.'

Understanding, Meg nodded. 'I'll see if they've got any news.' She ran off towards the other women and Lily set off across the field beside the car. On the grass, a little way away from the car, was a woman. She was sitting on a checked picnic rug, with her back to the road, wearing a pretty floral frock and a wide-brimmed straw hat.

'Excuse me,' Lily called. 'Have you seen a little girl?'

The woman turned round and Lily gasped. She was the woman she'd seen staring at her on VE Day, and there behind her, munching on a bar of ration chocolate, was Hope.

'Hope!' Lily said, weak with relief. 'You found her. Oh thank you.'

'Mummy!' Hope shouted. 'The lady did give me chocolate!' She waved the bar at Lily. 'I will share.'

She struggled to her feet, still holding the chocolate bar like a trophy, but as Lily, crying with happiness, held out her arms to her daughter, the woman stood up too. When Hope went to run to Lily, the woman scooped up the little girl and held her tight.

'Stay here,' she said.

'No,' said Hope, struggling to free herself. 'Get down.'

'Give her to me,' said Lily, bewildered at what was happening. She took a step towards the woman. Hope reached out for Lily, but the woman shifted her grip so she was holding the little girl's arms tightly.

'Mummy,' Hope whimpered.

'Who are you?' Lily said. 'What are you doing?'

The woman ignored her and instead she spoke to Hope sternly. 'Enough wriggling. Goodness me, you're just like your father. He never listened to anything I said either.'

And like the final piece in a horrifying jigsaw, Lily suddenly realised who this woman was. She had recognised her on VE Day, she'd been right. It was Hazel Mortimer – Derek's wife. The woman who Derek had cheated on. Lily had only met her once, when she'd found out Derek had been lying to her about – well, everything really. She'd been pretty then. Pretty and vivacious and full of life. Now she looked old and tired, with dark circles under her eyes and lank hair.

Lily might have felt sorry for her, if she'd not been holding her little girl.

'Hazel?' Lily began, then trailed off as she took in what the woman had said about Hope's father. She felt a rush of cold, hard fear and stared at Hazel, not knowing what to say. How did she know the truth about Derek being Hope's biological father? Was that why she was here? For some awful revenge?

'Don't look at me like that, all wide-eyed and innocent,' Hazel said, her tone harsh. 'Don't pretend. I know what you and Derek did.'

Lily couldn't find the words to explain that she hadn't known Derek was married. Instead she held out her arms to Hope. 'Please . . .' she begged.

'Mummy,' Hope said in a small voice that broke Lily's heart.

'Don't come any nearer,' Hazel said. She glanced behind her, where the field fell away down to the riverbank. The river was wide here, as it swept round in a bend before it reached Beckindale, and the water was deep and fast-moving.

Lily felt her legs begin to shake uncontrollably. She had to keep Hazel away from the river.

Still holding the little girl tightly, Hazel stroked Hope's fringe away from her face and gazed at her. 'She looks like her father,' she said to Lily.

Lily took a small step towards her daughter and Hazel backed away.

'Stay where you are,' she warned.

'Lily!' Meg called from the road. 'You've found her. She's found Hope!'

Startled by the sudden shout, Lily turned round to see Meg, followed by Nancy and June, making their way towards her.

When she turned back, though, Hazel was gone, walking quickly down the field and heading for the river. Lily saw Hope's small, scared face over the woman's shoulder and screamed. 'Stop it! Come back.'

Suddenly she was filled with strength. That woman had her daughter and she was going to get her back. She half ran, half threw herself towards Hazel, but the woman teetered on the edge of the riverbank and, not wanting to startle her, Lily stopped.

'It's all right, Hope,' she said to her daughter, whose face was white with fear. 'It's all right. Mummy's here.'

Behind her, Lily could hear Meg breathing. 'What's going on?' Meg said in a low voice. 'Who is she?'

Lily kept her gaze fixed on Hazel. 'She's Derek's wife,' she hissed.

Meg reached out and gripped Lily's fingers, showing she understood.

'Keep Nancy and June back,' Lily said.

Meg let go of her hand and Lily heard murmured voices.

At the edge of the water, Hazel was looking at Hope. 'She's got his eyes,' she said. 'Just like my boys. Such pretty blue eyes. Derek died. Did you know that?'

Lily nodded. Perhaps if she could keep Hazel talking, she could get close enough to grab Hope, she thought. Very carefully, she took a tiny step forwards.

Hazel started to cry. 'He died. And the army sent back all his things.'

'It must have been so hard for you,' Lily said, feeling sorry for the broken woman in front of her but desperately wanting Hope back in her own arms. 'You must miss him.'

'Ha!' said Hazel. 'I miss what I thought he was.' Her harsh voice made Hope jump. The little girl squeezed her eyes tightly shut and started to cry. And abandoning her plan to creep forward slowly, Lily sprang across the grass and tried to take her daughter.

'Give her to me,' she said, trying not to sound too panicky in case she upset Hope even more.

'Stay away,' Hazel said again. Unsteadily, she took a few steps down the riverbank so she was right at the edge of the water.

Lily breathed in sharply. She knew the river was dangerous here. Shallow enough at the edges but falling away sharply in the centre, with a strong current that meant no one swam here. 'Be careful,' she begged.

Behind her, Nancy spoke quietly to June. 'Let's get help,' she said. Lily heard the two women run off, back towards Beckindale.

Next to Lily, Meg spoke. 'Hazel?' she said, in her gentle way. 'I'm so sorry to hear that Derek died. But please let Hope go to her mother. She's scared.'

Hope wriggled in Hazel's arms again, and the woman gripped her tightly, making both the little girl and Lily cry out at the same time.

Lily felt like time had slowed down. She could see everything so clearly. The way Hazel's bony fingers were clutching Hope's soft arms. The tears on Hope's chocolate-stained cheeks. The shadow that the broad brim of Hazel's hat cast across her angular face. The grass rippling in the breeze. And the river behind Hazel, the brown water swirling and churning. She could see everything, and yet all she was focusing on was Hope. All her instincts were to rush to her daughter and grab her from Hazel, but she didn't want to risk her falling into the river. She took a deep, shaky breath.

'Hazel, your feet are getting wet. Why not come out of the

water and we can have a chat?' Carefully, Lily edged down the steep bank, not wanting to fall, and held her hand out to Hazel.

'Derek was a liar,' Hazel said, as though Lily hadn't spoken at all and ignoring her outstretched hand. 'He lied to you, I bet.'

Lily nodded. Perhaps if she could find common ground with Hazel, she could take Hope from her. She moved down the bank a tiny bit further.

'I didn't know he was married,' she said. The hot shame she'd felt when she'd first found out how Derek had fooled her flooded her again. 'I'm so sorry.'

'Not as sorry as I was,' Hazel said, her voice harsh. 'My whole life was a lie. Everything. The whole lot. Everyone knew what he was like. Everyone was laughing at me. And now he's dead.'

'She's mad with grief,' Meg murmured behind Lily. 'Poor woman.'

'No one was laughing,' Lily said to Hazel.

'I loved him,' Hazel carried on. 'I loved him and he wasn't the man I thought he was at all.' She started to cry again. 'But I miss him so much.'

Lily lost her footing and, with a gasp, she slid down the bank towards Hazel. The other woman waded out into the river. 'Stay back,' she said, holding Hope in front of her like a shield.

Lily could hear her breath coming in short, shuddering gasps. 'Don't go any further,' she begged. 'The water is deep. It's not safe. Just give me Hope.'

'She's all I have left of Derek,' Hazel said.

'You have your boys,' Lily said. She knew Derek and Hazel had two sons.

But Hazel shook her head. 'No,' she said. 'No.'

'Did they . . . ?' Lily said, not wanting to know the answer. 'Are they . . .'

'Anthony was killed in France,' said Hazel, talking to a spot over Lily's shoulder in the far distance. 'He was in the first wave at Normandy. Didn't make it off the beach, apparently. I didn't want him to go, but he wanted to make his daddy proud. He was eighteen. Still a baby.' She sobbed. 'Then Peter lied about his age and joined up. He was sixteen.' She looked fierce. 'Why didn't they check? Why didn't someone check how old he was?' She stroked Hope's hair and Hope looked at her in alarm, flinching away. 'I don't know where Peter is. I don't know if he's alive. He didn't even say goodbye.'

Lily's heart ached with sadness for Hazel, who'd suffered so much, but she just wanted her out of the water and for Hope, who was clearly not happy in the woman's arms, to be safe. Hope kicked out and Hazel wobbled, taking a step further into the river.

'Stay still, sweetheart,' Lily said desperately. 'Stay still. I'm coming.'

She looked round wildly, trying to work out what to do. Talking obviously wasn't working. Hazel was edging closer to the deep water. Could Lily rush her and try to grab Hope? It might work, but it would scare her daughter and it could send all three of them plunging into the rushing river.

A movement down by the road caught her eye and she turned, hoping Nancy and June had reached Beckindale and it was Jack coming, or her father, or someone neutral who could help talk some sense into this sad, dangerous woman. She saw a blond head and heard Meg gasp next to her and Lily blinked, thinking she was hallucinating.

But there, coming up over the field, was Rolf.

Chapter Twenty-Five

Lily thought she was dreaming. Why on earth was Rolf here? He stopped walking as he noticed them, clearly surprised, and she let out a breath, still balancing halfway down the steep riverbank.

Meg, seeing Lily's attention behind her, turned and her face went white and then pink as she saw Rolf. For a frightening moment, Lily thought her friend might faint. She swayed slightly and then gathered herself and ran to the approaching man.

'Rolf,' she heard her say quietly but desperately. 'She's got Hope. Talk to her.'

Rolf hesitated, taking in the situation. 'Who is she?' he asked in a low voice to Meg.

'She's Derek's widow,' Meg said.

Lily watched Rolf's eyes widen. He'd met Derek when Lily was working for him, and he knew the truth about Lily's unexpected pregnancy.

'Please,' she begged. 'Rolf, please.'

She turned back to Hazel and Hope. The woman had waded further into the river now and the water reached her knees. Her summer dress was swirling as the current tugged her. She was so thin, Lily worried that she would simply be washed away.

Holding on to an overhanging tree trunk, Lily edged down the bank a little further. The water lapped at her feet and made her gasp with the cold. Hope was completely silent now, shocked into being quiet by the events. Lily found that more frightening than if she'd been crying.

Behind her, Rolf made his way down to the water too. He'd dropped his rucksack at the edge of the river and now he stood next to Lily. She thought she'd never been so grateful to see anyone and marvelled that it was Rolf, of all people.

'Don't take her,' Hazel said as Rolf approached. She took another step away from them and almost lost her footing on the slippery riverbed beneath her feet. Hope gave a little shriek and Lily tasted bile in her mouth.

'Hazel?' Rolf said, ever so gently. 'Hope must be heavy. Why not come out of the water and give your arms a rest. You must be cold.'

'No,' said Hazel.

'Hope is scared. She's only a little girl and you're frightening her.'

Lily could see the whites of Hazel's eyes. She looked mad with grief and despair. Desperate to get to Hope, she went to move forward and Rolf stopped her.

'Stay there,' he said quietly. 'Don't startle her.' He turned back to Hazel. 'I know you don't want to hurt Hope,' he said.

But Hazel grimaced. 'Why shouldn't I?' she said. 'That tart took everything from me. Why shouldn't I take the thing she loves most?'

Lily stifled a small whimper. 'Please don't hurt her,' she prayed under her breath. 'Please don't hurt her.'

'Because you're better than that,' Rolf said to Hazel. 'You're a good person, who fell in love with the wrong man.'

Like me, Lily thought, holding her breath.

Hazel eyed Rolf suspiciously. 'You're German.'

Lily let out a sob. Of course Hazel would hear Rolf's accent. How could she think he would help?

'I am German,' Rolf said calmly. 'But I am not a Nazi.'

'You killed my boy,' Hazel said. 'And my Derek.'

'And the Allies killed my mother, and my sisters.'

'That's not the same.'

'Isn't it?'

The sun had gone behind a cloud and, in the water, Lily shivered.

'We've all suffered,' Rolf went on. 'We all know heartache.' He paused. 'It's the things you don't expect that make it difficult, isn't it?' he said. 'I found it very hard not having a funeral. No proper goodbye.'

Hazel nodded. 'There is to be a cemetery in France,' she said bleakly. 'But I know I will never visit.'

'Sometimes,' Rolf said, 'I see my mother. In the distance, walking along the road. Or on a bus that passes by. I see the back of someone's head and think "oh, there she is", as though I've been waiting for her. But then I remember that she is dead, and it must be someone who looks like her. And it breaks my heart all over again.'

Lily looked at Hazel, who was crying. Hope was still quiet, gripping the woman's shoulders tightly, holding her legs up so her feet didn't get wet.

'The soldiers are coming home,' Hazel said. 'And I watch

them come and I hope that Anthony walks up the path to my front door. Or that Peter gets off the train. Or Derek drives up in his car. But then I read the telegrams again. Dead, dead, missing. And I know there is no hope.'

Rolf shook his head. 'There is always hope,' he said.

Hazel looked in his direction and Lily thought she'd never seen anyone look so completely stricken by sadness. 'There is no hope,' Hazel said again.

Rolf took a step towards Hazel. They were so close now, Lily thought he might reach out and take Hope from Hazel's arms.

'The children give us hope,' Rolf said.

Hazel looked down at the little girl in her arms and, to Lily's relief, she nodded.

'Can I take her?' Rolf said. 'Can I take Hope?'

There was a moment when Lily thought Hazel was going to refuse, but instead she nodded again. Rolf took another step closer and Hazel turned to him. But, as she moved, a startled Hope arched her back, trying to get away from the woman that held her. Hazel lost her footing, teetered and fell, plunging into the deep, rushing water in the centre of the river.

Lily screamed, a loud, piercing sound that sent birds soaring up from the trees and tore the sky.

Hazel and Hope disappeared under the water. Lily screamed again. Rolf didn't hesitate. He pulled off his jacket and plunged in too.

Next to Lily, Meg slid down the bank. 'Stay here,' she said firmly. 'Think of your baby. I'll get Hope.'

Meg kicked off her shoes and waded into the water, too, wobbling as the current pulled her. Frantic, but knowing she had to think of her unborn baby, Lily stayed where she was, feeling her feet sinking into the river mud.

'Hope!' Meg shouted. Lily gasped as Hope's little blonde head popped up above the murky water, much further down the river. The current was so strong and Hope so small, it had dragged her along. Hazel was nowhere to be seen.

Hope was crying, and then spluttering as she went under again.

'Get her!' Lily screamed. 'She's there!'

Rolf was already on his way, slicing through the water with firm swimming strokes, Meg was following behind, her swimming less certain, but still strong.

'Hope, I'm here,' Rolf shouted. 'Stay still, don't struggle.'

She won't understand, Lily thought in despair. *She won't know what he means.*

She couldn't see Hope's bunches at all now. Just the brown water, topped with bubbles as it frothed and flowed over the rocks.

Rolf dived under the surface, looking for Hope and Hazel, and didn't come up again.

Far, far away, Lily could hear Meg wailing, but the pounding in her own ears drowned out the sound. Her vision was fading. 'She's dead,' she said. 'She's dead, she's dead, she's dead.'

And then, like a miracle, Rolf surfaced, holding Hope in his arms.

Lily let out a strangled moan. 'Is she breathing?' she shouted desperately. 'Is she alive?'

'Mama,' Hope spluttered and Lily sank down on to the muddy riverbank, because her legs could no longer support her.

She watched as Meg struggled through the water to help Rolf pull the little girl out. With new-found strength, Lily staggered to her feet and ran along the edge of the river to her daughter.

Meg held Hope out to Lily and the little girl grabbed her mother. They were both crying now, Hope burying her face in Lily's neck, and Meg too as she crawled out of the water and on to the bank.

Rolf stood up to his knees in the water.

'Hazel,' Meg said. 'What about Hazel?'

Lily let out a gasp. Where was Hazel? She watched over the top of Hope's head as Rolf plunged back into the freezing water, diving and resurfacing once, twice, three times. Shaking his head as he came back up each time.

Lily was holding her breath. She clung to Hope and Meg as they sat at the top of the bank and watched Rolf's fruitless searching, until eventually he shouted.

'I've got her.'

Meg stood up and waded back into the water and Lily turned away and hid Hope's face from the awful sight before them. Feeling her little girl shiver, Lily wrapped her in the picnic blanket where Hazel had sat, and held her like a baby in her arms. Then, with growing horror, Lily watched Meg and Rolf pull Hazel from the water and lift her up on to the grass at the top of the bank.

The woman looked so small as she lay on the field. There was nothing of her. Her arms were like twigs and her cheeks were hollow. Her hair was spread out around her, bits of river weed in it, and her skirt clung to her legs, making her look like a macabre mermaid. Her eyes were open and her lips were blue.

'Is she . . .' Lily began, but she knew the answer. There was no doubt at all that Hazel was dead.

Chapter Twenty-Six

Meg found she couldn't stop shivering. Or crying. She was shaking and sobbing and she wasn't sure exactly what was going on. What had happened here? Why was Rolf here? What were they going to do about Hazel?

'I know first aid,' she said vaguely. 'We had a course when I did my teacher training. I could try . . .'

But Rolf just shook his head. 'She's gone,' he said. 'I wasn't quick enough.'

Lily seemed more in control now, cradling Hope, who was wrapped in a blanket, and keeping her face away from the sight of Hazel as she lay on the ground 'Look,' she said, pointing towards the road. Coming towards them was Jack's police car, followed by a second car.

Well done, Nancy, Meg thought.

There were a few minutes of quiet, as they all sat still on the grass, thinking of what had happened. Poor Hazel, Meg kept thinking. Poor woman. And then there was a flurry of activity as Jack got out of his police car and Dr Black – who was in the car behind – arrived too.

Meg's head span with relief and sadness. Lily, still clinging on to Hope, ran to Jack and sobbed in his arms. He spoke quietly and comfortingly into her ear. Meg couldn't hear what he was saying, but she knew he would be choosing exactly the right words; he always did. Dr Black was crouching beside Hazel's body, speaking to Rolf. Meg could see an ambulance coming down the road from Hotten, but it was too late for that. Dr Black reached out gently and closed Hazel's eyes, then he went to his car and took a red blanket from the boot and covered her up.

Even though there was activity all around her, she felt as though it was all slightly out of focus. As though no one was really there on the field with her, except Rolf. Now he'd finished explaining what had happened to Dr Black, he was standing to the side, quietly, with his head bowed and his hands clasped behind his back. Meg's feet seemed to have a mind of their own. They carried her across the grass to where he stood. And then her arms took over, reaching out and giving Rolf a resounding slap across his wet shoulders.

'Why are you here?' she said. Her voice sounded harsher than she'd intended, but she didn't care. What was he thinking? Waltzing up the road to Beckindale as if he hadn't a care in the world? 'You shouldn't be here.'

Rolf looked completely wretched. 'I came to say goodbye,' he muttered.

'We said goodbye,' Meg replied. 'And Wally Eagleton and his friends attacked us. I'm surprised you don't remember.'

She knew she was being horrible, but the emotion of the day, her fears for Hope, and the terror she'd felt when she'd seen Rolf submerged in the water and not come up again, all combined to make her absolutely furious.

'Meg . . .'

'No,' she said. 'No, this isn't fair. I've spent six weeks feeling horrible, and then just as I started thinking I had to pick myself up again, you arrive.'

Rolf hung his head. 'This was a mistake. I'm going to go.'

He turned away, but Meg pulled his arm. 'Go where? Back to Berlin? Again.' She spat out the last word.

'I thought I might go to Canada,' Rolf said.

Meg's jaw dropped in surprise.

'Canada?'

'Berlin was a wonderful city, and I'm sure it will be again,' Rolf said. 'But the scars are too deep. The wounds are too raw. I can't live there. It's not my home any more.'

Meg could barely keep up. 'But Canada?'

He shrugged. 'There are not many countries that would welcome a German.'

'Would Canada?'

'Apparently.'

Meg glared at him. 'You still haven't explained why you're here.'

'I'm getting a boat from Liverpool in a few days,' he said. 'I thought I'd come to Beckindale on the way. I didn't mean to bump into you. I wasn't going to see you at all. I just wanted to walk along the river, where we had our last time together. And I half thought I could watch you without you seeing me. Check you were all right.'

'Check I was all right?' Meg said. Her fight was ebbing away as she looked at Rolf, and now she just felt exhausted. 'Of course I'm not all right, Rolf. I don't think I'll ever be all right.'

Rolf nodded. 'I feel the same.'

Meg looked up to the blue sky in despair. 'But what can

we do? We can't be together. And now you've made it all harder again.'

'I'm going to go,' Rolf said.

Not trusting herself to speak, Meg nodded.

Rolf turned away. He picked up his jacket and rucksack from where he'd thrown them and walked along the grass, squelching in his wet shoes. Meg watched him go. That was that, then. She'd never see him again.

Up ahead, Dr Black was helping as Hazel was carried into the ambulance. Meg wondered what would happen to her. She hoped there would be a funeral. She hoped Hazel had someone who would miss her and remember her fondly. This bloody war, Meg thought fiercely. This bloody war, still hurting people, even though it was over.

'Where's Rolf going?' Lily, her face still tear-stained and grubby though she was smiling, rushed over. 'Jack wants to thank him.'

'He's going to Canada,' said Meg. She sounded matter-of-fact, though she felt anything but. 'He's off to the new world for a new life.'

Lily looked at her as though she'd grown an extra head. 'No he isn't,' she said. 'He's coming back to Beckindale.'

'No he's not.'

'Meg, I was wrong. Rolf's a hero. He saved Hope's life, and you and him belong together. He'll come back to the village with you.'

Meg shook her head, feeling utterly hopeless and very close to tears. Her teeth were chattering and her skirt hung damply around her knees. Everything was hopeless. 'He can't come to Beckindale, Lily. He's a German. No one will accept him. No one will accept us.'

Lily started to cry. 'No,' she said. 'I can't bear it. I can't bear for you to lose him after all this. He's a hero and he saved Hope, just like he saved Ruby when she was little. I'll make sure everyone in Beckindale knows it.'

Meg felt the tiniest, teeniest, glimmer of hope. 'He's a hero,' she said softly. Like a news reel running through her head, she saw pictures of Rolf, giving up his chance of freedom to help her look for Ruby back when the war was new and Ruby was a sad, surly schoolgirl. Putting a smile on Stan's face by teaching him to play the violin. Stepping in to help Wally Eagleton's friend, who turned on him in reward. And bravely plunging into the churning waters of the River Emm and saving little Hope. 'He's a hero,' she said again. She remembered the feel of his lips on hers. How could she let him walk away?

Lily thumped her once more. 'Go and tell him.'

'Really?' said Meg, suddenly less sure.

'Go!'

'Rolf!' Meg shouted. She raced across the grass and down on to the street, where Rolf had started walking towards Hotten. 'Stop!'

Rolf stopped, but he didn't turn round.

'I need to tell you . . .' Meg began. She faltered.

Rolf turned to face her. 'What?'

She took a breath. 'Stan got into music school,' she said. 'He wanted me to tell you.'

Rolf's mouth curled into a brief smile. 'That is good news.'

There was a pause as they looked at each other.

'Was that it?' he said, his expression serious again.

'Pardon?'

'Was that why you chased me? To tell me about Stan?'

233

Meg looked at him carefully. Was he teasing her? His lips twitched and Meg, feeling more confident, took a breath.

'Actually,' she said. 'I wondered if you might want to come for tea. At mine. The children would love to see you.'

'Tea?' said Rolf.

Meg swallowed. 'And perhaps you could stay for a few days. Longer, if you fancied it. You don't have anywhere you need to be, do you?'

Rolf reached into the pocket on his knapsack and pulled out a long ticket. Meg wasn't sure what a passenger ship ticket looked like, but she imagined it looked almost exactly like the paper Rolf was holding.

'What's that?' she asked.

'Nothing important,' said Rolf. He crumpled it up.

'So do you have anywhere you need to be?' Meg asked.

Rolf took her hand. 'Right here,' he said.

Chapter Twenty-Seven

Lily's emotions were veering wildly between sheer blessed relief, giddy happiness, icy-cold horror at what could have happened to Hope if Rolf hadn't been there, and sadness about Hazel. She held her little girl tightly in her arms, watching Meg and Rolf chatting a little way along the road, and thought about poor Hazel – who hadn't meant any harm, not really. How could someone's life just end that way? It was so sad, she thought. So very sad.

'Dr Black and I need to go to the hospital with, erm, with the body.' Jack appeared at her elbow, making her jump. 'We need to make sure it's all recorded properly. There will be an inquest at some point, so I need to do everything by the book. I thought I would drive and Dr Black wondered if you'd be all right to drive his car back to the village for him?'

Lily nodded. 'Of course.' She had a sudden thought. 'Hazel had a car,' she said. 'It's parked in the lay-by.'

'I'll take care of it.' Jack wrapped his arms around Lily and Hope and kissed the top of Lily's head. 'I hate leaving you after all this.'

Lily smiled, thinking for the thousandth time how lucky she was to have him. 'We'll be fine. Just hurry back.'

'I will,' he said. He waved to Dr Black, who was closing the ambulance door, looking exhausted. Lily wasn't surprised. She also felt like she could sleep for a week. 'Lily's taking your car. I'll follow you.'

Lily held out her hand for the car key and Jack dropped it into her palm. Then he jogged over to the police car and got in.

'I'm driving back to the village,' Lily called to Meg. 'Come on.'

Meg and Rolf came over, both looking flushed and happy, and still dripping wet. Lily was glad they seemed to have sorted things out. She knew it wouldn't be plain sailing for them, but they had to give things a try. How much would they regret it if they didn't?

'Meg, could you take Hope and sit in the back?' she said.

Meg slid on to the back seat of the car, and Lily handed Hope in to her. The little girl had fallen asleep, still wrapped in the picnic blanket. Lily wondered how she'd be when she woke up. It had been a confusing and frightening day for her.

She got into the driver's seat and adjusted the position of the chair, while Rolf sat in the passenger seat. And they set off to Beckindale.

'Do you think Hope will be all right?' Rolf said, glancing over his shoulder.

'I'll get her home and put her in the bath, then we can have a quiet tea and she'll be right as rain,' said Lily. Then she gasped. 'Oh my days, I'd forgotten about the party.'

'The party,' said Meg. 'Oh good lord.'

'The party?' said Rolf.

'There was a party going on in the village,' Lily explained. 'Music and games and all sorts. To welcome the troops home. There was a parade first with prayers for the fallen, then a celebration.'

Rolf's eyes widened. 'And this will still be happening?'

Lily nodded. 'Well, I expect everyone's waiting to hear what's happened with Hope.'

'Everyone will be so relieved she's safe,' said Meg. 'I reckon your poor dad will have been frantic. And Nina. And Jed and Larry.'

'They will be pleased to see her,' said Rolf. He sounded nervous, Lily thought. It must have been the idea of a whole welcoming committee waiting in the village. Any hope he'd had of sneaking in quietly had fallen by the wayside.

'Goodness, Hope will be overwhelmed,' she said, thinking the same could be said about poor Rolf. As she took the turning to Beckindale, she glanced in her rear-view mirror and saw her daughter was sitting up and blinking. 'Hello, sweetheart, did you have a nice sleep?'

Hope looked at Lily with a frown. 'Why is you driving Daddy's car?'

'It's Dr Black's car,' Lily said. 'We're just borrowing it. We're almost back in Beckindale now, look.'

Hope looked out of the window. 'Are we going to the party?'

Meg chuckled. 'She seems fine.'

'I did have chocolate,' Hope told Meg. 'And we went in the water.'

'I know,' said Meg. 'You were awfully brave.'

Hope nodded. 'My dress is wet.'

'It doesn't matter,' Lily said. 'We'll dry it on the washing line.'

'But what will I wear?'

'You can put your nightie on.'

Hope laughed and Lily's heart lifted. She'd thought she would never hear that lovely sound again.

'Silly Mummy,' she said. 'I can't wear my nightie to a party.'

It was Lily's turn to laugh, marvelling at her daughter's resilience.

Lily parked outside Dr Black's house and Hope scrambled out of the back seat, followed more elegantly by Meg. Rolf stood nervously by the car.

'I'm not sure . . .' he began.

'It's fine,' Lily said firmly. 'Let's get dry first and then we'll go and let everyone know Hope's safe.' She looked at Rolf. 'And why.'

She dashed up Dr Black's path and posted the car key through his letter box, then, taking Hope by the hand, she led the way to her cottage. She found towels for everyone, and a dress for Meg to borrow. She looked in Jack's wardrobe and pulled out a shirt and some trousers for Rolf to wear, and she gave Hope a good rub with a towel and brushed her hair. She'd lost her ribbons, so Lily found some more in the little box on her dressing table. Hope seemed none the worse for her ordeal. She was just keen to go back to the party and do some dancing. Rolf, though, was quiet and nervy as they headed outside and across the village to The Woolpack.

Outside the pub, Lily could see groups of people milling around. The music had stopped and the games and stalls were quiet, but there were plenty of villagers waiting to see what had happened to Hope.

'Oh heavens,' Meg muttered.

'It's fine,' Lily said.

Hope spotted Mick, who was sitting with Nina and Jed. 'GRANDAD!' she bellowed, making everyone turn. 'I did have chocolate!'

The joyful look on Mick's face made Lily's heart almost burst with happiness. He leapt on to his feet, then crouched down and opened his arms and Hope raced over and cuddled him tightly.

Lily, Meg and Rolf hurried over. Lily was nervous about answering the inevitable barrage of questions about what had happened, dragging up the story of her ill-advised romance with Derek again, but at first most people just seemed happy to see Hope safe and sound. Lily took a deep breath and let it out slowly.

'What happened?' asked Nancy. 'Who was that woman?'

Lily swallowed. 'She was Derek's widow,' she said quietly. 'Derek was Hope's biological father.'

'Goodness.' Nancy's eyes widened.

'She took Hope and she waded out into the river,' Lily said, her voice cracking as she remembered the fear she'd felt. 'Out where the river bends, past Mr Butler's fields.'

'The water is so deep there,' Mick said, shuddering. 'And the current is so strong.'

Lily found she was crying again, telling the story. 'I couldn't get to her,' she explained. 'And then . . .' She took a deep breath and glanced round at where Meg stood under a tree a little way from the group. Rolf stood next to her, his hands in the pockets of his borrowed trousers. 'Hazel fell into the water with Hope. I was terrified, Hope was dragged along by the current, and she can't swim yet . . .'

She looked round at the faces of the villagers, everyone hanging on her words.

'Rolf was there,' she said. 'He was really brave. He dived straight in,' she said. 'He didn't even hesitate. He went after Hope so fast and pulled her out of the water. He saved her life, and Meg helped him too. I don't know what would have happened without them. A second or two longer and Hope would have drowned.'

Mick held Hope closer to him, kissing her hair as she wriggled in his arms.

Nina, who'd met Hazel back when Derek was billeted with her, spoke up. 'And Hazel?' she said. 'Is she all right?'

Lily couldn't speak. She shook her head slowly. 'She died, Nina,' she said. 'She drowned. Rolf looked and looked for her, and he and Meg pulled her out of the water, but it was too late.'

Nina's face twisted with sadness. 'Oh, Lily.'

'I know.'

The hubbub around Lily grew as the villagers talked about what had happened. But Lily became aware that everyone was looking at Rolf. Gradually, the muttering stopped, dying away until the villagers were silent, staring at the German as he stood awkwardly, looking at his feet.

'How do, Rolf?' her father said and Rolf nodded to him in response. Lily smiled at Meg. Perhaps it was going to be all right.

But among the people of the village, the muttering started up again in response to Mick's greeting.

'He's a Kraut,' she heard someone say. 'A German.'

'He saved that little lass's life,' someone else pointed out.

'So he says. Happen he pushed her in the water himself.'

'We should get rid,' another voice said. 'We don't want his sort here.'

The mumbling was getting louder, so, taking a deep breath, Lily clapped her hands for quiet.

'It's Rolf,' she said in a shaky voice. 'Not just any German. Rolf. You remember him? Remember how he went searching for Ruby when she ran off when she was little?'

Nobody spoke. Lily felt everyone's eyes on her.

'Rolf turned up when Hope was in trouble today.' She swallowed. 'A woman took her. Not a bad woman, but she wasn't thinking clearly because she was so sad about the war and the losses she'd suffered.'

'Because of the Germans, like him,' someone shouted. Lily thought it might have been Wally Eagleton, but she wasn't sure.

'Rolf stepped in and helped,' she said. 'I don't know what would have happened if he'd not been there.'

There was a pause and then Maggie Sugden walked over to where Lily was standing. 'I know Rolf too,' she said. 'He helped us so much on Emmerdale Farm at the start of the war. We'd not have a farm now if it wasn't for folk like him working hard for us.'

Lily nodded. She remembered Maggie standing up for Rolf when he'd been in the village before. She knew right from wrong, did Maggie, and where she went, others often followed.

Rolf was standing still. He didn't look defiant exactly. More that he was letting everyone speak. Letting them say what they had to say.

Nick Roberts joined Rolf under the tree. 'I reckon we've got a lot in common,' he said. 'I bet you've got some stories to share about the camps you've been in.'

Rolf nodded and Nick held out his hand for Rolf to shake. Lily felt a rush of emotion. Beckindale people were good people, she thought.

Now it was Seth Armstrong's turn. He stood up too. 'Welcome to Beckindale, Rolf,' he said. 'Will you need work?'

Rolf, looking slightly overwhelmed, nodded.

'I'll put a word in for you with Mr Verney,' Seth said. 'We could do with more hands up at the estate.'

'I'm here,' Mr Verney appeared from behind the crowd, waving a hand at Seth. 'And Seth's right. There's a job for you at Miffield Hall if you want one.'

'Thank you,' said Rolf.

'Rolf doesn't want to go back to Germany,' Meg said, her clear schoolteacher's voice ringing out over the crowd. 'He wants to stay here in Yorkshire. I reckon we should welcome those who want to be here.'

For a second, Lily thought that was it. Everyone was on board and everything would be all right. But then Wally Eagleton pushed his way through the crowd.

'No,' he said. 'No way.'

Meg moved so she was in between Wally and Rolf. Meg wasn't big anyway, but next to Wally she seemed even smaller. Lily felt a moment of fear for her friend. Wally was one of those that had been changed by the war. He had a devil-may-care attitude about him now, as though the worst thing imaginable had happened already, so why worry?

'It's not up to you, Wally Eagleton.'

'It ain't,' Wally agreed. 'But there are lads that left this village and won't ever come back. And there's others who won't ever be the same. And you expect us to welcome in a Kraut?' He raised his voice. 'A stinking Kraut?'

'I understand,' Meg said. 'But Rolf's lost people too. There were no winners in the war, Wally. Not really.'

Wally snorted. 'We won,' he said. A few people cheered, but mostly everyone stayed silent. 'Ah, just look at him, standing there like butter wouldn't melt.' He turned round and spoke to the other villagers and Lily caught a whiff of beer on his breath. He was drunk. Unsteady on his feet and aggressive. She felt that flicker of fear again and wished Jack was here. Wally jabbed with his finger at no one in particular. 'You don't want him here, do you? Or you?' He span round, back to Rolf, and nearly lost his balance. 'You're a murderer,' he hissed. 'A murdering bloody Kraut. And you're not welcome in Beckindale.' He took a deep breath and then he shouted, 'Get out.'

'You get out.' Lily looked round to see Seth Armstrong squaring up to Wally. 'Rolf's worth two of you, Wally Eagleton,' Seth said. 'And he's staying.'

'Not if I have anything to do with it.' Wally stepped closer to Seth. He was taller, but Seth's arms were lean and sinewy. And he wasn't steaming drunk.

'No one's interested in what you have to say, Wally,' Seth said. 'Go on, clear off, before you make a fool of yourself.'

Wally gave him a slow, languid smile. 'Funny,' he said. 'Your Betty seemed very interested in what I had to say. Not that we did much talking, of course.' He gave a throaty chuckle. 'We found other ways to pass the time. If you know what I mean?' He turned to his group of friends and gave a couple of thrusts of his pelvis to make sure everyone knew exactly what he meant. His friends all whooped.

Seth's face turned red.

'Wally?' he said.

Wally turned round to face Seth, still grinning. And *bam!* Seth punched him square on the jaw. Wally dropped to the

243

floor like a stone and Seth turned away, rubbing his knuckles. He held his hand out to Rolf.

'Welcome to Beckindale,' he said.

Chapter Twenty-Eight

Birmingham

Betty was tired and grumpy as she got off the train. The hospital was only a couple of stops along the line and she could walk it, but she didn't have long before her shift at the jazz club started. She marched up the path to the little terraced house she shared with Margaret and Margaret's friend Thora, who was deeply religious and regarded everything Betty did or said with equal amounts of disgust and suspicion.

But Betty knew both Thora and Margaret were still at work, so she would have the place to herself. She was longing for a bath and an early night, but she had to simply get changed and go out again.

Birmingham was not as much fun as Betty had hoped it would be. Margaret had been overjoyed when Betty arrived on that snowy night after Christmas. She was thrilled to bits that Seth and Betty had broken off their engagement and excited to show Betty the sights of the city. She'd even pulled some strings to get Betty a job on reception in the hospital.

So Betty had gone from making appointments for sick animals to making them for sick people. She supposed it was a step up, of sorts.

She still dreamed of being on stage, though. Which was why she'd got the job in the jazz club. She was just working behind the bar, but there were dancers there, and musicians, and the smoky, sophisticated atmosphere made her feel like it was a place where she belonged.

She headed upstairs to her room, and peeled off her hospital tunic. She hated her uniform so much. She'd tried taking in her skirt to make it hug her hips in a more flattering way, but her boss – Mrs Trentham – had frowned and suggested Betty had been overindulging, and asked 'sweetly' if she could order Betty the next size up.

Luckily, at the club, she could wear anything she wanted. It was one of the reasons she liked it so much. She had a quick wash, brushed her hair and tied it up again, then she put on a dark blue dress that showed off just enough cleavage, and flat shoes – she'd learned early on that heels just made her feet and back ache after a shift – and a bit of make-up. Some of the other girls at the club had worked in munitions factories during the war, where they were given cosmetics as a bonus. They were generous and savvy about swapping their loot for other things, and Betty found herself giving dance lessons in the stockroom during breaks in exchange for a lipstick or some mascara.

The club was in the city centre, which was about twenty minutes on the bus from where Betty and Margaret lived. Betty hadn't been sure about living in a city when she first arrived. It was so dirty. And crowded. And there was rubble everywhere because Birmingham had been bombed during the Blitz. It was so different from Beckindale, with its sweet cottages and acres of farmland. At first, Betty had felt as though she couldn't breathe in the city centre, but now she had grown to like it. She liked the energy and the noise and the way no one knew everything about everyone else. That was very different from Beckindale too, and in a good way.

It was Friday night, so it was busy at work. Betty enjoyed the first hour, stocking the bar with drinks and making sure everything was ready for when they opened. The club didn't even unlock its doors until nine o'clock, which Betty thought was the height of sophistication. It would be frantic once the customers started coming in, but at first there was just chatter with the other girls behind the bar, and some flirting with the musicians. Betty was very fond of them all. She loved the other barmaids and waitresses, who were all so much fun to be around. They reminded her of her dancing friend Pamela, who she'd met when she was with ENSA.

And the musicians. Well, they were something else. They wore sharp suits and smoked cigarettes and they were so polite to the girls. Betty thought they were wonderful. One of them in particular, a lad called Jonah, who played the trumpet, was her favourite. He was really young – just nineteen – and so talented. Betty thought he was as cute as a button. She had tried to take him under her wing and give him advice on girls, but though he seemed to enjoy chatting to her, he never wanted to talk about romance. Betty thought that was sweet too. He was so shy.

Tonight, though, Jonah was on stage with the other musicians and Betty was dashing about serving drinks. Sometimes she worked behind the bar, and sometimes she worked at the tables, delivering orders. She liked that better when it was busy. She always got flustered with too many cocktail orders being shouted at once when she was serving drinks. Tonight she was on the tables and she'd been pleased because she loved chatting to the customers. That was what she was good at really.

She'd been running around for hours, and her feet were burning, when she took some drinks to two men sitting at the side of the dance floor.

One of them was older – in his late forties or early fifties, Betty thought – and the other was maybe ten or fifteen years younger. They both had an air of being well looked after. Their shirts weren't fraying around the collars, their faces weren't just the wrong side of too thin. They were laughing uproariously and not paying the slightest attention to the musicians on stage.

Betty put their drinks in front of them, and the younger man looked up and smiled at her. She felt an immediate pull of attraction. He was very handsome, with dark reddish-brown hair. His eyes sparkled as he looked at her.

'Thank you,' he said.

Betty leant over to put his glass on a coaster, making sure he got a glimpse of her low-cut top. She was pleased to see he'd noticed, his eyes flickering from her face to her bosom. She gave him another smile and sashayed off to fetch another tray.

Later, when the club was emptying and the music had finished, she walked by the table again. This time, the older man had gone and the younger man was sitting by himself.

'Where's your friend?' Betty said.

He put his head on his hands glumly. 'Gone home,' he said. 'He's got a wife waiting for him.'

'And you don't have anyone waiting for you?' Betty asked, daringly.

'Nope,' said the man. He had a soft Scottish accent that Betty found very endearing. He looked up at her, meeting her gaze, and again she felt that tug of attraction. 'Not yet.'

Betty gave him a slow smile as she leaned forward and wiped the table. 'I don't imagine you go home alone very often.'

He reached out a hand and stroked her fingers. 'Not if I can help it.'

All of Betty's senses fizzed and popped.

'What's your name?' the man asked.

Betty smiled. 'Elizabeth.' She liked using her proper name when she was at the club. She thought it sounded more grown-up and worldly.

'Roderick,' said the man. 'Do you work here every night?'

'No,' said Betty.

'What nights are you here?'

Betty took her hand away from his and grinned at him. 'You'll just have to keep coming back until you've worked it out, won't you?'

Roderick sat back in his chair and gazed at her in admiration. 'Well, perhaps I will.'

Betty walked away from his stare until she was standing behind him, then she leaned over his shoulder. 'I'd like that,' she said.

The next day was Saturday and for once Margaret wasn't working. Betty was looking forward to spending some time with her sister. They'd barely seen each other for weeks. Betty's job at the club meant she hardly had any free time anyway, and when you added that to Margaret's shifts, and the fact that she spent all her days off with her boring boyfriend, then the sisters were like ships that passed in the night.

'Just got up?' Thora said as Betty staggered into the kitchen the next morning and filled the kettle with water.

Betty looked down at the dressing gown and slippers she was wearing and gave Thora her best, dazzling smile.

'No,' she said. 'I've been out playing golf this morning.'

Thora sighed as though Betty's mere presence was a cross she had to bear. She was sitting at the kitchen table sorting through knitting patterns. Betty hoped she was making something for one of the old ladies she looked after at the hospital, because the patterns did not look like outfits a young woman should be wearing.

'Where's Margaret?' Betty asked, looking for a clean mug for her tea.

'She's gone out to meet Mr Bartlett,' Thora said.

Betty groaned. 'Boring Dr Bartlett.'

'He's not a doctor, he's a mister,' Thora said. 'Because he's a surgeon.'

'I don't care. He's still boring.'

'You've not even met him,' Thora pointed out.

'He sounds boring,' said Betty with a shrug. 'I thought we could spend some time together.'

'You and Mr Bartlett?'

God, Thora really was the most infuriating person Betty had ever met. 'No,' she said patiently. 'Me and Margaret.'

'She's bringing him back here for lunch,' Thora said, her attention fixed on her patterns.

Betty closed her eyes briefly. She did not want to spend her day off with Margaret and her boring boyfriend. Perhaps she could join them for lunch, then go into town to do some shopping. She was very taken with the huge department store in Birmingham city centre called Rackhams. It was like a treasure trove and she loved to wander round, looking at all the exciting things on offer.

She glowered at Thora. 'I'm going to have a bath.'

When Margaret came home, she bounced upstairs and rapped on Betty's bedroom door. 'Ready for lunch?' she sang. 'Betty, your room is such a mess.'

Betty was lying on her bed, reading a magazine. 'I never have time to tidy it.'

'How long have you been reading that?' Margaret said. 'You could have tidied up instead.'

Betty sat up and threw the mag at her sister, who ducked out of the way, laughing. 'You sound like Mam,' she said, knowing that was the worst insult of all.

Margaret made a shocked face. 'I do not.'

Betty chuckled. 'Is he here, then? Do I have to come and meet boring Dr Bartlett?'

Bouncing on her toes like an excited schoolgirl, Margaret clapped her hands. 'Mr Bartlett,' she said. 'But yes, he's here. Come downstairs. He's dying to meet you.'

'Fine,' Betty said, getting up off the bed dramatically as if it was just too much effort. 'But when old Barty has gone, I want to tell you about this gorgeous man I met in the club last night.'

'Ooh yes,' said Margaret as they went downstairs. 'Was he really handsome?'

'Handsome and sophisticated,' said Betty. 'Just my type.'

Margaret laughed as they went into the tiny living room. 'Betty,' she said. 'This is my boyfriend, Roderick Bartlett.'

And there, standing by the window, looking just as gorgeous as he had the night before, was the man from the club.

He gave her a smile that made her stomach flip over with desire. 'Hello, Betty,' he said, emphasising her name. 'It really is lovely to meet you.'

Chapter Twenty-Nine

SEPTEMBER 1945

'You look so smart.' Meg gazed at Stan in approval, her heart contracting a little as she realised how grown-up he appeared in his new school uniform. 'Have you got everything? Your satchel? And your violin?'

Stan nodded, looking pale and nervous. 'Will they tell me where to go?' he said. 'Because it's a big school and I'm not sure I remember my way round.'

Meg straightened his tie and gave him a kiss. 'They said there will be prefects on the gates to greet the new first formers, so don't worry. And Lily's going to wait until you're safely inside.'

Normally, Stan would get the school bus, but Lily was driving him today, as it was his first day. Meg wished she could go too. She was so proud of Stan, she thought she might burst with it, but it was her first day back at school too, so she had to go to work.

'Look at the state of that,' said Ruby, bouncing into the room, munching on some toast. She was wearing overalls and was giddy with excitement because she was working on her own at the garage all day today. She gave Stan's tie a tug and he aimed a punch at her.

'Geroff,' he said.

Ruby grinned at him. 'Proud of you though.' She ruffled his hair and he ducked away.

'Oi, don't, Ruby.'

'Leave him alone,' Meg said. 'He's nervous enough.'

'No need to be nervous,' said Ruby, jamming her feet into her work boots. 'You're the best.' She kissed Meg on the cheek, thumped Stan affectionately on the arm, and flew out of the door.

'She's right,' said Meg. 'You are the best.'

'What if no one speaks to me?' said Stan in a small voice. 'What if I don't make any friends?'

'Rubbish,' Meg said briskly. 'You, Stanley Dobbs, make friends everywhere you go. You'll know everyone's name by lunchtime, and the names of their brothers, sisters and family dog by the end of the day.'

A car horn blared outside.

'That's Lily,' Meg said. 'Ready?'

Stan bit his lip. 'Ready.' He picked up his bag and his violin case and he and Meg went outside.

Lily was standing by the car, looking beautiful as always, and happy. Her loose frock hid her swelling belly, but there was no mistaking her pregnancy glow.

'Oh Stan, you look great,' she called. 'Put your bags in the boot if you like. Will give you more room.'

Stan did as she said and as he shut the boot with a thud, he waved madly at an approaching figure. 'Rolf!' he shouted. 'It's my first day!'

Meg's heart lifted as it always did at the mention of Rolf. He was sauntering down the road, wearing a suit. A suit. She'd never seen him wear anything so smart before. And – she blinked in surprise – he was holding a violin case, too.

'What's this?' she said. 'Are you going to school, too?'

'I am.'

Meg frowned. 'Don't pull my leg, Rolf. What are you doing?'

He beamed at her and Stan. 'I've got an interview to be a violin teacher at Stan's new school.'

Stan looked delighted. 'That's wizard.'

'Wizard?' Rolf looked confused and Lily giggled.

'He means good,' she explained. 'Come on, Stan, let's get in the car and I'll tell you what's going on.'

Meg gave Lily a stern look. They were supposed to be friends. Why hadn't she told her what Rolf was up to? But Lily pretended not to see and got into the car. Stan followed. Meg, still bewildered, turned her attention to Rolf. 'But how . . .' she began.

Rolf grinned. 'Mr Verney.'

Rolf had been working with Seth Armstrong up at Miffield Hall since he returned to the village. He liked being outdoors and he was a hard worker, so he'd been getting on well, as far as Meg knew. He certainly seemed happy enough. He'd moved in with Nancy because she said she needed a lodger. Meg wasn't sure she really had needed a lodger – Nancy always seemed happy enough by herself – but she appreciated her opening her home to Rolf. With the exception of Wally and his friends, everyone had welcomed Rolf into Beckindale. Eventually.

'Tell me what happened,' she said to him.

'I got chatting to Mr Verney about music one day and he told me his father was a violinist too. He asked if I'd play his father's violin for him, so I did. And it became a bit of a regular thing. He liked hearing me play and I was so glad to have a chance to get a bow in my hands again.'

Meg nodded. She knew how important music was to Rolf and how much he'd missed it when he was in the POW camp.

'As it happens, Mr Verney is a friend of the headmaster at Stan's school. He mentioned me. What's the phrase? Put a word in?'

'That's right.'

'Mr Verney put a word in. I've spoken to the headmaster on the telephone, but I am meeting him today to play for him.' He made a face. 'I'm very nervous.'

Meg squeezed his arm. 'You're a wonderful violinist,' she said. 'They'll be lucky to have you.' She paused. 'What about . . .'

'Me being German?' Rolf said, making a face. 'The headmaster said it might be best if he lets everyone believe I am Swiss.'

Meg raised an eyebrow. 'Are you all right with that?'

He shrugged. 'I will do what I have to do.'

'And the violin?' Meg asked. She knew Rolf's own instrument was long gone.

'Mr Verney's father's,' he said.

'He gave it to you?' Meg gasped.

'Loaned it to me,' Rolf corrected. 'Just until I can buy a new one of my own.' He stepped forward and took Meg's hands in his. 'I have to go,' he said. 'Can we see each other this evening? Nancy is having dinner with Susan and her family to celebrate her exam results. I thought perhaps I could cook for you? We've not had a chance to spend much time together.'

Meg nodded. It was ironic that as soon as Rolf had returned to Beckindale she'd been so busy she'd barely seen him. She'd been responsible for finding billets for the evacuees who'd come to the village and surrounding areas early in the war, so she'd spent the summer sending them home again. It wasn't an easy job. Some of them had no family to return to. Others had parents who were missing, or who had been bombed out and relocated, and needed to be tracked down. It had taken up all of Meg's time, and left her so tired at the end of each day that she'd had little energy for anything else. Rolf, though, had been just as busy. He'd been working long days at the estate, helping Nancy at the vet's and settling back into life in Yorkshire. Ruby and Stan had seen more of him than Meg had. He'd spent hours listening to Stan play his violin and had been out cycling with Ruby, exploring the countryside. Meg had tried very hard not to feel envious when the children dashed off to meet him and she sat down with piles of evacuee paperwork to sift through.

Now, she smiled at Rolf. 'I'd love to have dinner with you,' she said.

'That's settled then.'

Lily beeped the car horn again.

'I must go,' Rolf said.

'Good luck,' Meg said. She stuck her head through the open car window and gave Stan another kiss. 'Good luck to you too!'

Rolf and Stan waved, Lily beeped the horn again, and off they went. Meg watched them go. She hoped they'd both have a successful day.

*

As she had predicted, Stan loved every minute of his first day. Meg met him from the bus and he hurtled down the steps and out of the door, already talking before his feet even hit the pavement. His hair was messy, and his tie was skew-whiff, but his smile was broad.

'The other boys are all wizard,' he said. 'I've made lots of friends. Hal lives on Treetops Farm, just past Emmerdale Farm. You know it? He plays piano. He's ever so good.'

Meg nodded.

'And a couple of the boys live in Hotten. There's Tim, he plays violin too, and Philip, and Jonathan . . .' He reeled off a list of names that Meg knew she wouldn't remember. 'What's for tea, Meg? I'm ravenous.'

Meg grinned. 'Chicken pie and mash.' She paused. 'But just for you and Ruby. I'm having mine with Rolf.'

They'd reached home now, and she opened the door to let Stan inside.

'Nice,' he said. 'What's he cooking?'

'No idea,' Meg said. 'Go and get changed out of your uniform – hang it up, don't just drop it on to the floor.'

Stan gave her a quick hug and she squeezed him tightly. How long would it be before he stopped wanting to cuddle her?

Both Stan and Ruby were exhausted after their exciting days. Meg sat at the kitchen table with them while they ate their tea, listening to them chatter and watching their eyelids drooping.

'Early night for both of you, I think,' she said.

She left the children playing cards in the lounge, the wireless on in the background, and went upstairs to get ready for her evening with Rolf. She brushed her hair until it shone, then tied it up neatly, and put on one of her favourite dresses from before the war, pulling in the waist with a belt because – like all of them – she was so much thinner now. She felt strangely nervous, as though this evening was important; not just dinner. She wanted to be with Rolf, there was no doubting that. Circumstance, time, Ruby and Stan, Rolf's nationality, had all got in the way, but now all the obstacles had gone. Would this evening be the start of something? She shivered in anticipation. She hoped so. She was nervous and excited all at once.

Rolf opened the door wearing a frilly pinny, with flour all over his face. Meg laughed out loud at his odd appearance, all nerves gone. He rubbed his nose, spreading more flour, and grimaced.

'My mother always made this look so easy.'

Meg followed him inside to the kitchen, which was also covered in flour. And potato peelings.

'What are we having?' she said, looking round at the devastation.

'Kartoffelpuffer.'

Meg was none the wiser. 'Potato . . .?'

'Potato pancakes,' said Rolf. 'They're so good. Puffy and golden with cheese. They sell them in the squares in Berlin from stalls.'

Meg's mouth watered. 'They sound delicious.'

'They remind me of home,' Rolf said.

Meg felt a rush of sorrow about Rolf losing his mother and his sisters and the place he'd grown up.

But Rolf just shook his head. 'At least they will, if I can cook the blooming things.'

'Blooming,' said Meg with a chuckle. 'You're picking up the Yorkshire phrases already.' She saw another apron hanging on a peg and slipped it over her own head. 'Let's cook them together, shall we?'

Swiftly, she swept all the potato peel into the bin and gave Rolf room to stir the pancake mixture.

'How was the interview?' she asked, picking up the cheese that was on the side. 'Shall I grate this?'

'Yes please.' Rolf stood up a bit straighter. 'The interview was a big success. They offered me a job teaching violin and piano.'

'Oh Rolf, that's wonderful,' Meg said. 'Are you pleased?'

'Relieved, I think,' Rolf said. He leaned against the worktop, looking tired for a second. 'I feel like my life can start again now.'

Meg nodded. 'A new start.'

'Exactly.'

'And they're all right, with you being German?'

Rolf made a face. 'Mr Potter, the headmaster, he's told everyone already that I'm Swiss. And he suggested I change my name. Because Schreiber is so obviously German, he thinks it'll cause problems. He said I should make it more English.'

'I've heard of others doing that,' Meg said.

'Seth told me he has a friend called George who did the same,' Rolf said. 'His father changed their name from Braumann to Brown.'

'Will you change yours?'

'I wasn't keen at first,' Rolf admitted. 'But, Meg, I want to stay here and build a life here.'

'So, what are you going to do?'

'Schreiber means writer,' Rolf said. 'So Mr Potter suggested Clark.'

'Rolf Clark,' Meg said. The name sounded odd, but not in a bad way. 'Mr Clark.'

'At your service,' Rolf said with a smile. 'Now, let's mix the cheese in here and we can cook.'

They had a lot of fun, making the pancakes. Meg ended up just as covered in flour as Rolf had been when she arrived. They ate them sitting together on the sofa, drinking beer that Rolf had bought from The Woolpack. They tucked napkins into their collars because the cheese oozed out of the pancakes and Meg laughed as she tried not to let it drip down her chin.

'I don't think you've ever looked so beautiful,' Rolf said to her.

'With flour in my hair and cheese grease on my face,' Meg said.

'Honestly,' said Rolf. He lifted the napkin from her collar and dabbed at her chin. 'You're the most beautiful woman I've ever seen.'

Meg's heart was thumping as he leaned forward and kissed her gently. She felt dizzy with happiness. Was this finally happening?

'Annie Pearson is in love with Jacob Sugden,' Rolf said.

Meg blinked at him in surprise, having no idea why he'd suddenly brought up her friend at such an intimate moment.

Rolf laced his fingers through Meg's, and carried on. 'I've seen her looking sad,' he said. 'She loves him, but they're not together. That's no way to live.'

Meg bit her lip. 'It's complicated with Annie,' she said. 'She's had some awful things happen to her in the past and she's still getting over them. But you're right. It's sad they're not together when they so clearly want to be.' She took a deep breath. 'I don't want to live like that.'

A smile played at the edges of Rolf's lips. 'What are you saying?'

Meg shifted along the sofa a little bit so she was closer to Rolf. 'I'm saying I want us to be together, Rolf. Properly. Forever.'

There was a pause and for a horrible moment she thought Rolf had changed his mind. That he'd come back to Beckindale just because he liked Yorkshire. That all the things he'd said that awful day by the river when they'd said goodbye to each other were forgotten. But finally, after what seemed like an age, he smiled, his blue eyes shining.

'I want us to be together too,' he said. 'Forever.'

They kissed again, longer and deeper than before. Meg sank into the embrace, marvelling at how it made her tingle from the top of her head to the tips of her toes. She'd never felt like this before.

'Meg Warcup,' said Rolf as they broke apart. 'I love you. Will you be my *mädchen*? My girl?'

'Rolf Clark,' said Meg with a smile. 'There's nothing I'd like more.'

They kissed again. Rolf wrapped his arms around Meg and pulled her closer so their bodies were pressing up against each other. Meg drank in the sensation. After so long apart, she just wanted to be with the man she loved, in every way possible.

'When will Nancy be back?' she asked breathlessly.

Rolf looked at her, his eyes full of love. 'Not until late,' he said. 'She's having tea with the Roberts family, then she said she was meeting June.'

'So we've got the cottage to ourselves?' Meg said.

Rolf kissed her. 'We have.'

Feeling bold, but not afraid, Meg stood up and held out her hand to Rolf. She wasn't at all nervous now. She knew this was the right thing to do. 'Show me your bedroom,' she said.

Rolf took her hand and stood up too. 'Are you sure?' he asked.

Meg kissed him, a long and lingering kiss. 'I've never been surer of anything in my whole life,' she said.

Chapter Thirty

Annie knew she was being miserable. She knew she was walking around under a dark cloud, but try as she might, she couldn't shift the gloomy mood that had settled on her since she realised she had fallen in love with Jacob.

She lay in bed every night, thinking about him. She imagined being close to him, kissing him, and more. And every time she did, Jacob's face was replaced in her mind with Oliver Skilbeck's scowl. She tried to think of being with Jacob, but instead she just remembered Oliver as he stood over her in the muddy field all those years ago, unbuckling his trousers, the leering grin on his face and the horror she'd felt as she'd realised what he was going to do.

'Everything is spoiled,' she'd said to Jacob later, when she'd told him what Oliver had done to her. She'd meant her relationship with Edward, at the time. Because the one time she and he had made love after Oliver attacked her, all Annie could do was cry. Of course, then Edward had been killed and she'd never had the chance to put it right. And now Oliver's actions were spoiling any chance she had of romance with Jacob, too.

She'd not thought about it much when she was in Portsmouth. She'd been too busy for romance, and there was no chance of bumping into Oliver, of course. So she'd been able to stick a bandage over the scars he'd left on her and carry on. But now she was back, it was like her wound was raw and exposed once more, and it hurt more than ever.

She had thought about getting a job on a different farm. Or leaving Beckindale behind and going somewhere else. Back to Portsmouth, perhaps? Or to visit Patricia, who'd gone home to Wales. She could start again, somewhere she had no history. Perhaps in time she'd meet someone new.

But the fact was, she loved Yorkshire. She loved Beckindale. She loved Emmerdale Farm. She sighed, staring out over the fields from where she stood at the top of the hill. This was her home and she didn't want to leave. She felt a surge of anger at Oliver Skilbeck. He'd taken so much from her – her dignity, her last night with Edward and now her chance of happiness with Jacob. She wasn't going to let him take her home from her, too.

She thought she could get over Jacob eventually. She could go back to seeing him as a friend. She'd have to really; it was the only solution, if she couldn't take things further. And, for now, she'd carry on avoiding him as much as possible, offering to do the jobs that took her to the fields at the very edge of the farm, and working until it was getting dark.

Today, Annie was getting some of the higher fields ready to sow winter wheat and barley. It was all new to her – something Maggie and Jacob had introduced after she'd joined up. But it was working so well, they'd decided to carry on with it even though the war was over. With the Sugdens still harvesting some crops, with the help of Ned Barlow and Annie's father Sam, Maggie had got her former Land Girl, Audrey, in to give Annie a hand.

Now Audrey and Ned were married, they had their own farm, but they'd taken it over after the crops had all been harvested. They intended to grow mostly fruit and vegetables – Ned's family owned the greengrocer in the village – so with just a few crops to plant and nothing to harvest, they had time to help the Sugdens. Thank goodness, Annie thought. Because it wasn't an easy job. She and Audrey had been working hard since dawn and it was now after eleven o'clock. She wiped her brow and waved to Audrey, who was standing a little way away, checking the seed drill.

'Audrey,' she called. 'Is it time for a tea break?'

Audrey waved back to show she'd heard and came marching up the field. Annie had a lot of time for the new Mrs Barlow. She was so determined and focused. Such a hard worker. She'd made the world of difference to Emmerdale Farm in the darkest days of the war, and Annie was fairly sure she was the person responsible for smoothing some of Jacob's prickliest corners. He'd become a much easier person to be around since he'd met Audrey. Less likely to blame others for his shortcomings and more willing to admit his mistakes.

Audrey's dog, Winston, came bounding over and Annie gave his ears a rub. He was a funny little thing with a wonky leg but so sweet-natured that everyone adored him. Annie knew Jacob had given him to Audrey and that made her feel uncharacteristically envious. Jacob had never given her a dog. Edward had rescued a donkey for her once, though. Neddy, he was called.

Audrey sat down with a sigh. 'We've done well this morning.'

'We've got more done than I expected.' Annie looked round, pleased with what they'd achieved.

'Was that what was making you smile?' Audrey said, unscrewing the flask of tea Annie had handed her.

'No,' Annie admitted. 'I was thinking about Edward.'

'Nice memories?'

'He rescued a donkey for me once. Neddy.'

'Aww, I remember Neddy,' Audrey said. 'He lived in the field with the carthorses when I first got here.'

'I was really sad when Maggie told me he'd died,' said Annie. 'He had such a character.'

'Jacob gave me Winston.'

'I know.' Annie gave Winston's tummy a rub. 'That's what made me think of Neddy.'

'And he gave Midnight to Susan.'

Annie nodded. 'I know that, too.'

'He comes across as grumpy, but he's got a good heart, has Jacob.'

Annie passed Audrey a piece of fruit loaf that Maggie had made and took the flask of tea to pour herself a cup.

'I know,' she said again.

Audrey gave her a funny look. 'So why are you avoiding him?'

'I'm not.'

'I've not seen you together since you came home,' Audrey said. 'He's always at one end of the farm and you're at the other.'

'So?'

'So, you spent the whole war writing to each other and now you're ignoring each other.' She took a bite of the cake and munched for a second. 'What's that all about?'

Annie regarded the other woman through narrowed eyes. 'Did Maggie tell you to ask me these questions?'

'No,' said Audrey defensively. But then she laughed. 'But she did say something, yes.'

Annie felt nervous suddenly. Maggie was so important to her, she didn't want to think that she'd been worrying over what she was up to.

'What did she say?'

'Just that you obviously weren't happy, and had you said anything to me?'

'And what did you say?'

'That I'd try to find out.' She looked at Annie carefully and Annie glanced away, feeling uncomfortable under her scrutiny. 'But I don't need to find out, do I? It's because of Jacob.'

Annie thought about denying it but changed her mind. Audrey was a good friend of Jacob's, and she might be able to shed some light on what he was thinking.

'It's Jacob,' she admitted.

Audrey nodded. 'You've realised how he feels about you and it's making you feel uncomfortable?'

Annie was shocked. 'No,' she said quickly. 'That's not it at all.'

'Then what?' Audrey frowned.

'It's nothing.' Annie popped the last bit of cake into her mouth and stood up. 'Shall we get on?'

'Really?' said Audrey. 'That's it? That's all you're going to tell me?'

Annie sighed and sat down again. 'You might know already,' she said, looking at the ground underneath her feet. After all, Oliver's sweetheart, Elizabeth Barlow, was Audrey's new sister-in-law.

Audrey gazed back at Annie, looking none the wiser.

'There was an incident,' Annie began. 'Between me and Oliver Skilbeck.'

Understanding grew on Audrey's face and she looked slightly awkward. 'Oh, yes, I heard.'

Annie raised her chin. 'He raped me,' she said, trying not to wince at the ugly word. 'And then he told everyone I was asking for it. Jacob almost killed him when he found out.'

'I heard that, too,' Audrey admitted. She paused. 'Ned said Jacob should have finished him off when he had the chance.'

Annie closed her eyes. 'That would have made everything a lot worse.'

'Would have made Beckindale a nicer place, though, I reckon,' Audrey said. 'Oliver's a nasty piece of work.'

Annie nodded, feeling heartened by the other woman's support. 'He's that all right.'

'So what's that go to do with Jacob?' Audrey asked. 'Are you in love with him?'

'In love with Jacob?' Annie said, feeling her cheeks flush bright red. She screwed up her face. 'I think I am.'

Audrey gave a little whoop of happiness. 'This is wonderful,' she said. 'He's been in love with you for years. Oh this is such good news.'

Annie put her head in her hands. 'It's not, because as soon as I even think about getting close to him, Audrey, the memories of Oliver come flooding back. I can't tell him the truth about how I feel, knowing I can't act on those feelings. It just wouldn't be fair.'

'Goodness,' said Audrey. 'That's awful.'

'I know,' wailed Annie.

'So you've not . . . since the incident?'

'Once, with Edward, before he went away. But it was terrible.'

Audrey made a face. 'What are you going to do?'

Annie felt completely hopeless. She shrugged. 'I'm just going to put one foot in front of the other and carry on, and hope Jacob meets someone else one day.'

'But that's not right,' Audrey argued.

Annie, though, had had enough. She didn't want to think about it any more. 'Come on, let's go down to the bottom of the field and carry on,' she said.

She walked off, taking big, purposeful strides to get her far away from Audrey and her questions.

Audrey laid off the topic for a while, to Annie's relief. They finished the sowing and Annie was careful only to talk about things that weren't so personal. Like the weather, or what crops the Barlows were planning for their new farm. But as they finished up and made their way back down to the farmhouse, Audrey started up again.

'Have you thought about talking to Oliver?' she suggested. 'Maybe you could tell him how his actions have affected you.'

'What good would that do?' Annie said, shuddering at the thought.

'I don't know,' Audrey said. 'It might help you put it all to bed.'

Annie winced at her choice of metaphor and Audrey flushed.

'Sorry,' she said.

Annie opened her mouth to say something else, then shut it again as she saw Nancy coming towards them from the farmhouse, holding her black bag full of her veterinary equipment.

'Hello there,' she called. But as she got closer, she looked at Audrey and Annie's faces and grimaced. 'What's going on? Are you arguing?'

Annie winced. 'No,' she said. She looked at Nancy. 'Why are you here?'

'Nice,' said Nancy with a smile. 'I came to see Jacob. He and Maggie have been talking about getting some sheep again, now the war's over, and he wanted me to check a few that Mr Smithers has for sale. I've been there this morning, so I just popped in to tell Jacob what I thought.'

'Have you seen him?' Annie said, glancing over Nancy's shoulder at the farmhouse.

'Yes, I saw him.'

Annie felt the fluttering in her stomach she always felt when she thought about coming face to face with Jacob Sugden.

'But he's gone back out to harvest the sugar beet,' Nancy carried on.

Annie felt deflated. Honestly, she spent all her time avoiding Jacob, only to feel let down when she didn't see him. She was a walking contradiction.

'I had dinner with Susan and her family yesterday,' Nancy said. 'A sort of goodbye before she goes off to university.'

Annie wasn't sure why she'd changed the subject so suddenly, but she was glad of it. 'Go on.'

'I was out for the whole evening. Didn't get back until late.'

'And?' Audrey looked as bemused as Annie felt about where Nancy was going with this.

'And Rolf invited Mcg round,' Nancy said. 'Judging by the big smile on his face this morning, their evening was a success.'

Annie was thrilled. 'Thank goodness for that. Meg deserves some happiness at last.'

'So do you,' said Nancy. 'It's clear you and Jacob adore each other. Why not tell him how you feel?'

Annie groaned. 'It's complicated,' she said.

'If Meg and Rolf can get over him being a German – a blooming Luftwaffe pilot no less – then you can get it together with Jacob Sugden,' said Nancy sternly.

'Annie's got a few issues,' Audrey said. Annie knew she was trying to be helpful, but she glared at the younger woman anyway.

'I have,' she admitted, after a long pause. 'Issues with Oliver Skilbeck.'

Nancy's puzzled face cleared. 'Oh, yes,' she said. 'I remember.'

'I think she should speak to Oliver,' Audrey said. 'Confront him.'

'Oh, I don't know about that.' Nancy shook her head. 'What if he's dangerous?'

'Exactly,' said Annie. The thought of being alone with Oliver made her feel sick and shaky.

But Nancy was thinking. 'What if someone went with you?'

'Nancy . . .' Annie began.

'Look,' Nancy said. She sounded firm and determined. 'I just think it's hard to find the right person, and if that person comes along, you should do whatever you can to grab your chance of happiness.'

Distracted for a second, Annie wondered why Nancy was so adamant. Had she found the right person? The only man she'd ever seen Nancy with was Nick Roberts and they seemed more like brother and sister.

'Or you could write him a letter,' Nancy said. 'Write Oliver a letter, telling him how he made you feel. You don't have to send it. Just getting your feelings out will help.'

That seemed a lot less frightening. Annie nodded. 'I could write a letter,' she said.

They were standing in the farmyard, and Nancy looked round. 'Here, use this to lean on,' she said, pulling a folder out of her bag and putting it flat down on a hay bale. 'I've got a pen and some paper.'

'Now?' said Annie.

'Yes, now.' Audrey nodded vigorously. 'Get it all out.'

'I don't want to.' Annie didn't like to think about the feelings Oliver stirred up inside her.

Audrey grasped Annie's hand. 'It might hurt at first, but I think it'll help. And then you can move on.'

Annie looked at her two friends and she sighed. 'All right,' she said. 'Give me the paper.'

She picked up the pen and wrote 'Dear Oliver,' at the top of the sheet. Then she scribbled out the word 'dear'. He wasn't dear to her.

'Oliver,' she said out loud.

'Go on,' Nancy said encouragingly.

'You hurt me,' Annie wrote. Her hand was shaking and her writing was wonky on the page. She didn't care. 'You took something from me that day in the field . . .'

And she was off. For a while she was back there, lying in the mud as Oliver sweated on top of her, thrusting painfully and not caring when she cried out. Then vomiting when he walked off and left her where she lay. Then she was cuddled up with Edward in the barn, sobbing her heart out because nothing felt the same, and he hadn't noticed. Or frantic with worry that Jacob was going to go to prison for smacking

Oliver on her behalf. Then she was on the hill with Jacob, after D-Day, desperate for him to kiss her and terrified that he would. She wrote it all down.

She wrote about the nightmares she'd had for months afterwards. How she was still jumpy if someone came up behind her suddenly. How she didn't like to be alone in a room with a man she didn't know. How she wanted to make things work with Jacob, but she didn't know how. And finally, as her hand began to ache, and tears fell in big splatters on to the pages, she wrote her final line.

I am not going to hate you any longer, Oliver. You are not worth my hate. Instead I am going to concentrate on my own life. You're worth nothing and you can't take anything else away from me.

She signed her name and looked up at Nancy and Audrey, who were watching her closely, both looking terribly worried.

'Now what?' she said.

'Did it help?' Nancy sounded concerned.

Annie thought for a second. She felt warmer, somehow. As though she'd closed a door that was letting in a draught. 'I think it did,' she said.

Audrey grinned. 'So now we burn it.'

She found a metal bucket and Annie screwed up the pages and threw them inside. Nancy gave her some matches and Annie lit one with a flourish and dropped it on to the paper. It caught immediately, sending orange flames up towards the women and making them all step back.

'It's over,' Annie said, watching the letter curl and turn black in the fire. 'It's over.'

Chapter Thirty-One

Annie felt so much lighter as she pulled on her overalls ready for a day on the farm, but she still had a niggle at the back of her mind. She may have put her feelings about Oliver to bed, but the only way to know for sure was to tell Jacob how she felt. Could she do it? What if he said he didn't feel the same? How humiliating would that be?

Mind you, she thought, if she did tell him the truth and he turned her down, she could leave Beckindale. She could go and see Patricia. Or visit Betty and Margaret in Birmingham. It wasn't what she wanted, but she knew more than anyone that life didn't always work out as you'd planned.

She glanced at herself in the mirror on her dressing table. Her face was pale and she had dark circles under her eyes from her disturbed night.

'You're not looking your best, Annie,' she said out loud. 'But you'll have to do.'

She would make sure she worked with Jacob today and when the moment presented itself, she'd tell him how she felt. Then, if he was horrified – or, she thought with a shudder, if he felt the same but those memories of Oliver showed themselves again – she could leave early and send a telegram to Patricia asking if she'd put her up for a while. There were plenty of farms in Wales. She could easily find herself a job.

But what would she say? She couldn't even remember telling Edward she loved him for the first time. It was just something they always knew.

She looked at her reflection again. 'Jacob, I've felt for a while now that I have been developing feelings . . .' she began. Urgh. That was too wordy. She'd have bored him half to death before she got to the point.

'Jacob, since Edward was killed . . .' No, absolutely not. Bringing up Edward was the last thing she should do.

'I've got something I need to talk to you about,' she said, in a serious tone. Goodness, he'd think she was dying or something.

She sat down on the bed and put her head in her hands. Maybe she should just be direct. 'I . . .' she began weakly. She sighed. If she couldn't say it here in her bedroom on her own, how would she ever say it to Jacob?

She took a deep breath. 'I love you,' she said. 'I love you.'

'Annie, is someone in there with you? Who are you talking to?' Her mother knocked on her bedroom door, making her jump and squirm with embarrassment.

'Just me, Mam,' she called. 'Talking to myself.'

'Your dad's about to leave,' her mum said. 'He says to hurry up if you want to go with him.'

Annie rolled her eyes. Her dad was working up at Emmerdale Farm again today and he liked to be early.

'I'm coming now, tell him,' she said. She had no more time to practise what to say to Jacob, she'd just have to see what happened. If she plucked up the courage to speak to him, of course.

She was quiet all the way up the hill to the farm. Sam asked her several times what was the matter, but she just told him she was tired. She wasn't lying; she was exhausted after her sleepless night. She hoped she could get away with doing something that didn't require too much concentration today. Whatever job Jacob was doing, she'd volunteer to help.

But when they were all gathered in the kitchen at the farm, drinking their morning cups of tea, Annie was annoyed to hear that Jacob was going to mend some broken tiles on the farmhouse roof.

'It's leaking,' he said to Maggie. 'That damp patch in the bedroom's getting bigger and, with autumn coming, I need to see to it as soon as I can.'

'You're right,' his mother said. 'That's fine. The sugar beet's all in now, and Audrey and Annie sowed the wheat yesterday. Sam and I can do the barley today.'

Sam nodded without speaking and Annie saw her chance. 'I'll help with the roof, Jacob,' she said. 'If you like?'

Jacob glanced at her sharply and Annie felt her cheeks flush. 'It'll be quicker with two.'

'You don't like heights,' he said.

Annie made a face. That was true, but if everyone else was up in the fields, it was a good opportunity to talk.

'I'll stay on the ground.'

Jacob looked like he was going to argue, then he obviously changed his mind. 'If you're sure.'

'Course.'

He drained his mug of tea and put it in the sink. 'Come on then,' he said. 'Let's get going.'

Obediently, Annie followed him out into the farmyard.

'Are you sure you're up to this?' he said. 'You look beat.'

'Didn't sleep very well,' Annie muttered.

'Don't nod off while you're holding the ladder.'

'I won't.'

'You'd better not.'

Annie tutted. He really was infuriating. She helped him pull a long ladder out of the barn and carry it round to the other side of the farmhouse.

'Careful,' Jacob said as she stumbled on an uneven bit of ground and let her grip slip a tiny amount. She tutted again.

'I am being careful.' Honestly, he really was a surly bugger. She was starting to think she wouldn't say anything at all. Did she honestly want to be his girl when he was so grumpy all the time?

'I can't afford any mistakes,' Jacob grumbled. 'These tiles were expensive.'

'I won't make any mistakes,' said Annie, through gritted teeth.

Jacob sighed as they carefully put the ladder up against the farmhouse wall. 'I'll go up and check what we need to do,' he said. 'You stay here and hold the ladder. Don't let it move, I don't want to fall.'

Annie gave him a sarcastic smile. 'No, that would be terrible.'

He huffed at her and climbed up to the roof. Annie stayed down below, trying not to look up for too long. He was right, she wasn't keen on heights. She didn't envy Jacob being up there. But he seemed fine. He'd got himself on to a flat bit of roof next to the gable window, and he was peering at the broken tiles.

'It's worse than I thought,' he called down. 'Might take a while.'

Annie shrugged. 'Fine.'

'I'll need at least ten of those tiles,' he said.

'Right.'

There was a pause. Annie, still gripping the ladder tightly, watched the horses in the field next to the house, their tails blowing in the wind, and thought she might like to take up riding again. It had been ages since she'd been on a horse.

'Annie,' Jacob shouted from the roof. 'Ten tiles. Go on.'

She looked up at his reddening, irritated face and scowled at him. 'Coming right up, master.'

The tiles were heavy and tricky to carry, so Annie had to go back and forwards to the barn where Jacob had stored them, ten times. Meanwhile, he was chipping away at the damaged bits on the roof, and throwing down the old tiles, so Annie was constantly dodging chips and shards as she carried her load.

Well, she thought as Jacob grumbled that she wasn't moving fast enough, that was one way to deal with this whole being agonisingly in love problem. She glared at his back while he climbed the ladder, muttering under his breath. Just spend a bit of time with the man you're in love with and he'll soon put you off him.

'Nancy said you're getting more sheep,' she called up to him.

'Coming next week.'

'Can I look after them?' Annie loved all kinds of farming, but she had always been keener on the animals than on growing crops.

Jacob tutted so loudly, the sound echoed around the yard. 'What do you know about sheep?'

'I know plenty,' Annie said. 'More than you.'

'I need another tile,' he said.

Annie held one up to him, her shoulders aching, and he clambered down the ladder to get it.

'What did you know about growing sugar beet?' she asked. 'Or flax?'

'WarAg told us what to do,' he muttered, snatching the tile from her so hard it grazed her fingers. 'We learned.'

'Then I'm sure I can learn how to look after sheep.'

He glanced over his shoulder at her as he went back up to the roof. 'P'raps.'

'Ned and Audrey are going to grow vegetables,' she said. 'Audrey says she wants to plant an orchard . . .'

'Annie, would you please stop blathering on,' Jacob snapped. 'I'm trying to concentrate and all I can hear is your chatter.'

Annie shut her mouth firmly. Horrible blooming man. She was just making conversation; there was no need for him to be so rude. What on earth had she been thinking, that she'd fallen in love with him? She watched him on the roof through narrowed eyes. He wasn't even handsome, not in a film-star way. He was more . . . What was the word? Rugged? Brooding. That was it. Like Heathcliff in *Wuthering Heights*. Annie wasn't much of a reader, but Meg had convinced her to read that one, and she had pictured Heathcliff as looking just like Jacob, all sullen stares and silent sulks.

No, Jacob was more brooding than handsome. She looked at him again as he stood, one foot braced against the top of the ladder. His legs were strong and the muscles of his thighs bulged against the fabric of his trousers. She tested her feelings. No, there was no fear there. No memories of Oliver. Just an . . . appreciation of what she saw. Annie swallowed, moving her eyes away, higher up his body. But the way his broad shoulders contrasted with the narrowness of his waist made her feel slightly breathless.

'For heaven's sake, Annie,' she muttered to herself. But she somehow couldn't drag her eyes away.

'What are you gawping at?' Jacob shouted down.

Ah, that did it. She glared at him. 'Just watching to see you're doing it right,' she said.

'Stop it, you're making me uncomfortable.'

Annie turned her attention back to the horses, until eventually Jacob called down to her. 'What do you reckon?'

She looked up. He'd done a good job, she had to admit. He replaced the tiles very neatly and you could hardly see the difference between the old roof and the new bits.

'You'll have to wait until it rains to check if it's watertight,' she said.

He nodded, straightening up and gazing across the fields, where Annie could see her father driving the tractor up and down in straight rows. 'It'll rain later, I reckon.'

Annie looked at the clear, hazy blue sky and screwed her face up. 'No chance. There's not a cloud to be seen.'

Jacob pointed at the trees in the distance. 'Birds are quiet,' he said.

'That's an old wives' tale.'

'Old Harry told me that, and he's never wrong.'

Annie actually had a lot of time for Harry, who'd lived in the village since he was a boy and was a fount of knowledge about the countryside. But she wasn't going to tell Jacob that. Not while he was being so bullish.

'I saw two crows flying together earlier,' she fibbed. 'That means it'll be fair. Harry told me that.'

Jacob looked down at her. 'The squirrels started burying their nuts early this year,' he said. 'That means it'll be a bad winter.'

'Ah, but there are lots of spiders spinning webs,' Annie said. 'All over the bushes in the village this morning, they were. That means a dry spell's coming.'

'You are infuriating, woman,' Jacob said with a groan. 'The leaves haven't started falling yet, have they? That means a bad winter.'

With a flourish, he flung his arm out and pointed to the woods in the distance, which were, indeed, still green. But the dramatic gesture made the ladder wobble. Annie tried to keep it straight, but Jacob's weight and the height of the ladder meant it slipped against the brick of the farmhouse and veered to one side. To Annie's horror, Jacob lost his footing and fell, his hands flailing in vain for the ladder. He landed with a sickening thump on the cobbled ground and lay still.

Annie let out a scream and raced to his side, throwing herself down. 'Jacob?' she gasped. 'Jacob, are you all right?'

He didn't move. Annie's heart lurched.

'Jacob,' she begged. 'Please say something, Jacob.'

Starting to cry, she put her ear to his chest. 'Breathe,' she said. 'Breathe.'

She could hear his heart beating. Relieved, she looked up at his face and saw his eyelids flicker.

'Jacob?' she said.

Slowly, he opened his eyes. Annie held her breath. Was he all right?

He frowned at her. 'I think I've broken my bloody arm.'

Annie let out a gasp of laughter. 'At least you've got something to complain about now,' she said. She flung herself on to him, laughing and crying at once. 'Thank goodness you're alive,' she said. 'Thank goodness.'

Jacob struggled to sit up and Annie helped him.

'I'll fetch Maggie and Dr Black,' she said. 'Don't try to stand.' She went to move, but with his good arm, Jacob reached out and held her close.

'Stay,' he said. His face was close to hers. She could feel his breath on her cheek and smell his sweat. Her torso was pushed up against his and his arm was warm on her back. 'Stay.'

Annie leaned forward and, gently, tentatively, touched her lips on his. Then, shocked by her own boldness, she pulled back again.

But this time Jacob leaned in and now their kiss was deeper. Annie wound her arms around his neck, stroking his thick hair just as she'd imagined. She was giddy with shock at his fall, and full of happiness, and longing, and sheer utter relief that the only person she was thinking about in this moment was Jacob. She pressed against him, letting herself relax into the kiss.

She wasn't sure how long they stayed there, on the hard ground of the farmyard, but eventually Jacob pulled away from her.

'Annie,' he said. His face was pale and his dark eyes looked enormous.

She smiled at him. 'Jacob.'

'Could you go and get Dr Black now, please? It really hurts.'

And then he fainted.

Chapter Thirty-Two

'I can't believe you fainted,' Annie said much later, after Jacob had come home from the hospital with his arm in plaster and gone to lie down.

She'd crept into his bedroom to see if he was asleep. Jacob had been propped up on his pillows, but his eyes were closed. Annie had made to close the door and sneak away without disturbing him, but he'd opened his eyes and looked at her. 'Come in,' he'd said.

She'd sat down next to him – carefully – so she didn't hurt him, and felt a bit silly. As though she wanted him to mention their kiss but also that she didn't. It was awkward and uncomfortable.

And then he'd smiled at her and she'd teased him about fainting and suddenly everything seemed more normal between them.

'You daft bugger,' Annie said fondly. 'I can't believe you'd go this far just to get a bit of time off. Honestly, as if I don't do enough around here already, and now you've just gone and doubled my blooming workload . . .'

Jacob didn't say anything. Instead he reached out and took

Annie's hand with his good hand and pulled her forwards and kissed her again. Annie's head span, convincing her that this was so right. She wanted to be with Jacob.

They stopped kissing and Annie grinned at him, feeling happier than she'd felt, oh, since Edward went away. He smiled back, his normally sullen face looking younger and more handsome.

'Can I sign your cast?' Annie said suddenly. She groaned inwardly. What a silly thing to say at such an intimate moment.

But Jacob just laughed. 'There's a pen on the bedside table, I think.'

Annie had a look, lifting up seed catalogues and a newspaper from two weeks ago to find it.

'Annie?' Jacob said as she was tutting about how untidy he was. 'Will you be my girl? Officially, like?'

Annie turned to him, a pen clutched in her hand. 'Pardon?' she said.

'Will you be my girl?'

Annie smiled at him and then she took the cap off the pen and scrawled 'yes please' on his cast.

They stayed together for a while, chatting and laughing and making plans.

'We should tell Maggie,' Annie said.

Jacob made a face. 'I suppose.'

'What?' Annie felt a prickle of unease. 'Do you think she'll be annoyed?'

'She wanted you to marry Edward,' Jacob said. A shadow crossed his face. 'What if she thinks I'm not good enough?'

'That's rubbish and you know it,' Annie said. 'You're being silly because you're tired and you need more painkillers.'

'Perhaps.' Jacob's eyelids were drooping.

Annie got up from the bed and found his bottle of pills. She shook out two and left them next to his glass of water.

'Here,' she said. 'Take these and get some sleep. You'll feel better tomorrow and we can tell your mum when you're stronger.'

Jacob nodded sleepily and Annie blew a kiss at him.

Annie had been fairly sure that Maggie would be thrilled to see Jacob settled, but his words about Edward had made her worry that she was wrong. What if Maggie didn't approve of Annie taking up with Jacob, when she'd once been engaged to his brother? What if everyone in Beckindale thought she was doing something wrong? Betraying Edward's memory. She'd tossed and turned in bed, and eventually she'd got up and gone over to her dressing table, where she had a photograph of Edward, looking handsome in his navy uniform.

'What do you think?' she asked him. Edward stared out at her, his serious expression not managing to hide the mischief in his eyes.

Sighing, Annie looked at her first love. He'd never grow old, she thought. But she and Jacob had a lot of life still to live. She touched a finger to his face in the photograph. Edward had been the nicest man she'd ever met. Still was. He was so kind, so caring, so thoughtful. Always a sunny smile for everyone he met. And even though his relationship with Jacob wasn't easy, he'd thought the world of his older brother.

'He'd be happy for us,' Annie thought. She was sure of it. She just hoped Maggie would feel the same.

*

Despite her conviction that she and Jacob were doing nothing wrong, Annie was relieved that Maggie was nowhere to be seen when she arrived at Emmerdale Farm. She poked her head round the kitchen door and said hello to Joseph, who was in his chair.

'Jacob . . .' he said. 'Looking for you.'

Annie felt a flutter of nerves. 'Where is he?'

'Barn,' said Joe. He gave Annie a sly look. 'Combed his hair.'

Annie reddened. 'I'll go and find him,' she said, backing out of the kitchen hurriedly.

She darted across the yard and into the barn. Jacob was in there, stacking hay bales with his one good arm. He looked round as his dog, Bella, barked to announce Annie's arrival, and for a second, Annie thought he'd changed his mind about everything. His expression was gloomy and he snapped at Bella to be quiet, which he never did.

But then he looked at Annie and smiled, his whole face lighting up, and Annie was flooded with relief.

'You look much better,' she said.

'Doesn't hurt so much now,' he said. 'It's just awkward. We're going to struggle a bit with me out of action.'

'I thought about that,' Annie said. 'Rolf's not starting his new job at the school for a while. I wondered if he'd help out.'

Jacob nodded. 'Not a bad idea,' he said. 'He was useful when he worked here as a POW.'

'And you and Maggie have a lot of clout in Beckindale,' Annie pointed out. 'You welcoming Rolf into Emmerdale Farm would really help him become part of the village.'

Jacob looked at her in a way that made her feel warm from the top of her head to the tips of her toes.

'You're a marvel, Annie Pearson,' he said. He opened his arms to her and she ran to him and he kissed her.

'I thought you'd had second thoughts when I saw you look so gloomy,' she murmured against his lips.

He held her at arm's length and regarded her thoughtfully. 'Well . . .' he said.

She gave him a nudge. 'Don't joke.'

They kissed again and Annie thought it felt like coming home.

'I haven't told Meg and Lily or my parents yet, but I will,' she said. 'Did you tell your dad?'

Jacob nodded. 'He'd worked it out, the old bugger. He sees more than we give him credit for, you know, sitting by that window, listening to everyone's conversations.'

Annie chuckled. She was very fond of Joseph.

'Still want to tell Maggie?'

Jacob took a deep breath. 'I think so.'

'I'd understand if you want to wait a while.' Annie bit her lip. Of course, she knew that Jacob and Maggie had a complicated relationship. He'd always been convinced his mother favoured Edward – that was why he was worried she'd think he wasn't good enough for Annie – and when Jacob had found out that Joseph wasn't Edward's father, things had got even more tricky.

As it turned out, during the Great War, Maggie had fallen in love with a conscientious objector called Hugo, who was working on the farm while Joe was away in the trenches, and he was Edward's real father. Hugo had died from Spanish flu just after Edward had been conceived and, actually, once Joseph returned from the war, he and Maggie had repaired their marriage. Joseph's experiences at the Front had changed him. It was a sad story of lost love, and Annie hated to dwell on it. But she knew that just as the last war had changed Joseph, this one had altered Jacob forever. He'd softened, and found forgiveness – for himself and for his mother.

'I want to tell her,' Jacob said. He played with Annie's hair, winding a strand round his finger. 'I want to tell everyone.'

Annie felt a tiny shiver of uncertainty. Once everyone knew about her and Jacob, there was no going back. Was this really what she wanted? But then she looked at him, standing there, his face flushed with love, and she smiled. 'Let's go and find her then.'

Maggie was by the empty sugar beet field, standing on the stile and looking out over the land.

'I can't face planting more beet,' she called as Annie and Jacob approached. 'Do you think we can stop growing it now the blooming war's over?'

'It's good feed for the cattle,' Jacob said, surly as ever. But he turned to Annie and gave her a tiny wink, letting her know he was teasing his mother.

'I want to grow more wheat,' Maggie said, then she saw Jacob's face and groaned. 'Are you pulling my leg?'

He laughed. 'A little bit.'

There was a pause while Maggie jumped down from the stile and looked at them both. 'Is everything all right? I thought you were off today, Annie?'

'I am,' Annie said. 'We just wanted to . . .' She stopped, looking at Jacob for guidance. They should have rehearsed what to say.

'Mam,' said Jacob. 'Something's happened.'

Maggie looked worried. 'What's happened?' she said. 'Is it Joe? Is he ill?'

Jacob put his hand on her arm to calm her. 'No, it's not Pa, it's me.'

Maggie opened her mouth again and Annie jumped in. 'And me.'

Tentatively, Jacob slid his good arm around Annie's shoulders. 'We've fallen in love,' he said. It sounded defiant, the way he said it, which made Annie wish he'd chosen a different tone, but no matter. It was done now.

'We have,' she added. 'I'm sorry.'

Gah, why had she said that? What did she have to be sorry for?

Maggie looked from Jacob to Annie and then back again. Annie felt like she was shrinking under the older woman's steady gaze. She spoke, just to break the silence.

'I loved Edward with all my heart,' she said, feeling close to tears. 'And when he was killed, I thought I would never be happy again. But since my time away with the Wrens, and coming home, I've realised I can find happiness with Jacob.' She faltered. *Please say something, Maggie*, she thought to herself. *Please say something*.

Maggie took a deep breath and Annie realised with a shock that she was trying not to cry. Oh god, they'd upset her. This was awful.

'Oh Jacob,' Maggie said softly. 'This is wonderful.'

Annie's heart thudded and she felt light-headed with relief.

'This is wonderful,' Maggie said again, more loudly this time. She threw her arms around both Annie and Jacob and squeezed them tightly, smothering them both with kisses. 'Oh my darlings, you deserve such happiness,' she said. 'I'm so pleased for you both.'

'You're not angry?' Annie said, untangling herself. 'I know you thought I would marry Edward.'

'Angry? Not at all. You can't spend your life grieving for Edward. And I'm so pleased you'll still be part of the family. You were always meant to be a Sugden.'

'Steady on, Mam,' said Jacob, but he was grinning broadly and Annie smiled too. She belonged at Emmerdale Farm.

Chapter Thirty-Three

Birmingham

Betty was feeling wretched. She couldn't believe her bad luck – she'd come to Birmingham to escape man problems and she'd just found more trouble instead.

The truth was, she'd fallen hard for Roderick. Since that first meeting in the club, he'd visited regularly and she'd spent more time with him, laughing and enjoying the way he looked at her. She was absolutely sure she wasn't imagining it. His admiring glances when she served his drinks. And last night he'd run his hand up her leg as she cleared the table, making her jump as heat coursed through her and drop her tray with a clatter.

She sighed and turned over in bed. But, of course, the awful, terrible thing about it all was that Roderick was still stepping out with Margaret. She called him Roddie. It made Betty want to throw up, how giggly and simpering Margaret became when she was with him. He was a strong man. Clever and thoughtful, with noble good looks. He deserved something more than a silly girl like Margaret.

'Stop it, Betty,' she told herself out loud. 'Stop it.'

Margaret thought Roderick was going to propose. Betty thought that he should probably stop looking at her the way he did if he was going to marry her sister. But she kept her mouth shut about that because, the truth was, she enjoyed him looking at her that way. She liked him an awful lot. She thought about him all the time. Dreamed about him. And last night she'd fallen into bed after her shift at the club feeling her leg burn where he'd touched her.

She loved Margaret and she would never want to upset her. But she was finding it so hard to be around Roderick without acting on her feelings. She was even starting to feel sorry for Jacob Sugden, who'd been in love with Annie Pearson for a hundred years and never done anything about it. Suddenly she understood why he was so grumpy all the time. Watching Annie so happy with Edward must have been hard for him. She hoped he and Annie would get it together. See! That's how out of sorts she was. Wishing happiness for Jacob blooming Sugden.

Margaret was working an early shift today, thank goodness, so she had already gone to work. And Betty was working at the club later, so they'd not see each other.

Roderick turning out to be Mr Bartlett had made Betty's work at the hospital more exciting. She'd seen him a few times around the corridors and felt a little thrill. She wondered if he'd be there today. She hoped so.

Betty dragged herself out of bed and threw on her uniform. Then, thinking about the possibility of seeing Roderick, she did her hair and face more carefully than usual.

*

293

The morning went so slowly, she wanted to cry. Betty worked in the outpatients department and Roderick was a surgeon, so he didn't have any need to come in to her part of the hospital. It didn't stop her hoping, though. She kept looking up every time someone walked by, until Mrs Trentham complained that she was like a jack-in-a-box and could she please stay still.

After lunch, Mrs Trentham, who was still annoyed with Betty for being too fidgety, said she could use up some of her energy and take a load of X-rays up to a ward.

Betty took the folders and wandered off to the lifts. She was going to a ward on the top floor and she wasn't climbing up all those stairs and getting sweaty.

She got in the lift and pressed the button for the sixth floor. The lift went up to number one in its usual juddery fashion and then stopped. Betty sighed. The stairs would have been quicker. But the doors opened and there, looking devilishly handsome in his white coat, was Roderick.

Betty was so surprised to see him that she let out a little gasp.

He smiled at her. 'Hello there, Miss Prendagast,' he said. Then he turned to the person next to him – a man on crutches – and asked, in his charming fashion, if he was going up. The man shook his head, so it was just Roderick who got into the lift with Betty.

The doors closed slowly. Betty could smell Roderick's cologne. She thought she'd never been so aware of the sheer presence of a man before. She tried to keep her eyes on the floor, and not meet his gaze, but as the doors shut, and the lift began to move, he turned to her and suddenly they were kissing, deeply and frantically, leaning against the wall in the lift. Betty's X-rays dropped to the floor because she needed both her hands to hold on to Roderick and she felt dizzy with desire.

Then, with a ting, the lift creaked to a halt. Roderick let go of Betty and straightened his white coat. Betty scrabbled on the floor for the fallen X-rays and watched as he got out of the lift without a word.

'Good heavens,' Mrs Trentham said, when Betty got back to reception. 'You look like you've been dragged through a hedge backwards. What happened to your hair?'

Betty's curls were hanging over her face, because Roderick had run his hands through them, and her lipstick was gone, because he'd kissed it all off. And she didn't care one tiny bit. She beamed at Mrs Trentham and the older woman stared back disapprovingly.

He kissed me, Betty kept thinking all day. *He kissed me.* Her heart was singing and she pushed away any guilt she felt about Margaret. Roderick wasn't good enough for her anyway. Margaret was far too sweet and pure for a man like him. She'd even confessed to Betty that she didn't want to do anything more than kiss Roddie until he asked her to marry him. 'It wouldn't be right,' she had said to Betty. Betty had groaned inwardly at that, wondering how on earth Margaret could resist. But she thought it just proved that Roderick wasn't right for poor Margaret. She deserved someone who didn't make eyes at her sister and kiss her in a lift.

Betty's giddiness lasted all day and into the evening, until Roderick didn't turn up at the club. Betty felt gloomy. Why wasn't he here? Why hadn't he come to see her after their illicit kiss. Betty had a little shiver of excitement, thinking about the feeling of his body pushed up against hers in the lift.

Maybe he was feeling guilty, she thought. Maybe – her heart lurched – he was off confessing to Margaret right this minute. Urgh. Nothing was ever easy, was it?

She was so fed up that she asked to move from serving tables to making drinks behind the bar, just so she didn't have to smile at the customers, and her boss let her go early because he thought she was poorly.

Betty took her coat and her hat from the cloakroom and went out into the dark city-centre night. She was still amazed every time she stepped out into the night without needing a torch. She loved that the blackout was over and that she didn't have to worry about being mowed down by a dark bus every time she crossed the road.

The cold took her breath away and she pulled her hat down over her ears as she climbed the steps up from the club's basement entrance to the street. She hurried out on to the pavement, still a bit annoyed that Roderick hadn't showed up. Oh goodness me, it was cold. She hoped she didn't have to wait too long for a bus.

But it definitely wasn't her lucky night. She had been standing at the bus stop for at least half an hour, and her head was aching with the cold, when a car pulled up in front of her. Betty looked in the other direction deliberately. Surely the driver hadn't mistaken her for some sort of working girl?

Out of the corner of her eye, she watched as the door to the driver's side opened and a man got out, wearing a thick coat and a hat.

And then, with relief and joy, the man took his hat off and she realised it was Roderick.

'Fancy a lift?' he called.

Betty looked at him, thinking carefully. She wasn't stupid. She knew if she got in the car with him, then chances were she'd be powerless to resist if he tried to kiss her again. That would be wrong, she thought. If Margaret ever found out, then well . . .

She shivered, half with cold and half with the thought of what Margaret would think of her.

'Come on, Betty,' Roderick called. 'You must be freezing.'

'I can't feel my toes,' she told him.

He grinned at her, and came round to the passenger side of the car, opening the door for her like a chauffeur.

Betty paused for half a second, then she danced over the pavement and got into the car.

Roderick got in to the driver's seat, but he didn't start the engine. Instead they looked at one another.

'You finished work early?' he said.

Betty nodded. 'I wasn't feeling well.'

Roderick winked at her in a way that made her giggle. 'Maybe you should see a doctor.'

And then his lips were on hers again and they were kissing so fiercely that Betty thought she might pass out. Her heart was thumping and she wondered if Roderick could feel it against his chest.

'Not here,' Roderick murmured against her neck. 'Come back to mine?'

This time Betty didn't hesitate. 'Drive on,' she said.

Chapter Thirty-Four

DECEMBER 1945

'I told you it'd be a bad winter,' said Jacob, from where he was sitting on the fence, watching Annie dig the feed they'd stored for the cows.

Annie glared at him. 'Old Harry said that, did he?'

'He did actually.'

'And did he tell you that watching while your girlfriend does all the work is a very bad idea?'

Jacob jumped down from the fence with a grin and came properly inside the feed shed where Annie was working. 'He didn't have to.' He picked up a spade and Annie shook her head.

'Don't worry. It's done now. Where have you been all morning, anyway?'

'Had to see Dr Black about my arm,' Jacob said, pulling up his sleeve and showing Annie that his cast was gone. 'He says it should be back to full strength in no time.'

'That's great news,' Annie said, dropping a kiss on his bare forearm. She tugged his sleeve back down and shivered. 'It's too cold for exposed flesh.'

'Shame,' said Jacob. He pulled her close and kissed her properly. Annie melted against him, snuggling into his thick jumper.

It was freezing. The temperature had dropped suddenly a few days earlier and now a heavy frost sat across the fields. The ground was frozen solid and the animals were all inside, where they could keep warm. Everything was iced over, but there had been no snow. Not yet.

Jacob pulled Annie's woolly hat over her ears and kissed her nose. 'Are you finished for the day?'

'I guess so, there's not much more to do.'

He grinned. 'Come with me then.'

Annie hung her spade on the hook on the wall and followed him out of the feeding shed and across the yard towards the farmhouse.

'Wait here,' he said.

'I thought we were going for a cup of tea?'

'No,' Jacob said with a mischievous glance over his shoulder. 'This is so much better than that.'

Annie was wearing gloves, but her hands were still cold. She shoved them under her armpits and stomped her feet to keep her toes from freezing while she waited for Jacob to come back. They'd been a proper couple for a while now, though actually it felt so normal it was almost as though they'd always been together. Jacob surprised Annie every day. He had his moments, obviously, where he went back to his old surly self. But when he was with her, he was sweet-natured and caring.

Jacob had been odd for the last few days, though, distracted and a bit 'off' with her. And though he'd obviously been telling the truth about seeing Dr Black this morning, he kept disappearing and she wasn't sure where he was going. All in all, she was beginning to worry he'd changed his mind. Perhaps he didn't want to be with her after all? Annie thought. Perhaps he'd realised he preferred being single. Or maybe he'd met someone else? The thought made her feel queasy.

She peered through the window of the farmhouse, trying to see where he'd gone, but she couldn't see him. What was he up to?

Jacob appeared, wearing a thick winter coat and scarf, and carrying Annie's overcoat, which she'd left in the kitchen that morning. She didn't like to wear a coat while she was working, preferring to put on a thick jumper that didn't get in the way. Jacob had a large parcel, tied up in fabric, in his arms too.

'Here,' he said, awkwardly juggling the parcel so she could take her coat. 'You'll need this.'

'Where are we going?' Annie put on her coat, gratefully. 'You'll see.'

Off he strode. Annie had to jog to catch up with his long legs. They walked down the hill, hand in hand, their boots crunching on the frosty grass and their breath puffing in clouds. Jacob's dog, Bella, darted around their legs, enjoying the exercise.

'Where are we going?' Annie asked again, as they skirted the woods that hugged the river. 'Where are you taking me?'

Jacob was infuriatingly silent.

'Jacob,' said Annie. Once more she felt nervous. Was he going to tell her it wasn't working? Say he thought they should break up?

But he led her through the trees to the edge of the river. Normally, the water where they stood widened and slowed into a broad pool, popular with swimmers in the summer because it was deeper there than under the bridge near the village where the children played, and calmer than on the bend where little Hope had her frightening adventure. But today it was completely frozen.

'Oh my goodness,' Annie sighed. 'I've not seen it like this since we were children.'

'I know.' Jacob looked delighted. 'I stumbled on it when I was out walking with Bella yesterday.'

'Is the ice thick?'

Jacob nodded. He pointed to the centre of the pool. 'Can you see that the ice is kind of transparent?'

Annie looked. He was right. It looked clear and blue, rather than frosty.

'That should mean it's safe. But just to be sure, I checked. It's four inches deep.'

'Four inches?' Annie was astonished. 'I knew it was cold, but, goodness, that's really solid.'

'Want to skate?' Jacob said, his eyes glinting with fun in the weak sunshine.

'I don't have skates.'

'Ah, but you do . . .' Jacob put his parcel down on the ground and unwrapped it. 'I went up into the loft and found these.'

Annie crouched down. There, nestled in the fabric, were her old ice skates. She'd not worn them for a long time. Maybe ten years. Maybe even longer. A sudden memory of gripping Edward's hand while she taught him how to move his feet on the ice, and tried not to laugh at his frightened face, hit her and she felt dizzy.

Jacob put his hand on her arm, ever so gently. 'I know,' he said. 'I felt the same.' Now Annie remembered Jacob had

been there too. He was a better skater than Edward and had
shown off, racing round and trying to make Edward fall over
so he could laugh at him. But that was then, Annie thought.
It was time to make new memories now. She smiled up at
Jacob, letting him know she was grateful.

'I can't believe you found them,' she said.

'They were with Edward's things.' Jacob frowned. 'Mam's
packed everything away, but it's safely stored.'

Annie thought she'd quite like to have a look at Edward's
things one day, but she wasn't sure how she would be able to
ask. So instead she picked up one of the skates and looked
at it. 'They're good as new.'

'So, do you want to skate?'

Annie looked at the pristine ice and decided she did want
to skate, very much.

'Let's go.'

They pulled off their boots and laced up the skates. It was
funny, Annie thought, how your muscles remembered just
how tightly to pull the laces, and how to bend the leather
at the top to make it easier for the foot to slide in.

'Sure it's safe?' she said, looking at the ice.

'I'm sure,' said Jacob. 'But I'll go first if you like.'

He went to step forward and Annie caught him round the
waist. 'Just be really careful,' she begged. 'You don't want
to fall on your arm.'

Jacob looked down at her and smiled and Annie caught
her breath as she saw the love in his eyes. She'd been so silly
to doubt his feelings. She was lucky to have him.

Carefully, Jacob stepped on to the ice and pushed off. He
was wobbly at first, but as he skated round the edge of the
pond, his confidence grew.

He stopped beside Annie and held his hand out. 'Come on,' he said.

Trusting him completely, she stepped out on to the frozen pond and she was off, gliding across the ice just as she had all those years ago.

Round and round they went, gasping with the cold, and laughing when one of them stumbled. It was exhilarating being out there on the ice, with her nose red from the icy wind and her cheeks glowing.

'Race you,' Jacob said and he sped off, his skates sending up a shower of frozen drops as he went.

'Oi,' shouted Annie. 'That's not fair!' She put her head down and raced after him, her breath ragged and her legs aching from the effort. Edward, she thought, would have let her win. She quite liked that Jacob didn't.

She reached the far side of the pond just seconds behind Jacob. He threw his arms up in triumph.

'Jacob Sugden takes the title of Beckindale's champion ice skater,' he declared.

Annie bent over, with her hands on her knees, trying to catch her breath. 'Unfortunately, you've been disqualified for cheating,' she said.

'Is that right?'

Annie grinned at him. 'Rematch,' she shouted and headed off back the way they'd come. But Jacob was too fast. He caught up with her, grabbed her arms and span her round until she was dizzy from the turning and from laughing so much. Jacob let go of her and the sudden difference in his balance made him stumble and slide inelegantly down on to his backside.

Annie giggled and he pulled her down next to him and kissed her.

'I love you,' Annie said, resting on his chest and looking into his dark eyes, so often hooded and sullen, but today sparkling with fun and mischief.

'Annie . . .' Jacob began. 'I wanted to . . .'

The sound of voices stopped him. They both glanced round and there, coming towards the pond, was a group of people from Beckindale.

Jacob looked cross for a second and then he gave Annie a quick kiss. 'Later,' he said.

With a bit of ungraceful effort, he got to his feet and helped Annie up too.

'Hello there!' he shouted to the approaching villagers. 'I knew having the pond to ourselves was too good to be true.'

Annie spotted Stan Dobbs, and lots of his friends from the cricket team. There were some older children too. Ruby and Susan, who was home from her first term at university and looked quite the young woman now, along with some of Susan's schoolfriends and a couple of Ruby's cycling club pals. Annie watched them all with a touch of nostalgia. They were just like she, Jacob and Edward had been during the last big freeze, she thought.

'Having fun?' Annie turned to see Nancy Tate and her friend June.

'It's silly, but it's wonderful,' Annie said. 'Can you skate?'

Nancy made a face. 'Not well,' she admitted. 'But June's going to teach me some moves.'

June was sitting on a tree trunk lacing up skates that were the most beautiful white leather, rather than Annie's utilitarian brown boots.

'She looks like an expert,' she told Nancy.

Nancy grinned. 'I've yet to find something that June's not good at.'

June looked up. 'Two left feet,' she said. 'I dance like an elephant.'

Nancy beamed at her friend. 'If Betty Prendagast ever comes back, I'll get her to give you some lessons.'

'Betty Prendagast is no match for my disastrous dancing,' laughed June.

Annie watched the two of them chatter back and forth. They'd become very good friends since June came home from the WAAF, she thought. That was really nice for them.

She waited for June to get up, then plonked herself down on the tree trunk she'd been sitting on. She needed a rest.

Contentedly, she watched the skaters take to the ice. Ruby was, predictably, not graceful but totally fearless, whizzing across the ice. Susan was more cautious, following behind slowly as she gained confidence. Stan and his cricket friends were more interested in pushing each other over. Annie laughed to herself as she watched.

Jacob stood to one side, chatting to Nick – Susan's father. He wasn't skating, but, like Annie, he seemed to be enjoying watching. Annie eyed him curiously, wondering if there was something going on between him and Nancy. She watched as Nancy skated past him and he pretended he was going to trip her up. She stuck her tongue out and whooshed past, and Annie frowned. They seemed more like brother and sister than lovers, she thought. Their gentle teasing and silly games reminded her of how Lily was with Jed Dingle, who was more like a brother than a cousin to Lil.

On the ice, Nancy had stopped and was watching June spin in tight circles. Annie looked at Nancy's face and, with a start, she realised the expression she wore as she watched June was just the same as the way Jacob looked at her.

'Well I never,' she said out loud. 'Well I never.'

She watched as June finished her spin and stopped, looking to see if Nancy was impressed. Nancy clapped wildly and June gave a little bow. Then, the women, both laughing, gripped hands and set off round the ice once more.

Annie wasn't sure what to think, or even if she'd really seen what she thought she'd seen. Two women? Was that legal? She knew two men who fell in love could be thrown in prison. She looked at Nancy and June again, holding hands and gliding over the pond together. They both looked very happy, she realised. And Nancy, who'd always been on the tetchy side, was calm and content these days.

'To think I thought it was Nick,' she said under her breath.

'What are you muttering to yourself about?' Jacob said, crunching over the frosty ground in his skates.

'Nothing,' said Annie.

Jacob narrowed his eyes at her. 'It wasn't nothing.'

Annie sighed. He knew her too well to be fooled. 'I'm not sure,' she said in a quiet voice. 'But I think there might be something going on with Nancy . . .'

'And Nick?' Jacob said. 'Nah, he says they're just mates.'

'Not Nick,' Annie said. She stopped for a second, wondering if she should say anything.

'Who is it?' said Jacob, sounding like he wasn't that interested.

Annie nodded her head in the direction of Nancy and June. 'I think it's June.'

Jacob's eyes widened. He looked at the women and then back at Annie. For a second she regretted telling him, unsure how he'd react. Goodness, she wasn't even sure how she felt about it. But then he shrugged. 'Good luck to them,' he said.

'Do you think so?' Annie said. 'Isn't it . . .'

'What?'

'Wrong?'

Jacob shrugged. 'Don't bother me,' he said.

Annie was surprised by his reaction. 'She looks so happy, doesn't she?'

'She does.'

'And you really think it's all right?'

'None of our business, is it?' Jacob said. 'You might be wrong, anyhow.'

Annie doubted that. There was no mistaking the love in the women's eyes as they gazed at one another. But Jacob was right. It wasn't any of their business.

'Don't say anything to anyone, will you?'

'Who do you take me for?' Jacob said. 'Nora Prendagast?'

Annie chuckled. Betty's mother was the most notorious gossip in Beckindale.

Jacob stood behind her and put his hands on her shoulders. She leaned back, her head resting on his firm stomach, and looked up at him.

'It's been the most perfect day,' she said.

Jacob grinned. 'It's not over yet.'

'What else have you got up your sleeve, Mr Sugden?' Annie was charmed by how sweet he was being.

'Budge up,' Jacob said.

Annie shuffled along the trunk a little so he could sit next to her, and he turned to face her. He looked slightly odd, she thought. Nervous and out of sorts again.

'Annie,' he began. 'These last few months with you by my side have been the happiest of my life.'

Annie smiled at him. Her romance with Edward had been happy and carefree. And while being with Jacob wasn't the same, there was no doubt it was . . . What was the word? Restorative. Bringing hope where there had been none.

Jacob took a deep breath and felt in his pocket, wriggling so much on the tree trunk that he almost shoved Annie off.

'Careful,' she started to grumble but then stopped short as she realised he was holding out a ring. A tiny gold circle, with a red stone in it that caught the light and sparkled in the hazy winter sunshine.

'Annie, would you marry me?' Jacob said in a rush, his words tumbling over each other.

Annie stared at him. Of all the things she'd been expecting him to say, a proposal hadn't entered her head.

'That's where I was this morning,' Jacob said, still looking worried. 'I went to Dr Black and then I had a chat with your dad. Asked his permission, you know? And then I spoke to Mam and got the ring. It belonged to my gran. I was going to ask you earlier, but then everyone arrived and ruined it.'

He was babbling because she wasn't answering, Annie realised, but she still couldn't speak. Memories of Edward flooded her mind, but then new memories too, of Jacob. And, slowly, she nodded.

'Yes, Jacob,' she said. 'I will marry you.'

Chapter Thirty-Five

Lily was staring up at the bare branches of the large oak tree in the centre of the village, where a small cat was mewing pitifully.

'I can't climb up because I'm too pregnant. If you come down a few branches, I'll be able to reach you,' she said. The cat looked at her in disdain and she tutted. 'I'm trying to help you.'

'What's going on, Lil?' said a voice behind her. She turned to see little Stan Dobbs. Not so little now. He was taller than she was and growing into such a nice young man. Lily was very pleased to see him.

'There's a tiny cat stuck up there, and it won't come down,' she said. 'I think it might belong to Nora Prendagast.'

And, sure enough, Nora was coming along the path, calling: 'Smudge! Smudge!'

'He's here,' Lily shouted. 'I think he's stuck.'

Nora came hurrying over. 'Honestly, I got this kitten to keep me company when our Betty went to Birmingham,' she said. 'But I think he's more trouble than she is.'

Lily snorted. 'Doubt that,' she said with a giggle.

Nora rolled her eyes. 'You're right.' She looked up at the cat and he looked back at her. 'I can't climb up and get him.'

'I can,' said Stan, already shrugging off his coat. 'Hold this.'

He threw his coat at Lily and clambered up the trunk like a monkey. He reached Smudge just as the kitten was about to jump up to a higher branch. 'Oh no you don't,' he said. He grabbed the cat and held him with one hand against his chest, and then shimmied back down the tree.

'Here he is,' he said triumphantly, handing the little animal to Nora.

'Thank you,' Lily said to him, as Nora took Smudge and held him up to her face.

'You silly thing,' she said, then she gasped. 'Oh, he's bleeding.'

'We should take him to Nancy to check him over,' Lily said.

'It's lunchtime,' Nora said. 'I don't like to disturb her.'

'Oh get away, you're Betty's mam. Nancy won't mind one bit,' Lily assured her. 'If the front door is locked, we'll go in the back way. She'll just be eating a sandwich at her desk, if I know Nancy.'

She gave Stan back his coat, and he tied it round his waist, making Lily worry about what Meg would think of him treating his good duffel like that, said goodbye and ran off.

'Come on,' Lily said. 'Let's go and find Nancy.'

They walked over to the vet's surgery. Nora chattering all the way.

'Annie Pearson and Jacob Sugden are getting wed,' she said. 'Isn't that something? Reckon Maggie will be pleased. Mind you, must be strange, to have had both sons engaged to the same woman at one time.'

'Maggie is pleased,' Lily said.

'Have you spoken to her about it?' Nora asked. 'What did she say?'

Lily didn't reply. Having been at the receiving end of rumours and chatter when she was pregnant with Hope, she didn't like to join in with gossip if she could help it.

'Let's go to the main entrance first, shall we?' she said instead, going up the path to the surgery. She tried the front door, but it was locked, as Lily had thought it would be. 'Come round the back way,' she said.

She led Nora past the side of the surgery and round to the back door. It was open and the women went inside. The back door led straight into the treatment room, with its steel table and cages for the animals. Lily could hear muffled talking and laughing in the other room.

'She's in reception,' she said to Nora. 'Go on through.'

Lily opened the door and let Nora, still cradling Smudge to her chest, go ahead of her. Lily followed behind.

They both saw them at the same time. Lily and Nora stood by the door, staring in shock at Nancy and June.

June was sitting on one of the comfortable chairs where people waited for their animal's name to be called. And Nancy was sitting on her lap, her arms tightly wound round June's neck, kissing her deeply. June's hand was on Nancy's thigh and, as Nora and Lily watched, both frozen with shock, she moved it higher up her leg . . .

'Oh my goodness,' Lily gasped and the two women sprang apart. Nancy leapt to her feet, her face bright red.

'Lily,' she said, 'I didn't know the door was open.'

'That's obvious,' snapped Nora.

June and Nancy both turned to stare at Nora, who was looking at them with a mixture of disgust and delight.

'What on earth were you doing?' Nora asked. 'What disgusting scenes have I just walked in on?'

She's going to tell everyone, Lily thought to herself. *The whole village will know by tea-time.*

'This isn't how it looks . . .' Nancy said vaguely.

June stood up too, looking pale and worried. 'Nora,' she said. 'I'm not sure what you thought you saw, but . . .' she trailed off. Lily wasn't surprised. There was absolutely no doubting what they'd seen.

Nora looked sick. 'I think it was exactly how it looked,' she said, turning to leave. 'I'll take Smudge to the vet in Hotten.'

'No, don't do that, please,' Nancy said. She sounded a bit desperate. 'I can help. Is he ill?'

'He got stuck up a tree,' Lily said faintly. She was finding it hard to make sense of what she'd seen. Nancy and June? Kissing like that?

Nancy took a step towards Nora, and Lily noticed that some of the buttons on her blouse were undone. She felt her cheeks flame. Nancy's eyes followed Lily's gaze and she reached out, pulled on her white coat and did it up, all the way to her neck.

'Let's have a look at him,' she said, holding her arms out for the cat.

Reluctantly, Nora handed him over, and Nancy held him up to her face.

'He's a sweetie,' she said. 'Come through to the treatment room and I'll check him over.'

'Maybe I'll go,' Lily said.

'Stay, please,' Nancy begged.

She went out to the back room and Nora followed in silence. Lily and June looked at each other. Lily was never short of something to chat about, but she couldn't think of a single word to say to June now.

June shifted from one foot to the other and then she picked up her coat and hat. 'I'm going home.'

She went out of the surgery like someone was chasing her, and Lily watched her go, hurrying through the cold village, her breath making little puffy clouds as she went.

'Has June gone?' Nancy came back into the waiting room.

'She said she was going home.' Lily's attention was caught by Nora, who she could see through the window. She'd obviously gone out the back way and round to the street. She was still clutching Smudge, who looked none the worse for his escapade, and she was talking to Mrs Connor from the butcher's. 'Heavens,' Lily muttered. If Nora Prendagast was a gossip, then Mrs Connor was even worse.

Nancy looked out of the window and went pale.

'Lily,' she said. 'Do you hate me?'

Lily wasn't sure what to say. She wasn't completely sure how she felt about two women doing . . . well, whatever Nancy and June had been doing. But Nancy was her friend. She shook her head. 'Of course I don't hate you.'

Nancy looked relieved.

'Will you go to prison?' Lily said. She knew that men could be locked up for having a relationship with someone of the same sex. Was it the same for women? She felt a sudden rush of fear at the idea of losing her friend.

'No,' Nancy said. 'Thankfully.'

'Do you love her?' Lily said. 'Do you love June?'

Very slowly, Nancy nodded her head. 'I do.'

Lily's head span.

Nancy shrugged. 'You can't help who you fall in love with, Lily. You know that better than some people.'

Lily winced at the comparison. This was nothing like her and Derek. But then she thought again. In a way, it was. In fact, in a way, it was less harmful and immoral than her romance with Derek had been. Nancy and June weren't hurting anyone. Neither of them were married. She looked at Nancy, who was biting her lip and watching out of the window as Mrs Connor and Mrs Prendagast said goodbye and hurried off – no doubt to spread the word to everyone they saw. Nora stopped to chat to Elizabeth Barlow and Lily shuddered. She would delight in spreading the word. She imagined the gossip being shared around the village like poison coursing through infected veins.

'Lily?' said Nancy.

Lily sighed. She was a romantic at heart and she knew that Nancy had been happier these last few months than she had been since she'd come to Beckindale.

'You can't help who you fall in love with,' she repeated. She reached out and gave Nancy's arm a little squeeze to show her support.

Nancy gave her a small, sad smile. 'Thank you,' she said. 'Do you think everyone else will feel the same?'

Lily couldn't lie to her. She made a face. 'I don't think so.'

Nancy looked like she was going to cry, then, with a huge effort, she managed to fight the tears. 'I think I need a drink,' she said. 'Woolie?'

Lily was horribly aware how fast a juicy piece of gossip like this could spread round the village. She thought that it could already have reached The Woolpack. But she nodded. 'Woolie,' she said.

It took them a while to get going. Almost as though they were putting off going out in public. Nancy cleaned up the treatment room where she'd looked after little Smudge, then she had some paperwork to finish, and Lily helped with a bit of filing.

Eventually, Nancy was ready to go. She found her coat, and Lily reminded her to lock the back door, and Nancy did so with a roll of her eyes.

'Puts me in mind of stable doors and horses,' she said wryly.

Then, arm in arm, the two women walked across the village. Well, Lily waddled – because she was really very pregnant now. There was no sign of Mrs Connor or Nora, and Elizabeth Barlow had gone, but Oliver Skilbeck was coming out of the pub as they approached. He looked at the women with a leering smile.

'Careful there, Lil,' he said. 'Pretty girl like you. She won't be able to resist.'

'Shut up, Oliver,' Lily spat. 'No one's interested.'

'Shame,' he said, walking past them and looking at Nancy with undisguised lust. 'I'd have liked to have seen that.'

His raucous laugh echoed round the houses as he swaggered away.

Nancy's hand tightened on Lily's arm. 'How does he know?' she said. 'It's only been a couple of hours. Has Nora told everyone already?'

Lily felt sick. 'Word spreads fast,' she said.

Nancy sat down on the bench outside the pub. 'June's mother is in a sewing bee with Mrs Connor.' She swallowed. 'They're good friends.'

'Are they?' said Lily, though she knew that and had been worrying about it since she saw Nora chatting with the other woman outside the surgery.

'She might already have told her.'

'She might have.'

Nancy stood up again. 'I should go and see if June's all right.'

Lily reached out a hand to stop her, thinking that wasn't a good idea, when the sound of shouting made them both look round.

June was standing on the path of her parents' cottage. 'You're not listening,' she was shouting.

Lily couldn't see Mrs Butterfield, but she could hear her wailing like a banshee. June's father appeared in the doorway and spoke to his daughter. June stood, head down like a scolded schoolgirl, and nodded as he talked. He went back inside the house and came out again with a small suitcase, which he put down on the path next to June. Then he pulled out his wallet and handed June some money and without saying anything else he went inside and shut the door. June stood looking at the house for a minute or two, then she picked up the case and started walking towards the bus stop.

'June!' Nancy called. She got up and dashed down the stairs from the pub and over to where the other woman stood, shoulders slumped. Lily followed, much more slowly, and when she got to the bus stop, June and Nancy were standing close together, but not touching. Both of them were crying.

'I'm going to stay with my horrible grandmother in Sheffield,' June was saying. 'Everyone knows, Nancy. Everyone's talking about us. My mother said she was going to put a bath in the centre of the village and scrub me clean in front of everyone.'

Lily winced. Mrs Butterfield was well known to be a stern mother, who believed firmly that if you spared the rod, you

316

spoiled the child. She had no doubt that she would carry out her threat, and more besides.

'Will you come back?' Nancy whispered.

June shrugged. 'One day, maybe.'

'I'm so sorry,' Nancy said.

June scoffed. 'Never be sorry.'

Lily found she was crying too. She was so sad for them. They hadn't meant for any of this to happen. She turned away as they hugged, feeling like she was intruding on a private moment, and then the bus pulled up at the stop.

'Goodbye,' June said in a croaky voice. She blew a kiss to Nancy, picked up her case, and climbed aboard.

Nancy waited until the bus doors had shut, and then she threw herself into Lily's arms, sobbing her heart out. Lily held her friend tightly, wishing she could do something to make her feel better, but knowing there was nothing to be done. It was over.

Chapter Thirty-Six

Meg tied her scarf more tightly and shoved her hands into the pockets of her cardigan. It was freezing in the village hall and she was starting to lose the feeling in her fingers.

'Can we do it all the way through once more,' she said to the children. 'I know it's cold, but let's just make sure we've got it all right.'

The children all groaned, but as Stan played a chord on the piano to get them ready to sing, their faces lit up. Meg smiled as she listened to them singing 'Away in a Manger'. She had organised so many nativity plays in her time at the school, but she never got bored. The children were so sweetly eager to get it right, and everyone loved Christmas, didn't they? Especially this year – the first without the war casting a shadow over the festivities. So many families reunited after years apart. Meg thought that was definitely worth celebrating, even if there was still some sadness.

She let the children's singing wash over her as she thought about her plans for Christmas. It was still three weeks away, but it was always good to have things worked out. She had planned a double celebration. A German Christmas on the twenty-fourth and then British festivities the following day. Meg had written to Rolf's sister Liesbeth to ask for the recipes of some of Rolf's favourite festive treats, copying the address from a letter Rolf had written. She knew Klara, one of his sisters who'd been killed in a bombing raid on Berlin, had loved something called stollen. Rolf had explained it was a type of cake with dried fruit inside, but Meg had no idea what it was supposed to look like, so she was keeping her fingers crossed that Liesbeth understood her request. Rationing was still in force, of course, but Meg was hoping that she could make her own version for Rolf, to make him feel more at home. Then, the next day – Christmas Day – there would be church in the morning, of course, and then Rolf was going to come for a slap-up lunch.

'Lovely,' she said as the children finished. 'You all sound like little Yorkshire angels.'

'Miss, do you think it will snow?' asked Jimmy Jones from the farm cottages on the estate. 'My da says it won't.'

'He's wrong. My mam says it'll snow today,' said Agnes Bulliver. She was a tiny slip of a girl, with enough courage to stand up for herself against anyone, much to Meg's delight. 'My mam never gets things wrong.'

Meg looked out of the window at the leaden sky. It had been heavy with snow for days, and the temperature was so low, it hurt to be outside for long. Stan and Ruby had been skating on the frozen pond more than once, and Rolf and Meg had plans to go themselves if the cold snap continued. But there had been no snow. Not yet.

'Miss, Agnes is being mean,' said Jimmy.

'Is she really being mean, or is she just disagreeing with you?' asked Meg with a grin. She exchanged an amused glance with Stan over the top of the piano and felt a pang. He was so grown-up now; thriving at his new school, taller than she was. But it only felt like five minutes since he'd been one of the little ones in her class, cowering away from attention and crying himself to sleep.

'I heard the most wonderful sound and had to come and see who was making it,' said a voice.

Thrilled, Meg turned to see Rolf coming into the hall. He was wearing a new overcoat with a furry lapel and a warm deerstalker-style hat. He looked extremely handsome, she thought.

'It was us,' said Jimmy proudly. 'And Agnes.' Agnes glared at him and he shut his mouth tightly.

'Never,' said Rolf. 'I thought it was a group of professional singers.'

'Hello, Mr Clark,' said Stan, waving at Rolf from where he sat on the piano.

Meg made a face, wondering if she'd ever get used to hearing Rolf called Mr Clark. Perhaps she would. It was astonishing what you got used to when you had to. The war had shown her that.

'You can call me Rolf, out of school,' he said to Stan. 'It sounds odd to my ears, hearing you speak so formally to me in Beckindale.'

Stan grinned. 'Hello, Rolf,' he said.

It wasn't just Stan who was thriving at the new school; Rolf had fitted right in and was thoroughly enjoying being involved in music again. He'd had a chance to join an orchestra in America before the war but had chosen to stay and fight for Germany instead. Meg wasn't sure she'd ever quite understand that decision, but in a funny way she was glad. After all, it was because of him choosing to join the Luftwaffe that they'd met.

'We were just finishing up,' she told him. 'But I can get the children to sing another song, if you'd like?'

'I would like,' he said.

'How about "While Shepherds Watched Their Flocks", children?' Meg said.

Stan played the first few bars, the children all opened their mouths and the carol swelled through the village hall. Meg felt absurdly happy. Proud of the children, thrilled to bits with how well Stan was doing, chuffed that Rolf was in her life.

'Miss, miss!' One by one, the children were stopping singing and chattering excitedly. 'Miss, look!'

She turned to the window and there – finally – were fat snowflakes drifting down.

Agnes nodded and turned to Jimmy. 'Told you,' she said.

Keen to avert another argument, Meg clapped her hands. 'You can all go,' she said. 'Coats on first, though!'

Cheering madly, the children all scuffled for their things and then dashed out of the village hall, leaving the doors wide open.

Meg went over and pulled them shut, noticing the snow was coming down heavier now and beginning to settle on the ground. How lovely. Maybe they were in for another white Christmas.

'Are you busy?' she asked Rolf. 'I just need to tidy up here, and then we could go for a drink, if you're free?'

'I'm free as a bird,' said Rolf. 'Shall I help pick up the music?'

'Thank you.' Meg went to where Stan was loitering by the piano, looking hopefully at the falling snow. 'You go,' she said to her son, giving him a kiss that he immediately rubbed away with the heel of his hand. 'Don't get too cold and wet.'

'See you later,' Stan called over his shoulder as he dashed off. 'Bye, Mr Clark. I mean, Rolf.'

With the hall to themselves, Meg found herself wrapped in Rolf's arms.

'Hello,' she said, giving him a kiss. 'I've missed you.'

Rolf looked at his wristwatch over her shoulder. 'You saw me three hours ago.'

'Too long,' Meg joked.

They kissed for a while and then broke apart as a polite cough echoed round the village hall.

'Sorry to interrupt,' said Nancy, who was standing by the door, bundled up in an enormous scarf.

'Don't be sorry,' said Meg, reluctantly letting Rolf go. 'Were you after Rolf?'

'I was,' said Nancy. She waved a small package at him. 'This arrived for you,' she said. 'I know you were waiting for it.'

Rolf virtually snatched it from her hands. 'Oh thank you,' he said. 'I have been hoping this would arrive soon.'

Meg watched curiously. 'What is it?'

'Just something from Germany,' Rolf said vaguely. He took one of Nancy's hands. 'How are you doing?'

Nancy gave him a tiny smile. 'Not great,' she admitted. 'Just putting one foot in front of the other.'

Meg had been astonished when she'd heard about Nancy and June. Astonished and a little bit ashamed that their friend hadn't felt able to confide in them. Annie had confessed that she'd worked it out, but Lily had said she hadn't a clue until she saw them together. Meg had also been unaware, though Rolf, being Nancy's lodger, had an inkling. Meg thought she was in no position to judge anyone on their romantic choices, and she just felt very sorry for Nancy, who was still the talk of the village.

'Are you missing June?'

Nancy pinched her lips together. 'Madly.'

'Have you heard from her?'

'Not yet.'

Meg gave her friend a little squeeze. 'Things will work out,' she assured her. 'They always do.'

'Not this time,' Nancy said bleakly. 'I've written to Mr Walters.'

Meg widened her eyes. Mr Walters was the owner of the vet's practice. Despite being in his fifties, he'd joined the Royal Army Veterinary Corps and spent the war caring for the animals who were part of the campaign. Meg knew he'd gone up to Scotland, where his wife had spent the war, when he was demobbed, and that Nancy had been hoping he would decide to stay there.

She narrowed her eyes. 'Why did you write to him?'

Nancy shrugged. 'Beckindale is June's home,' she said. 'She belongs here. If I go, she can come back.'

'Oh Nancy,' Meg said. 'Where would you go?'

'Back to Scarborough. My father says he could do with my help in his surgery now.'

Nancy's father was a vet too and though he'd doubted her abilities at first, thinking women weren't up to the job, she'd proved her worth.

'Is that what you want?'

Nancy shook her head. 'I want to stay in Beckindale with

323

June,' she said bitterly. 'But that can't happen now.'

'Don't make any hasty decisions, will you?' said Meg. 'You never know what could happen.'

Nancy nodded, but she didn't look convinced. 'I'll let you get on,' she said, and headed off.

Meg looked out of the window, where Nancy was hurrying past, hunched down against the bitter wind. 'I'm so sad for her. It's heartbreaking when people find love and they can't be together.'

'I agree,' said Rolf.

Meg tugged his sleeve. 'So what's in the package?' she asked. 'Who's it from?'

'It's from Liesbeth in Berlin.'

'Open it.'

Rolf slid his finger under the flap of the packet and upended it. Out fell a smaller package and a brown envelope.

'This has your name on it,' he said, turning it over and looking at it quizzically. 'Why is Liesbeth writing to you?'

Meg tried to grab the letter, but he was too fast, holding it up and out of the way.

'Are you expecting her to write?'

'I am,' said Meg, totally unable to lie to him when he looked so baffled. 'It's a surprise for you.' She looked at the small packet. 'What has she sent you?'

Rolf grinned. 'It's a surprise for you.'

Meg sat down on one of the chairs they'd been using for Mary and Joseph in the stable. 'Is it a Christmas surprise?'

Rolf sat down next to her and put his feet up on the box that was standing in for the manger.

'Geroff,' said Meg, slapping his legs away. 'That's baby Jesus.'

'Oops, sorry.' Rolf gave her a cheeky grin. 'So tell me why

324

my sister is sending you a letter.'

'It's for Christmas,' Meg said. 'What's in the package?'

Rolf shifted his chair a little closer. 'It's for Christmas.'

There was a pause.

'You know,' said Meg, casually, 'Christmas is still three weeks away.'

'It is.'

'That's a long time to wait.'

'It is.'

She grinned. 'I'll show you mine, if you show me yours.'

'Or,' said Rolf, 'I could just see yours.'

In one swift move, he snatched the envelope from her hands and darted across the hall, tearing it open.

'Rolf,' Meg protested, but she wasn't really cross. She didn't mind if he knew what she'd asked Liesbeth for.

She looked over to where Rolf was standing very still, staring at the sheet of notepaper.

'Rolf?' she said again, worried this time.

He looked up at her and, to her distress, she saw tears shining in his eyes.

'Stollen,' he said.

'I remembered you telling me that you had it for Christmas, and that it was Klara's favourite,' Meg said carefully, worried she'd upset him. 'I wanted to make it for you, to bring back some happy memories.'

Rolf frowned. 'And you wrote to Liesbeth? How did you know where to send the letter?'

'I copied it from one of your letters to her, a few weeks ago.'

His face twisted, as though he was trying very hard not to cry. Rolf looked at Meg. She looked back, scared she'd made a huge mistake.

But then he spoke. 'This is the most thoughtful thing anyone has ever done for me.' He came over to where Meg stood and wrapped his arms around her. 'You are the kindest woman, Meg Warcup. Thank you.'

Meg sank into his embrace, thankful that he wasn't sad.

'And now,' said Rolf, 'your letter from Liesbeth has made me see that I should not wait a moment longer to show you what is in my package.'

He turned away from Meg a little bit and tore off the paper. Meg heard him sigh in contentment and then he faced her again.

'Meg, I love you very much,' he said. 'Will you be my wife?' He held out his hand and nestled on his palm was a thin gold bracelet. 'I don't have a ring,' he said. 'But Liesbeth sent me this to give you. It belonged to our mother; she was given it on her twenty-first birthday by my grandparents.'

Meg was speechless with happiness. She nodded so vigorously she thought her head might fall off, and held out her wrist for Rolf to fasten the bracelet around it.

'Is that a yes?' Rolf said.

Over the moon, Meg threw herself into his arms and kissed him. 'Yes, a thousand times yes,' she said, laughing and crying all at once. 'The children will be thrilled,' she said, when she felt a bit calmer. She admired the bracelet glinting on her wrist. 'We should tell them first, before anyone else.'

Rolf cleared his throat. 'They already know.'

'What?'

'I know in England it is traditional to ask the bride's father for permission,' Rolf said. 'But I asked Ruby and Stan instead.'

Meg was charmed. 'What did they say?'

'Stan slapped me on the back like a man, and said well done,' said Rolf, smiling at the memory. 'And Ruby very seriously told me that I had to look after you, or she would – let me remember the precise words she used – sort me out?'

Meg laughed. 'That's exactly what I would have said they'd both say.'

'Shall we go to The Woolpack and have a drink to celebrate?'

'Excellent idea.'

They bundled themselves up in their coats and hats and headed out into the snow. It was settling thickly on the ground beneath their feet and on the cottage walls. It was quiet and beautiful in the village and very cold.

They scurried across to the pub, taking care not to slip, and Meg pushed open the door. Inside was warm and cosy, a fire burning brightly in the hearth. She stopped for a second, enjoying the heat, and then blinked in surprise, because the drinkers were all raising up a toast.

'Congratulations!' Jed was saying.

Meg turned to Rolf in confusion. How did they all know?

Rolf looked blankly at her. 'It's impossible. I didn't know myself.'

And then Annie flung herself at Meg. 'Where have you been? Did you forget we were having drinks to celebrate our engagement?'

Meg actually had forgotten. She'd been so busy with the nativity rehearsals, and worrying about Nancy, and planning the perfect German Christmas for Rolf, that Annie and Jacob's engagement party had completely slipped her mind.

She felt awful.

'Gosh, I'm so sorry,' she said. 'But we're here now and ready to celebrate with you.'

'Come and have a drink,' Annie said, pulling Meg's hand.

'Hang on.' Meg looked at Rolf and he gave a tiny nod. 'I've got something to tell you, too.' Annie looked at her and Meg smiled. 'We're engaged, too!'

With an ear-piercing shriek of joy, Annie gathered Meg and Rolf into a hug. And then Lily was there, and Jack, and Maggie Sugden. Jacob hovered close by, smiling broader than Meg had ever seen him. Jed slapped Rolf on the back and said well done, Nick Roberts bought him a pint, and Annie's father shook him firmly by the hand. Meg was delighted. It seemed Rolf really was part of Beckindale already.

'The future Mrs Sugden and Mrs Schreiber,' Lily said later, when all the hubbub had died down and the three women had a chance to chat.

'Clark,' Meg reminded her. 'I'll be Mrs Clark.'

'Annie Sugden,' said Annie dreamily. 'It sounds exactly right.'

Lily's eyes filled with tears and Meg gave her a shove. 'Stop being so soppy,' she said. 'The sooner you have that baby, the better.'

Lily giggled, stroking her rounded belly in contentment. 'Have you and Jacob set a date, Annie?'

Annie shrugged. 'Whenever we can,' she said. 'No point in waiting. What about you, Meg?'

Meg thought. 'I always wanted to get married at Christmas,' she said. 'It's such a special time of year, and Christmas Eve is my birthday, too. And the children's, of course, now. And I love Christmas carols.'

Lily grinned. 'So why not?' she said. 'Why not do it at

Christmas?'

'It's only three weeks away,' Meg said.

'We'll all help,' Lily said. 'Won't we, Annie?'

Annie was looking thoughtful. 'Or,' she said, 'we could do it together.'

'A double wedding?' Lily said. 'Is that even allowed?'

'I don't see why not,' Annie said. She reached over and took Meg's hand. 'What do you say, Meg? Fancy walking down the aisle together on Christmas Eve?'

Meg felt a surge of excitement. She was so happy she wanted to scream it from the rooftops, but instead she just squeezed Annie's fingers.

'Absolutely,' she said. 'A Christmas wedding. Could anything be more perfect?'

Chapter Thirty-Seven

Birmingham

Betty was trying her hardest to stay away from Roderick. Trying but failing. She kept telling him that enough was enough. She'd told him that if he was still with Margaret then she couldn't keep seeing him, but somehow fate just kept throwing them together.

But not today, she thought with determination. Margaret was working and Betty had the day off from the hospital and the evening off from the club. She was going to stay at home and tidy up and maybe even do a bit of cleaning. That should stop Thora looking at her in that disappointed way at least.

But first she was going to have a bath, and wash her hair.

She lay in the water and read a magazine until her fingers got wrinkly, then she got dry and put on her underwear and her dressing gown, and wrapped a towel round her head, and sat in front of the fire to dry her hair. Christmas was almost here. She'd thought about going back to Beckindale for the festivities. But Margaret had to work, and Betty had said she would stay in Birmingham to keep her company. The fact that Roderick was going to be there too hadn't played a part in her deciding to stay. Not at all. Well, maybe a tiny bit.

Once she was warm and her hair was almost dry, she went to make herself a cup of tea. While she was waiting for the kettle to boil, there was a knock at the door. She sighed. She wasn't expecting anyone. Perhaps someone was lost and needed directions.

But there, at the door, stood Roderick.

'Hello there,' he said jovially as she answered. 'Just got up?'

'Just had a bath,' Betty said, trying to ignore the thumping in her chest as he glanced at her bare legs.

'Is Margaret in?'

'She's working.'

'She is?' Roderick put his hand to his forehead in mock surprise. 'Goodness me, I'd forgotten.'

Betty rolled her eyes, and then shivered as a blast of icy wind whipped round her.

'Let's get inside,' said Roderick. 'It's freezing.'

Betty thought about saying no, and telling him to come back later. That's what she knew she should do. But the kettle was whistling. Where was the harm in having a cup of tea with him? There was nothing wrong with that, was there? Just a cup of tea.

'Let me go and put some proper clothes on,' Betty muttered, showing him inside.

'No need,' Roderick said. 'Honestly, don't go to any trouble on my account.'

Roderick sat in the lounge as Betty made the tea, leaning back against the corner of the settee, arms above his head. Betty found her eyes drawn to him as he sat there. He knew how good-looking he was. He wore his handsome face like a badge of honour. He was so different from Seth. And Wally. And all the men she'd known in Beckindale. Self-assured, charming, fond of the finer things in life . . . She shook her head. And Margaret's boyfriend, she reminded herself. That kiss in the lift had been an accident. And the time in the car, well, it was cold and she wasn't feeling her best. And going back to his house instead of letting him drive her home had just been an error of judgement.

But as she put the tea down in front of him, he put his arm around her waist and pulled her towards him.

'How can you look just as lovely in your dressing gown as you do in your glad rags?' he said.

Flattered, Betty slapped his hands away. 'Enough,' she said, firmly. 'I'm off limits.'

Roderick grinned. 'You're right in front of me.'

Betty knew she should move away, though she didn't.

He reached for her again, and this time she let him pull her down on top of him, kissing her and pulling her dressing gown off before she'd even realised what he was doing.

Roderick's shirt soon joined her dressing gown on the floor. Betty was lost in the moment, enjoying the way his skin felt against hers and the way his hands explored her body. She didn't even hear Margaret open the front door. Didn't even realise she was there, until she was standing right beside them, her face white with shock.

'Margaret,' Betty said in horror. She scrambled for her dressing gown and pulled it over herself, hiding her bare skin.

Roderick sat up more slowly. Betty reached for his shirt and threw it at him. Margaret still hadn't said a word. She was just staring at them, a tear snaking down her cheek.

'Why aren't you at work?' Betty said. 'You said you wouldn't be back until after tea-time.'

'I'm not feeling well. Sister sent me home.' Margaret's voice was heavy with tears. 'How could you, Betty?'

Betty felt a rush of shame. Worse than she'd felt after her night with Wally Eagleton. Why did she keep doing this to people she loved? she wondered.

'I'm sorry,' she whispered.

Margaret's face went from white to red. 'You're the worst person I know,' she said to Betty. 'You don't care who you hurt, as long as you're happy.'

'That's not true,' Betty argued weakly. She felt awful. Margaret's disappointment was so much harder to cope with than her anger.

'It is true,' Margaret said. 'You cheated on Seth, and now you've seduced my boyfriend.'

'I didn't mean it,' Betty said. Her argument sounded pathetic to her own ears. 'Margaret, you're my sister. I would never do anything to hurt you.'

Margaret snorted. 'You have,' she said. 'You've hurt me more than anyone else has ever hurt me. You've broken my heart just like you broke poor Seth's.'

Betty started to cry and Margaret stared at her in disgust. 'You can't be sad now, it's too late.'

'I'm so sorry,' Betty sobbed. 'How can I make it up to you?'

'You can't,' Margaret said coldly. 'We're done.'

Betty felt sick. 'Do you want me to leave?'

'There's a train to Leeds at six o'clock,' Margaret said. 'You'd better start packing.'

Going back to Yorkshire was the last thing Betty wanted. But perhaps it was for the best, just for a few weeks. She'd been writing to her dancing friend Pamela and they'd made a few plans that Betty had put on hold because of the lure of Roderick. But perhaps she could go back to Beckindale for Christmas, and then see how things were in the new year. She nodded at Margaret. 'All right,' she said. 'I'll go.'

Roderick had put his shirt on and his coat, and now he was edging towards the door. 'I'm going to leave,' he muttered.

Margaret turned to him, her face suddenly twisted in anger. 'Yes, you'd better go,' she said fiercely. 'Get out. I never want to see you again either.'

'Margaret,' he said, looking devastated. 'I'm so sorry. Darling Mags, you know you're the girl for me. I came to see you, forgetting that you were working today. Betty invited me in, and she was prancing around half-naked, flirting with me. I couldn't resist, and I'm sorry. I'm so weak. You have to forgive me.'

Betty tutted in disgust. 'Don't believe a word he says, Margaret,' she snarled. 'This wasn't a one-time mistake – we've been doing it for weeks. And he made the first move. He's not good enough for you, Margaret. I've done you a favour really. You can't trust him.'

But Margaret was staring at her sister, shaking her head. 'That doesn't make it better, Betty,' she said, sounding totally astonished. 'It makes it worse. Much worse.'

'Does it?' Betty was genuinely confused. 'But he seduced me, Margaret. He was flirting with me at the club before I even knew who he was.'

'And once you knew, did you come to me and warn me? Or did you jump into bed with him as soon as you could?'

'You wouldn't have believed me,' Betty said. 'You were so starry-eyed over your Mr Bartlett that you wouldn't have believed me if I'd told you the truth.'

Margaret looked straight at Betty, her eyes red and sore from crying. 'I would have believed you,' she said. 'Because I trusted you, Betty. But not now I know you've been sneaking around for weeks with my boyfriend. In fact, I don't think I'll ever believe anything you say, ever again.'

Chastened, Betty nodded. 'I'll go and pack.'

'I'm going to the post office to send a telegram to Mam,' Margaret said. 'I think she should know why you're coming home, don't you?'

'Oh Margaret, really?' Betty didn't want to have to face her parents with them knowing the truth.

'You can't just do as you want and not face the consequences, Betty,' Margaret said. 'I'm going out and then I'll go for a lie-down. Please don't disturb me when you leave.'

'I'll give you a lift,' Roderick said to Margaret.

Betty snorted. 'She doesn't want a lift,' she said.

But Margaret simply nodded. 'That would be helpful, thank you.'

'You know what?' Betty said, suddenly full of rage. 'You two deserve each other.' She glowered at Roderick. 'I hope you're very happy together.'

Then she turned and ran upstairs to her bedroom to pack her bags. It seemed she would be back in Beckindale for Christmas after all.

Chapter Thirty-Eight

Betty stepped down from the bus and looked around. She'd been away for a year, but Beckindale didn't seem to have changed a bit. Except for the lights. When she'd left, everything had been in darkness, because of the blackout. Now, lights flooded out of every cottage, making the falling snow shimmer.

'Home sweet home,' she said, with more than a little touch of bitterness. She pictured Margaret's tear-stained face again and shoved the memory aside. It was done now.

Betty held her suitcase in frozen fingers and glanced over to where her parents' cottage was. The curtains were drawn – normal curtains, not blackouts – but she could see light leaking out round the edges. They were home, of course. They'd be expecting her. She took a breath. Time to face the music, she supposed.

A burst of laughter from the pub made her look round. Perhaps she should have a drink first? Bit of Dutch courage before she went home to see her father's disappointment and her mother's disapproval. Yes, a drink was a good idea.

Slipping in her unsuitable shoes, she made her way across the village. The snow reminded her of last Christmas, when she'd spent the night with Wally. She screwed her face up as the guilt and sadness she'd felt over her break-up with Seth came flooding back.

'Oh Betty,' she said to herself softly. 'What are you like?'

Well, that was it for a while, she thought. She'd sworn off men; they just caused trouble and made her feel wretched. She was going to concentrate on herself for a while. Margaret's face appeared in her mind's eye again, blotchy and ugly with anger as she shouted at Betty and Roderick. She grimaced at the memory.

So, yes, she was off men for a while. And, actually, Margaret should do the same, because Roderick had been very quick to succumb to Betty's charms, so she was willing to bet she wasn't the first woman he'd been with behind her sister's back. He really was a rotter. Margaret should be grateful.

The buzz of conversation from the pub was louder now and for a second Betty faltered, her courage deserting her. Did she want to go and see everyone? Face a barrage of questions about why she was back?

She paused by the door, looking from The Woolpack to her parents' cottage and back again. She didn't really want to go into the pub, but she wanted a drink. So The Woolie it was. She took a deep breath, pulled back her shoulders, lifted her chin and painted on her best smile.

'Let's go,' she said out loud.

Inside was mercifully cosy and busier than usual and no one noticed Betty when she walked in. She was both pleased about that and slightly disappointed. She'd half expected everyone to turn and stare at her as she arrived.

In the corner, she could see Lily – who was enormously pregnant – chatting in an excited fashion with Meg Warcup and Annie Pearson. They all looked flushed, happy and giggly. It made Betty feel a little envious. She knew all about Annie and Jacob, of course, her mother had written a long gossipy letter about them getting together. And what about Meg Warcup! Betty had been astonished when her mother wrote to say she'd taken up with a German. Though, according to her mother, his name was Clark, so Betty thought he must be at least partly English.

She thought about going over to say hello, but changed her mind. Instead she went to the bar, where Jed Dingle was serving.

'Looking good, Betty,' he said, as though he'd just seen her yesterday. 'Just back for Christmas, are you?'

Betty thought about saying that actually she was back because her sister had very unfairly blamed her for what was, at worst, a tiny error of judgement and, at best, an act of sacrifice on Betty's part. But instead she just smiled. 'Might stay a while, perhaps. I'm bored of Birmingham now.'

Jed looked pleased. 'We've all missed you,' he said. 'What can I get you?'

Betty gave him her most dazzling smile. 'Can I stash my case behind the bar first?' she said.

Jed rolled his eyes, but Betty knew he didn't mean it. 'Hand it over, then.'

Betty passed him her case, which was, she noticed, rather small considering it contained all her worldly goods. 'Gin and orange, please,' she said.

Jed made her drink and gave her a wink as she paid him. He was rather handsome, Betty thought, and then chided herself. No more men. She had a plan to get her life back on track and men would only distract her.

She took a gulp of her gin, thinking she would go and chat to Lily and the others, but as she moved through the crowded pub, she felt someone's gaze on her and turned to see Seth, his eyes boring into her. He did not look pleased to see her. She screwed up her nose. She'd assumed a year away would have given Seth time to get over her, but apparently not. She was actually quite pleased about that and she wondered if Roderick was still thinking about her. She thought he probably was and she was quite pleased about that, too.

She drained her drink and then, feeling bold, she weaved through the people until she was at Seth's side.

'Hello, Seth,' she said. She kissed him on the cheek, lingering a second too long as she breathed in his familiar smell. He stayed still as she leaned into him. In fact, she thought he pulled away from her slightly. Surely not?

Seth gave her a small, polite smile. 'How do, Betty?'

'Better for seeing you,' she said. She flashed him her best Judy Garland smile. 'Any chance of a drink?'

'Jed, get Betty a gin and orange, will you?'

'Thanks, sweetheart,' she said to Seth. She smiled at him. 'So what's new with you?'

Seth looked slightly uncomfortable. He took a mouthful of his ale.

'Nothing doing,' he said. 'Home for Christmas, are you?'

Betty shrugged. 'Might stay a while longer,' she said. She put her hand on his arm. 'If there's anything worth staying for.'

Again Seth shifted on the stool, looking uncomfortable.

'It's nice to see you,' he said. He sounded dismissive. Clearly Betty needed to up her game.

'You too,' she purred.

'Hello, Betty,' said a voice.

Seth shook Betty's hand from his arm, and Betty looked round to see little mousey Meggy Harrison. She vaguely remembered her from school, mostly because her father was involved with the Salvation Army and Betty remembered teasing Meggy about his silly uniform.

'Hello,' she said, wondering why on earth Meggy had come to speak to her.

She turned her attention back to Seth, but he was sliding off his bar stool and standing up. And – horror! – he was putting his arm around Meggy's shoulders.

'Meggy,' he said, sounding rattled. 'You remember Betty?'

Meggy gave Seth an odd look, but then she smiled. 'I do.' She looked Betty up and down. 'Everyone remembers Betty.'

'This is Meggy Harrison,' Seth said, very formally. 'She's my girlfriend.'

Betty's head span. What on earth was he talking about? How could he go from her – Betty Prendagast – to mousey, downtrodden Meggy Harrison? Surely she'd misunderstood. But no, Seth kissed Meggy's cheek and Meggy simpered.

'Well, it was lovely to catch up, Seth,' Betty said, matching his formal tone. 'I must say hello to the girls. I've heard we've got some celebrating to do.'

Ignoring Meggy's icy stare, she turned and, as quickly as she could without running, headed to where Lily and the others were chatting.

'Quick,' she said, squeezing herself into the corner beside their table and perching on a chair. 'Talk to me. Is she still giving me a filthy look?'

Lily rolled her eyes. 'Hello, Betty, nice to see you.'

Betty waved her hand. 'Yes, yes, hello. Laugh, like I've said something hilarious.'

To her relief, the three women all giggled, even though they looked a bit baffled.

'What's going on?' said Annie.

'Seth's over there with his new girlfriend,' Betty said with a grimace. 'I just wanted him to know I wasn't bothered.'

'And yet you do seem bothered.' Meg gave Betty a sly look.

Lily was peering over Betty's shoulder. 'Meggy Harrison?'

Betty groaned. 'Apparently.'

'Aww, she's a sweetheart,' Meg said. 'We always used to laugh when people mixed us up at school.'

'Hilarious,' Betty said drily.

'So you're home then?' Lily said.

'For a while.'

'At a loose end?'

'We've got a wedding to plan,' said Lily, flinging her arms out in a 'ta-dah' gesture. 'A double wedding.'

Betty looked at Meg and Annie, both of them grinning away, and felt the corners of her own mouth start to lift. Their happiness oozed out of them and it was infectious. She smiled. 'Both of you on the same day?' The women all nodded. 'When?'

'Christmas Eve,' said Meg. 'I've always wanted a Christmas wedding and Annie didn't want to wait too long, and Rolf and Jacob were all for it.'

'What about Reverend Thirlby?' said Betty. 'Did he agree?'

'He wasn't keen at first, but Jacob bought him a drink and he came round,' said Annie, grinning. She tilted her head to where the vicar was talking animatedly to Jacob Sugden, who looked far less surly than usual.

Betty felt a tiny shiver of envy at everyone's happiness, but she pushed it aside. 'That's wonderful.'

Lily clutched Betty's hands. 'Will you help with the planning?' she said. 'There's so much to do and you're so good at this sort of thing. I'm no blooming use with this getting in the way.'

She gestured to her pregnant belly and Betty smiled. 'I heard you were expecting again. Congratulations.'

'Any day now,' said Lily.

'Let's hope it doesn't happen at the wedding again, eh?' Annie said. Lily had gone into labour at her own wedding to Jack.

Lily looked alarmed. 'No, we've got three weeks to go still. And I went early with Hope, so I reckon this little one will be here sooner rather than later.' She wriggled on the chair. 'So will you help, Betty?'

It was nice to be wanted. Betty smiled. 'Of course. I can help with dresses, and I can do your hair, and we can practise some dancing if you like?' Meg and Annie both nodded and Betty sat back in her chair. 'That's settled then.'

Lily gave Betty a sideways look. 'What brought you home, then? If it wasn't Seth?'

Betty sighed. 'I had a little bit of bother in Birmingham,' she said.

She told them the story of what had happened with Roderick, embellishing it slightly – well, more than slightly – so it sounded as though she hadn't known he was Margaret's boyfriend.

'Poor you,' said Lily, her eyes shining with tears. 'Margaret will come round, I know it.'

'Lily's a bit overemotional,' said Annie. 'She cried at a squirrel the other day.'

'A squirrel?' Betty raised an eyebrow.

'It was scurrying round under a tree and I thought it had forgotten where it buried its nuts,' said Lily. 'I know it sounds ridiculous, now, but it looked so sad.'

The women all laughed and Betty felt much better. It was surprisingly nice to be back in Beckindale.

A draught blew in as the pub door opened and, just as Betty had imagined, everyone stopped talking and stared at the person who'd just entered. Except in Betty's head it had been her that everyone was looking at, not Nancy Tate.

She stood there for a second, scanning the room, two bright red spots on her pale cheeks. Then Meg waved. 'Over here, Nancy!'

Looking grateful, Nancy hurried over. 'Oh god,' she said, sinking down into a chair. 'This is awful. Everyone hates me.'

Betty's mother had, of course, filled Betty in on every detail of what she'd seen at the vet's. Betty had been shocked and felt embarrassed for her old boss. And, she had to admit, she'd felt the tiniest glimmer of envy. Who knew staid, stern Nancy had such a wild side? Still, despite that, Betty was fairly disgusted about the whole thing. Two women? That wasn't right. She wasn't surprised everyone in Beckindale was still talking about it.

'Hello, Nancy,' she said.

Nancy looked at her in surprise. 'Betty,' she said. 'I didn't know you were coming home.' She flushed red again. 'I suppose you've heard?'

Betty wasn't sure what to say. She gave a small nod.

'I thought you were avoiding the pub,' Lily said to Nancy. 'I'm surprised to see you here.'

Nancy took a deep breath. 'I've just come to say goodbye,' she said. 'My dad's come to collect me and I'm going back

343

to Scarborough tonight. Mr Walters is coming back to reopen the surgery in the new year.' She looked at Betty. 'He'll probably need a receptionist.'

Betty did that same small nod again. She felt awkward around Nancy now and, to her shame, she found she was relieved she was going.

Meg was looking sad. 'We'll miss you, Nancy,' she said. 'But I understand why you have to go.'

Nancy pinched her lips together and Betty thought she was trying not to cry. 'I've written to June and said she should come home,' she said. 'I've told her to tell everyone it was my fault. This is her home and she shouldn't feel unwelcome.'

'Maybe you and June could go somewhere together?' Lily suggested. 'Start again, somewhere no one knows you, where they might be more accepting. Leeds maybe? Or London?'

Betty thought that even with Lily's love of happy ever afters that was a step too far.

Nancy just looked really sad and shook her head. 'Maybe one day,' she said. 'But not yet.'

'We'll come and see you off. Come on, girls,' Annie said, getting up and giving Lily a hand. 'You can't go without a proper goodbye.'

Together, the women all filed outside into the snow. Nancy gave them all a quick hug at once. Betty stayed stiff-armed as she did. Then Annie, Meg, Lily and Betty all stayed by the pub and watched as Nancy walked over to where her father was waiting in his car and got in. The engine started and slowly the car pulled away.

The women all watched the lights disappear out on to the main road.

'I wonder if she'll ever come back,' said Meg.

'I think she might.' Lily looked thoughtful as she gazed at the marks in the snow left by the car's tyres. Betty thought Nancy would have to be mad to come back to Beckindale after everything that had gone on, but stranger things had happened.

'Time to call it a night for me,' Annie said. The others all murmured their agreement, said their goodbyes, and headed out into the night, back to their warm homes. Betty glanced over at her parents' cottage and shivered. Ah well, she couldn't put it off any longer.

She went back into the pub, avoiding looking at Seth and Meggy by the bar, and got her case from Jed. Then she went back out into the snow.

Once she was outside, she paused in the light from the pub's windows and pulled a piece of paper from her handbag. It was a letter her friend Pamela had sent her. Since the war had ended, Pamela had been doing the rounds of auditions, trying to make it as a dancer – just as Betty dreamed of being.

'I've got twelve weeks at the end-of-the-pier show in Scunthorpe for the summer,' Pamela had written. 'They're still auditioning. I can put in a word for you, if you like?'

Betty had been going to say no thanks, she was settled in Birmingham. But this afternoon she'd scrawled a note to Pamela saying yes please. She'd missed out on her chance to dance for the troops during the war, and she wasn't turning down any more opportunities. Not for Seth, not for Roderick, not for anyone. Summer season in Scunny didn't sound the most glamorous of jobs, but Betty knew it could lead to bigger and better things and maybe – maybe – one day help her realise her dream of becoming a Tiller Girl.

She nodded to herself, and put the letter back into her bag. She just had to keep her head down, work hard, practise her dancing every day, and make it through the audition. Then she'd be on her way. And this time she wasn't going to let any man come between her and her career.

Taking cautious steps through the snow, she walked across the village towards her parents' cottage. Her case was small, but it was heavy, and as she shifted it in her cold hands, her right foot slid on some ice. Betty tried to stay upright, but it was too slippery and she tumbled, falling hard on to her backside in the wet snow.

'Urgh,' she said.

'I knew you'd fallen for me,' said a voice. A large hand reached out and Betty grasped it gratefully and got to her feet. There was Wally Eagleton, grinning at her. His hair was dusted with snowflakes and in the light from the street lamp he looked like a sort of burly angel.

Betty smiled at him. 'Hello, Wally,' she said.

Wally offered her his arm. 'Can I walk you home?'

Betty tucked her freezing-cold fingers into the crook of his elbow. 'That would be wonderful,' she said.

Chapter Thirty-Nine

A WEEK BEFORE THE WEDDING

Lily thought Annie looked absolutely lovely as she span round, showing off her outfit.

'Is that comfortable round your waist?' Nina said, standing back and looking at Annie with a critical eye. Annie was wearing the suit Nina had worn to her own wedding, but thanks to Betty's clever ideas and Nina's artistic flair, it looked totally different. Nina had added a peplum that hugged Annie's hips, and Betty had found some old earrings that she'd sewn on to the lapels, giving the suit a touch of sparkle.

'You're so clever,' Lily said in awe. 'I'd never have thought to alter the outfit in that way.' She was sitting on Nina's sofa, counting coupons that the villagers had donated to help with the wedding party. She was uncomfortable in late pregnancy, feeling aches and cramps every time she moved, so she was grumpy and horribly aware that she wasn't being of any real use to anyone. She was trying her best to be as sweet-natured as she could. It was not easy.

'I think it's fine around my waist,' Annie said. 'It fits perfectly.'

Betty was leaning against the wall, overseeing proceedings. Now she shook her head. She went over to Annie and ran a critical finger around the waist of her skirt. 'I think it needs taking in a fraction to be perfect,' she proclaimed.

Lily rolled her eyes. Betty was very good at giving opinions, but not so good at offering solutions.

'What do you think?' Meg came into the room, wearing a draped, dusty-pink dress.

'Oh my goodness.' Lily was delighted by how beautiful her friend looked. Poor Meg never spent any time on herself – she was always worrying about Stan and Ruby, or the children at school – so to see her looking glamorous was really something.

When they'd first talked about outfits for the big day, Meg had shyly shown Nina a picture of Judy Garland on her wedding day, back in the summer, and asked if she thought she could wear something like she had.

Nina and Betty had gone off to Leeds, armed with as many clothing coupons as they could gather, and come back with the most perfect fabric, which Nina had fashioned into the dress Meg was wearing now.

Betty, who was a huge fan of Judy and who Lily thought looked a little like her too, clapped her hands with pleasure.

'That is absolutely perfect,' she said. She went to Meg and gathered some of her hair back, leaving the rest on her shoulders. 'With the little pillbox hat and the veil, it'll look precious.' She turned to Lily. 'Where's the hat, Lil? Do you have it?'

Lily groaned. 'Oh bother. I left it on the kitchen table at home. Don't worry, I'll waddle on over and fetch it.'

With some effort, she struggled to her feet, but as she did so, she felt a trickle of wetness down her leg. She stood still, recognising what was happening, but not wanting to alarm the others.

'Are you all right?' Nina looked at her, concerned, and Lily made a face.

'Erm, I think my waters have just gone.'

Annie gasped and Meg looked worried. Betty's eyes were wide. Thankfully, Nina took charge.

'Can you walk?' she said. 'I'll help you home. Where's Jack?'

'Working,' Lily said. 'I'm fine to walk.'

Betty, clearly glad of a reason to leave, was already putting her coat on. The snow was still deep in the village, with no sign of a thaw, and it was freezing outside. 'I'll get Jack,' she said.

'And Dr Black,' Nina added. 'Get them to meet us at Lily's.'

Betty gave a cute salute and headed out into the cold.

'Where's Hope?' Meg asked.

'With Dad at the garage,' Lily said through gritted teeth. She felt very peculiar, as though her skin was too tight for her body.

'I'll get changed, then take Hope back to mine for her tea,' Meg said.

Lily reached out and grasped her friend's hand. 'Stay with me,' she begged.

If Meg was alarmed, she didn't show it.

Annie was already wriggling out of her wedding suit and pulling on the skirt and jumper she'd been wearing before. 'I'll help you across to your cottage,' she said.

With a grateful nod, Lily went to pick up her own coat and stopped short as she was hit with a wave of pain. Still hanging on to Meg's hand, she leaned over the back of the sofa, breathing deeply, until the contraction stopped.

'Nina,' she gasped. 'I don't think I can make it home. Oh god, here comes another one.'

Thankfully, Nina didn't argue. In her calm way, she hurried round Lily as she hung off the sofa, gathering up Annie's wedding suit, and the coupons, and all the other things that were lying around.

Back in her normal clothes, Annie took over from Meg, rubbing Lily's back as she breathed through the contraction, and Meg went to get changed.

'We need towels, and blankets,' Nina said to her. 'Let's get Lily comfy.'

Betty burst through the door, looking panicked.

'Dr Black's over with Mr Smithers, the other side of the hill,' she gasped.

Lily felt relieved. That wasn't so far. 'So he won't be long?'

'Phyllis is phoning now,' Betty said. 'But she said he might even already be on his way back.'

'Jack?' Lily said. 'Where's Jack?'

Betty made a face. 'He's gone to speak to some farmer in Hotten about some stolen sheep, but I've left a message for him at the police station.'

'Come and get yourself comfortable, Lily,' Nina said. 'Would you rather stand or lie down?'

Lily wasn't sure. She sat down and then stood up again when that made her more uncomfortable.

'Walk, I think.' She started shuffling round the room and found, to her relief, that it was slightly better that way. 'Can everyone talk or something,' she said. 'I need a distraction.'

The women all started jabbering at once, and Lily put her hands over her ears.

'Not all together,' she begged. 'Meg, tell me about Ruby's bike race.'

'It was another one where she wasn't allowed to take part because it was men only,' Meg began.

Lily carried on walking backwards and forwards, half listening to Meg's tale of Ruby standing up for herself, and half just concentrating on her own breathing. She stopped when another contraction gripped her, gritting her teeth through it, and then carried on.

Betty was hovering by the door, looking dreadfully uncomfortable, and after a while, when Dr Black hadn't arrived, she put her coat back on and headed out into the village again to check where he'd got to.

She'd not been gone long – just long enough for Lily to have another searing contraction – when she was back, looking even more worried than she had before.

'Snow's coming down so heavily, the pass over the hills is blocked,' she said. 'Dr Black's stuck with Mr Smithers until the plough can get out.'

Lily glared at her. 'What?' she barked. 'What are you saying?'

Betty bit her lip. 'Dr Black's not coming.'

'What about Jack?'

Betty looked relieved to have some good news. 'He's fine,' she said. 'The road to Hotten's still clear and he's on his way, apparently.'

Lily doubled over as another contraction hit her. 'What about Mrs Connor?' she gasped. 'Wasn't she a nurse?'

'Didn't she remove people's corns?' said Meg. 'I don't think she was a *nurse* nurse.'

Lily was feeling so desperate now that she didn't care what medical qualifications anyone had, as long as they could get this baby out safely.

She shuffled over and gripped Betty's sweater in her fist. 'I. Am. Having. A. Baby,' she growled. 'Help me.'

Betty looked down at Lily's hand. 'I'll find someone,' she said.

She dashed off again and Lily groaned through another contraction, hanging on to Annie's hands as the pain gripped her.

The front door slammed and in came Betty again.

'Dr Black?' asked Annie hopefully.

Betty shook her head. 'No chance,' she said. 'It's like a blizzard out there. But I brought someone.' She stepped aside and there behind her was Susan Roberts, looking pinched and nervous as she took in what was going on.

'Betty, what on earth?' Her voice was shrill. 'I thought it was a cat having kittens you wanted me to help. You never said it was Lily.' She took a step back towards the door. 'Sorry, Lily.'

'Susan's a vet,' Meg said, staring at the young woman, who looked completely terrified.

'A student vet,' Susan pointed out faintly. 'I can't help here. I'll go.'

Lily wanted to scream. In fact, she thought she might scream any second. But first she needed to make someone understand that her baby was coming. Now.

'Don't move a muscle,' she shrieked at Susan. 'You're the best I've got.'

Susan went white. 'Oh no,' she said.

Lily let out a roar as another contraction gripped her. She was shaking uncontrollably and starting to panic. 'Stay here,'

352

she gasped at Susan. 'I don't care if you've only delivered calves and lambs.'

'One calf,' Susan said. 'And no lambs.'

Lily roared again. Her contractions were close together now. This baby wasn't hanging around.

'Please, Susan,' she panted.

To her immense relief, Susan snapped into professional mode. 'I think I should have a look,' she said. 'See what's going on. Would you mind, Lily?' Unable to speak, Lily shook her head and Susan patted her gently on the shoulder. 'Back in a second.'

She headed into the kitchen to wash her hands.

'There are too many people in here,' Nina said to Meg and Annie. 'You two put the kettle on. Betty, can you go and tell Mick what's happening, just so he doesn't arrive with little Hope in tow. And then go and wait for Jack in the village. He won't know where we are unless someone tells him.'

Betty didn't need to be asked twice. She gave Lily's arm a gentle squeeze and whispered 'Good luck,' then she fled.

Lily tried to speak, but she could only make that same roaring sound again as another pain tightened across her abdomen.

Susan came out of the kitchen, looking determined. Lily almost kissed her, she was so pleased to see someone taking charge. Even if that someone was an eighteen-year-old trainee vet.

'Could you lie down on the sofa, do you think?' Susan asked. 'Or is the floor more comfortable?'

'Floor,' grunted Lily. With some help from Nina, she got down on to the blankets Meg had spread out.

Gently, Susan eased off her underwear. Lily didn't care that someone she'd known since she was a little girl was peering up under her skirt. She was too busy being frightened that the baby was coming too fast and that something was wrong.

'Please,' she said to Susan. 'Please.'

Nina sat down by Lily's shoulders and cradled her head on her lap. Her hands were cool on Lily's hot brow and Lily realised she was so very pleased her stepmother was there.

Susan sat back on her haunches. 'You're fully dilated,' she said. 'I can see the baby's head. It's time to push.'

Lily began to cry. 'I don't want to.'

'Rubbish,' said Nina. 'You've done it before. When the next contraction comes, you hang on to my hands and push.'

Lily thought about that and decided that, actually, she wasn't going to do what Nina said. She shook her head. 'No,' she said. 'No.'

'Come on, sweetheart,' Nina said softly. 'It's time to meet your baby.'

'I've already got a baby,' Lily said, knowing she was being irrational and not caring one tiny bit. 'I don't want another one.'

'We're here,' Susan said. She was white-faced with worry, but Lily felt an air of calm coming from the young woman. 'It's all going to be all right. I just need you to push.'

Another pain gripped Lily and suddenly her body took over and she pushed.

'That's it,' cried Susan. 'That's it. Keep going.'

Nina stroked Lily's head. 'Well done, darling girl. Push.'

It took a few excruciatingly painful minutes, but eventually Lily pushed again, screaming with the effort, and with a gush of fluid she felt the baby slide out into Susan's waiting hands.

There was silence. A terrible, lengthy silence that went on and on.

Lily watched, terrified, as Susan wrapped the baby in a towel, with shaking hands, wiped its tiny nose and mouth, and rubbed it.

'Come on, little one,' she murmured. 'Come on there.'

Lily was crying now, watching Susan. But then the tiny red creature opened its mouth and yelled.

Lily fell back against Nina, sobbing with happiness and relief, just as Jack burst into the cottage.

'Lily,' he said, rushing into the lounge. 'Are you all right?' And then he stopped in the doorway, as the baby's cries filled the room. 'Ohhh,' he said in wonder.

Susan held her precious bundle up. 'Do you want to check if it's a boy or a girl?' she said to Jack.

With an expression of sheer awe, Jack peeked under the towel. 'It's a boy,' he told Lily. 'A beautiful bouncing brother for our Hope.'

He took the baby from Susan and brought him round to Lily. Nina moved over so he could hold her, and she leaned against him, staring down at the baby's perfect little face and tiny fingers that gripped the edge of the towel.

'He's the most wonderful Christmas present anyone could ever dream of,' said Lily.

Jack kissed her. 'Reckon Hope will still want her bike, though.'

Lily laughed. 'Reckon you're right.'

Jack took the baby while Susan cut the cord, and then he sat on the sofa, cradling their son. Nina helped Lily on to the sofa, too, wrapped in a blanket, as she gave her baby boy his first feed, gazing at him in wonder.

'Susan, I can't thank you enough,' said Jack.

'Me too,' Lily added. 'I don't know what we'd have done without you. You were wonderful. Are you sure you want to be a vet? I think you'd make an excellent doctor.'

Susan grinned. 'Every part of nature is amazing,' she said. 'But I'm sticking to kittens and calves from now on.'

'And you, Nina,' Lily said. 'I'm so pleased you were there with me.'

Nina nodded, her lips pinched tightly together. She was so obviously moved by the afternoon's events that she couldn't speak.

'Knock knock,' called Meg from the kitchen. 'Can we come in?'

'Of course,' cried Lily. 'He's a boy. Come and meet him.'

Meg and Annie crowded round.

'He looks just like Jack,' said Annie. 'Poor bugger.'

Lily grinned. 'He really does.'

Jack looked at the tiny boy, whose head was covered in white-blond fuzz. 'He's got your hair though, Lil.'

'His hair is like a halo,' said Meg. 'He's a little Christmas angel.'

'Is it safe?' Betty stuck her head round the door.

'Oh Betty,' said Lily. 'Thank you for fetching Susan and I'm sorry I shouted at you.'

Betty gave her a little wave as if to say it was nothing. 'He's lovely,' she said. 'Do you have a name for him?'

Lily looked at Jack. 'We talked about calling him Victor, didn't we? Because we found out he was coming on VE Day.'

Jack nodded. 'Victor Dingle Proudfoot.'

But Lily made a face.

'What?' said Jack. 'What are you thinking?'

356

'Meg gave me an idea,' she said, stroking the baby's soft fuzzy head. 'Our little Christmas angel . . . Gabriel.'

Jack looked down at the baby and then up at Lily. He leaned over and kissed her very gently on the lips.

'Gabriel Victor Dingle Proudfoot,' he said. 'That's perfect.'

'Bit of a mouthful,' Betty grimaced and Annie picked up a cushion and hit her with it, making Lily laugh.

'Gabriel,' she said. The baby opened his eyes for a second, frowned and then snuggled into her chest and went back to sleep. 'I think he likes it.'

Chapter Forty

23RD DECEMBER 1945

Meg looked out of the window at the snow-topped cottages of Beckindale. She couldn't believe that tomorrow she'd be Mrs Clark. Or Frau Schreiber, as Rolf had called her quietly when it was just the two of them.

It was going to be the most wonderful day. Her Judy Garland-inspired dress was perfect. Ruby – her bridesmaid – had turned her nose up at a frock at first but had then given in when Betty had produced a dress in a rich red fabric.

'It's the colour of a ruby,' Betty had said with a flourish. 'So you can't say no.'

With her clever eye, Betty had Nina shorten the skirt and nip in the waist and Ruby was going to look as pretty as a picture.

And as for Stan. Oh, Meg's heart swelled just thinking about him. He had his first suit. Well, he had a jacket that Betty had found somewhere, and a new tie to wear with that and his school trousers. He was determined to look smart because he was going to walk her down the aisle.

It had been the obvious choice, because her parents had passed away years ago now, and there was no one else she wanted to give her away. But she'd still been nervous when she'd asked Stan, and thrilled to bits when he'd said yes.

She was still a little sad, though, that her parents and her twin sister Rosie weren't there on her special day. Though she no longer blamed herself for Rosie's death in a cycling accident when they were fifteen, she still missed her sister every day. And never more so than on their birthday, or on other special occasions.

'I wish you were here, Rosie,' she whispered up at the bright stars. 'Happy birthday.'

Snow crunched outside the window and, with delight, she saw Rolf coming up the path. She waved at him through the window and darted into the hall to open the front door. But Ruby got there first, leaping down the stairs and barring Meg's way like a guard dog.

'Absolutely not,' she said.

'It's Rolf.' Meg was confused.

'You can't see him the night before your wedding,' Ruby said. 'It's right bad luck.'

Meg fixed her daughter with a stern gaze. 'I'm marrying a Luftwaffe pilot, just six months after the war. I think we can handle trouble.'

Ruby screwed up her face. 'Fair dos,' she said, chuckling. 'Go on then. But don't blame me if something awful happens.'

Laughing, Meg shoved Ruby aside and opened the door. 'Ruby says this is bad luck,' she said.

'We've had all our bad luck already.' Rolf gave Meg a kiss. 'That's what I said.'

'I won't stay,' Rolf said. 'But I've brought you your birthday present. I thought you might want to wear it tomorrow, so I wanted to give it to you early.'

Meg steered him into the lounge and Ruby blew Rolf a kiss and ran back upstairs to her room.

'Here.' Rolf handed Meg a small parcel, tied up with ribbon.

She unwrapped it and opened the box it held. Inside was a brooch. It was in the shape of a pink rose, with coloured glass for the petals. It was very pretty.

'Ohhh,' Meg breathed.

Rolf looked slightly uncomfortable. 'I didn't want to upset you,' he said. 'But I know you are missing Rosie and I thought this brooch could . . .' He frowned, thinking of the word. He always forgot some of his English vocabulary when he was nervous. 'Stand for her?'

'Symbolise,' Meg said. 'It can symbolise her.'

'Yes.' Rolf made a face. 'Do you like it?'

Meg looked down at the brooch in her hand and then up at Rolf's handsome face, so earnest and full of love. 'I adore it,' she said. 'You really are the kindest, most thoughtful man.' She pulled him into a hug and kissed him. 'I will wear it tomorrow and it'll remind everyone that Rosie's still in our thoughts.'

'I'm glad you're not sad.'

Meg thought for a moment. 'Not sad, exactly, no. But always sorry that she's not here.'

'I understand,' Rolf said. 'I feel the same about my sisters and my mother.'

They sat there for a moment, hand in hand, thinking about their lost loved ones. And then Rolf stood up.

'And now, I must talk to Ruby and Stan.'

'Really? What about?'

Rolf tapped his nose with his forefinger. 'Family business,' he said.

'I'll get them,' Meg said, making to stand up too, but Rolf put his hand on her shoulder to stop her.

'No,' he said. 'I'll get them. This is just for me, Ruby and Stanley.'

'All right,' said Meg uncertainly.

Rolf went out of the lounge and shut the door behind him. Meg sat on the sofa obediently for a second, then deciding she was too curious to resist, she opened the living-room door again the tiniest amount, and stood with her ear to the crack, straining her ears to listen.

She shrank back as Ruby and Stan came hurtling down the stairs and went into the kitchen. She heard the kitchen door shut, and knowing she wouldn't hear what was going on through two doors, she crept out into the hall, hoping that from there she could hear what they were discussing.

'I have something to say.' Rolf's tone was serious as it floated through the kitchen door, and Meg felt nervous for a second. What was this about?

'Are we in trouble?' Stan said, and Rolf laughed.

'Not in the least.'

In the hallway, Meg smiled. Stan always assumed he'd done something wrong.

'I just wanted to tell you that tomorrow I am marrying Meg,' Rolf went on in that oddly formal way.

'Well, yes, we knew that,' Ruby drawled and then added 'Ouch, Stan,' as – Meg assumed – her brother kicked her under the table to stop her interrupting.

'I am marrying Meg, your mother, but I want you to know that I am also marrying you two.'

There was silence from the kitchen. Meg inched closer to the door. Were they still talking? Why couldn't she hear? But it seemed they'd just all stopped talking for a minute because she heard Rolf speak again.

'You two are the most important people in Meg's life, and I know you come as a package.'

Meg heard a sniff through the door. Was Ruby crying?

'So, tomorrow I don't just get a new wife,' Rolf said. 'I get a whole new family.'

Meg heard the sound of chairs being scraped back and muffled chatter and sniffing as the children went to Rolf.

Keen not to be caught eavesdropping, she darted back into the lounge and sat on the sofa, looking at her Rosie brooch. Rolf was the most wonderful man, she thought. And she couldn't wait to marry him.

Chapter Forty-One

24TH DECEMBER 1945

Annie woke up with a start, her heart pounding. She'd had the most awful dream that she was walking down the aisle to marry Jacob. But when she reached the altar, she'd seen that he was Edward, his face tear-stained. 'How could you do this, Annie?' he'd sobbed. 'I thought it was me you loved.'

She lay there for a second, concentrating on her breathing and feeling her heart rate return to normal. This was nothing to worry about, she told herself. This was just her subconscious playing tricks on her.

Rolling over in bed, she looked out of the window. When the war ended, she thought she would never tire of being able to see outside at night. She thought the years of blackout would mean she would appreciate it forever. But already she'd grown accustomed to being able to leave her curtains open an inch or two – like she'd done when she was a little girl – and seeing the sun rise.

This morning, though, it was still dark. Well, dark-ish.

The snow that still blanketed Beckindale was reflecting the moonlight and giving the village a cold, grey glow.

'It's my wedding day,' Annie whispered to herself. 'The happiest day of my life.'

The words felt odd in her mouth, as though someone else was saying them.

She sat up, hugging her knees under the covers. She was happy. There was no doubt about that. She and Jacob had a good relationship. They had a history together. They'd both had awful troubles and they'd got through them together. They had a shared past, and now a shared future. She loved him. And she loved Maggie, and Joseph, and Emmerdale Farm. It was where she was meant to be.

There was a soft knock on her bedroom door and her mother Grace put her head round. She was still in her nightie and dressing gown, with her hair in curlers.

'You're awake,' she said. 'I thought I heard you stirring.'

'Come in,' Annie said, moving over so there was room for Grace to sit on her bed.

Her mother sat down and put her hand on Annie's leg under the blanket. 'My little girl, getting wed,' she said with a smile. 'Who'd have thought?'

Annie tried to smile, but instead – much to her surprise – she burst into tears.

'Oh, now, what's this?' said Grace. She put her arms around Annie and held her until Annie's sobs started to ease. Grace gave her a handkerchief from the pocket of her dressing gown and Annie took it gratefully.

'Thank you,' she sniffed. She felt a bit silly. What sort of bride cried on her wedding day?

'Thinking about Edward?' Grace said.

Annie nodded. 'I dreamt that he was upset that I was marrying Jacob.'

Grace thought for a moment. 'I know that if Edward was still alive, you'd be marrying him, not Jacob,' she said. 'Everyone knows it. Maggie and Joseph know. And so does Jacob.'

Annie bit her lip. That was true.

'But Edward's not here,' her mother went on. 'And you have a long life to live, Annie.'

'What if I'm making a terrible mistake?'

'Do you know what I think?' Grace said with a weary smile. 'I think little girls grow up with pictures in their heads of fairy tales and happily ever afters. But that's not what marriage is like at all.'

Annie looked at her mother through narrowed eyes. She knew her parents' marriage hadn't always been good. And she had always – without meaning to – blamed her mother for that.

Grace sighed. 'When your father had all that trouble, things were bleak.'

'I remember,' Annie said. Back when Annie had been much younger, the Pearsons had their own farm and things were good. But then Sam had broken his leg and been unable to work, their debts got too large, and the local bigwig, Clive Skilbeck, had swooped in and bought the farm.

Sam had worked for Maggie Sugden for a while at Emmerdale Farm – which was why Annie spent so much time there with the boys – and she'd even given the Pearsons their shepherd's cottage to live in.

The humiliation had been hard for Sam. And things were even worse for him when Grace had taken a job as Clive Skilbeck's housekeeper.

Annie swallowed. Then Oliver Skilbeck – Clive's son – had raped her. She may have put that behind her now, but it would always be with her. Just like she would always remember the dreadful thing he'd told her – that Grace and Clive were having an affair. It had been one of the hardest times in Annie's life. She shuddered now, thinking of it.

Grace put her hand on Annie's shoulder. 'I know,' she said, softly. 'But here's the thing. We got through it, didn't we? Your dad and me.'

It had been the war that had been the making of Sam Pearson. His farming know-how was suddenly in great demand, and even though his leg still caused him bother, he was recruited by the WarAg and quickly rose through the ranks. As a surveyor, he travelled round Yorkshire, advising farmers on how to make the most of their land, and his confidence had come back in spades.

Meanwhile, Grace had taken a job with Mr Verney instead, organising his paperwork and doing his typing. And suddenly, at least as far as Annie could see, things had taken a turn for the better. They still lived in the little shepherd's cottage, but they paid Maggie proper rent now, and no longer felt like she was doing them a favour – though, of course, Sam still helped out when he was needed.

'Marriages last a long time,' Grace said. 'There will be good times and bad times. And you'll say some awful things to one another. Sometimes you'll feel far apart and sometimes so close you're almost the same person.'

Annie nodded slowly.

'What I'm saying, Annie, is that it's not all sunshine. But you can make it work, if it's what you really want.'

Annie looked at her mother, and thought about the hardships she'd been through and how she'd kept fighting through it all. And she smiled. 'It is what I really want,' she said, truthfully. 'I want to be Mrs Sugden of Emmerdale Farm.'

Grace breathed out slowly. 'Good,' she said. 'Now, you best get up, because we've got a lot to do before the ceremony.'

'Hold still,' Betty said, jabbing Meg in the head with a hairpin.

'Ouch.' Meg rubbed her scalp and Betty slapped her hand away.

'Don't touch.'

Meg rolled her eyes at Ruby, who was watching with amusement.

'You're next,' she said to her daughter. 'So don't look so smug.'

'Ruby is a natural beauty,' Betty said. She looked at the women, so comfortable with each other, and felt a pang. She and Margaret had got ready for dances together, until Betty had ruined everything. And even Betty's relationship with her mother had taken a nosedive since 'all that bother in Birmingham', as Nora kept calling it. She wanted Betty to apologise to Margaret, but so far Betty had refused. Because Margaret, the silly girl, was back with Roderick and they were engaged. They were planning to move to Scotland once they were married. Betty thought Margaret was making a very big mistake, but what could she do?

'What does that make me, then?' Meg made a face at herself in the mirror and Betty blinked at her, not understanding. 'If Ruby is a natural beauty, what am I?' Meg said. 'A natural ogre?'

'Well, I didn't like to say . . .' Betty joked. 'There, you're all done.'

Actually, Meg looked very pretty, Betty thought. Her hair curled perfectly under the hat, and her dress was lovely, draping around her hips and legs in a very flattering way. Her sparkly rose brooch set everything off perfectly.

Meanwhile, Ruby was looking very grown-up in her red dress.

'You won't put too much make-up on me, will you?' Ruby said.

Betty tutted, but she nodded.

Her expression full of emotion, Meg stood up and gave Betty a tight hug. 'You're a good friend, Betty Prendagast,' she said. 'Thank you for everything you've done for Annie and me.'

Betty was pleased. "S'nothing,' she mumbled. She was grateful for the praise. She'd been feeling rotten since she'd heard Margaret was back with Roderick.

'Perhaps one day, you and Seth will find your way back to each other,' Meg said.

Betty doubted that very much. Seth was smitten with boring Meggy. But Betty found she didn't mind too much. Not while Wally was around to distract her. She hoped she'd see him later. She thought they could celebrate Christmas together. Hopefully in the same way they'd celebrated last year . . .

Betty gave a little shiver of anticipation, tidied a loose strand of Meg's hair and smiled. 'Go and find Stan while I sort out Ruby's hair,' she said. 'We'll be ready in five minutes to walk across to the church.'

Meg felt a rush of excitement. It was happening. Soon she and Rolf would be husband and wife, ready to share the rest of their lives.

'Urgh,' said Betty. 'You look sickeningly happy. Go away before it gets too much for me.' Then she gave Meg one of her beautiful dazzling smiles. 'I'm really chuffed for you and Rolf, you know.'

Meg blew Betty and Ruby a kiss and headed off downstairs to find Stan. She found him in the kitchen, looking handsome and smart in his suit, pacing backwards and forwards.

'Easy,' she said. 'You'll wear out the floor.'

Stan looked at her. 'You look very pretty,' he said. 'Prettier than I've ever seen you.'

Meg dropped a little curtesy. 'Why, thank you.'

'Can I hug you or will you crease?'

'I don't mind a couple of creases,' Meg said, opening her arms. Stan cuddled her gently. He was taller than she was now, but he would always be her little boy.

'Meg,' Stan said. 'Ruby and me, we love you, you know that?'

'I do,' Meg said. 'And I love you both too.'

'And we'll always be grateful to you for giving us a home.'

Meg put her hands on Stan's shoulders and gave him a stern look. 'Now, you listen to me, Stanley Dobbs,' she said. 'You have nothing to be grateful for. The way I see it is we all found each other when we needed someone.'

Ruby appeared in the door of the kitchen, looking like one of Betty's film stars.

'Did you ask her?' she said to Stan. 'What did she say?'

'Not yet,' Stan hissed. 'I was working up to it.'

Meg looked at her children and raised an eyebrow. 'Ask me what?'

'We know Rolf's name isn't really Clark,' Ruby said. 'But he's chosen that, and now you're choosing it too.'

369

'Yes?'

'Can we be Clarks as well?' Stan blurted out. 'So we can be a family?'

'We'd keep Dobbs as a middle name. To remember our mam,' said Ruby. 'But we want to be the Clark family.'

Meg couldn't find the words she wanted to say. She was so full of love for these children that she couldn't speak. She wrapped one arm around Stan and the other around Ruby and held them tightly.

'I think that would be absolutely precious,' she said, eventually. 'Precious.'

Betty had come downstairs behind Ruby. She'd been leaning against the door frame, watching the emotional moment. Now she straightened up. 'Do not cry,' she said firmly. 'I've got no mascara left.'

Annie stood in the church porch with her parents. She had arrived earlier than Meg, who wasn't there yet, so she had to wait, which wasn't doing much for her nerves.

Inside, she could hear the organ playing and the buzz of chatter from the congregation. She peeked through the glass panel on the door and saw Jacob and Rolf standing at the front. Rolf was turning round, talking to Nick Roberts, who was sitting in the front pew, while Jacob was standing silently, his hands clasped behind his back.

He's just as nervous as I am, Annie thought. And the realisation comforted her. Perhaps her life hadn't turned out as she'd thought it would when she was running around with Edward, before the war, carefree and young. But that didn't mean it wouldn't be a good life.

'All right?' Grace said.

Annie turned to her mother. 'I'm fine,' she said. 'Honestly.'

Grace nodded. 'Good.' She kissed Annie on the cheek. 'I'm going to sit down now, but you should know that I am very proud of you.'

Annie squeezed her mother's hand.

Sam, who'd been chatting with Reverend Thirlby, came over. 'Meg's on her way,' he said. 'Are you ready?'

Annie grinned. 'As I'll ever be.'

Her father put his thumb on her chin and tilted her face up so he could look straight at her. 'You can say no, you know. If you want to. You don't have to go through with it.'

Annie felt a rush of love for her father, who said few words but who saw a lot.

'I had a wobble,' she said. 'But I'm fine now. Really.'

'Sure?'

Annie looked through the glass panel again. Up towards the front of the church sat Lily with baby Gabriel in her arms, Hope next to her, and Jack next to Hope. Jack was obviously explaining something to Hope, as he was pointing to the stained-glass window and Hope was looking up at him adoringly. Annie thought about having her own children, and Jacob teaching them all the things he knew about farming and nature. She imagined her family growing up on Emmerdale Farm, just as she, Edward and Jacob had done, and she nodded.

'I'm sure.'

'I'm glad,' Sam said. They smiled at each other, enjoying the calm before the wedding began properly.

'We're here!' Ruby's voice rang out over the quiet snowy village.

Annie and Sam turned to see Meg and the children hurrying towards them, along the frosty path.

'Oh my goodness, it's so cold,' Meg gasped, coming into the porch and stamping snow from her boots. 'I need to change my shoes.'

'Here, let me help you,' said Annie.

She helped Meg off with her winter coat and gave it to Ruby to hang up. Then Meg balanced on Stan's arm while she took off her boots and swapped them for pretty pumps.

Annie took her friend's hands. 'You look absolutely beautiful,' she said. Meg's face shone with happiness and Annie thought she'd never seen her look so radiant.

'So do you,' Meg said. 'I'm glad we're doing this together.'

The friends shared a hug.

'Shall we do it, then?' Annie said. Her stomach flipped over with nerves.

'Let's.'

Reverend Thirlby, who'd been standing by quietly, gave a nod and hurried off down the aisle. The organ struck a chord and they were off.

Annie and Sam led the way down the aisle, followed by Ruby, then Meg on Stan's arm. Annie's legs felt wobbly, but she was happy. She saw Betty sitting at the back, next to Wally Eagleton, and as far away as possible from Seth and Meggy, who were on the other side of the aisle. Mick and Nina sat with Lily and Jack, and right at the front were Maggie and Joseph, holding hands. Annie didn't think she'd ever seen them hold hands before. The thought made her smile.

And then, there was Jacob, looking strong and handsome in a smart suit. He really did scrub up well, when he had to. He was gazing at her in a way that made her heart lift.

'You look wonderful,' he whispered to her as she took her position next to him.

'I'm so nervous,' Annie murmured.

Jacob took her hand. 'Oh god, me too,' he said, smiling at her. 'Let's get through it together, shall we?'

Lily sobbed her way through the whole wedding. 'It's so lovely,' she kept saying to Jack. 'I'm so happy.'

Jack passed her a handkerchief. 'You're giving a whole new meaning to the phrase wetting the baby's head,' he said, dabbing poor Gabriel's damp hair with his sleeve.

Lily grinned. She was absolutely content with her new baby and her little girl, and her caring husband. And Ruby's determination to make it as a cyclist had given her lots of ideas about how to grow her business, too. She missed Nancy, but other than that, she felt like the future was bright for her in Beckindale. It could have all been so different, she thought with a shudder. Hope could have drowned that awful day when the troops came home. She could have been the one who died that day, not poor Hazel. She reached out and tweaked one of Hope's pigtails and her daughter turned and gave her a cheeky grin.

Gabriel gave a little snuffle and as Jack put his arm around them both, holding them close, Lily looked down at her baby boy, feeling her heart swell. Life was good, she thought.

The ceremony passed in a blur for Meg. It felt like one minute she was standing in the church porch, shaking the snow from her boots, and the next, she and Rolf were kissing as Reverend Thirlby declared them man and wife.

'It's perfect,' Rolf said to her. 'Today is the perfect day.'

Meg couldn't stop smiling. Still standing at the front of the church, gripping Rolf's arm, she pulled Ruby and Stan in to them for a hug.

And then their friends and family were clapping and shouting 'congratulations!' as the brand new Clark family walked down the aisle, followed by Jacob and Annie, who were hand in hand and smiling broadly.

Meg thought her heart might burst, she was so happy. She was Mrs Clark – Frau Schreiber – and she had Ruby and Stan, and who knew? Maybe a baby one day soon.

'Can we make it to the village hall without our coats and boots, do you think?' Annie said. She was rosy-cheeked with the excitement and looked young and pretty.

'I think so,' said Meg.

'I'd put them on if I were you,' said Lily, emerging from the church and giving Annie a smacker of a kiss on her cheeks. 'Congratulations, both of you. And happy birthday, Meg. And you, Stan and Ruby.'

Meg grinned. Christmas was such a special time of year for her and now it was even more precious. 'Why do we need our coats?' she asked Lily.

Lily glanced at Ruby and Stan. 'Ready?' she said. The kids both nodded, and huddled together, full of purpose, they headed out into the snow.

'What's going on?' said Annie.

'You'll see.'

They all bundled up in their coats, and the brides pulled on their boots, not caring how odd they looked with their special outfits.

'Do you know what this is about?' Meg asked Rolf, but his face was as blank as hers. With their warm clothes on, the two happy couples followed Lily outside and up towards the main part of the village. The sky was dark and heavy with snow, and even though it was the middle of the day, the light was dim. But it didn't matter, because there, in the centre of the Beckindale, were all their friends, and the children from Meg's class, holding candlelit lanterns and books of carols.

'Did you organise this?' Meg asked Lily.

'Me, Stan, Ruby, Maggie . . . even Jed had a hand in it,' she said.

At that moment, snow began to fall. Meg laughed in delight, holding her hands out to catch the flakes.

From the pub, Jed shouted: 'Three, two, one,' and suddenly the Christmas tree outside The Woolpack lit up.

Stan, who was standing at the side of the villagers, holding his violin, drew his bow and together everyone opened their mouths.

'Joy to the world,' they all sang.

Meg was charmed. She stood wrapped in Rolf's arms, listening to the singing as the snow fell. It was magical.

Next to her, Annie wiped away a tear. 'Joy to the world,' she sniffed. 'That's simply perfect.'

Lily nudged her. 'Don't start me off,' she joked.

Meg reached out and took Lily's hand in one of hers, and Annie's in the other, and the women all smiled at one another. They had their husbands, their families and Beckindale. And, most of all, they had each other. Whatever the world threw at them next, they would get through it, together.

Acknowledgements

I am so lucky to have been given the chance to write these stories based around my favourite soap. Thank you to my agent Felicity Trew for giving me the opportunity, and to Katie Brown and Sam Eades at Trapeze for their amazing editing talents. Thanks also to Holly Foster, who named baby Gabriel for me.

Finally, this book is in loving memory of Paula Tilbrook, who brought Betty to life so brilliantly in *Emmerdale* and who will be missed.

Credits

Trapeze would like to thank everyone at Orion who worked on the publication of *The Emmerdale Girls*.

Editorial
Sam Eades
Sarah Fortune
Charlie Panayiotou
Jane Hughes
Alice Davis

Copy-editor
Laura Gerrard

Proofreader
Karen Ball

Audio
Paul Stark
Amber Bates

Contracts
Anne Goddard
Paul Bulos
Jake Alderson

Design
Loulou Clark
Lucie Stericker
Rachael Lancaster
Joanna Ridley
Nick May
Clare Sivell
Helen Ewing

Publicity
Patricia Deveer

Finance
Jennifer Muchan
Jasdip Nandra
Afeera Ahmed
Rabale Mustafa
Elizabeth Beaumont
Ibukun Ademefun
Sue Baker
Victor Falola

Marketing
Tanjiah Islam

Production
Claire Keep
Fiona McIntosh

Sales
Jen Wilson
Laura Fletcher
Esther Waters
Rachael Hum
Ellie Kyrke-Smith
Ben Goddard
Georgina Cutler
Barbara Ronan
Andrew Hally
Dominic Smith
Maggy Park
Linda McGregor

Rights
Susan Howe
Richard King
Krystyna Kujawinska
Jessica Purdue
Louise Henderson

Operations
Jo Jacobs
Sharon Willis
Lucy Brem
Lisa Pryde